CAT'S
MASQUERADE

CAT'S MASQUERADE

Thea Girard Marshall

To order additional copies of this book, contact:
Xlibris Corporation
1-888-795-4274
www.Xlibris.com
Orders@Xlibris.com
27176

CONTENTS

A Daring Plan 9
Escape 28
The Accident 38
Discovered 49
Cat In London 60
Encounters 69
Fairfax & Montclair 83
Inquires 94
Deceptions 108
Hyde Park 118
Scandals 129
Returns 142
Appearances 158
Conversations 172
Acquaintances 175
Preparations 181
Presentations 184
Strategies 197
The Opera 210
The Ball 227
Rivals 241
Desires 249
The Contest 266
Bal Masque 277
Captive 297
Resolution 319
Last Masque 331
Unmasked 344

To Patti,

For my friends

I hope you enjoy
the Rowaster journey!
Best wishes,

[signature]

July 18, 2008
Pie Town
NM

A DARING PLAN

T he grey rain beat its cold tattoo upon the mullioned panes where Caitlyn sat, curled like a kitten in the window seat, staring disconsolately across the trees of the Park to the mist-enshrouded hills beyond. Her long auburn hair hung loose in heavy waves down her back. Her green eyes sparkled beneath finely arched brows.

"Why, oh why, won't Father let me go?" she thought. "I am seventeen, and he treats me like a child! Everybody goes to London for the Season and Bath for the summer, while he buries himself here at home with his musty old books and his antiquities. And I must stay here too."

She sighed and stretched her legs, propping her back against the stone of the arched windows. The partly drawn dark green curtains formed a bower that concealed her from the rest of the library. Nobody walked the garden in the rain anyway, and her father, Sir Merlin Llewellyn, lord of Eldertree Manor, never cut back the trees. Caitlyn felt like the princess in a fairy tale. "Perhaps I should take a nap," she thought with a certain tart humor, "but then I would probably sleep for a hundred years and never get to Bath or London at all."

She sighed again and began to twist her long hair into a braid. Her father preferred her to wear it loose, like one of the heroines in old Celtic romances. He simply did not understand that women now wore their hair pulled up with little curls about their ears and foreheads. Her neighbor

Clarissa Thomas always had her hair done in the latest fashion, and her clothes were of the newest cut. She would be going to London for the Season. She would not be buried here in Wales.

Above Caitlyn, the device of some ancient ancestor, set in the window in stained glass, took fire from the flames that burned brightly in the library fireplace. The cat, *sejeant guardent*, shone red as blood in its milky white glass background, surrounded by three red stars and bordered by green. She had always liked this window best because of that design, although the rest of the household thought it was the view. She closed her eyes, picturing the brave knight who must have carried this device on his shield.

She stood on the battlement of the tower. He knelt before her, all in silver, his helm decorated with a cat crest. He raised his visor, and she looked into his face. High cheekbones shadowed his face, giving him a ruthless look. Black eyes beneath thick straight brows looked at her with longing and passion. His wide mouth curved in a tender smile. He removed his helm, and she saw the black glory of his hair, which curled about his temples and ears. The sharp line of his square jaw bespoke of strength and determination. He would surely rescue her from her lonely tower.

The gentle drum of the rain was soothing. Caitlyn's thoughts became calmer, as she watched the white mist curl about the huge dark trunks of the ancient trees. Her father was a gentle old man, white-haired and dignified, renowned as a scholar and often consulted by other scholars as far away as the Continent. His country neighbors thought he was a bit dotty because he did not share their interests in hunting, shooting, and gambling. He preferred a book to a brook, they said, shaking their heads, and who could understand that? All the tenants knew him as a good master nonetheless, and he kept Eldertree Manor well. Although he delighted in Celtic antiquities, his farming methods were the most modern in the county.

Caitlyn was his only child, born of a late marriage to a well-connected London heiress. The beauty of the Season, she had startled the *ton* by marrying an old man of forty-five instead of one of the many young bucks who sought her hand. The lovely Charis Lovelace did not hesitate to turn her back on London to accompany her husband to the deep shade-sequestered Eldertree Manor. They had but three years of love and companionship before Charis died in childbirth.

Sir Merlin loved his newborn daughter, but the loss of his beloved wife was too difficult a burden to allow him to take an active interest in Caitlyn's young life. He retreated to his books and farming, but he made sure that little Caitlyn had all the physical and mental necessities. She received an excellent education in the classics. She could read both Latin and Greek, as well as speak French and Italian.

At seventeen, she felt bored by these things. It was all perfectly well to know so many things, but rather useless, really, if you never had a chance to use them! True, the current state of affairs with Bonaparte forbade a visit to France, but surely, Italy was not yet an impossibility. Since she had been fourteen, her father had been enjoying her company more. Perhaps it was true what Bessie said, that Caitlyn was the exact semblance of her mother.

She examined her face in the little mullioned panes, small dark mirrors now as the grey day faded to deepening twilight. She saw herself, skin white as ivory, tinged with a darker damascene rose. With long slender fingers, she touched the wide high cheekbones and delicately molded chin that gave her face the feline quality that had led Bessie to call her "Cat." The flickering light of the fireplace flames threw shadows that shaded the strong planes of her face, the delicate hollows of her cheeks. Her mouth was wide, the upper lip drawn as a graceful bow, the underlip full, with the sensual ripeness of a cherry.

Perhaps they would both go to Italy, she thought. Had not Sir Merlin received a letter from Firenze some months ago? Then there had been a flurry of missives, and, in the last week, he had positively beamed at her over the dining room table at dinner. When she had asked about the correspondence a fortnight ago, he had merely rubbed his hands together and replied that she would know soon enough.

Bessie, calling Caitlyn's name and bringing the tea tray, interrupted her reverie. Caitlyn stepped out of her hidden bower, which had become decidedly chilly with the approaching evening.

"Oh there ye are, Missy. I brought ye a bit o' tea and cakes to keep ye until dinner. 'Tis a cheerless day, and I know how little ye like to be shut up in the house." She poured tea from a blue-and-white chinaware pot into a delicate fluted cup.

Caitlyn sat upon the large burgundy satin sofa and chose carefully from among the small desserts set out so temptingly upon the tray. "Look, Child, Mrs. Congdon has made a few cream cakes just for ye," Bessie said, pointing out the round flaky pastries stuffed with whipped cream. Caitlyn paused, a small apple tart in her graceful hand. "Oh, Bessie, I am not that hungry," she said, noting the look of desire that Bessie cast upon the tempting pastry. "You take it, and sit a bit with me. What is the news with Mrs. Congdon and the others?"

"Well, there has been an awful to-do over at Squire Thomas's. It seems that Miss Clarissa was all set to leave for London, when her maid up and married a cottager on the estate. She was already with child, so it wouldn't have been fittin' to go with Miss Clarissa anyway, but now the young Miss is without a maid and furious to have to do without during her trip! Everyone has been telling her she is like to be the white ewe lamb of the Season, and she has set her mind to go handsomely." Bessie wiped her fingers on the apron and looked at the remaining cream pastry.

Caitlyn smiled as she finished her tart and choose another, cherry this time. It was easy to find amusement in the follies and mishaps of others when sentenced to remain constantly in the audience of life, only witnessing, never acting in any role. She smiled at Bessie and nodded toward the remaining pastry. Bessie bobbed a grateful nod and continued with her tale. "Miss Clarissa is hot to make a good match. She is sure to be the most beautiful debutante of the Season. O' course that would not be true if you were going to London. You would quite put her in the shade. O' course there is no reason fer ye you to go to London to find an eligible match. Sir Merlin is looking after you, rightly enough. He's already found you a good husband." Bessie clapped one rough work-worn hand to her mouth. She was not supposed to have said a word, and here she had said all. Still, it was a shame that the coming of Lord Falconbridge, Sir Merlin's long-time friend and the proposed husband of his daughter, was known to all the servants belowstairs, but not to the young lady herself.

"Husband!" exclaimed Caitlyn. "Who is this husband my father has found for me? Why did he not mention this to me?" She put down the fragile cup with a small snap and strode about the room.

"He meant to, I warrant ye," cried Bessie in alarm, as she wrung her hands. "He meant to tell ye tomorrow night after his lordship arrived."

"Arrived! Tomorrow!" cried Caitlyn. "He is to come tomorrow! Who is he? Why did Father fix upon him as my intended?"

"He is the Earl of Falconbridge, lord of Foxearth, the manor next to Eldertree! He has been residing in Italy these last twelve years. I am sure he is a goodly man. Sir Merlin was uncommonly fond of him in the old days!"

Caitlyn felt her heart leap in tumult in her bosom. Surely her father couldn't expect her to marry some lord simply for the sake of joining their land together! Foxearth had pleasant pasturelands and woods all around it, and she had often ridden her horse over to the great park, where she sometimes caught a glimpse of the grey turrets of the old manor house. But to marry now, before she had seen anything of the world, and to settle down right next door with a man probably old enough to be her father! It was unbearable. Her entire tempestuous spirit rebelled at the idea. It must not happen! She composed her rebellious expression, carefully smoothing her frown, replacing the fierce scowl with a pleasant noncommittal smile.

"Well, Bessie," she said quietly, seating herself gracefully and pouring herself and the old nurse another cup of tea. "How does everyone know of these matters? Father does not approve of his personal papers being read."

"'Twas nothing like that, Miss," said Bessie, a tinge of fear creeping into her voice. "'Twas himself that said the very same as I said to you to Mr. Jones two nights ago. Oh, Miss, he is going to be ever-so angry. You won't tell, will you?"

Caitlyn thought swiftly. She needed time. "Of course not, Bessie," she said kindly, giving the old woman a kiss on the cheek. "I will say nothing at all about it to Father. You have nothing to fear. Please take away the tea things. I am quite finished with them."

"Yes, Miss," Bessie said and bore away the tray with the remains of the tea, glad that the young miss had been so understanding. She vowed to herself never to listen to backstairs gossip again. 'Twas a pity just the same, she thought. No doubt, Sir Merlin had the best of intentions, but he was not a willful, headstrong girl of seventeen, full of life, with all her dances yet to be danced!

Caitlyn sat curled on the large sofa and stared into the flames. Certainly she had no desire to marry some elderly man and retire to the manor house right next door! Why, she would be buried alive. A nebulous plan was taking shape in her mind, one that boded well to solve all her problems. Her Aunt Henrietta lived in London as a respectable young widow. Her husband Charles had died in the Continental wars, leaving her with a substantial fortune, a large town house in London, and a goodly manor in Devonshire. Why could she not sojourn with Aunt Henrietta for a time? She would surely present Caitlyn for the Season.

But how to get to London? Caitlyn was sorely puzzled, although something Bessie had said tickled at her mind like a light feather. How unfair that Clarissa Thomas would be going to London on the morrow, with nothing to worry about save for her lack of a maid.

Caitlyn sat up suddenly as the solution ran through her body like a flash of lightning. She could be that maid! By the time they discovered that she was missing, she would already be on her way. But how to reach Westmarch Manor, some three leagues beyond Eldertree? Certainly, she could not order the carriage. But she could ride! She could pack a small bundle of clothes, slip a horse out of the stable, and ride there. Then how would she explain her arrival on horseback? Caitlyn shook her head. There had to be a solution.

She closed her eyes, laying her head on her hands and staring sightlessly into the flames, as she used to do when just a child. Within the heart of the fire, a red glow against her closed eyelids, she saw the image of a horse, a great stallion, as deeply red in the sun as the sizzling coals in the fire's heart. Meteor! He was her father's breeding stallion, descended from the great Eclipse. And he had the habit of jumping his paddock fence in search of neighboring mares!

Pleased with herself, Caitlyn rose from her warm nest in the cushions and went lightly up to her room. She needed to go though the wardrobe in search of some proper clothes to add to her traveling bundle. She would leave in the last hour of darkness before sunrise. No one would miss her until nearly luncheon the following day!

She ran quickly through the Great Hall, her slipper-shod feet making little noise on the old flagstones. She ran lightly up the old staircase with the wood-paneled walls. The ancestral portraits stared down at her. Slowing to a fast walk, she passed the great archway from the older part of the manor house to the newer wing. She opened the great door to her own room, with its large oriel windows and tall canopied bed. Going to the wardrobe, she thrust her hand feverishly through the frocks hung there until she came to the last garments. She pulled them out eagerly. Yes, she thought, these would do. She laid them out upon the bed, two plain work gowns of grey woolsey.

Sir Merlin had insisted that Caitlyn learn everything about running a house, and, to that end, she had been put to apprenticeship in kitchen and scullery, poultry yard and garden. "If you don't know what you're about," he had chuckled, "the servants will take advantage." So she had accompanied Mrs. Congdon to market, with a basket on her arm to purchase spices and copper pots, and inspected the kitchen garden. She weeded and cut the fine herbs to flavor the game or fowl served at Sir Merlin's table. None of the other young ladies in the district had such duties, she knew, but Sir Merlin had dismissed them all as "too missish by half, a great flock of namby-pambies not worth a man's time." And, as a reward for her efforts, she had been given leave to go to the stables and ride any horse she chose.

The beautiful animals so delighted Caitlyn that she eagerly inquired of the head groom all there was to know of their care and feeding, of spavins and colic. "She's like no other young lady I ken," he said to Sir Merlin when he made his weekly inspection of the stables and tack. "And she has real talent for the beasts too, Sir Merlin. Not a one of them will kick or even flatten an ear. The beasts take to her, Sir."

The most beautiful of all was the great stallion Meteor. Sired in the line of the greatest racehorse ever bred, the Duke of Cumberland's Eclipse, he was the pride and joy of Sir Merlin, second in his affections only to Caitlyn herself. He had grave doubts when she requested that she be allowed to ride Meteor, but seeing the real affection and rapport between them removed all trace of fear for either. "You can ride him, my Dear, but I beg you keep close! There is as much danger to him from rabbit holes as there is for you, and," he added with a twinkle in his eye, "I intend to breed you both to advantage."

Caitlyn's face had suffused with a delicate pink glow, which betrayed the treacherous beating of her heart, but Sir Merlin remained oblivious to her feelings, amused by his own joke. Caitlyn had barely dreamed of that shadowy male who lurked somewhere in her future. She felt caught between her fear and her desire for the unknown bridegroom.

At times like those, she saddled Meteor and rode him astride round and round the spacious paddock, glorying in her freedom of power and control, all the more precious to her because she knew that she would not always possess it. One day, she must give up her freedom to become wife to some squire or lord, bear his children, manage his house, and submit to his desires. Yet as she groomed Meteor and curried the sweat off his gently glowing red coat, she wondered how that unknown man would look and what it would feel like to have his hard body under her hand as she had the stallion now. Then she would go back to the great grey manor house, and Bessie would prepare her a bath. Caitlyn would soak all the smell of sweat, leather, and horse off her delicate skin in the lavender-scented water, thereby returning to her civilized and demure self, the memory of the rocketing power of the great horse between her thighs buried deep behind her conventional dinner conversation and sweet smile.

Caitlyn could ride Meteor over to the Thomases' manor house. The great stallion teased the head groom and his stableboys. He had learned to slip the bar of his stable door and walk out of the barn down to the paddock. From there, if he desired, he could leap the white fence and gallop freely all over the great park or over the county, if he chose. Not that any of the other landowners minded if Meteor felt compelled to visit their mares unbeknownst to them or his owner. They too might have the good fortune to breed into the best line of racing horses in the world!

Caitlyn realized that she would have to appear at dinner, or someone would miss her. It would be better to retire to her room in the early evening, pleading a headache. If she left before dawn, it would be at least six hours before they missed either her or the great stallion. Clarissa would want to leave early in the morning. Caitlyn could arrive and be accepted before they found anyone else. Then, when they were safely on their way, she would tell Clarissa who she really was. What a delicious joke it would be! Caitlyn smiled as she imagined herself and Clarissa conspiring together, making wonderful plans of what they would do in London.

Caitlyn added other articles to her small bundle, some knit cotton stockings, a comb, two cotton chemises, all wrapped in a shawl. Next to the little bundle, she placed a cloak and scarf. When she arrived in London, her Aunt Henrietta would supply her with beautiful new dresses and gloves. She would put her hair up in coils and cascades of curls, threading her glowing locks with ribbons and garlands of flowers and pearls. Perhaps her father would be so glad to hear that she was in London after all that he would send her some of Mama's jewelry to wear. Caitlyn imagined herself and Clarissa standing side by side, her own deep auburn hair contrasting with Clarissa's pale champagne blonde. She would be in light seafoam green, Clarissa in pale blue, together attracting all the beaux, the cynosure of all eyes.

Caitlyn hid the tidy bundle deep within her wardrobe. It would not do for Bessie to come in to prepare her room and herself for bed, as she did every night, and see that bundle. Nobody must even suspect until Caitlyn was safely on her way. She could ride Meteor to the gates of the Thomases' park and walk thereafter. But how would she explain her sudden appearance to Lady Thomas? "I could be from a neighboring manor, Foxearth perhaps. I know Mrs. Carstairs, the housekeeper, I could say she referred me! Better than that!," she thought suddenly, "I can write a letter of recommendation! Nobody would think a servant could write, and nobody will send all the way to Foxearth to check."

Caitlyn walked over to the small writing desk that she kept in her room and pulled out several sheets of London's finest writing paper and a fine-nibbed writing pen. She composed her thoughts. She began to write, taking great care not to blot her words: "To Whom it May Concern, The bearer of this letter, Miss—" Caitlyn stopped in mid-sentence. She would need another name. Something a country girl would have, something like Bessie or Rose. She shook her head almost imperceptibly. Not even for a day would she go by either of those names. She wanted something that she liked, even if 'twere only a brief fiction. She put the pen down and thought. Nothing came.

Caitlyn heard a faint respectful scratching on the door. "Missy Cat," Bessie said, "have you forgotten you dine with Sir Merlin tonight? Do you need help getting ready?" Bessie waited quietly on the other side of the door. Despite their easy informality, born of long acquaintance and mutual respect, Bessie would not overstep her bounds. The young Miss was also the Mistress of the Manor, on the verge of being quite grown up and soon to be married! Bessie would wait outside. Brief noises came from the other side of the closed door. A chair scraped, a drawer shut.

"I'm coming, Bessie. Thank you, I had quite forgotten!" Bessie heard the light steps of her mistress running across the floor. The key turned in the lock, and the door was flung open. "Come in," Caitlyn said and pulled the nurse gaily into her elegant bedroom, softly glowing of polished wood, with soft carpets of woven red and green. "I am quite late, Bessie, do help me dress! I have already chosen this. Will it do?" Caitlyn pointed to the modest sprigged muslin gown with the blue pelisse.

"O' course, milady. Let me help you dress, and I'll brush your hair for ye. I think we have that much time."

"Are you sure, Bessie? I don't want to be late," said Caitlyn with a trace of anxiety, which she was trying unsuccessfully to conceal.

"O' course I'm sure. Trust old Bessie," replied the old nurse with a smile as her fingers deftly wove Caitlyn's long hair into a neat coil, which Bessie pinned at the nape of Caitlyn's neck. The child was nervous, of course. She already knew of the impending announcement and naturally wanted to know more about her intended husband. What girl wouldn't be anxious? But there was something else, something different and troubling, which lurked just below Bessie's consciousness. She shook her head, but could not dismiss the notion that something highly unusual had just happened.

"What's the matter, Bessie? Is something troubling you?" Caitlyn asked, her voice low with concern.

"Nothing but a wee bit of wonder that you are all grown up so fast and ready to embark on a woman's life. I'm going to miss you after tomorrow." In the mirror, Caitlyn's answering smile was weak, and her color drained, leaving her skin pale as pearls.

"What do you mean?" Caitlyn whispered, her hands on the vanity table to steady herself. Nevertheless, she swayed a bit where she sat, and Bessie feared that she might faint.

"Why, Darlin', only that you are a woman ready to be married. I am sure your father's done well by you. During your courtship and after your marriage, you won't have time for poor old Bessie. Why, you shall be the greatest lady in the county, with horses and carriages, gowns for every day, and a great ball on your birthday every year! Now, see how pretty you look!" Bessie stepped away so that Caitlyn could admire Bessie's handiwork.

In front of the mirror sat a young woman of startling beauty. The simple dress showed off Caitlyn's graceful form admirably. It was cut low enough to reveal the gentle curve of her bosom, as sweet and ripely swelling as country apples. Her long graceful neck was accented by a small necklace of gold, ornamented by a single cameo that had once belonged to her dead mother. In her delicate ears, Caitlyn wore earrings of small square-cut garnets surrounded by pearls, their colors refracting the glint of her hair, the glow of her skin.

"Sure and ye look like the grand lady ye will soon be," said Bessie, stepping back to admire her charge. "He will but lay eyes on ye and fall head over heels in love. Ye have no ta fear of the morrow, Lass."

Caitlyn stood up and put the lace shawl about her shoulders. The tall slender woman who stared back at her from the mirror had a queenly hauteur, belied by the swift smile and the quick laughter that lit her face and eyes. If Bessie only knew her thoughts! Caitlyn turned this way and that to view herself. Her long thick hair, simply dressed in a large chignon, left the nape of her neck bare, accentuating her slender figure.

Bessie worked the long kid gloves up over her shapely hands, over the forearm to the elbows, smoothing the wrinkles. Her slender arms and bare shoulders had none of the fashionable plumpness of other young girls. Caitlyn was lithe and strong. "Yer father, Sir Merlin, will be pleased that you have grown into such a lovely young woman. Many's the day I worrit about you, out with them horses in the paddocks or walking in the park. Ye might have been a boy for all ye cared of the things a young lady of quality ought to know. But ye've turned out fine, every bit as beautiful as your mither afore ye."

Caitlyn descended the grand staircase slowly, conscious of the dignity of her gloves and gown, as well as the heavy coiffure into which her luxuriant hair had been painstakingly pinned. To her left were the ancestral portraits, faces she knew well, who had been almost playmates throughout her lonely childhood. Frown though they might, she could not, would not accept an arranged marriage with a kindly old man for the sake of property and an heir! She would find love's excitement, even if she must risk heartbreak. Her thoughts whirled to the hidden bundle in her wardrobe and her plot to escape.

Descending the final step, she turned right through the massive stone archway into the large vaulted great hall, with its minstrel gallery and heavy iron chandeliers. Once it had been the great hall of the castle keep, but Llewellyn ancestors had added other wings, and the Great Hall had become a stately dining room.

Before her stretched the long table of polished wood with heavy silver candelabra and fine china set on snowy linen. She slipped gracefully into the chair that Jones, the butler, held for her at the foot of the table. Caitlyn felt faintly foolish. Usually she dined with her father at the much smaller table in the library or even with Bessie in the servants' dining room near the kitchen. Many evenings, Sir Merlin, often busy with his studies in his stuffy little office, took only a bit of bread, meat, and cheese on a tray. Here she sat, with nearly twenty feet of space separating her from her father at the other end of the table. She unfolded the white linen napkin as Jones poured the claret into the delicate Venetian wineglass.

From the head of the table, Sir Merlin raised his glass to Caitlyn. "Well, my dear Girl, here is to the future." He drank a sip and added, with a twinkle in his eye, "No doubt you've already heard something about your future."

Caitlyn blushed. "I've heard that our neighbor and your old friend Lord Falconbridge is returning from Italy and is coming for a visit here tomorrow." She patted her lips with the napkin to hide her lack of composure.

"And you haven't heard that I've settled upon the Earl of Falconbridge as your future husband?" Sir Merlin chuckled. "I've done well by you, see if I haven't, when he arrives tomorrow." His speech was briefly interrupted by the footman's passing him the platter of pheasant. "That one," said Sir Merlin, pointing to a golden roasted plump breast of pheasant.

"Very good, Sir," said the footman, who then placed the indicated portion upon his master's plate.

"Never did hold with soup," said Sir Merlin, cutting a tender morsel out with the heavy ornate silverware. "A very uninteresting liquid that adds nothing to a meal."

The same footman presented the platter to Caitlyn, who indicated a leg. She felt that she could hardly eat anything, her heart was beating so heavily. So, it was true! Her father fully intended to marry her to his old friend. She must flee tomorrow at dawn. "Yes, Father," she murmured, spearing a small piece of the succulent fowl on her fork, but chewing it without interest. It felt as dry as splintered wood in her present state of near panic. Another footman brought a bowl of roast potatoes to her, garnished with fresh sprigs of parsley and paprika. Caitlyn took a small one. If she ate nothing, her father might notice and have her kept under watch, lest she take ill. And that would ruin her plans. A little more wine would strengthen her, and she beckoned to Jones.

"Well, what do you think of my idea, eh? Have I not done well by you?" Sir Merlin beamed down the expanse of white napery and crystal at her, waiting expectantly for her reply.

"I have no reason to doubt your good judgment, Father," Caitlyn replied, laying down her knife and fork and hiding her hands in her lap to conceal their trembling. "I am sure Lord Falconbridge will have every requisite to recommend him to my good opinion. When does he arrive?"

"He'll not be keeping town hours here in the country, though he will have just arrived this afternoon from London. No, I expect we'll not be seeing him here until after luncheon. And we have business matters to discuss in my study." Sir Merlin winked. "So I think you will meet him tomorrow at dinner."

Caitlyn carefully took another sip of her wine and blessed the feeling of warmth that filled her, for she had gone cold with her father's words. At dinner tomorrow. No wonder her father had wanted her to dress for dinner. It was a rehearsal for her first meeting with her future husband. "Will I do?" she enquired with more animation than she felt and helped herself to the trifles that were passed to her on a silver platter.

"My dear," said Sir Merlin, "no man who saw you could fail to love you immediately. I am so proud of you." He signaled to Jones for more wine. Caitlyn noted the gleam of a tear on her father's old cheek. "You look so like your mother," Sir Merlin murmured before downing the wine in three gulps. "May we never grow apart. I could not bear to lose you."

Caitlyn got up quickly and ran down the long table's length to where her aged parent sat. "Oh, Father, I love you so!" she exclaimed while putting her arms about him. But she felt an ache in her heart. What would he think when he found her gone, even if it were not forever? What else could she do? She must have a life and love of her own. Resolutely, she kissed him on the forehead and said, "May I take my leave now? I am very tired, perhaps with the wine, and would like to retire to my bedchamber."

"Of course, my darling Child. Go along, and may your dreams be happy." He patted her hand saying, "Trust me, Child."

"Of course," she said softly, but her feelings were a riot of impulses. She turned and fled the great hall.

She reached her room in a state of breathless excitement. She felt the rapid beating of her heart. Her hands trembled as she unloosed the chignon and her thick coils of hair tumbled down over her shoulders.

"Cat? 'Tis me, yer old Bessie. Can I not come in and help ye? I've brought ye a little tea to settle yer nerves."

"Bessie?" Caitlyn looked about, but nothing that would give away her plan was in sight. Her bundle of clothes was tucked out of sight in the back of the closed wardrobe. "Yes, please come in. I would be grateful for some tea."

Bessie entered and closed the door carefully behind her. She set the tray down carefully upon the marquetry table. "What's this, then?" she said, looking at the pens and paper. "Do ye intend to make up your list for bridal clothes? Ye should know that Sir Merlin loves ye dearly and will ge' ye anythin' ye'd ask."

Caitlyn smiled a small smile, but to Bessie's critical eyes, she looked far too pale, save for the feverish red that burned upon her cheeks. "Here," she said. "Take this, 'twill have a calming effect on ye." Bessie handed Caitlyn a small glass full of a light amber liquid, which had been hidden beneath a linen napkin.

"What is it, Bessie?" said Caitlyn as she lifted it to her lips. The strong odor of spirits caused her to wrinkle her nose.

"'Tis some of the Master's very best brandy. 'Twill steady yer nerves. Take a sip," Bessie replied, watching Caitlyn kindly. Caitlyn obediently took a very small sip. "Ye'll not be tellin' on me now, that I took some of his lordship's best brandy? Mr. Jones would have me out o' here before ye could say 'Jack Robbins.'"

"Thank you, Bessie. I feel much better now. Of course, I'll not say anything to Jones." The drink was strengthening, but Caitlyn suddenly got the idea that it might be wiser to save it until she really needed it on the morrow. "Will you help me get ready for bed? I would like to undress."

"Sartinly, me darlin' child. Let old Bessie undo yer laces here and help ye out of this muslin. Ye have a lovely figure," she said approvingly as she viewed Caitlyn in her white undergown. Womanly, but slender. Not overripe, like some misses. "'Tis a lovely bride ye will be." Bessie took the silver brushes from the mirrored vanity. "Now set yersel down here, and let me do yer hair for bed." Caitlyn sat in front of the silvered mirror. Her hair spread its silken sheen across her shoulders. Bessie stood behind her and brushed the shining waterfall of fire. "I am beautiful," thought Caitlyn with despair. "I am lovely enough to draw my knight to me, but instead, I am to be married to an old man." Tears began to brim in her sea-green eyes as she watched Bessie braid her hair for bed.

"There now, ye are all ready. Shall I take away the brandy and blow out the candle?"

"Oh please no, Bessie. I feel much better now, but I would like to write a bit before I sleep. And the brandy will calm my nerves. Will it be all right if I drink it just before I sleep?"

"Yes, Miss. I think it will be fine. Donna worry yersel any. All maids are nervous near to meeting their husbands. 'Twill pass. Good night to ye, and blessed dreams." Bessie left quietly. Caitlyn, staring into the mirror, saw Bessie go.

Caitlyn darted over to the table, moving the nearly full glass of brandy to a safe distance. It would never do to spill such a wonderful liquid. The little she had swallowed had first burned her tongue, throat, and belly, but now she felt the pleasant afterglow of that fire warming and strengthening her. It would be good to have tomorrow morning. She looked at the rest of the things on the tea tray that Bessie had brought. There were a few biscuits there. Even better. Now she would have a bit of something to break her fast. Caitlyn took up her pen and, organizing her thoughts, pulled out the unfinished letter and began where she had left off.

"To Whom it May Concern, The bearer of this letter, Miss—" Caitlyn paused and nibbled the end of her pen. What to call herself? Her delicately arched brows drew together in concentration. The image of the red heraldic cat in the stained glass in the library came to her mind's eye, along with Bessie's voice and the rain-washed griffins that guarded the entrance to the park at Eldertree Manor. She put her pen to paper and wrote, "Cat Gryffyn has worked at Foxearth these past four years. She is trained in all the duties of a lady's maid." Caitlyn thought a minute. She was not exactly trained, but she did know what was expected. Anyway, it was only a ruse, one that she would end as soon as she could. She continued to write. "She is neat and clean and well-spoken. I have had every satisfaction with her during her employment here and can fully recommend her."

"That should suffice," thought Caitlyn. "Do I sign it, I wonder?" She had never seen Mrs. Carstairs' handwriting. "But I don't think Lady Thomas has either." In her best script, Caitlyn signed "Elizabeth Carstairs, Foxearth."

She blotted the paper carefully and folded it. Using the candle, she melted some red sealing wax and dripped it upon the letter. With her own seal, a beautifully engraved and fanciful "C," she imprinted the hardening wax. "They will take it to mean Carstairs," she reasoned. Weighing her work critically in her hand, Caitlyn thought that it looked quite genuine.

Climbing into bed, she blew out the candle. Beyond the drawn drapes, the waning moon was rising. "At least there will be some light to see by tomorrow," she thought thankfully. "I hope I do not oversleep." But her excitement was such that she felt that she could hardly close her eyes the whole night long.

ESCAPE

Caitlyn awoke with a start. She hurried over to the window and parted the curtains. In the eastern sky, the morning star shone brilliantly white, heralding the dawn. Fearing to light a candle, Caitlyn dressed as quietly as she could in her darkened bedchamber. The servants would be stirring soon, she thought as she picked up the clothes bundle in one hand and her shoes in the other. The crystal glass with the brandy caught her eye, along with the biscuits on the tray. She swallowed the fiery amber liquid in two swallows, trying not to choke on the strong drink. It made her breathless while it burned through her body. She bit into a biscuit, and some of the fire dissipated. She felt less lightheaded. Noiselessly, she slipped out of her room and down the back stairway.

With great caution, she unbolted the scullery door. When the scullery maid did find it unbolted, she would be unlikely to mention it, fearing the scolding that she would get from Mr. Jones, the butler. It was her duty to see that it was locked for the night.

The dawn air was cold, and the dew of the kitchen herb garden was heavy, chilling Caitlyn's bare feet and soaking her skirt hem. She bent and wiped her feet dry with her cloak and put on the stockings and shoes that she had carried. The stable yard was just beyond the garden gate.

Moving silently over the brick paths between the tidy rows of herbs, Caitlyn opened the wooden gate as quietly as she could. In the chicken yard beyond, a rooster crowed, warning her to make haste. She ran lightly over the cobblestones of the stable yard, slipping like a shadow into the musty darkness of the stone stables.

Within the stables, she heard the soft sounds of the horses munching their hay, the whisk of tails. From the box stalls, the mares softly whickered at her, recognizing her scent. At the end of the row, she heard Meteor's greeting neigh. Picking up her skirts, she walked quickly to his stall. "Hush now," she said, putting her hand upon his silken nose. "Don't you make a fuss." Meteor blew a soft greeting through his nose and nuzzled her clothes, looking for treats. "None of that now," Caitlyn said. "We have to ride."

She deftly slid back the heavy bolt that closed the box stall. It had been firmly latched, but Meteor had slipped his bolt before. Taking him by the halter, she led him out of the stable into the dark shadows of the lightening grey dawn. Looking fearfully around, but seeing no one, she led him to the mounting block and lightly swung herself astride his bare back. Crouching as low to his neck as she could, she rode him slowly over the cobblestones and out to the paddocks beyond.

When his iron-shod feet touched the turf, she sat up and, with a high whistle and a kick of her heels, spurred him into a canter, then a full gallop. Meteor headed toward the white paddock fence. The whitening sky and mist obscured distances, and Caitlyn's heart felt squeezed by fear. She felt the muscles of the great stallion bunch under her as he galloped toward the white railing, felt him gather himself to leap. She leaned over his neck, holding on to his mane as the powerful horse sailed over the fence, landing with a rocking jolt on the other side.

"We did it." She patted his neck, and the stallion regained his stride. The ragged ends of the mist drifted by them as they galloped across the rolling meadows towards Westmarch Manor. With every league they traveled, she felt the cold hands of her unwanted bridegroom, like night's ragged thinning mists, diminish their grip upon her young life. With her night terrors now past, she gloried in this mad gallop across the rolling fields, which were still dangerously wet with dew. Meteor was as surefooted as if he had wings, and Caitlyn felt invulnerable to Fate and its minions.

The sun had just cleared the horizon, washing the grey stones of the great house with thin light as Caitlyn first glimpsed it. Caitlyn drew the stallion from a canter to a trot, then to a walk. She patted his neck again as she let the halter reins rest upon his neck. "Good boy," she whispered. "You know what to do next." The magnificent horse stopped, his ears flicking at the sound of her words, snorting a reply. Caitlyn slid down from him, her bundle still slung securely across her hip. Beyond the wall that enclosed the back gardens and stable area was the servants' door, where her masquerade would begin. She stroked Meteor's velvet nose. "Go on." She slapped him lightly with the reins. "Go on home." The great horse nuzzled her one more time, then smartly turned about and trotted away toward the far-off pastures of Eldertree Manor.

Caitlyn stood behind the wall, listening, as Meteor's hoofbeats grew fainter as he trotted away over the turf. She drew several deep breaths to calm herself. Her heart was beating furiously. The early morning felt chill and dank. Smoothing her skirts and inspecting her bundle, she checked herself to make sure that her dress had not become disarranged. She re-coiled the two thick braids of hair that had come loose when she jumped the first fence. After straightening her grey cloak, she stepped around the wall into the courtyard beyond.

Stepping boldly up to the shut door, she knocked firmly. "Someone should be stirring by now," she thought. The door was opened by a severe-looking woman with grey hair pinned back tightly under her cap.

"And what do ye be wantin' this morning?" the woman asked brusquely, her narrow gaze intently taking in every article of Caitlyn's dress and deportment as she stood before the half-open door. "We serve no beggars here."

Biting her underlip, Caitlyn bobbed the gaunt woman a brief curtsey. In an imitation of Bessie's speech, Caitlyn said, "An' it please ye, Ma'am, I come over from Mrs. Carstairs at Foxearth. I heard they were lookin' fer a maid for the Young Miss, an' the housekeeper, Mrs. Carstairs, said I might apply, as I was a likely lass, and perhaps could do better in the world."

"Well, Girl," said the woman, her face registering no change in attitude, the door still held half open, "do ye have any references from this Mrs. Carstairs, who thinks so highly of ye that she'd let ye go, slipping over the fields at dawn?"

Caitlyn drew in a long breath. "Aye, an' I have it right here, Ma'am. And Mrs. Carstairs herself had me driven to the park gates by Foxearth's own coachman, that I might get here early before any other girls." She withdrew from her bundle the long sealed paper that she had written the night before and gave it to the stern servant woman.

After the woman took it, she opened the door and gestured Caitlyn in. "Shake the dews and damp off yer cloak, and sit down by the hob over there. I am just getting the porridge ready for the other servants. Have a cup of tea to warm ye. I'll give yer letter to Mr. Wright, the butler, and he can ge' it to Lady Thomas." Caitlyn gratefully took off the woolen cloak and hung it on a hook near the door. She was surprised by the woman's new friendliness and glad to be accepted by her. Her plan was going well.

"And what be yer name, Girl?" asked the woman. "I am Mrs. Gwyn, the cook." She held out a cup and saucer filled with fragrant, steaming tea.

"I thank ye, Mrs. Gwyn. I am called Cat Gryffyn," Caitlyn said, pleased with the sound of her new name, even though it would be hers for only a matter of hours. "Me Dad is a cottager on Foxearth Estate," she continued after a sip of tea, relishing the chance to embroider her story. "Me mum is dead. I have been working at the house since I was just a girl. Mrs. Carstairs has been very good to me."

"Well, ye are not much more than a girl now. How old are ye?"

"I have 18 years, come this summer."

Mrs. Gwyn took the cup and saucer, now empty, back to the basins. "Perhaps ye could busy yerself with setting the table for eight. The other servants will be down soon, and ye might as well make yerself useful if ye want to work here."

Upstairs, Mr. Wright stood respectfully before Lady Thomas, the mistress of the house. She was a heavy florid woman with a large bosom, a haughty manner, and a disdainful look. She perused the letter that Mr. Wright had handed her through her lorgnette, which she affected because it gave her more dignity. Her eyes, however, were excellent, so the device only made the words blurry and hard to read.

"This is quite impressive, Wright. Did you say she is down in the servants room at this minute?"

"Yes, your ladyship," he replied.

"Send her here immediately!" Wright made a quick bow. Turning smartly upon his heel, he walked rapidly towards the servants' staircase. Finding a suitable maid for Clarissa on such short notice would put both the Thomas ladies into better humor, which made everything more pleasant belowstairs. He just hoped that Mrs. Gwyn was not filling the young thing's ears full of tales. It would be awkward if she ran off without even setting eyes on her ladyship and Clarissa.

Caitlyn was seated in the kitchen, pouring a cup of tea for Mrs. Gwyn. He noted with approval her clear-eyed direct look; her straight-backed, yet elegant, posture. "Miss Clarissa could learn a thing or two about grace and composure from this one," he thought.

"Cat Gryffyn, her ladyship will see you now," he said. He was pleased to see that she did not stutter or become flustered, but simply put down the teapot and rose gracefully from her chair. She followed him quietly up the backstairs to the morning room.

Caitlyn's heart was beating furiously as she climbed the stairs behind Mr. Wright. She had not seen Lady Thomas or Clarissa since the Assembly Ball almost three months before. Would they remember her? She patted her primly pinned braids. If she could convince herself that she was Cat Griffyn, she could convince them until they were all well on their way to London. Taking a deep breath and folding her hands in front of her, she looked gravely at the floor and stepped lightly and quickly into the imposing room.

The interview was surprisingly short. Lady Thomas did all the talking. Clarissa merely stared at her with disdain.

"Well, after inspecting yourself and your credentials, I find that you will do. Mind that you remember your station at all times. You have a proud look about you. I cannot abide self-serving, forward girls. You must know your place and keep to it."

"Yes, your ladyship," Cat had murmured, her eyes on the floor. She was puzzled as to what she had done that seemed forward. Afraid of being recognized, Cat had kept her head bowed for the entire interview.

"Remember that, Girl," Clarissa had interjected. "You are not very pretty, and if you lose this post, you will not have much to recommend yourself to another in London. Do you hear?"

"Yes, m' lady," Cat replied, eyes down. Her plan was already going awry. How different Clarissa was now to the simpering young woman Caitlyn sat next to at the Assembly Ball. Then Clarissa had complimented her on her beauty and her dress, laughing behind her fan.

An hour later, Caitlyn stood at the front door with Clarissa and her ladyship, surrounded by boxes and trunks, waiting for the coach to be brought around. Clarissa and Lady Thomas were standing a little way off; both were bundled in hats, scarves, and gloves against the still cold and damp west winds. Standing over by the baggage, Cat stole surreptitious glances at them as they talked together. Lady Thomas fussed with Clarissa's traveling bonnet, straightening the deep indigo velvet ribbons.

The carriage drew up in front of them, and the footmen began loading the baggage onto the roof. Cat handed up some of the smaller pieces and stepped away to judge with a critical eye the horseflesh harnessed to it. They were a flashy team of greys, well matched in size and strength, but Cat could see immediately that they were green and unsteady. The harness too was ill cared for, the leather showing small cracks, and the hold-back straps looked worn and in need of replacement.

She thought about drawing her ladyship's attention to it, but remembered the woman's warning about keeping her place. Cat glanced up to where the coachman sat on the box. His hard-set face did not look open to receiving advice, especially from a lady's maid. How different things were from this position, Cat thought wryly. If she were at home and the coachman had presented her with such a lax exhibition, she would have immediately ordered him to change the harness or delay the trip to mend the old one, if necessary. Nothing like this would ever be allowed at Eldertree Manor. Both she and Sir Merlin were too conscientious to allow teams and harness to be treated in such a slipshod way.

The Thomas ladies had entered the coach, and Cat hurried over to the door to join them. The footman was just closing the door, with its intricate heraldic design and folding the steps back up. Clarissa glanced at her once through the carriage window and turned her head away with an audible sniff.

"On top, my Girl," the footman said to Cat, who was still standing bemused at the pavement. "Yer to ride on top with the coachman. The weather is good enough for the likes of you." He took her arm and steered her to the box where the driver sat. "Climb up wi' ye, then," he said and gave her backside a shove.

Cat turned angrily to look down upon him, but he had already walked to the back of the carriage to take his stance at the rear. His familiarity rankled Cat. Had such things gone on at Eldertree Manor? Sadly, she realized that she did not know for sure, but looking carefully at all her memories, she could recall nothing of the sort. How different the rest of the world was from her home!

There everything was kindly and orderly. Servants were treated well, and discipline was maintained. Women of every class were safe from men's unwelcome attentions. Apparently, this was not so in the outside world. Cat would be careful to give no offense, to arouse no man's interest until she could shed this dubious masquerade. For the first time, she began to doubt the wisdom of her plan. Certainly, Clarissa did not appear likely to greet her announcement of her identity with enthusiasm. In fact, Cat realized with a great shock that Clarissa was jealous of her looks. She would not welcome a rival in London and would probably do everything she could to destroy her!

As the carriage jounced out of the park, past the high gates, Cat pulled her scarf tighter about her throat. The air was still chilly, and the newly risen sun had yet to pour any real warmth upon the morning.

The coachman whipped the horses into a brisk trot. Her ladyship had very little notion of the limitations of horseflesh, or human flesh either, for that matter, and had set her mind on arriving at Wrexham for luncheon and Shrewsbury by eventide. The horses had heart, but they were skittish as a team. But it did no good to tell her that. No, she would have him drive them even if they was just green broke and likely to bolt.

He spat and hoped that if the horses did bolt, it would be her bleeding ladyship and her spoilt daughter who took the hurt of it. He looked quickly at the girl beside him as he drove. Now she was a piece. All modest and yes, ma'am, and no, ma'am, not saying boo to a goose. There was something else about her he could not quite put his finger on. She had a knowing look about her, that one.

Cat began to relax as they drew further away from the neighborhood of Eldertree Manor. The sun gently warmed the air, and she began to enjoy the views from her perch on the box. Freed from the meeting with the Earl of Falconbridge, she began to dream of the yet-to-be-found knight-errant who would rescue her from the fusty old hall. The hours passed by as agreeably as the landscape and her romantic imaginings.

The sun had passed the meridian when from below them there came a rap on the carriage roof. Her ladyship's walking stick, a-thumping on the roof, the coachman thought. She wanted more speed. He sighed and chucked the reins, urging the greys into a slow canter. He wished that her ladyship would let him do the driving. These roads was tricky, and with a raw team, ye never knew what accident might be around the bend.

He glanced again at Cat. She was staring intently at the team, now quickening their canter. His eyes followed her glance down to the harness. The hold-back straps were fraying! He had told those stable lads again and again to oil the harness. With all his trouble to oversee the teams at Westmarch, he couldn't see to everything himself.

He pulled back on the lines to get the horses to slow their pace, but the outside front runner sped up instead. That one always did take the bit between his teeth. Their speed increased, and the carriage rocked upon its springs as they swept into the wide curve of the road. The left horse closest to the carriage stumbled briefly, causing his outside partner to lurch violently.

The coachman endeavored to rein in his pointers, but they had begun to shy toward the verge, pulling the bouncing carriage across the deep mud ruts that scored the country roads in early March. Cat held on to the box as best she could. The carriage swayed in an alarming fashion, and the screaming of the two ladies within did nothing to promote tranquillity.

She could see that unless their coachman could stop the greys, they should soon be overset in the road.

"Pull up your seconds," she cried, for in his concern to check the gallop of his pointers, he had unaccountably given his wheelers a slack rein, and they were adding their weight and strength to the dangerous course of the lead horses.

"I know my team, Miss," cried the coachman, but Cat was gratified to see that he did begin to rein them in as well. She thought that they were quite going to continue without oversetting, when a horse and rider cantered around the narrowed bend of the road dead in front of them.

THE ACCIDENT

Many things happened at once. The intruder expertly wheeled his mount out of their way in a consummate piece of horsemanship. The unfortunate coachman was not so talented, and in his panic threw the brake on the carriage. This caused the frayed hold-back straps to snap in two, The horses, frightened by the unexpected gentleman's flaring redingote pulled sharply to the left, heedless of the drag of the carriage. The wheel bounced into a deep, water-filled rut. The horses lunged, and the carriage majestically fell upon its side.

Cat found herself flung out of the box and landed on her back with a hard impact upon the grassy verge of the road. She lay dazed for a moment, her grey woolen skirt pulled halfway up her thigh, revealing to the stranger a long slender and shapely leg clothed in a black cotton stocking. Despite the pandemonium about him, the handsomely dressed gentleman noted the girl's lovely form with approval, even as he swiftly dismounted from the prancing chestnut, quickly assaying the entire situation with the practiced eye of an impeccable horseman. The ladies inside the carriage were screaming and wailing now, but Vere Courtenay Fairfax rapidly determined that they were in no danger other than being severely inconvenienced.

The immediate problems were the fallen coachman, who lay partially pinned under the box by the accident, and the rearing, snorting horses, now in a froth of panic. The threat of their trampling hooves must be dealt with first. Fairfax moved quietly toward the nearest of the bucking, whinnying greys, making low, soothing noises in his throat.

Cat sat up, feeling the ache of her impact with the ground in her back and shoulders. It was not the first time that she had fallen to the ground at speed. Certainly, she had taken enough purlers while learning to hunt. Gingerly, she tested all her muscles, ascertained that she had no broken bones, and stood, shaking her head to clear the slight dizziness that she felt.

There by the lead horses' head stood the silly fool who had caused the entire disaster. He had seized the bridle in one black gloved hand, and speaking gently, was endeavoring to calm the maddened animal. The brisk March winds, blowing wide the folds of his elegant seven-caped redingote, further panicked the other point horse, denying success to his efforts.

Cat felt about her neck for the scarf that she had tied there and unwound it hastily. Stepping decisively up to the plunging horse, dodging its iron-shod hooves, she dexterously threw it about its eyes. The horse immediately ceased its mad panic and stood snorting and blowing, trembling and still.

With its partner suddenly quieted and docile, the other grey became calmer at the hands of the imposing stranger. The unknown gentleman cast an astonished and appreciative glance at his sudden assistant. Even in her drab clothes, she was remarkably beautiful. The heavy long braids of her russet hair hung down her back, and her green eyes were full of fire under the fierce arch of her brows.

She quickly stepped away from the horse, her scarf still about its eyes, giving the stranger a brief contemptuous look. "If you are quite finished with causing mishaps, I beg you to hold these horses while I tend to the unfortunate coachman."

Fairfax looked over this fiery girl with admiring amusement. By her clothes, she appeared only a pretty servant girl, but her clear voice had conveyed an authority that suggested a cool head in an emergency and that she expected obedience. He had rarely been treated to such a raking by a member of his own class, let alone a serving wench. He admitted himself intrigued as he watched her stride away. In all, she was as charming a wench as he had ever seen. The groaning coachman, having come to consciousness and extricated himself from beneath the box, now sat by the side of the road. He rubbed his leg and moaned, but did not seem seriously injured. The footman, who had stayed prudently out of sight while the horses were still in their dangerous maddened state, now slipped forward to assist the girl with the coachman. From inside the overturned carriage came a thumping and a female wailing.

"You there," Vere commanded the footman. "Come hold these horses, while I tend to your mistress. Coachman, can you stand?"

"I think so, Sir," replied the Coachman with a deferential tug at his forelock. "I think I may have sprained myself, but I might rise with a little help."

"Very well. Girl," he said, looking at Cat for the second time, with a very long and intent gaze, deliberately perusing the piquant charms of her slender lithe figure: the defiant uptilt of the delicately rounded chin, the opulence of her braids, which confined in their coils all the fire of her magnificent auburn mane, and the imperious blaze of her bright green eyes, darkened with pique. "Go tend to your mistress and her companion while I assist the coachman. He is too heavy for you."

She bobbed her head once in acknowledgment only, with not a trace of the submissiveness with which servants usually treated him. He watched her walk gingerly over the deep mud ruts to the carriage. Just as she reached for the door handle, the head and shoulders of an enchanting porcelain doll of a girl appeared.

Seeing her maid, Clarissa scowled, distorting her pretty features. "Cat, where have you been? Did you not think we might have been killed in here? Mama may be terribly injured by the fall. I have been ever so frightened, exhausted by knocking and crying for help. What took you so long, you dirty sloven? Look at your hair, all tumbled down."

Vere approached the two women and removed his high crowned hat as he did so. "Your pardon, Miss, for being so overbold to address you, but in this juncture, I think circumstances would allow me to petition to be of assistance, even if we have not been properly introduced. May I present myself? I am Vere Courtenay Fairfax, at your service."

Clarissa turned to look at him with amazement and then simpered her thanks. "Oh thank you, Sir, for your kind offer. I find we are truly in a difficult situation and do require masculine assistance. Your offer is gratefully accepted, with thanks."

Both girls stood silently by, regarding him, the porcelain white and rose-pink blonde from beneath fluttering eyelashes, the splendid auburn-haired incognito goddess with a direct censorious green-eyed stare.

He was a man above six feet in height, his aristocratic chiseled features crowned with midnight black hair, curling locks *à la Brutus* framing a fine forehead, deeply set and heavily lidded black eyes, a high-bridged, nearly aquiline nose, and a thin-lipped wide mouth set in a slightly sardonic smile.

Beneath the woolen seven-caped redingote, he was wearing an exquisitely cut coat of impeccable broadcloth of the deepest black over his wide shoulders. Narrowly cut, it displayed to advantage his trim waist and narrow hips. His long legs with well-muscled thighs were encased in tight grey breeches. His polished top boots, now spotted by the mud that he had walked through, showed off his muscular calves.

From within the disabled carriage came a loud moan and a furious rapping. "Help me, Child," wailed Lady Thomas. "I cannot bestir myself without your aid."

"Oh dear," whispered Clarissa. "What is one to do? Cat is outside, and I cannot get out, nor can she get in." She looked beguilingly at Vere from under lowered eyelashes.

"Well, give me your hand yourself, Girl," her parent bawled in tones of exasperation. "You are not so strengthless as all that!"

"But Mama," protested Clarissa, who looked anxiously at Mr. Fairfax. "I may not be as strong as you require."

"Girl, you will help your parent or suffer the consequences. Give me your hand!"

Clarissa gave the attractive stranger a swift smile and to Cat a venomous look. She then turned her back to them both and stretched her hand downward towards her fallen mother. She felt herself suddenly bent double by the heavy weight of the elder woman and gave a dreadful grunt as she attempted to heave her ladyship to her feet. The effort was too much for her. Her mother's weight was far too great, and Clarissa slipped, lost her own footing, and tumbled down in a heap beside her moaning parent. From within came a short sharp cry that could have been an oath.

Vere smiled briefly at the ridiculous scene, catching the eye of the beautiful girl he had heard addressed as Cat. He caught a quick glimpse of the laughter in her eye.

Unable to resist the comedy of the situation, Cat was, nevertheless, torn by anxiety at the delay that he had caused. Cat marked the insult that his rude interest added to the injury. She disliked him intensely.

"My ladies, let me help you. I can climb in and be of assistance," she said hurriedly, resuming her role.

"There are already far too many of us in here," Lady Thomas bawled from within, her aggrieved tones betraying her displeasure.

By the temper already shown by the younger lady, Fairfax thought, the beautiful servant maid would be likely turned out for her lack of speedy action.

Swiftly, he stepped between Cat and the carriage door. "My ladies, allow me to extricate you from your unfortunate situation."

Clarissa stood up. "My lord, thank you for your offer. If I could but get out of this carriage, there would be room for a stronger arm to assist my mother."

"Of course." He looked appreciatively again at Cat. "Please help your mistress out of the coach, and escort her across the ruts while I aid her ladyship."

Clarissa's face fell in disappointment. She had imagined the tall handsome stranger sweeping her up in his arms and carrying her across the road with its deep spring ruts and mud. Now she would surely spoil her pink slippers, which she had worn against the advice of her mother, who had recommended sturdy traveling shoes.

Clarissa carefully composed her face to one of sweet sorrow and replied, "Thank you, kind Sir, but I fear my footwear will not bear me on such a perilous journey." She gave a little hop, and the strong arms of Cat embraced her about the waist. With that assistance, Clarissa used her arms to boost herself upon the ledge that was the carriage step. Then she tried to swing her legs gracefully outward to show off the delicate slippers and the pretty ankles above them, when she lost her balance and nearly fell backwards, displaying an uncouth amount of leg and petticoat.

Fairfax looked discreetly away while Clarissa tried to regain her dignity. Across from him, Cat was gazing unsmilingly into the distance, but he could tell by the merry light in her eye that she was struggling with her hilarity at Clarissa's misfortune. He bowed deeply to both women.

"May I be so bold as to carry you across?" he asked Clarissa, but he looked swiftly again at Cat, another meaning implicit in his glance, before either could reply. Clarissa was deeply flustered. He had asked her, but she had intercepted his swift glance at Cat. Nevertheless, she, Clarissa Thomas, was the lady, and it was she to whom the offer had been made.

"Of course you may, Sir. It is an undue familiarity for such a short acquaintance, but the circumstances are rare enough to make it quite acceptable." From within came the querulous tone of Lady Thomas. "Help me, someone. I am growing cold and damp down here on the ground."

"Please decide, Sir, on your course of action," said Cat dryly, "as the lady is in true discomfort."

Clarissa looked shocked, but Fairfax was merely amused at the presumption of the lovely girl before him.

"By all means. The girl is quite correct," he agreed quickly, hoping to forestall the anger of her mistress at the servant's temerity. "You there, Footman, come quickly and help your mistress across the road."

Cat watched from under thick eyelashes with secret amusement as dismay and anger flashed across Clarissa's face.

Stripping off his coat, Fairfax stepped up to the coach and leaned in. "Madame, will you take my hand?" Cat could see the muscles of his back swell as his shoulders took the strain of Lady Thomas's considerable bulk. He braced himself upon the carriage edge with his other hand and gripped it tightly. "My lady, get your feet under you if you can, and prepare to stand when I give the word." Lady Thomas murmured something indistinct from within.

"Ready and go," said Fairfax.

Cat saw him throw his back and thighs into the smooth lifting motion. With so much grace as to belie the effort, he assisted Lady Thomas as she clambered to her feet. Cat, still standing by, dangerously heedless of Clarissa's petulant looks from the edge of the road, was struck in spite of herself by the powerful masculinity of that gesture. She felt a little breathless.

Fairfax bowed to Lady Thomas, who appeared slightly askew, but remained formidable nevertheless. He smiled again at Cat, a quick humorous and conspiratorial smile, and then bowed to Clarissa. "Your parent is nearly restored to you," he said with exaggerated and slightly mocking gallantry. Clarissa's simper immediately returned.

"Footman," Fairfax commanded. "Bring the carriage step that her ladyship may descend. The footman hurried back across the road, almost floundering in one deep rut, to detach the carriage step block from the boot and bring it to his mistress. With far more huffing and puffing, but withal a great deal more dignity, Lady Thomas stood at last on the road.

"Thank you, Sir," she said, her flinty eye raking him through the ever-present, although now slightly bent, lorgnette. "I am not so unprepared as my dear child and have no fear of crossing this road." She turned and viewed the carriage wreck from the safety of the verge and sighed. "I am afraid this must end our journey for now. I am sure I do not know how to proceed."

Cat went white with fear. Her plan depended on vanishing from the neighborhood. By evening, her disappearance would be known. Her masquerade would be discovered. Even now, perhaps, her intended was driving toward Eldertree Manor! Her mind sought desperately for an alternative.

Clarissa stamped her foot and let out a great sob. "Oh, Mama," she cried, tears coursing prettily down her cheeks. "We must find a way to go on. Invitations to the balls at Almack's are only issued to those who have been seen and judged during the first weeks in Town. You do not wish me to miss making my entrance. My life will be ruined!"

"Hush, Child, hush," said her mama, with more annoyance than tenderness. Cat thought that Clarissa had used pretty tears often before to get her way, and Lady Thomas knew it. "How badly damaged is the carriage, Coachman?" she demanded in rising tones.

"Not seriously hurt, your ladyship," he replied, "I have been walking around it these past ten minutes and see no great damage other than to the paint. 'Tis the harness that is ruined, and that cannot be mended."

"It will take hours to send back to Westmarch," wailed Clarissa. "We shall be here all night," she cried, beginning to shiver and making a rare ninny of herself, thought Cat.

"Hush, Child," said Lady Thomas, ignoring her daughter's emotional display. "Let me think."

"Allow me, your ladyship. I believe that I can be of some assistance. I have just left the post house not an hour's ride from here. I believe that you might procure some new harness there, along with whatever is requisite to repair your carriage and thus continue your journey."

"Thank you, Sir. I shall send the coachman upon one of the horses immediately."

"Beggin' your ladyship's pardon," that worthy interjected, "I have sprained my leg something fierce and don't feel meself up to ridin' yon broad horse bareback any way a t'all. Perhaps Roberts may make the ride."

The footman quailed immediately. "And it please yer ladyship," he said tremulously, "I am not at all good with horses, even those properly saddled and bridled."

Lady Thomas's mouth fell open with a pop. Never in her life had a servant been so disrespectful, but she could see that the footman was indeed trembling, and her loyal coachman was in deep pain. Although arrogant, she felt compelled to act modestly before the calm, somewhat amused stare of the man before her. "Sir, you have put yourself to a great deal of trouble upon our account. I would not ask you to do this if it were not of the utmost necessity. Could I apply to you to ride to the post house and procure aid for us there?"

Fairfax bowed deeply over her hand. "I should be happy to do so. I shall return with aid as soon as possible. Ladies," he said as he swung up into the saddle of his horse and tipped his hat to them. As he wheeled the tall gelding, he looked directly at Cat and smiled at her. His look was so naked with amused desire that she blushed to the roots of her hairline.

The three women sat under the trees on the grassy bank by the side of the road. Cat sat a little apart, as became her humbler status, as she brushed the dried mud off Clarissa's slippers. As she worked, she smiled to herself. How comical Clarissa had looked, trying to be so graceful and nearly falling backwards into the carriage. Cat noticed with some satisfaction as she turned the nearly cleaned slipper in her hand that her unshod foot was far smaller than Clarissa's. She had laid her sturdy plain shoes aside to dry out and saw with pride that her foot, with its high instep, was far more beautiful as well.

She heard Lady Thomas and Clarissa's whispered words about the mysterious stranger. They both seemed quite taken with him. She herself had no interest in such an ill-bred person. The insolent way in which he had looked at her confirmed that he could be no true gentleman.

Still, he had been a bold rider. She could tell that by the way he held his hands, long-fingered, strong and graceful in their black leather riding gloves. He was not a mere country beau, but someone who had acquaintance with the wider walks of the world. "Who is Vere Courtenay Fairfax?" she thought, unconsciously echoing the conversation of the Thomas ladies behind her.

She had just finished cleaning the last of the dried mud from Clarissa's slippers when she heard the sound of horses approaching. Mr. Fairfax, accompanied by the post-house groom, was returning with the replacement harness. He reined in his tall horse and dismounted in front of the three ladies. Taking off his top hat, he made a respectful bow to them, marred only in Cat's opinion by the intense way his eyes met her own.

"Ladies, your horses will be harnessed in a trice, and you shall soon be able to resume your journey. I have business in this neighborhood, but I do not expect it to be of long duration. Perhaps you will permit me to call upon you in London?"

"Certainly, if you find yourself there, we shall be most happy to repay your kindness with what hospitality we can offer," Lady Thomas replied in the most ingratiating tones she could manage. "Our town house is in Portman Square. If you find yourself nearby, your visit would be welcome."

Mr. Fairfax bowed again and took the hand that the dowager offered. Clarissa, standing beside her parent, offered her hand also. Standing behind them both, Cat examined his polite and noncommittal expression as he made his farewells to them. Mounting his powerful horse, he wheeled the beast toward the direction from which they had come. The animal snorted and pranced as his rider once more tipped his hat to their party. But before he left, he deliberately looked deeply into Cat's green eyes, the slightest of sardonic smiles playing about his lips. The invitation and the insult were unmistakable to Cat. She turned abruptly away, picking up some of the smaller cases of the Thomas ladies. Those worthies, seemingly entirely unaware of what had transpired between Fairfax and Cat, remained lost in their own dreams and suppositions.

"Odious man," Cat thought. Her dislike of the entire passage between them gave her the requisite energy to pack up the cases with dispatch, the sooner to continue her journey.

DISCOVERED

F airfax kept his tall chestnut steed in a trot until he was safely away from the scene and then drew up into a meditative walk. He was faintly chagrined at his behavior toward the young servant girl. At thirty-and-three, he was far beyond the point of allowing mere physical lust to dictate his course of action, nor was he interested in seducing woman of the lower classes, no matter how beauteous they might be. If he wished lights of love, he had found Italian contessas and Austrian grafen who were both beautiful and titled, who understood how to both enjoy and take leave of a moment of love. He knew the titled ladies of the English *ton* to be much the same. He had absolutely no interest in spoiled young girls, no matter how white and gold might be their charms. Empty-headed child wives and formidable mother-in-laws were not something he wanted to entertain, even in thought. In fact, he had already negotiated a highly suitable match for himself with a wealthy young heiress.

Therefore, it was greatly to his surprise that he found himself offering to continue their acquaintance in London. In truth, he admitted to himself, the beautiful servant named Cat had captured his fancy. Even more than her slender beauty, the imperious bravery of the auburn-haired girl had taken him by surprise, first drawing his interest and then his desire. She was self-possessed far above her station and age. There was steel in her, and those deep green eyes met his own black ones with high-mettled challenge. The man who had the breaking of that filly would have to be skilled indeed. Vere smiled to himself, knowing his own pride in his horsemanship. His upcoming marriage need cause only a slight delay. Her hair was nearly the color of his chestnut hunter, he mused. All unawares, he spurred the horse into a brisk canter, soothing his agitation with its rocking gait.

The land with its bare trees, their rain-soaked bark black in the chill lowering air, challenged him. Overhead, low-rolling grey clouds dampened the thin rays of sunlight that had touched the delicate furled green of the few plants that had leaves. The open meadows of the south, with their stately stands of beech groves, gave way to thicker woodlands. On the verges of the road, gnarled oaks writhed as if in pain. Beneath them, he could see the delicate scrolls of ferns just beginning to show above the ground.

In his villa in Tuscany, the air would already be gay with bird song and wild flowers nestling among the shrubberies of the English garden. The rose bushes would be in tender leaf upon the trellises that led into the walkways of their garden. On the south side, the Provençal garden was planted with rosemary and lavender, bright with potted geraniums of deep ember orange and sunset glowing red, where graceful espaliered fruit trees made green shadows upon the sunny wall that enclosed it. He had loved the gardens best.

Each room of the villa had a door leading to a terrace or garden. His mother had Lancelot "Capability" Brown, the most famous of gardeners, come to lay out the grounds. She had even planned two of them herself. The first, a somber walk under yew trees, among cypresses and broken marble statues, led to a small colonnaded Roman temple set beneath towering pines.

"For your father," she had said in explanation, "if he ever comes. He loves melancholy antiquities. This should please him, *no?*" She looked back over her shoulder as she spoke, as she led him, her skirts swaying like a bell, up the shadowed path.

It had, Vere thought bitterly. His father had spent his last days there, carried down to the little temple on his pallet by the silent stolid servants, the bright flush of fever on his cheeks giving his wasted face an illusion of health and youth. Vere had remonstrated with him, telling him that the site with its looming trees and cold marble was too damp, begging his father at least to lie in the sunny garden that opened off his own sitting room, all to no avail.

"She built this for me," the old man had whispered. "She did love me; she knew what pleased me." He turned his failing gaze outward past the yews to where a sullen pool overgrown with waterweeds lay dankly in the shade. Vere had turned away in disgust from the old man and his foolish denial of the truth of his marriage in his final days.

"Here, he can rest content in his own world and not bother me in mine," Vere's mother had laughed after touring the finished temple. "What does he care of me, when he has his dreams? Truth is not important to him where 'ought' suffices. Well, he may spend his time here in solitary contemplation, while I enjoy the sun somewhere else."

"The sun somewhere else," for his mother, had been her lovers and the other garden, a conceit entirely of her own devising. From the doubled doors of the great central ballroom, a set of stone steps led down to a long terrace. Along the sides, stone balustraded arbors entwined with ancient grapevines led to a central garden of hedges. At first, the hedges, dense and green, were low, with walkways decorated by bright plantings in stone urns. As the brick walkway continued inward, turning this way and that, the hedges grew taller, until they became a dark maze, leading the unwary into unexpected dead ends among their menacing green shadows.

"There is a secret center," Vere's mother had laughed at Vere, as she watched him walk in, then walk out, having come again to another path that led nowhere. "Shall I show you the way to the heart?"

"No," he had scowled, turning bitterly upon his heel and striding off to his own rooms. It had been at the end of his squalid love affair with the countess, when the mystery of love had become a fool's maze that left him confused and abandoned in a mannered wilderness, reft of love, but not desire. He had left shortly thereafter for his father's house and Oxford, without ever seeing what lay in the center of his mother's private garden.

Only after both of his parents' deaths had he penetrated to its center. He had been sorting through their private papers. Most he burned without reading. He did not care to know what the passions were that had trapped two such different people in an unsuitable, unhappy union. He had come across the plans for the garden maze in a small secretary where the estate papers were held. The sight of her handwriting upon a set of drawings caused him to scrutinize the text more closely.

"*Mon Cher*," she had written, but to which beloved, he had no idea. "Here is the map to the labyrinth. I think I have been rather clever, for although the prototype for my maze is rather common, I have by the expedience of using a left-hand direction rather than a right made it quite difficult to gain the center. Is it not so in life, as in art, that a man frequently takes the wrong direction to arrive at the secret at the center of a woman's heart?"

Vere had taken the map with him and through its direction threaded the tall green corridors of the hedge maze. The hedges had grown taller the farther inwards he had penetrated, giving him the uneasy feeling of being lost within dream corridors of a haunted castle. A strange conceit, he thought, as he followed the turnings marked on the map. She had been clever, for at each turning his instinct had usually been to take the right-hand path, which would have taken him to another dead end. But two out of three turnings were always made to the left hand, and the sequence was cleverly built on the previous sequence. Who had helped her, he wondered, for her cleverness alone was not sufficient for this. How many of her lovers had passed this test? Had any?

At length, he reached the center. There, in a little square of lawn stood a life-sized statue. It was of Carrera marble, so white and smooth that it looked like flesh. The naked woman modeled in Greek fashion stood modestly before him, eyes down, one rounded arm hiding her breasts, the other modestly obscuring her sex. Yet her slight mocking smile beckoned him to look again. He saw that while her upper hand was clasped palm inward over her left breast, her left hand was stretched palm outward, offering an apple to whomever completed the quest. An inchoate raged burned in his bosom. Turning sharply on his heel, crunching the gravel underfoot, he left the maze.

Sitting in the fading sun later that day in the Provençal garden, with only the cook's white cat for company, Vere made his plans to flee Napoleon's approaching reconquest and reclaim his father's northern lands, to become his son rather than hers. He had written to old Sir Merlin that very evening, reminding him of their families' ancient promise, advising him of Vere's future arrival.

Now he rode through this foreign silent countryside, which was just awakening from winter's hand. Faded memories from his earliest youth stirred in his mind, sweeping aside the bitterness of his recent years. He rode over roads that became more familiar with each mile. By the time he glimpsed the top of the turrets of Foxearth, he felt the deep peace of homecoming, and the events of the past months, including the morning's carriage disaster, were temporarily forgotten.

The accident on the road had made him later in his arrival than he had anticipated, but he arrived home at last, pausing only to bathe and change his clothes. Mounting a fresh horse from his stables, he rode to his appointment. It was nearly four o'clock before he approached his destination. At sixteen, he had ridden this road often enough to visit Sir Merlin. As he now rode up the deeply wooded drive toward the manor house, he perceived that something was wrong. Several carriages were drawn up front, along with a small troop of men and horses. Vere was puzzled, then worried, as his last communications had plainly stated that all was well. He hoped that nothing had happened to the old man.

But no, there was Sir Merlin himself, older than Vere remembered, standing in the middle of the little group. Vere spurred his horse into a brisk trot and arrived in time to hear Sir Merlin say, "We will have to widen our search for her."

Quickly, Vere drew up. In dismounting, he threw the reins to one of the grooms who stood nearby. "Sir Merlin, old friend," he said clasping Sir Merlin's thin hands in his own. "What has transposed? Why all this pother?"

"Who are you?" Sir Merlin challenged him.

"My father's son and your sometime fosterling. Do you not recognize me?"

"Vere! Lord Falconbridge!" exclaimed Sir Merlin. "I fear my daughter is missing This morning, Meteor was absent from his stall. We found him in the far paddock. When Caitlyn had not come down by luncheon, I sent to her room. She had vanished. I fear that she took the stallion out for an early morning ride and has been injured."

"Come," replied Vere. "Let us ride down to the paddock where he was found. Perhaps we may find a clue. Is this something that your daughter does often, riding stallions out before anyone is awake?"

"No, I fear this is strange behavior indeed. I told her of the proposed marriage and of your coming visit today." He coughed in embarrassment. "But I fear that she may have taken it amiss. Perhaps I did not make it clear that the marriage would take place only if both of you were agreeable to it."

Vere smiled a chill smile. "I have never thought my person so repulsive to the fairer sex. Quite the contrary. What sort of female has your daughter grown into? I have not seen her since she was but a child of three. Certainly to a youth of then nineteen years, an alliance to a mere baby was not a concept that I took seriously. However, as my father pointed out to me during the long years of your correspondence, she grew into a very accomplished young lady. I have offered for her on the strength of that reputation and other matters to our mutual advantage. However, this behavior has put a very different face upon our old promises."

"Let us talk while we ride, Fairfax," said Sir Merlin testily. "I would not have heeded that old promise had I not thought it would be suitable for both of you." Motioning to the groom to hold his horse, the old man mounted with surprising agility. Fairfax swung up upon his own tall grey, and together they set off at an easy canter to where Meteor had been found.

The great stallion was cropping grass contentedly in the paddock, surrounded by his harem of mares and foals. Vere looked appreciatively over the herd, noting the strong limbs of the sire and his brood. Certainly, he could see the advantage of an alliance with Sir Merlin. He intended to improve his own stables now that he had returned to England. As his practiced eye examined the horses that were spread about the paddock, he noticed deeply cut earth by the western fence.

"Over there," he pointed. "It looks as if a horse has been jumped there." Swinging down lithely from his horse, Vere strode across the paddock to the patch of churned earth. Squatting on his heels, he examined the now-drying, but still damp, deeply cut imprints of hooves. "By the look of it, these prints would have to have been made before sunrise." He moved along the fence, his eyes sweeping the ground. "Here are the return marks," he pointed. "The turf is less cut, and the prints are less sunken. He is not carrying a rider."

"You are right, Fairfax. She must have taken him over at that spot. And from here is only a quarter mile to the road."

"Sir Merlin, if she did not come off after that jump, she probably did not fall off at all. She in all probability turned him loose. She would not go towards the road if she meant to travel on foot. In what condition was Meteor found?" asked Vere, "and where?"

"Right here," replied Sir Merlin, "exactly as you see him."

"With no bridle, or saddle?" Vere asked incredulously. "With only a halter?"

"Exactly as you see him now," said Sir Merlin with a touch of pride. "My daughter is a horsewoman."

Fairfax reeled with the information. To jump a stallion bareback over a three-barred fence before dawn, with only a halter to control him; why the girl must have been a Valkyrie! A sudden image overcame his mind. "Sir Merlin, do you have a recent portrait of your daughter?"

"This is no time to wonder if she's beautiful enough for you to wed," Sir Merlin snapped. "If she is not lying dead in a ditch somewhere, she may be carried off."

"If my supposition is correct," Vere replied smoothly, hiding his excitement, "she is both well and found. Come; let us return to Eldertree for a drink and a bit of luncheon, for I have had none since I arrived. If I am correct, you at least need fret yourself no more for her life. Listen and judge for yourself."

An hour later, the two sat comfortably in the sitting room, drinking a fine claret, with the remains of a light luncheon between them. Vere stretched his long legs negligently in front of him as he meditatively sipped the claret. "A toast," he proposed, "to the successful conclusion of our pledge." Sir Merlin raised his glass in return and smiled.

On their return to the manor house, Sir Merlin had taken Fairfax into the morning room. There, above the fireplace, hung the portrait of Caitlyn he had commissioned on her sixteenth birthday. As Vere contemplated it, he had no trouble recognizing the beautiful girl who had intervened with the maddened horses this morning. Only a horsewoman of consummate skill could have jumped the great stallion, as this girl had demonstrated. There was no doubt. The painted semblance proved them one and the same.

As the two men stood silently in contemplation, each one with a different portrait in his heart and thoughts, Jones approached deferentially. "Your pardon, Sir, but Bessie is upset. She is crying this past hour and blames herself for Miss Llewellyn's disappearance. She was found by one of the maids in Miss Llewellyn's room."

"I think we ought to hear this story now, "Sir Merlin said. "Bring her here, if you please."

"I wonder why she blames herself," Vere mused.

Bessie stood in the doorway. "Come in, Bessie," Sir Merlin said. "We are not angry with you. What has happened that you think you are to blame for her disappearance?"

"'Twas I who first told her that his lordship was a'comin'. She was right shocked, jumped up, and strode round the room, nervous like a horse before a storm. Then she settled down, nice as you please, and asked me what I had heard and how. And I told her what you told Mr. Jones about his lordship and how he was an old friend. Beggin' your pardon, but I may have misspoke that. Then, when I go to help her undress after dinner she was writing something. I thought it might be a list of bridal clothes and thought nothing of it. But I knew she was worrit, so I brought her some of your brandy to drink before bed. I should have come to you, Sir, I know that now. This morning 'twas I who found her room empty and the brandy drained, as well."

Vere said dryly, "I would need a brandy myself if I planned to jump a three-barred fence bareback before dawn the following morning. Did she drink the brandy in your presence?"

"Just a sip, your lordship. She said she would keep it for later, before she went to sleep."

"It seems she had a plan," Vere commented. "I have never thought mere announcement of my approach would cause such panic," he added ruefully.

"But why are you crying, Bessie?" inquired Sir Merlin gently. "There is no real sin here. Jones, take her back to Mrs. Rhys."

"'Twas I gave her the idea to run away. 'Twas I told her she would be the white ewe lamb of the Season if she went to London," she wailed. As Bessie was led away, another more awful truth she had told came to mind. 'Twas that old tale of the unfortunate servant girl and the wild young gentleman. Sooner or later, Cat would learn the gentleman's name.

Sir Merlin had then listened grimly as Vere had recited his own encounter with Caitlyn upon the road, carefully editing his own response to the girl. Although the man was eager to have him for a son-in-law, Vere did not think that Caitlyn's father would appreciate the intensity of the lust she had aroused in Vere, though he felt free to express his admiration for her.

"We shall have to get her back," said Sir Merlin. "I will simply follow the Thomases and bring her home. She can't continue as a servant, and if her plan was to decamp to Henrietta's establishment upon arrival, she will find herself sadly frustrated. Henrietta does not go to London this Season. I am quite as shocked at this headstrong behavior as you must be, Falconbridge."

Vere, who knew how badly his own actions had already compromised his suit, needed time to change her impressions. Seizing on a plan, he made a proposal. "Sir Merlin," said Vere, indolently helping himself to some more claret, "I think we should let her believe she has gotten away with this little masquerade. If you bring her back to Eldertree and deprive her of the world of excitement that a London Season is for a seventeen-year-old girl, I fear that she would resent me as the cause, no matter what may be the charms of my person. On the other hand, if I were to meet her and woo her in London, she might be more amenable to our marriage and retiring here with me. Of course, I have already opened my London establishment, so she needn't fear rustication in the country."

"An excellent plan, Falconbridge. But how do you intend to keep your true identity from her?"

"No one but you knows that my father is dead and that I have inherited his titles. I stayed in London only long enough to instruct the servants on opening the house. She already knows me as Vere Courtenay Fairfax. Let her think me a cadet branch of the family, if she makes the connection at all. I can watch over her from a distance until you can inform your sister, and she can arrive to open her house."

"Done," said Sir Merlin.

CAT IN LONDON

The journey continued for two more days of jolting and swaying on the roads. Cat found the changing countryside interesting. The fresh air was brisk and oftimes sunny. She felt that she had the better of positions compared to the Thomas ladies, violently jolted about inside the airless closed carriage.

Cat also had time to consider her situation and lay her plans. It was quite apparent that Lady Thomas would never accept her masquerade with grace and humor. Cat had to leave Portman Square before they found her out. At the first opportunity, she would have to petition Aunt Henrietta. She simply must get a card to a ball at Almack's! Surely, Henrietta would sponsor her.

Conjuring up pleasant visions of herself at the ball, she found that the face of Vere Courtenay Fairfax kept intruding upon the form of her fantastical suitors. "*Peste,*" she thought, trying angrily to dismiss him. I want a knight, not some foul satyr, as he must surely be! No gentleman would look at a lady the way he looked at me. The fact that he thinks me just a poor servant girl makes it all the worse. I could not love a man who preys upon the helpless and yet parades in virtue among his peers.

The fact that both Thomas ladies were taken by him was not a recommendation. Caitlyn had decided that both women were insufferably vulgar and petty. Of course, it might have been the obvious air of wealth he had about him. Even a relatively inexperienced girl, such as herself, could tell that his clothes were well-cut, of good quality, and probably of the latest mode. She devoutly hoped that she would never encounter him again, as servant or as lady. He was too bold in his desires. Involuntarily remembering the look he had given her before he rode off sent a rising flush up the graceful column of her throat to darken her proud high cheekbones.

The house in Portman Square was imposing enough, with Corinthian columns at the entranceway. Although it was not situated in the most fashionable area of London, it was close enough to St. James to lend the Thomas women a certain dignity. All the other servants were lined up outside to meet the ladies' arrival. They had been sent ahead in the slower traveling-van, along with the ladies' clothes and other personal possessions.

The two ladies were already within doors as Cat descended from the box. As she clambered down, one of the footmen stood ready to receive her. "You will be needed immediately. One of the maids will show you the quarters in which you will be staying. If you please, I'll take your box down."

"Thank you kindly," replied Cat. "I just have this one bundle."

The footman sniffed when he saw her clever little clothes bundle. "You will be needing grander clothes than that," he said. "Just a country girl, are you?" There was something decidedly unpleasant in his tone, which put Cat on her guard.

"But not born yesterday," she said tartly, thinking again of the handsome gentleman and his frank look of desire. She turned to find a tall straight maid waiting for her, with composed features and quiet hands. "Let me show you first to where your mistress is staying and then backstairs to the servants' hall. After you have attended to Miss Thomas, you can repair there for a cup of cider, and I will show you the arrangement of the rooms. That was Roberts," she nodded towards the footman. "My name is Rose."

"Thank you, Rose," Cat replied. Together, they walked through the imposing arched doorway, which was flanked by its grandiose columns.

Two harrowing hours later, Cat sat at the servants' long table, enjoying a cup of fragrant hot cider. Miss Clarissa Thomas had proved to be a most demanding mistress. Cat worried that her masquerade was to fail immediately, so little had her handiwork pleased Clarissa.

After three changes of dress and one of hairstyle, Clarissa had finally declared herself satisfied. Cat was released to find her way to the servants' hall for dinner and a brief tour of her quarters, a small cramped attic room, which she was to share with Rose. Afterwards, she would have to repeat the process in reverse, undressing Clarissa and getting her ready for bed. Cat had never realized how difficult a servant's life could be and resolved immediately to be more thoughtful in the future.

For days, Cat had very little time to herself. She went through her duties in a fog of weariness. Rising early with the rest of the servants, she washed quickly from a little washbasin of cold water, rebraided her hair and dressed in one of the two grey gowns. Then descending the three flights of backstairs to the basement and the servants' hall, she had a quick breakfast of porridge and a small glass of cider. She enjoyed this part of the day, as she had a chance to converse with the other servants. In all, they were an agreeable lot, save perhaps for Roberts, the footman. A tall somewhat rawboned fellow of twenty-five, he had a sly sense of self-importance that made her impatient. Mr. Arbuthnot, the London butler, was correct and distant, as befitted his exalted position, but kindly withal, if you obeyed the rules. Rose was the head parlormaid and had another girl, Agnes, beneath her. Mrs. Congdon was the cook. She had a kitchen maid, Jane, and a scullery girl, Alice, to assist her. Lady Thomas's maid, Maude, was a very thin woman with a censorious glance. She had been with Lady Thomas many years and had adopted an attitude similar to that of her mistress. Among the servants, she was Lady Thomas's representative and, as such, was distrusted by even Mr. Arbuthnot. She rose later than the other servants and slept in a small cubicle off Lady Thomas's own bedroom.

Clarissa never woke before one, but Cat had many duties to perform before her mistress rang her bell. There were shoes to clean and gowns to press. There was mending, as Clarissa sometimes tore her clothes in impatience or ill temper when displeased. She had returned from the opera two nights before in a furious fit because all the better boxes had been taken, and she had been compelled to make do with a *baignoire*. Cat despaired of mending the delicate lace around the sleeve, but old Bessie had taken great pains to teach her needlework. The task was very time-consuming, and she had almost finished working on it when Clarissa's bell rang in the servants' hall.

"Alice, is there any hot water? Miss Clarissa will be wanting to wash."

"I set it to a boil a half hour gone by. Agnes can take it up for you."

"Thank you, Alice, Agnes." The bell rang again, more impatiently. Cat folded the nearly mended gown across her arm and hurried toward the backstairs. As she ascended, she noted that so far, all the servants accepted her has genuine, but she had had no leisure to put into action the second part of her plan. She had yet to have time to herself to set off for Aunt Henrietta's town house.

Clarissa was lying in bed, yawning sleepily. Cat stepped up quickly and turned down the covers. "The hot water is already on its way, Miss," she said, laying the gown upon the armchair. "Shall I brush out your hair for you?"

Clarissa rose from bed and slipped her feet into the dainty blue skippers that Cat had placed by the bed for her. Taking the sheer lace dishabille, she sat down before the large mirror and studied herself as Cat brushed her short shining curls.

Agnes knocked softly on the door. Cat opened the heavy oak door, and Agnes entered, bearing a large washbowl full of hot water wrapped in thick towels. Cat smiled at her. "Thank you, Agnes." Cat knew that the day would go better for her if Miss Clarissa had all of her desires attended to immediately.

Clarissa studied the girl behind her in the mirror's reflection. She was very lovely, which both pleased and piqued Clarissa. It was complementary to have a pretty woman as a maid, and she had to admit to herself that she was really quite capable. But Clarissa was jealous of anyone who presumed to a beauty beyond her own, and this girl certainly did. There was something vaguely familiar about her, but Clarissa never remembered seeing her among any of the villagers or tenants on fair days, when the entire county populace attended.

Nevertheless, as naturally lovely as she was, she could never hope to be desired by any of the handsome rich bucks of the *ton*. Clarissa decided that she would tell her lady's maid of her triumphant social evening at the Bellinghams'.

"I think I shall want to wear the pink pelisse over the white-sprigged muslin frock today. Also, I will want the lace-trimmed fillet, not the one with satin ribbons, but the other." She smirked at their joint reflection in the large mirror. "Mama and I are expecting several gentleman callers this morning."

Cat made no comment as she finished arranging the last curls of Clarissa's blonde hair about her forehead. Cat wished that she could share in the excitement, but she knew that Clarissa brooked no rivals, requiring only envious subordinates. Still, Cat felt that it would be appropriate to make a response. "And who are these fine gentlemen, and where did ye meet them?" The dialect came naturally now after nearly two weeks of use.

Clarissa brightened at the inquiry. She was longing to talk of her triumph. She could not discuss her feelings with Lady Thomas, who disapproved of flightiness. Cat would do well as a listener.

"Mama and I attended Lady Bellingham's rout last night. She has a quite beautiful large town house in Mayfair. The floors are all marble, and the chandeliers are crystal. Imagine, she had six footmen, all six feet in height, with crimson livery, at the entrance. So many grand carriages drew up, I vow I was quite overwhelmed! There was such a crush. Imagine, the Season has not even started yet, and there were near a hundred or more people there! It's really too bad Lord John Bellingham is married and to such a drab little thing. My dance card was filled by the third quadrille. There was an ever so handsome French count that claimed me for the fifth dance. He quite took my breath away. So polite, so complimentary. I wonder if he is rich."

Cat gently dropped the white frock over Clarissa's chemise and buttoned it up the back. She was hardly listening to the girl's chatter, although she tried to give every appearance of attentive interest. Clarissa was always in better humor when she was the center of attention, and Cat hoped that perhaps this day, she would get some time to herself to explore London and find Aunt Henrietta's town house in Berkeley Square.

"And I met that interesting gentleman who helped us on the road, Mr. Fairfax," Clarissa simpered as she studied her image in the mirror. Cat's only reaction was a slight narrowing of her green eyes. "He is going to call this morning. He is very handsome. I wonder if he is possessed of any fortune at all," she prattled. "But I would think so! After all, only people of consequence can be invited to parties like the Bellinghams'. He must be rich! And he seems to be well-liked. All the Exquisites were clustered around him just before supper. I heard he drives a four-in-hand as well as he rides."

Cat drew her brows together, as if concentrating on the artfully careless arrangement of curls she was making with Clarissa's rather thin blonde hair. As if, she thought to herself, Clarissa would know anything about horsemanship. The praise that she had heard merely reinforced her belief that he was a duplicitous rogue, hiding his dangerous nature. If he had money, which she doubted, he probably made it by cozening county innocents with wagers on horses and races.

Cat finished setting the last of Clarissa's curls in place and stepped deftly out of the mirror's reflection so her demanding mistress could study herself. Cat had left one tendril of curled lock to droop becomingly around Clarissa's ear, giving her a shy, innocent air. This met with her mistress's reluctant approval. Clarissa tossed her head coquettishly to see whether any lock escaped from its defined arrangement. The results satisfied her.

"Well, my girl," she said with an imitation of her mother's habitual arrogance. "It would seem that you know your business well enough." Her lips thinned a moment as she hesitated before continuing. Mama had said that Clarissa must reward good work with generosity, as befitting her station and prospects in life. Still, Clarissa clutched everything she owned closely to her, despising to part with anything. Yet as a lady, it was imperative that she obey the proper codes. "In thanks, I want to give you my old blue frock. You need something more to wear in London than your old dresses of gray woolsey. As my maid, you represent my family and me. I would not have it said we do not know how to keep our servants." Clarissa arose and went to the wardrobe herself, rummaged about, and emerged with the promised frock over her arm. Cat took it gingerly, with a quick bob of a curtsey.

"Thank ye, Miss. 'Tis truly generous of ye!" Clarissa basked in the pretty servant's gratitude, finding the picture of herself as a Lady Bountiful to be most agreeable. "I will take it away to my room, if ye have nothing more for me."

"Of course," said Clarissa graciously. The imminent arrival of Mr. Fairfax had put her in a forgiving and generous mood. "Perhaps you should put it on. I should like to see how it suits you."

"Yes, Miss. I will do that now, if ye wish." Making another brief bob of her head, Cat hurried out of the bedroom and mounted the narrow dark staircase to her own tiny room in the eaves of the third floor. Before a tiny sliver of mirror that Rose had salvaged from the shattered pieces of her ladyship's own broken glass, Cat turned herself this way and that, looking at her dim reflection in the mirror of herself in the blue gown. The neckline was modestly scooped, and a bit of white ribbon threaded through the blue ruffle around it. There were forget-me-nots of a darker blue embroidered about the hem and on the flounces of the three-quarters length sleeves. Assuring herself that every button was in place, Cat returned to her mistress's room, treading down the steep staircase as serenely as a queen.

Clarissa was not pleased by Cat's appearance. The periwinkle blue suited Cat's glowing copper hair and rose and ivory complexion far better than it had suited Clarissa's, which further vexed Clarissa because periwinkle blue was all the rage this season. She folded her hands in her lap, appearing grave and composed. "It is not a shade that becomes you, Cat, but it will do well enough for going out on errands." She paused to consider her next words. Mr. Fairfax was expected within the half-hour. It would not do to have Cat in the vicinity. She had appeared a little too familiar with him at their last encounter. Having a servant who even appeared to be a light-skirts would be an unfortunate reflection on the mistress. Perhaps, she thought, I can send her out to market.

Clarissa took up her little net purse. She drew out two bright coins and held them disdainfully between her fingertips. "Take these, and go to the drapers on Bond Street and purchase some colored ribbon to match my new blue frock. I shall be wearing it tomorrow for callers, so do not return without it." She slowly drew another small coin, a copper, from her purse. "Take this, and buy yourself some ribbons for your cap. If we walk in Hyde Park, we must look fashionable."

Cat made a quick bob to Clarissa, her eyes decorously cast down, looking at the worked threads in the carpet to hide her joy. A brisk half-hour walk should serve to arrive at Bond Street, where she could easily find at least half a dozen milliners' shops that carried blue and white ribbons. Another half-hour would serve to carry her to Berkeley Square, where Aunt Henrietta kept her town house. She carefully murmured a quiet and correct "Thank ye, Ma'am," to Clarissa and fled as decorously as possible back up the narrow staircase to retrieve her reticule and depart on her quest.

ENCOUNTERS

Vere Courtenay Fairfax rode the handsome black horse up the street toward Portman Square at a slow pace. He had stood up with the Thomas chit at the Bellinghams' rout the evening before partly out of curiosity. Unfortunately, his first impressions had been confirmed. Her prettiness merely hid a set of rattletrap brains and a cunningly disguised vicious streak. He was extremely relieved when the suavely sinister Comte du Foix claimed her for the next dance. He could think of no two better suited partners. In that brief encounter with Lucien Montclair, the Comte du Foix, Vere felt the instinctive antipathy a terrier feels for a rat, and he had long ago learned to trust his instincts. His business was not with Clarissa, however. He hoped that he could get another glimpse of Cat. The thought that Montclair, through his attentions to Clarissa, might also catch a glimpse of Cat disquieted him more than he expected.

Since his conversation with Sir Merlin, Vere had been endlessly reviewing his first encounter with the auburn-haired beauty. The surprising knowledge that she was actually his promised bride had increased his original desire for her. Knowing that she was destined to be his served only to relax his restraint upon his lustful thoughts. Again, in his mind's eye, he saw her strong lithe body, her firm high breasts, the lush ripeness of her full underlip, and the firefall of her braided hair. He imagined her yielding to him, opening up the softness of her parted lips within his embrace, as she smiled up at him with her green eyes, heavy lidded with desire. So absorbed in his own mental picture was he that he almost missed seeing her slip out among the crowds that eddied past Portman Square and joined the separate streams of people on London streets.

In one fluid motion, he pulled up his horse. Swinging lightly down from the saddle, he saluted her courteously. "Miss Cat," he said, raising his hat even as he blocked her passage. "May I say how good it is to see you again? Have you been well?" He took a step nearer to her, bringing himself close enough to catch her personal fragrance, a mixture of fresh cut grass and lavender, which intoxicated his senses, bringing his mental musings dangerously close to enactment.

"Mr. Fairfax, I beg your leave to continue upon my way," Cat replied coolly, stepping away from him. His physical presence, less than a foot from her own, intimidated her. Despite the courtesy of his address, the look in his eyes bespoke something else. "I am on an errand for my mistress and have no time to delay," she said sharply. "Please remove yourself from my path."

"Your pardon, Miss Cat," he replied, stepping back a foot, still smiling down at her upturned face. "I meant only to compliment you on your bravery with the horses the other day. Such a show of skill is surprising in a woman. May I ask you where you learned it?" Behind the suave tone of his voice, Cat detected a controlled watchfulness, rather like a cat at a mousehole. It seemed that he expected her to lie, which was exactly what she intended to do. Had this bold stranger somehow penetrated her masquerade? Did he intend to take advantage of his discovery?

Using her broadest west marches accent, she replied, "Me da was the head groom at Foxearth. I used ta watch him with the horses since I was just a wee lass. He said I had a way wi' the beasts an' let me feed and groom them as soon as I could swing a feed bucket." Fairfax raised his brows in surprise at her claim of belonging to Foxearth.

This interrogation might prove to be very amusing. "What of the master of Foxearth? He could not possibly approve of a young girl mixing so freely with the stablehands." He waited with interest for her reply.

"The old master was never there when I was growing up. He was off in Italy, fer his health or some such. Only Mrs. Carstairs was ta home, and she did not mind till I began to get grown. Then she took me in service inside the manor house. By then, I had already learned the ways of horses." She lifted her chin proudly, challenging him to dispute the truth of her words.

Vere flicked his riding crop impatiently against his boot. "And was there no other family at Foxearth, other than its absent lord?" he asked, looking deliberately into her wide green eyes.

"None other that I ever heard," she replied, dropping her gaze to escape his impolite stare. His questions came too close to the subject that she wished to hide. She heard the snap of the riding crop against his boot again.

"Well then, Miss Cat," he said, noting how the faint blush rose prettily about her alabaster throat. "Thank you for assuaging my curiosity." He swung up upon his tall black mount, which snorted and pranced with impatience. He held the horse steady as he looked down upon Cat, a most fetching vision in periwinkle blue upon the cobbled pavement. "If I did not have a call to pay upon your mistress, I would accompany you myself. A creature as lovely as yourself should not be walking about London alone."

"Pray do not give it a thought. I only mean to go to Bond Street to purchase some ribbons. And now, I am quite late. I beg you to let me take my leave," she added impatiently, as he showed no signs of riding on.

The horse whickered, but Vere held it firmly as he continued to stare down at Cat thoughtfully. She stepped forward, but he brought his mount about as if to block her path again.

"Sir, I really must insist," she said loudly, drawing the attention of several young gentlemen who were approaching.

A frown clouded Fairfax's countenance. He regretted having to let her go, but he could not ride after her. She should be safe enough in broad daylight, but every fiber of his being protested letting her roam unescorted through the streets of London. There was no help for it this time, he thought grimly, but on the next occasion, he would be prepared. "Your servant, Miss Cat," he finally said, raising his hat once again, and then, not trusting himself to look at her again, he rode onward to the entrance of the Thomas town house. Dismounting in one easy motion, he threw a penny and the reins of his horse to a ragged boy who was waiting there and swiftly ascended the steps. He had already seen what he came for, and his visit to Clarissa would be polite, but brief.

Cat breathed a heartfelt sigh as she hurried away from her strange tormentor. His impertinence seemed only to grow. In all his addresses, there was a hint of dangerous passion held under strict control. Cat had no experience with men, but she had heard tales of them from old Bessie. Gentlewomen were usually safe, unless they connived at their own ruin, but serving maids were another matter. Had not Bessie whispered a tale of some poor serving girl taken advantage of by the quality, left with child, and abandoned by her master's scapegrace son? For that poor servant, passion had equaled death; she had taken her own life. Cat shivered and wished that she had brought a shawl to wrap about herself. She had set off, proud of her pretty new dress, delighting in her own beauty in defiance of Clarissa's spiteful words. Now she thought better of her vanity. Walking quickly, she carefully composed her face into her most serious mien and hurried toward Bond Street to complete her purchases and begin her search for Aunt Henrietta.

Fairfax gave his card to the footman, who announced him. Fairfax was subsequently shown up to the morning room, where the Ladies Thomas were waiting in gracious tableau to receive him. Lady Thomas was sitting regally erect upon a pale blue watered silk ottoman. Miss Clarissa sat upon a Chippendale chair and pretended to work upon the embroidery screen in front of her. His glance idly took in the rest of the furnishings. He judged them to be a trifle second rate. Removing his hat, he bowed deeply to both women, carefully concealing his perceptions behind an inscrutable mask of exquisite politeness.

"Thank you for receiving me," he began smoothly. "Your kindness to me at the ball was much appreciated. May I ask you whether you enjoyed yourself?" he asked, addressing his remarks to the formidable Lady Thomas.

"Indeed, Sir, you may well ask. We were quite gratified by the many friends we saw at the Bellinghams' rout last evening. May I inquire the same of you?" Her small eyes betrayed a glint of rapacious curiosity as to the true status of this handsome, albeit mysterious, stranger.

Aware of the game that her ladyship was clumsily playing, Vere answered easily. "Indeed, your ladyship, I too enjoyed the company of many from whom I might claim acquaintance. As you saw."

They sat in stillness for some moments, Vere declining to break his silence while Lady Thomas futilely sought another gambit. Clarissa finally broke the silence. With a light toss of her curls and a falsetto laugh, she directed her question to Vere directly, despite her mother's startled look.

"Do you intend to stay for the Season, Mr. Fairfax?" She smiled at him from under trembling eyelashes. Fairfax glanced at her in mild surprise, but directed his reply to her mother.

"When I returned from abroad, I had merely intended to open my town house and then spend some time on my estates settling business affairs. However, I have since changed my mind."

Lady Thomas and her daughter were consumed by their mutual curiosity as to where Fairfax's estates and town house were located.

"Yes, I do remember your mentioning that you had business in the neighborhood upon the occasion of our first meeting. I hope that it has been successfully concluded?" Lady Thomas asked impertinently.

"That remains to be seen. May I call on you again?" Vere picked up his riding whip and hat from the small table beside him, rose, and made a brief bow to them. "With your permission," he added. Without waiting for Lady Thomas's nod of assent, he left the morning room and descended the stairs, intent on pursuing the true object of his interest.

"Well," said Lady Thomas to her daughter when she heard the front door close behind him. "I am not sure all this rude mystery bodes well for any hopes of him. I suspect there is something hidden about this Mr. Fairfax." She tapped her large horse-teeth with the edge of her fan. "Where have I heard that name before? Could he be a younger son shopping for an heiress? I wonder if he could be from a cadet branch of some great lord's family? I must ask Sir Thomas if he knows of any Fairfaxes and where they keep their town house in London. You do not wish to be a victim of a clever impostor." Clarissa looked crumpled in her pretty white and pink as she thought with dismay of her shattered hopes.

"Do not get yourself into a pother, Clarissa. He is not the only fish in the sea, though he is a most attractive man. However, the Comte du Foix is also very attractive, and I understand that despite his family's misfortunes, he remains most eligible. And your father will ferret out the truth of Mr. Fairfax." At this moment, the footman appeared, bearing another card, which he presented to Lady Thomas. "Straighten yourself up, Girl," she said to Clarissa. "It seems the Comte wishes to pay us a call. Show him up, Roberts."

Cat walked rapidly toward Berkeley Square. After escaping from Mr. Fairfax's unwelcome company, Cat regained her natural delight in her surroundings. She enjoyed the color and bustle of London's busy streets. The cries of the costermongers mixed with those of the street urchins who sold everything from oranges to shoelaces for a farthing. She enjoyed the passing parade of carriages, curricles, hackneys, and phaetons, with their colorful passengers. Young bucks in brightly-colored coats with buckskin breeches and polished top boots rode by on prancing bays, blacks, and chestnuts. One or two even drew rein and saluted her, but she walked by without showing that she had seen them. She had enough for one day of being taken for a light-skirts.

The stores on Bond Street displayed a vibrant profusion of goods: Alençon lace, feathers, bolts of watered silk, bolts of taffeta, fur muffs, and white kid gloves. She chose a store at random and entered. A pretty, young girl stepped forward to help her. Quicker than Cat would have liked, she found several lengths of ribbon in the desired colors. Cat would have enjoyed browsing further before completing her purchases, but she reminded herself that she had another important errand.

The sun had begun to decline in the sky when Cat arrived in Berkeley Square. All the houses were sedate, without the pretensions to grandeur that marked the Thomas residence at Portman Square. Nevertheless, the formal Georgian entries bespoke a long-standing wealth and nobility. Cat consulted the small scrap of paper in her reticule, upon which she had written her aunt's address. Number 44 was directly opposite her. The grey shutters closed over the tall windows were disquieting. Could it be that her aunt was not in town yet? She hurried across the street, not noticing the closed carriage that stood waiting at the corner. Disquieted by her growing suspicion, she nevertheless climbed the short flight of steps and knocked boldly on the grey door. At least the elegantly curved brass knocker had been polished recently, which meant that someone was at home.

From below, in the area, outside the basement kitchen, a man's voice called up, "May I help you, Miss?" Cat turned and looked down upon a neatly dressed fellow of some fifty years, probably by his dress a servant of some sort.

"I am inquiring after Lady Henrietta Leacock. Is she at home?"

"I am sorry to disappoint you, but Lady Leacock is not yet arrived in town. May I ask your name and your business?" He stared upward at her, wondering who she was among the quality, to be arriving alone and on foot. The dress was fine, and he could see that she had not been worn by hard work. A nasty suspicion began to grow in his mind about the young Lord Leacock and his doxies, but he kept his thoughts hidden.

Cat was uncomfortably aware of her equivocal position. She debated revealing her identity. Fearing the risk of his censure now and possibly her aunt's later, she thought swiftly. She needed to know when her aunt would arrive, but she could not reveal her identity, lest her father find her out and take her back to Eldertree Manor.

Mustering all the hauteur she could manage, she replied loftily, "I have a special message to deliver to your mistress of an extremely confidential and personal nature. I can deliver it only to her in person. As she needs to know this information as soon as she arrives, I would appreciate knowing when she is expected in London. If you wish to serve your mistress, you need to tell me this information."

The serving man considered her words and appearance thoughtfully. There was something familiar about the young auburn-haired girl. Quality, he decided. He looked down the street and saw the waiting carriage with its coachman. Probably a friend of the mistress from the country, in town for the Season, he thought. He cleared his throat.

"Lady Leacock does not arrive for another week. We received notice just this morning that she would be arriving for the Season Sunday sennight. May I have your name so I may mention your visit to her?"

The young woman's face briefly betrayed her dismay. Nonetheless, she composed herself and answered him calmly enough, "I shall return myself to see your mistress upon the day that she arrives. You have been most kind, and I will mention it to Lady Leacock." She smiled at him and turned to leave. He watched her walk gracefully down the steps toward the waiting carriage. Satisfied that she was indeed a lady of quality and most likely a family friend, the old servant descended the steps to the basement kitchen. He did not see her walk past the waiting carriage, nor did he see the tall gentleman descend from it to greet her.

Vere sat quietly in the closed carriage, grey-gloved hands clasping a silver-headed walking stick, a falcon of exquisite workmanship. His blue kerseymere coat and buff breeches were admirably cut and quite expensive. He had put on a fresh cravat as well to aid in the deception that he had just come from another engagement and was in the neighborhood by happy accident. He smiled a small smile of satisfaction. He had learned Lady Leacock's address previously from Sir Merlin. His assumption of her ultimate destination had been proved correct. He had both seen her arrival and had watched the little interplay between Cat and the servant caretaker. As she passed by the carriage, he opened the door and descended. "Miss Cat," he said, smiling as he bowed to her, "what a happy coincidence to encounter you a second time today. May I ask whether you are returning to Portman Square?"

Cat stood still, her way effectively blocked by Mr. Fairfax's body. She knew this second meeting to be no accident. Fairfax was deliberately stalking her. Although he was smiling at her with every appearance of gentlemanly attentiveness, she suspected that his motives were dishonorable. What other reason would he have for being so courteous to a young lady's maid of no fortune or family? Still, she endeavored to be polite. If he could keep up the fiction, so could she.

"Aye, Sir. I am in truth returning to Portman Square, as I have completed all my errands on behalf of my mistress. Please, Sir, I beg you to let me pass. The day grows shorter, and I need to be back to the house."

"Indeed," he replied, but he made no move to let her by. "I would think that the sun will be quite set before you are even a halfway back to Portman Square."

The dismay in her eyes showed that she agreed with him. To be abroad alone in London at night was no place for any respectable woman, be she lady or serving wench. Cat fumbled quickly at her reticule, hoping that she might have a shilling, enough to pay for a hackney. Her obvious distress provided Vere with the opportunity he desired. Making her a courteous bow, he offered her his arm and said, "May I offer you a place in my carriage? My coachman can get us back to Portman Square before the sun sets."

Cat looked at the closed carriage and then at the sky. The sun was low, and soon the western horizon would be streaked with red. The closed carriage seemed less a threat than the fast-darkening streets of London. Deciding her strategy, she pointedly ignored his offered arm, replying broadly. "An' it please you, Sor, I can ride as well with your coachman upon the box." To his astonishment, she then turned and made as if to clamber upon the coachman's box.

"You will do no such thing!" he roared in surprise. "I refuse to drive about the streets of London with a girl as pretty as yourself on the box in open display. I have my reputation as well, my girl. Your insinuations are most insulting. However, I will overlook them in view of your youth. Please desist in this young girl's foolishness, and enter the carriage."

Cat curtseyed, hiding her smile. By bringing his honor into question, she had put him on the defensive. Now his own pride would prevent him from making any ungentlemanly attempt upon her person. "Beggin' your pardon, Sor, I had no mind to offend ye. I thought only to take a place as befittin' my station in life. Such as we do not ride with the gentles. I am sure, if my mistress were to find out, I would be turned out of my place."

A small muscle twitched in Vere's jaw, betraying his displeasure at her cleverness. He saw quite well how this fetching minx had checkmated him. "Very well," he said a trifle coldly. "You shall ride in my carriage, but I shall let you out a safe distance from the house. Now kindly honor me with ascending into the carriage. We have been standing here quite long enough to be seen by half of fashionable London." He again offered her his hand, but the girl ignored it as if she did not see it and scrambled gracefully into the carriage, where she folded herself into a corner and stared out the window.

He sat opposite her, his hands upon his stick, which rested on his thighs. She presented him with a lovely profile; she continued to avoid his eyes, instead looking out at the changing London streets. His eyes followed the curve of her cheek, her lovely straight nose, with just the hint of an uptilt, the fullness of her lower lip, curved in a slight smile. Her self-satisfied coquetry challenged him.

"Are you smiling at my discomfiture?" he asked suddenly. "I am not unaware of the tricks women play upon men to arouse their interest. Do you suppose the same of me? Please remember that you are hardly more than a schoolgirl, and act accordingly."

She turned to him and asked, "What can you mean?" Her eyes blazed with the fire he had witnessed upon their first meeting. "How could you suppose such? I know only too well what a girl like myself could expect from a gentleman such as you. It is precisely that which makes me wish to avoid your company and your pretended 'kindness.' Please confine your coarse thoughts and actions to the Cyprians who welcome and profit from such attentions!" Saying that, she abruptly turned her head to resume staring out of the carriage window. Her mortification was complete. He could see, along with the sudden color that flamed her cheeks, small tears brimming from her eyes.

Vere sat in stunned silence. His anger at her rebuke fought with his self-control. Never before had his honor been so directly impugned in such a coarse way by anyone. That a female, a hoydenish schoolgirl, no less, should vilify him with such accusations of dishonorable intent was unbelievable. Yet there she sat, in his carriage, blinking back the tears that she was too proud to wipe off her cheeks.

Nonetheless, she had been correct, in a sense. Even now, he could feel the electricity that stirred within him at her nearness. Had not his courtesy also been an excuse to touch her, to feel the young flesh whose sight and smell had intoxicated his senses since first he saw her upon the highroad? He removed his cambric handkerchief from his coat breast pocket. Leaning forward, he offered it to her. "Here," he said, sternly. "I do not have patience with foolishness. Wipe your eyes like the good child that you are. I will endeavor to forget your ridiculous accusations if you will cease to carry on in such an undignified manner. Despite what tales you may have been told, not every gentleman who does you a kindness is intent on seduction." He was burningly aware of his own hypocrisy even as he spoke.

Sniffling a bit, she took the proffered cloth, barely daring to look at him "I apologize for my unacceptable behavior," she whispered, her words nearly muffled by his handkerchief. She wiped the tears from her cheeks and handed back the handkerchief. The brief touch of his fingers as he received it back felt to her like a burning brand. She hurriedly withdrew her hand as if from a fire. When she dared to look at him, he was sitting up quite upright, his hands on the walking stick between his legs, the handkerchief abandoned on the seat beside him. The decidedly peculiar gleam in his eyes made her afraid of him all over again.

"We are a safe distance from Portman Square," he said, rapping with the stick upon the carriage roof. The coachman obediently stopped the carriage. He leaned across and opened the carriage door. The groom waited outside to assist her out. "You need to learn to control your headstrong words," he said grimly. "Whatever you got up to in the wilds of Wales will not do here in Town. Such a passionate nature as your own is dangerous to both yourself and those around you."

"Do you include yourself in that category?" she said, lifting her chin in challenge.

Vere gave her a wintry smile. "Do not seek to interrogate me. We have already decided upon that matter." He motioned her to the open carriage door. "You have duties to attend to."

Quickly, without looking at him, she descended from the carriage and hurried off. Vere rapped upon the roof twice. The horses started down the street at a sedate trot.

Alone, in the cold dusk of the carriage, he picked up the abandoned handkerchief, still damp from her tears. Briefly, he put it to his face, seeking the ghost of her skin in the remains of her scent. The passage between them in the carriage had served only to further inflame his desire. It was cursed luck that she seemed to be able to read him so easily. The cultured mask of disinterest he assumed with such convincing success among the ladies of the fashionable world in which he lived was not sufficient to deceive this passionate schoolgirl. He laughed bitterly. Never had he been more ardently bent on seduction, never had he desired more to wed, and yet he was frustrated in both occupations by his damnable position. He rapped again on the roof of his carriage. "Charles," he said, "take me to St. James. I wish to go to my club." A few bottles in good company should serve to soothe the turmoil that the chit had created in him.

Cat hurried down the kitchen steps. She hoped that her late return would go unnoticed. "Well, 'tis time you returned, Cat," Mrs. Congdon said. "'Tis a good thing her ladyship and Miss Clarissa have lain down for long afternoon naps, or you would be in fair trouble. Take off yer bonnet, and help me get the tea things ready. The bell has just rung, and ye can help Rose with setting the table. Here, take your purchases. The young miss will want to see them."

Mrs. Congdon smiled kindly upon Cat. It was the young girl's first day out to get a glimpse of London, and Mrs. Congdon was not so old that she had forgotten her own feelings of wonder at being in the streets of London for the first time. One lapse was forgivable, but only one. "Do not let me catch ye again, though, or I will be obliged to report ye," she added severely. "Now hurry along. The bell has gone again, and Rose has already taken up the cups." Cat smoothed her braided hair and, taking the parcels, hurried up the stairs after Rose.

FAIRFAX & MONTCLAIR

Vere mounted the stairs to Brook's. Upon entering the gentlemen's club, he gave his hat and stick to the attendant. "Is there anyone in the sitting room, Richards?" he asked. "I am minded to get myself well foxed tonight, and I would prefer to do it in pleasant company."

"Lord Carleton is there, Sir, as is Mr. Darlington and young Viscount Stanhope. Shall I announce you?"

"No," replied Vere. "Just send up a few bottles of port from the cellars. 1789 was a good year, I think. I will see myself up." He climbed the staircase, hoping to find surcease from the disordered emotions his encounter with Cat Llewellyn had aroused in him. To preserve and increase his estates, Vere knew that he must marry. The alliance with Sir Merlin's daughter had been expedient and convenient. Eldertree Manor was not entailed. Caitlyn Llewellyn would bring nearly three thousand acres of good farm and pastureland adjacent to his own acreage and a large dower in money, plate, and good breeding stock. For that alone, he had planned to marry her. When first he saw her on the road, before he knew her identity, he had been taken aback by her beauty and vitality and had freely acquainted her with the fact. He had not recognized her inexperience and innocence. But she had assayed him, and he knew that all the gilt of his title would not now cover the dross. At present, while she still masqueraded as a lady's maid, he could not even pay court to her. However, he could not keep away from her. 'Twas the very devil that from the first instant he saw her, on the road to Wrexham, he had desired her utterly.

"Fairfax!" exclaimed Lord Carleton over the low buzz of conversation. "I thought you still on the Continent! Did Boney confiscate all your Italian estates?"

"No. Thanks to the good offices of the local magistrate, I was able to keep my fortunes there intact." Vere sat in silence and remembered the fighting that had convulsed northern Italy, the stream of refugees that grew to a flood as Napoleon's armies had marched steadily southward, conquering and burning cities and towns. As his father had lingered in his prolonged dying, so too had the old political order convulsed and finally succumbed. "I felt that it would be better if I left at the first opportunity. This truce will not last long. I have no wish to be interned in a pestilential prison for the length of the war. Napoleon is a madman. There is no agreement that he will not break."

"And your father, is he with you?" asked Carleton. Richards, bearing several bottles of port and a glass, interrupted their conference.

"Richards," Vere said, "bring extra glasses for these gentlemen." He gestured at the other three men.

"Alas, no," said Viscount Stanhope. "I must take my leave. Darlington and I are riding to a mill several leagues out of town. Have to get up early because the fight begins at 6:00 a.m. So far, the magistrates are not on to it. Tomkins has not been beaten yet, but Black George went seventeen rounds against Mackey and is slightly favored." The two young men rose, and made their way unsteadily out the door.

"What of your father, Lord Falconbridge? Is he in town also?" Carleton asked again, settling across from Vere in a deep red leather armchair. Vere took a sip of the port, contemplating his friend from under heavily lidded dark eyes.

"Can you keep a secret, Carleton?" he asked, looking at his friend with an imperturbable stare while swirling the port gently in the glass that he held.

"Certainly," Carleton replied. "Always keep a confidence. I discovered your indiscretion with Her Grace. Never breathed a word of it to anybody."

Vere emptied his glass and filled another one. He looked at it meditatively, then drank it down in one long draught.

"What is the secret that I am not to reveal?" Carleton prompted him.

"My titles, Carleton," Vere said flatly. "My father is dead. I beg you to keep this in confidence. I have reasons for wanting to keep the true state of my affairs a secret a while yet." He reached for the bottle and poured himself yet another glass of the ruby liquid as Richards returned with the extra glass.

"Sorry to hear it," Carleton murmured and helped himself to a glass of port. Fairfax was drinking three to his one, Carleton noted. Never seen his friend so determined to get quiffed. Losing a father could do that, although Carleton had never thought of them as especially close. Old Lord Falconbridge had disapproved of his son, with good reason.

Despising his father and disdaining even to use the courtesy title Viscount de Montferrato or to associate himself with the Falconbridge name, Vere was known at University and in Town simply as Mr. Fairfax. He had been a wild youth, dueling, racing, and cutting a wide swath among the Cyprians and gaming hells in his days at Oxford.

At nineteen, he had run riot with the Prince of Wales's set, Hellgate, Cripplegate, and all. As the most notable young whip in the Jockey Club, Fairfax's racing escapades were legendary. Fairfax's hot temper and skill with pistols and swords made him a feared duelist, and few cared to challenge him, no matter what the provocation.

When a family serving wench he had got with child killed herself, his father had banned him from the family estate at Foxearth for a wastrel and a libertine. Upon receiving the letter in his rooms at Bedford Square, Fairfax had merely smiled. He had commented, "It's five years past noticing," and had gone off with some of his raucous companions. The next news Carleton had of Fairfax was that he had returned to his mother's estates in Tuscany. He had visited London less than half a dozen times in the ten years since.

The two men drank together in silence, Carleton in respect for his friend's feelings, Vere himself, ever more morose as he thought of his impossible situation regarding Cat Llewellyn. Carleton wanted to ask Fairfax why he desired to keep his father's death a secret and his titles unclaimed, but Carleton forbore. His friend would tell him when he was ready. In the meantime, he had another glass of port and noticed the second bottle was nearly empty. Fairfax's eyes were closed, and his head was sunken upon his chest.

Watching him, Carleton wondered what could have happened to bring his friend to such a pass. It could not solely be the death of his father. Fairfax and his father had never been close. Old Lord Falconbridge had been a man of scholarship and temperate habits. He had married a tempestuous Italian beauty of ancient lineage, who was allied by blood to half the ducal households of Austria and France.

There was no doubt that it was a misalliance. She preferred the warm sensual climes of her youth, whereas Lord Falconbridge delighted in the cold mists of his great Welsh estates. She had returned to Italy, taking the child with her. Although husband and wife were periodically reunited during Fairfax's childhood, they lived apart until Lord Falconbridge contracted consumption and removed to Italy for his health, leaving the fortunes of Foxearth in the hands of his agent and to the oversight of his good friend and neighbor, Sir Merlin Llewellyn.

After his early childhood, Fairfax had spent comparatively few years in England: some summer months on the Welsh estates of his father from ages twelve to seventeen, then another three years while at Oxford. Carleton, who had met Fairfax at Magdalen, knew him to be wild and reckless, even then, and ferociously intelligent, with an especially cynical attitude toward authority and the fairer sex.

Carleton finished his glass and put it upon the table. It made a faint clink as he did so. Without opening his eyes, Fairfax asked, "Have you ever loved, Carleton? Or have you, like the rest of us damned mortals, known only lust and the waste of spirit that comes with satiation?"

The remark, so unlike his friend, took Carleton aback. Already a seasoned libertine from his youth on the Continent, Fairfax had grown more discreet with age, but had hardly lost his appetite for the pleasures of the flesh. Residing sometimes in London, often in France, but usually in Italy or Austria, he took his pick of titled ladies.

Six months previously, Carleton had heard from a friend returned from his Grand Tour that Vere had seduced an Italian countess while at the opera in Rome, during which her husband had sat, unaware, in rapt contemplation of the aria only a few feet from them. The affair resulted in a duel in which Fairfax had left a bullet in the aggrieved husband's shoulder.

Afterwards, Fairfax continued to enjoy the delights of his countess for a full fortnight at her country estate. In his recollection of all of Fairfax's escapades, Carleton had never heard from him one word of regret or remorse. Surprised, Carleton replied hurriedly, "You are out of my depth, Fairfax. I've taken my pleasures as other men do. Sleep it off. You'll forget all this in the morning." He got up to leave.

Without stirring, Fairfax made a request. "Send up Richards with another bottle when you leave. Some devils are not easily drowned."

Carleton realized that something or someone must have touched a deep, hidden chord in his friend's very being. Silently leaving the room, Carleton wondered, in vain, who that person could be.

The port brought a soothing numbness to Vere's senses, a respite from the agitation of his mind and body. Lust he had known often, love never, since his beautiful laughing mother had left him to the care of a succession of servants and turned away to pursue her own loves and pleasures. His stern father had spent money on him for tutors, for horses, for clothes, for education, but never had he reached out to him in affection or care. Perhaps he had not even believed that Vere was truly his son, but instead a nameless bastard foisted upon him by the faithless woman he had wed.

As a young man, Vere had experienced the bright brittleness of a society whose values were all appearance, whose loves and lusts were petty and indistinguishable from each other. Life was a vicious game of prey at which the young Vere Courtenay Fairfax had been singularly well-equipped by face and fortune to play and win, but ill-suited by temperament to enjoy.

At fifteen, left behind during one of his mother's rare trips to England, he had been seduced for the first time by one of her friends, a French countess of about thirty, powdered and patched, with both an aging husband and a vast appetite for young men. He had thought himself in love, for she was beautiful and, at first, kind. During the few months of the affair, their secret rendezvous and stolen caresses had vivified every nerve of his body. He loved her, ardently, obsessively, in the way that comes only with first love, when first passion awakens the senses to full erotic maturity.

When he had poured out the love of his hidden heart to her, his devotion and dreams, she had laughed mockingly, beckoning from across the room to a friend of hers, an old roué, who smiled behind his scented lace handkerchief as she repeated each word. He had stormed out, in the fury of youthful disillusionment. Later, when he had, heartbroken, told his mother of his affair, the tears coursing down his face, she had laughed at him! From that moment on, he had vowed never to love again, but to take what pleasure he could, caring nothing of the hurt he might give, rejecting all emotion save contempt, all values save pride.

He idly wondered what had become of that first woman he had loved. Had she been swept to her death in the tides of war and revolution that had raged on the Continent, along with so many others who had been his mother's friends? She herself had died of childbed fever, the result of an ill-omened affair with a young hussar of the Austrian army. At the end, when she lay dying, what had he felt? He looked at the dregs of the port in his glass. Nothing. He had viewed her lifeless body without emotion. His father had wept shamelessly, but the son had only turned away. Now both were dead. Throughout his father's prolonged final illness, while tides of refugees flowed past the estate, and Florence opened her gates to the triumphant French, Vere had held his lands and peasants safe, unaffected by the dangers of his situation, unmoved by the carnage and death that permeated every facet of daily life. Impassive, he stood by as his father breathed his last. Silent and dry-eyed, Vere watched as the old man's pitifully wasted corpse was laid to rest beside the grave of his mother. He had wealth in excess of 800,000 pounds, and he felt nothing.

Until he had seen Cat upon the road. Her courage, the vitality of her young life, as well as her ravishing beauty, had brought a warmth to Fairfax that had been suppressed all these long years. She was his to possess, and yet, for all his experience in Love's flowery combat, he had no idea how to proceed. She could be forced, by her father and by himself, but he did not want that. He wanted the gift of her heart and her love to be given freely. In the black night of his mind, all his sins, the secret scars of his soul, rose to reproach him. How could he offer love to this pure young girl, when he was disfigured by the loathsomeness of his diseased spirit, the baseness of his acts?

The candle burned low in its socket, its light wavering as it guttered out. In the dimness, he could make out Richards and his man Charles at his elbow. Nodding briefly in acknowledgment, he rose unsteadily from his chair. They reached out to help him, but he shook off their hands. However drunk he was, he would walk by himself. He slowly made his way down the staircase, past the raucous shouts of the gamesters playing hazard in the salon. His carriage awaited him outside the door. He allowed his footman to help him inside. He heard a light whistle, and the horses trotted off. Vere closed his eyes in weariness, holding off sleep until he arrived at his own door and climbed into his own bed.

Cat lay awake in the narrow bed that she shared with Rose. She was weary, yet unable to sleep. The strange encounters with Mr. Fairfax had left her in a state of nervous excitement. When she had arrived back home, she had obediently shown Clarissa her purchases, sewed the new ribbons onto the dainty cap, finished the morning's interrupted mending, and dressed her mistress for dinner, all the while listening to her tell of the two visits by Mr. Fairfax and the Comte du Foix. Cat thought Fairfax's behavior disquieting. According to Clarissa, even Lady Thomas's suspicions had been aroused. Cat kept her face carefully expressionless, murmuring "Yes" and "No" as Clarissa's commentary continued, but within she felt fear squeeze her heart. Cat was brave, fearing little in her childhood world. But Vere Courtenay Fairfax represented a danger that she had never encountered before, and she instinctively knew that she, not Clarissa, had become his quarry.

She turned in her narrow little bed, seeking the sleep that eluded her. Clarissa informed her that they were going to walk in Hyde Park on the morrow. Clarissa could see and more importantly be seen there by the world of London's gentry. Lady Thomas was feeling a touch of gout and would not consent to walk anywhere, so Cat would be Clarissa's companion. In a fit of generosity, Clarissa had presented Cat with yet another of her cast-offs: an ivory-colored gown trimmed with bright jonquil yellow ribbons through the bodice and sleeves. Its simple girlish innocence was not stylish enough for London, and the yellow color had never suited Clarissa. Cat had bobbed a curtsey to her mistress, thanking her in a nervous voice. Clarissa preened herself on her maid's overwhelming gratitude.

Cat feared that she would draw more unwelcome attention to herself with this dress. She dreaded another meeting with the sardonic, supercilious Fairfax, whose insolent dark-eyed stare stirred so many conflicting emotions within her. He both frightened and attracted her. He meant only ruin and death, yet she was drawn by his terrible fascination. She was cornered, with no place to hide until her aunt arrived. Even then, she thought, she might not be safe.

In the sunny morning, all Cat's spectral night fears melted like a late snowfall as she and Clarissa walked in Hyde Park. Although she was aware that this was another place in which Mr. Fairfax might suddenly appear, the beauty of the spring soothed her apprehensions. The sky was a bright robin's-egg blue, and all around, the nodding heads of the flowers from the formal gardens betokened a happy lightness of spirit. Cat was so taken by the lovely landscape that she paid scant attention to the passing parade of fashionables and Clarissa's chatter about them. Cat was only vaguely aware of Clarissa's constantly bobbing parasol as Clarissa saluted first one then another acquaintance who passed in one of the elegant landaus. Her chatter cascaded unheeded past Cat's ears like fine rain. Cat had only to murmur "Yes, Miss," or "No, Miss," at appropriate intervals to have her thoughts entirely to herself.

A slender handsome man approached them. Clad in subdued colors of grey, he was of only medium height, but well-proportioned withal, with fair hair and eyes as grey as storm-shifted clouds. Clarissa bent her head closer to Cat's ear. "That is the Comte du Foix, with whom I danced at the Bellinghams'. So handsome, don't you think? And polite too. He called on Mama and me just after that strange Mr. Fairfax left and was ever so much more amiable! Mama and I much preferred him to the other!" As the elegant slim figure drew abreast of them, Clarissa bowed her head in recognition and greeted him.

"Good Morning, Comte du Foix! How nice to see you." She extended her hand gracefully.

"*Enchanté,*" the count replied, taking her gloved hand and bowing low, "I am so delighted to see you this morning. May I inquire if you are enjoying your morning stroll?" said Montclair, falling in step with them.

"Very much, Comte du Foix," Clarissa said, smiling coyly. "May I ask the same of you?"

"Very much, more so, now that I am in your presence. May I hope to see you at Lady Delafield's supper party?" Cat watched him covertly from under lowered eyelashes. His smiling open countenance betrayed none of the sensual invitation that she had seen in Mr. Fairfax's smile. She warmed to him immediately.

"Indeed, Comte du Foix," replied Clarissa, with a toss of her shining curls, becomingly arranged beneath her gypsy bonnet edged with blue flowers. She had worn her sky-blue and white-stripped walking dress, with its matching pelisse, which became her fair coloring admirably. Clarissa was pleasantly aware of how she and the count matched each other in stature and coloring. Clarissa was a few inches shorter than Cat and of smaller build. Her neat figure complimented the Comte's own far better than did Cat's willowy height. Let that dark, difficult Mr. Fairfax be attracted to Cat, a mere lady's maid. Both of them were no better than they ought. However, Comte du Foix was real nobility, attentive, gently bred, a friend of the Comte de Artois, and, to be sure, rich.

"I shall look forward to greeting you there, Miss Thomas," he said, smiling gravely, and with a little bow, which included both girls, he again lifted his hat, and strode off.

"Is he not perfect, Cat?" giggled Clarissa in her triumph. "So much nicer than Mr. Fairfax, who is really frighteningly abrupt! I hope I shall have the pleasure of standing up with him again. What do you think of him?"

"He seems a goodly gentleman," Cat murmured, unwilling to volunteer anything more. Clarissa nodded, satisfied with Cat's reply, and they continued onwards, each lost to her own thoughts.

Cat found herself trying to remember each detail of the encounter that she had witnessed. Comte du Foix was indeed attractive. His courtly manners were both restful and pleasing, without the edge that characterized her exchanges with Mr. Fairfax. His politeness had been unexceptional, with the perfect correctness that should characterize a true gentleman. Although he had taken no personal notice of her, she felt that he had acknowledged her presence in his farewells. She hoped that she might meet him again in her aunt's company. As they walked deeper into the park, Cat forgot her fears of meeting Mr. Fairfax along the way. Although she had felt a certain apprehension that he might suddenly appear, as the morning wore on, her anxieties receded. Both girls walked onward, unaware that they both dreamed the same dream of the same man.

INQUIRES

Fairfax opened his eyes with a groan as shafts of the mid-morning sunlight penetrated the closed curtains of his bedchamber. His dry mouth and aching head told him in no uncertain terms that he had dipped too deeply into the bottle last night. He remembered very little of his evening after broaching his third bottle. At least the ache in his head seemed to dull the pain in his heart. He winced as he sat up and swung his long legs out of bed. The well-trained staff had already set out the tray with the pitcher of cold water and a plate of biscuits that were his preferred breakfast on late mornings that invariably followed such evenings.

After quenching his raging thirst and calming his stomach, he rang for his man. Stevens arrived nearly immediately, bearing hot water and shaving razor, his impassive countenance betraying nothing of his thoughts on his lordship's morning after-state. "Would your lordship care for a bath?" Stevens asked as he applied the white lather to Fairfax's cheeks.

"Yes, Stevens, I think that would do nicely. Lay out my claret-colored coat and blue waistcoat. I think I will go down to Jackson's boxing academy and find out who won this morning's mill."

"Very good, Sir," replied Stevens, as he skillfully scraped the lather from Fairfax's square jaw. Delicately, with small strokes of the straight razor, Stevens scratched the soap from around Fairfax's wide, thin-lipped mouth, from the flat hollowed cheeks. Vere stared imperturbably at his image in the mirror as this operation continued. Bit by bit, his harsh, arrogant features were revealed: the wide mobile mouth set in a dead straight line revealed neither kindness nor humor; a high-bridged, aquiline nose with slightly flared nostrils; large dark eyes, deeply socketed, brooding with the sullen fires of hell; the thick black straight brows set above them; the high forehead; his jet-black hair, which curled about his temples; and his close-set ears. A handsome, harsh face, he thought idly, one to inspire passion, perhaps, but too formidable to engender love's tenderness.

He rose and walked into the dressing room, where Stevens had poured the water for the hipbath. Dropping his dark purple dressing gown, Vere stepped naked into his bath. Stevens poured warm water over Vere's broad shoulders, which ran down his back, channeled by his spine, recessed in its cleft of muscle, and over his narrow flanks and powerful horseman's thighs, his long curved calves, and narrow feet. Taking a sponge, Vere washed his flat muscled chest and belly, with its line of curling hair, which trailed from his thickly furred chest to his abdomen and formed a dark shadow at his groin.

Stevens stood by, holding a towel. He thought his lordship a fine figure of a man, handsome and well-grown. It was common knowledge in the servants' hall that the Earl of Falconbridge had quite an appetite for the ladies and they for him. Standing stolidly by while his lordship washed himself, Stevens could understand why. He himself was above gossiping about his employer with the other servants in the house, but apparently his predecessor had not been, from the impression he gathered from certain remarks made by the undermaids in the hall one evening. Even housemaids could not fail to note the Earl's evident virility. As his lordship stepped out of his bath, Stevens handed him his towel and turned back to the dressing room, where he selected a white linen shirt to go with the frock coat and blue waistcoat.

The early morning walk had put fresh roses in Cat's smooth cheeks by the time she and Clarissa returned to Portman Square. Cat meekly followed her mistress up the steps to the front door and into the cold marble hallway. Clarissa took off her bonnet and handed it and her parasol to Arbuthnot, who waited solemnly to receive them. She primped in the dainty gilt mirror that hung just inside the great doorway, flashing a sweet simper, and fluttering her eyelashes. Miming her earlier conversation with the Comte du Foix and tossing her head in a saucy way, to judge the effectiveness of the gesture for future use, Clarissa finished regarding herself and turned once again to Cat, who was standing quietly aside.

"Go and inquire of Mrs. Congdon whether there are any scones left from breakfast. I would like to have my cup of tea early today. After that, lay out my afternoon tea dress, the white one with the lace-trimmed cuffs." As Cat hurried off on her errands, she heard Clarissa ask Mr. Arbuthnot, "Has anyone left cards in our absence?"

Two hours later, Cat sat down at the servants' long dining table and drank a fragrant, steaming cup of hot cider with Mrs. Congdon. No doubt Clarissa was entertaining callers with her mother. Cat was grateful for the respite. She wanted to be alone with her thoughts. Many new masculine faces had been introduced into the gallery of her mind, but none pleased her so much in recollection as that of the Comte du Foix. It was true that he in no way resembled the fanciful knight of her imagination; alas, that part was more nearly filled by the insufferable Mr. Fairfax, but the reality of the Comte was very agreeable indeed, and Cat fancied that if she might meet him in Society as an equal, she might find herself the object of his courtesy. Cat closed her eyes, seeing again the sleek blond head and the merry grey eyes, with their quizzical expression.

Roberts, the footman, arrived and laid the tea tray down between the two women who were sitting at the table. "If you please, Mrs. Congdon, her ladyship requests more tea and biscuits. Seems Miss Clarissa's walk was very profitable this morning." He winked lewdly at Mrs. Congdon. "There's two more gentlemen callers come round. Lord Carrington and Mr. Fairfax just went up. That makes four in all, counting the Comte du Foix and Colonel Percy." Looking toward Cat, he added, "You'll be wanted in the salon soon enough. Miss Clarissa asked me to tell you to fetch her blue shawl, as 'tis getting a bit chill."

Cat got up, albeit unwillingly. She had no desire to face Mr. Fairfax again, even with other people around for protection. Not only had she been unforgivably rude to the man, but also, she had betrayed thoughts that no lady ought to admit having in the first place. Far from discouraging him, her words could only serve to further embolden him. Hurrying toward the backstairs, she decided that she would be as self-effacing as possible, slipping in quietly and leaving quickly.

Pausing outside the salon door to still her too rapidly beating heart, Cat heard a loud female voice raised in boisterous laughter. "I'd have thought this a mill by the amazing presence of so much masculine company. Or the sitting of Parliament!" A loud caw punctuated this rather inelegant jest. Taking a deep breath, Cat slipped in the door, sidling around the wall toward Clarissa and Lady Thomas.

Sitting squarely upon the satin-striped ottoman was the strangest woman Cat had ever seen. Tall, broad-shouldered, and solidly built, she had iron-grey hair, a dark complexion, heavily painted and rouged, and dark eyes. She was dressed in a most astonishing peacock-blue walking dress, with a spencer of bright emerald green. Her hat was a turban of the same defiant shade, topped with an ostrich feather dyed in royal blue. Momentarily astounded by the outlandish figure, Cat forgot to slip out after silently handing the shawl to Clarissa. Disregarding any of the other guests, Cat stepped back against the wall to look again at the eccentric apparition before her.

Lady Thomas was smiling and offered the woman more tea. "Well," she simpered to her bizarre guest, "I, for one, cannot fail to be pleased by the hospitality and generosity of London society in making us feel so welcome here. It is most good of you to call upon us, Lady Bullstrode."

"Nothing to it, Lady Thomas. I enjoys callin' upon all the young debutantes and their mothers. Like to know which horse has the inside track in the marriage stakes, what?"

From under her fringed eyelashes, Cat noticed a certain subtle shifting in the postures of the men arranged about the room like so many courtiers. Colonel Percy grinned suddenly and flicked his handkerchief. The Comte du Foix merely smiled slightly and momentarily closed his eyes, as if in agreement with her ladyship's jest. The stranger, who must be Lord Carrington, a distinguished man of about fifty-five, chuckled in polite acknowledgment. Cat dared to hazard a glance at Mr. Fairfax. He sat beside Lord Carrington, one arm resting on the arm of his chair, the other lightly holding his riding whip, betraying not a flicker of movement. Silently, she edged away from Clarissa, and with a sigh of relief, Cat slipped out of the salon.

Bemused, descending the great staircase on light-slippered feet, Cat heard the discreet click of the salon door closing. The hairs on the back of her neck prickled, so sure was she that she would be overtaken by the despicable Fairfax. She quickened her pace and almost missed a step, when she slipped on the highly polished marble. Cat grasped the banister to steady herself as she heard a footfall directly behind her.

"Have a care, Mademoiselle," said a light voice at her ear as a slim white hand steadied her elbow. She turned around to face the slightly smiling face of the Count du Foix. His grey eyes looked into hers with concern. "Please slow your descent. You must not fall and injure yourself." Cat looked back at him, pleased by his recognition.

"*Merci*, your lordship," she replied, smiling and dropping her glance. They stood there a moment in silence upon the last steps of the staircase until the clatter of descending booted footsteps caused Cat to remember herself and scurry off towards the door of the backstairs to the servants' hall.

"Comte du Foix," said the familiar voice of Mr. Fairfax. "We seem to have many pursuits in common. May I interest you in broaching a bottle with me at a place I know, located quite conveniently close?" Her curiosity piqued by Fairfax's words, Cat paused briefly at the doorway and looked back at the two men, who stood together at the foot of the staircase. Fairfax's visage was set in grim harsh lines, but the Comte merely returned a bland smile.

"Alas, no," sighed the Comte. "I have another appointment, which I must keep. Perhaps we may meet again at another time. *À bientôt.*" Which said, the Comte du Foix made a quick, supercilious bow and departed speedily. Fairfax saw Cat still standing there, paused in her hurried flight.

"A minute, if you will," he called to her. Without waiting for reply, he strode over to her. Frozen, she faced him while her hand groped behind her, futilely seeking the door handle. Before she could reach it and escape to the safety of the servants' stair, his hand closed upon her wrist, warm fingers forming a loose bracelet about her suddenly galloping pulse. She gasped in surprise as he brought his lips close to her ear. "Do not become over-friendly with the fair Count," he whispered hoarsely, the warm thunder of his breath pouring over her shell-like ear. "He represents a danger that you cannot comprehend."

"And you do not?" Cat raged, endeavoring ineffectually to pull her wrist from his strong-fingered, tightening grasp. "He has only shown himself the gentleman, whereas your behavior respects no boundaries! Let me go now," she demanded with a toss of her head, "or I shall be forced to scream for help." His grip loosened, but his forbidding expression did not change.

"I have no wish to harm you," Fairfax replied. "On the contrary. I have your ultimate welfare at heart." Letting go of her slender wrist, he took her hand, bowed over her clenched fist and gently brushed her curled fingers with his lips, unable to resist briefly pressing a kiss upon them. His tone softened. "I know all too well what you think of me," he added with a brittle smile, letting her hand drop. "Nevertheless, on this point, I beg you to believe me."

"I shall believe as I choose. Do not try to seduce me with melodrama and pretended courtesy," Cat flung at him, as she pulled the wainscoted door open and fled down the servants' staircase. He hesitated, debating with his desire to follow her, but before he could take another step toward her, Lord Carrington descended the curving stairwell and called to him. Fairfax looked intensely again toward where he had last seen her, one muscle twitching in his jaw by the corner of his downturned mouth, then turned to follow the older man. Roberts, the footman, standing unobtrusively just inside the dining room, noted everything and watched as the two men departed.

Once outside, Carrington looked at Fairfax with a long, flat, speculative stare. Although Fairfax felt his cheeks burning, he returned that stare. His towering height gave him an advantage over the shorter man, but Fairfax suddenly felt ashamed of this. Carrington smiled then, a bright twinkle in his eye. "What do you think of Lady Bullstrode, eh? A Fantastic in the truest sense!"

Fairfax returned his smile and bowed. "A force of nature, Sir."

"Well, you can trust her," Carrington said. "She can be surprisingly helpful in a pinch."

Fairfax held his horse while Lord Carrington waited on his carriage. "A most interesting afternoon, Fairfax," he continued gruffly. "It appears that I must extend my regrets to the Delafields for next Saturday evening, but may I propose your name in my stead, as perhaps you will be so kind as to attend and keep an eye on this affair for me?"

"Certainly, Lord Carrington," replied Fairfax, baring his strong white teeth in a wolfish grin. "I have more reason to do so now than before. I am at your service."

Lord Carrington's carriage was brought. Fairfax swung up upon his impatient horse, tipped his hat, and departed homeward at a brisk trot to prepare to attend a supper party.

Upstairs, in the salon, Lady Bullstrode was finishing her second cup of tea while Colonel Percy bade gallant farewells to the Ladies Thomas.

"A pleasure and a privilege," he said as he bowed over Lady Thomas and Clarissa's hands. "I hope that on the next occasion of our meeting, you will allow me to claim a dance." Without waiting for a reply, but perhaps expecting none, he too left the salon.

"Well, that's a pretty fellow," commented Lady Bullstrode, as she put down her cup and saucer with a clatter that made Lady Thomas wince. "Which of them do you fancy, Girl?" she remarked to Clarissa in her loud voice, while peering shrewdly through her lorgnette. While Clarissa hesitated, Lady Bullstrode declaimed her own opinions of the possible suitors. "No doubt, the best of the lot appears to be the Comte du Foix. Foreign, but well-spoken, certainly rumored to be rich. Seen everywhere by everyone. Very fashionable. Of course, young Percy has a very fashionable name, but younger sons in the army are not held to be very good catches, unless the elder brother is sickly, which I happen to know is not the case in Percy's family. Now Mr. Fairfax, that is a name I do seem to know. Doesn't there happen to be a family of that name up your way, Lady Thomas?" she inquired, her eyes sparkling with curiosity.

"Fairfax, Fairfax," muttered Lady Thomas, as she stalled for time. Perhaps Lady Bullstrode could enlighten her as to the real identity of Mr. Fairfax. "Doesn't come to mind," she replied thoughtfully, "though it does sound familiar. I have been meaning to write Sir Thomas and inquire."

Lady Bullstrode narrowed her eyes as she looked at Lady Thomas. The woman's face was innocently blank of information. "Well, Lady Thomas, I wonder if that is not the family name of old Lord Falconbridge. Doesn't he have some estates up your way?" She watched as unfeigned recognition dawned in Lady Thomas's eyes.

"Of course, Lord Falconbridge. I should have known. But he has been absent from the neighborhood so long, one forgets his existence! Do you think that this Mr. Fairfax is directly related to him?" That would explain his presence on the high road that morning, thought Lady Thomas excitedly. And if he were related, Lady Thomas mused, with a smile of satisfaction, he would be very rich indeed. In addition, Clarissa could be settled very near home.

Lady Bullstrode settled her ridiculous hat at a more precarious angle upon her head. "Could be," she winked knowingly, "but relationships in that family were not always harmonious. Not every son who claims a name is born on the right side of the blanket." She stood up, a tall and imposing woman. "Must be going now. Hope to see you and your gel at Almack's come late April. I'll drop a wee word to Ladies Sefton and Cowper." Picking up her reticule and parasol, she resolutely left the salon, billowing like a ship under full sail.

Lady Thomas and Clarissa sat awhile together, each pondering Lady Bullstrode's revelations. "Well," said Lady Thomas, after a lengthy silence. "I wondered about Mr. Fairfax. Do not give him any further encouragement, Clarissa. He is probably nothing but a fortune hunter or worse. For the life of me, I cannot remember anything about Lord Falconbridge or any sons. We must be careful. Be polite, nothing more. Now, Child, we must hurry if we are to be dressed for the dinner party tonight." So saying, she rang the bell for her personal maid and bustled off to her rooms, taking Clarissa with her.

Fairfax rode his horse briskly through Oxford Street toward his town house on Park Lane. He had much to meditate on as he pondered the new developments that this morning's and afternoon's events had revealed. The sights and sounds of London faded from his consciousness as he ordered his thoughts.

After dressing that morning, Fairfax had gone to Jackson's Boxing Academy in Old Bond Street to inquire as to the results of the morning's mill between Tomkins and Black George. Like many another dandy in the London set, Fairfax attended Jackson's establishment to learn the finer points of fisticuffs. Unlike many of the other young dandies, however, Fairfax was quite adept at the bareknuckle sport. His punishing left usually took his opponents by surprise, and they rarely stood even five rounds with him. Even Gentleman Jackson himself had felt hard-pressed on a previous occasion or two when he actually consented to enter the ring with Fairfax, once going ten rounds before jovially waving an end to the contest, and declaring Fairfax "much improved." Fairfax had grinned a battered grin and had taken home several bottles of claret with which to nurse the split lip and cut above his left eye, along with his bruised ribs. Jackson himself had the dubious honor of sporting a splendid constellation of blue and purple bruises upon his right ribs. "You might try a little higher, say for the jaw, Mr. Fairfax. Save yourself a little time. On any other man, that is!" he had added with merriment, for Jackson's skill at evading blows to the head was legendary.

Today, Fairfax had come to listen, not to fight, and he was gratified to find that despite his late arrival, the main salon was still full of men talking over the surprising results of the morning's mill. Amid the babble of voices that filled the crowded antechamber, Fairfax picked out Stanhope and Darlington from the previous evening. As he approached, gingerly making his way through the crowd, he heard Stanhope's voice raised querulously in loud complaint: "I do not understand how he could have just folded up that way in the fifth round. Damned suspicious, especially after his fight with Mackey. I lost nearly a year's worth of rents on the bet!"

"Well, you are not the only one to be out of pocket on this," spoke up Darlington morosely. "Seemed good odds to me. I wagered a pretty sum, enough to buy a new team of carriage horses at Tattersalls'. How am I going to explain that, I ask you? And the tailor has begun to dun me for the coats I ordered last winter. What's the use of paying him now? They are already out of fashion."

"I gather this morning's results were not entirely satisfactory?" Fairfax said smoothly to them, his dark eyes surveying the rest of the crowd of young dandies.

"Hardly," replied Darlington petulantly. "It seemed such a sure thing, we all made side bets on which round Tomkins would fall. The earlier the round, the longer the odds. And it was Black George who crashed to the canvas, as if he had been poleaxed, in the fifth round. A lot of us got caught short by that!"

"The deuce of it is that blasted French comte cleaned out most of us. Made all sorts of ridiculous bets at the mill, giving long odds on rounds. Every man there thought him a prize fool. We were happy to take his money, or so we thought!" interjected Viscount Stanhope. "I hear he even got in some of the betting books around the clubs. I can safely wager that he is a happy man tonight. And quite a bit richer too!"

"Really?" Fairfax commented politely. "How very fortunate for him." He stood among them for a short time, letting the conversation swirl around him, listening for the technical details of the fight. As the conversation drifted into different channels, Fairfax slipped off. He made his way into Jackson's private rooms, reserved for Jackson and the more privileged members of his clientele.

Inside the well-appointed, high-ceilinged rooms, Vere had no trouble spying Jackson. The boxer sat enthroned in a large armchair, surrounded by his admirers.

His smiling visage was resolutely cheerful. In his middle thirties now, Jackson, with his solid, compact body, still had a fighter's power. Although he had gone ten rounds with Vere without even becoming winded, he had genially admitted afterwards he had to work for his fun.

"Well, now," he hailed Fairfax, "you have been away for long enough. Didn't even know you were back in Town, and that's a fact. Heard about the mill this morning, did you?"

"I have heard several things about it," replied Fairfax, taking a vacated seat beside Jackson. "I wonder what you have heard."

"Hmm," growled Jackson, as he touched his thumb to his nose, "Enough, Mr. Fairfax, I've heard quite enough." He grinned a lopsided grin. "If you take my meaning. Seems to my recollection Black George is from Martinique. Do you ken what I'm saying?"

"Yes, I believe I do. I'll be around next week for some sport," said Vere as he rose from his chair.

"You do that, Mr. Fairfax," Jackson retorted. "I'll see to it that you get some work. I have just the lad. Thomas Cribb is his name, one England will be hearing in the future." He rose and clapped Fairfax solidly on the back with one hand. "You come around; I'll see you have plenty of sport." He turned back to his other admirers, and Vere left the salon, with new information to ponder.

The mild sunny afternoon weather stimulated Vere's suppressed appetite. The moroseness of the previous night's indulgence evaporated as he contemplated the possibility of action. A dangerous smile touched the corners of his mouth, failing to reach his obsidian eyes. He felt a personal antipathy towards Monsieur Lucien Montclair, the Comte du Foix, beyond jealousy over Cat's affections. If it came to a contest between them, Vere had no doubt that he would be the winner. He had met too many men like Montclair, smooth and limpid in their affections, whose addresses were but pretense to gain advantage. If this were an ordinary love affair, the Comte du Foix would easily cede the field to him. Montclair's fancy would collapse against the strength of Vere's passion. Or from his bullet, fired in a duel at dawn. He would go willingly, even eagerly, to that extreme.

No, it was much more serious than a mere rivalry *d' amour*. Vere had known too many scoundrels in his travels, those whose deep-dyed duplicity hid an intent more dangerous than mere personal lust. He had seen it in the agents of Napoleon in Italy. He recognized in Montclair a danger to more than Cat.

Fairfax's father had had a friend highly placed in the unofficial councils at Whitehall. His father had often spoken of this well-placed friend as a man of good sense and great influence. Although Fairfax did not think he had met that man in fifteen years, he felt sure that the mention of his father's name would gain him entree. Except for his love for his wife, the late Lord Falconbridge had been quite intelligent. Luncheon with Lord Carrington might prove highly interesting to them both.

James Aubrey St. John, Lord Carrington, sat meditatively at his desk by the second floor bow window. He was a vigorous man of fifty-five years, large without being corpulent. The rays of the sun streaming in through the thick panes warmed him. He put down his quill pen and rubbed his cramped fingers. Too damn many proposals, no action whatsoever! This government knows nothing! he fumed. Wasting time with treaty proposals, when all they are is but a device to gain time for Boney. "He has no intention of stopping until he bestrides the entire continent! The time to act is now!" he had exhorted. However, woollier heads than his had prevailed, and now he spent his days writing, "Yes, Minister," and "No, Minister," and "I respectfully submit to your attention that . . . . " If he could only get some clear evidence to confirm his suspicions, he could convince the harder-headed members at Whitehall of the necessity to take up arms. As he leaned back, the chair creaked slightly with his weight. He rubbed his eyes tiredly. Certainly, he was not young anymore. Perhaps he was getting too old to ride with the hounds.

He heard a quiet knock on his door. "Come in," he growled. Bentworth, his butler, entered, and bowed slightly. "There is a visitor for you, your lordship." He held out a silver salver with a single white card upon it. *Vere Courtenay Fairfax* it read, in elegant printed script. "He says he is an old friend."

"Hmm," said Carrington, fingering the card. "I did know a Fairfax, many years ago. How old is this man?"

"Young, Milord." replied Bentworth. "Not a stripling, but a man in his prime. A dangerous-looking man, Milord."

"Dangerous, eh, Bentworth?" chortled Carrington, his good humor restored. "Well, he seems exactly the sort of man I would like to see right now. Send him up, by all means. Have no fear, he'd not attack me in my own house, and I have a small gun here in the drawer of the escritoire if need be." He put away the papers on which he had been working. No sense in courting unnecessary risks. Lord Carrington was a man who believed that daring was well served if it had prudence in the details. When Mr. Fairfax entered the room, Lord Carrington was seated upon one of the green armchairs, the white visiting card upon the silver tray on the table between them.

"Mr. Fairfax," Carrington said, "to what do I owe the pleasure of your visit?"

"Your lordship was once a friend of my father's. He spoke highly of you. I believe you are a man whose judgment is worth consulting." Mr. Fairfax held his gaze steady as the older man's eyes searched him intently. Lord Carrington reached for the card that lay on the table. "Fairfax," he murmured. "Refresh my memory of your father."

"Stephen Andrew Fairfax, Earl of Falconbridge, Count de Montferrato," Vere replied quietly, surprised at the emotion he felt in saying his father's name aloud. "Late of Tuscany and Wales." Carrington tapped the edge of the card between thumb and forefinger absently on the table. He recalled the name and man from the dim past. A keen intelligence, a penetrating eye, and as swift to strike as a hawk upon the wind. He stared reflectively at Fairfax, who sat in the Queen Anne armchair opposite with the alert grace of the natural hunter. "And have we met before?" Carrington asked.

"Some twelve years previously, my lord. I was at Oxford."

DECEPTIONS

As her tea grew cold beside her, Cat sat in silence, mending some of Clarissa's silk stockings. The chatter of the other servants cascaded heedlessly around her. With the mistress and her daughter out at the Delafields' supper party, the evening's workload had been considerably lightened for the other servants. There was no grand dinner to be prepared, served, and washed up after.

Cat had to prepare Clarissa for the party. While Cat dressed Clarissa's curls with a pink rosebud filigree, Clarissa had looked sharply at Cat in the mirror and spitefully said: "Your precious Mr. Fairfax is a bastard and a fortune hunter. Lady Bullstrode as much as said it during our tea. I saw you flirting with him that day. Oh yes, I saw how he looked at you upon the road. You deserve such as he." Cat was taken aback by Clarissa's sudden venom and frightened by her implication. Had Mr. Fairfax's unwelcome attentions become generally known?

Now Roberts, the footman, sat nearby, blacking boots. Rose and Agnes, the undermaid, had been given the evening off. Mr. Arbuthnot had slipped discreetly out to the public house on Tottenham Court Road. Jane and Alice were giggling together in the chimney corner. Mrs. Congdon was knitting nearby, listening to their chatter and occasionally adding a remark of her own.

Cat put down her mending with a sigh. She had been in London nearly a month, and so far her stay had consisted mostly of onerous tasks for Clarissa. Court presentation and the important first ball at Almack's were only two weeks away. She closed her eyes in brief prayer, hoping that nothing would delay the arrival of her Aunt Henrietta tomorrow evening. Save for a few errands and an outing with Clarissa, Cat had been a prisoner to her duties at Portman Square. After her unsettling meetings with Mr. Fairfax the day she had called at Berkeley Square, she nearly preferred it that way. Equally disturbing was the afternoon scene between Fairfax and the Comte du Foix. Worse still were the words that they had exchanged before she had managed to escape him. For a minute, she had been certain that he was going to attack her within the walls of Portman Square itself while the Thomas ladies were yet upstairs! Cat had been afraid of Mr. Fairfax, so darkly furious had been the light in his eyes. For the first time, at that moment, she had wondered whether she might be in physical danger from him, not mere seduction, but rape. When he had kissed her hand, her terror had been superseded by astonishment at his strange gentleness. Almost unconsciously, she brought her hand to her mouth, lightly touching her ring-finger knuckle where his lips had paused to kiss. She shivered, feeling breathless as she felt her heart, grown suddenly enormous, beat in her breast.

"Child," said Mrs. Congdon, interrupting Cat's train of thought, "Ye'll be ruining your eyes on such fine work in this light." Cat's tea sat untouched beside her. "And yer tea has gone cold. Is something troubling you?" she inquired kindly. The concern in her voice brought sudden unexpected tears to Cat's eyes. "Ye miss yer people, don't you, Lass?" she continued in a solicitous tone. "Well, it's to be expected. It's yer first time away from home, is it not?"

"Yes," whispered Cat, unable to resist the kindness in Mrs. Congdon's voice. "This is not . . . what I expected," she added truthfully, in a hesitant voice. She turned her head aside and surreptitiously wiped the rebellious tears from her eyes before they could spill down her cheeks.

"There, there," Mrs. Congdon clucked, leaving her chair and coming over to the long scarred wooden table where Cat sat. "Put aside that mending, child," she said in an authoritative voice. "Miss Clarissa can wait on those stockings, I reckon. Ye've hardly had a day to yersel since ye arrived. It would do ye good to get out and away from this house for a bit. Miss Clarissa will most probably sleep late tomorrer, if'n I understand anything about supper parties at all. So why don't ye take the air in Hyde Park? If Miss Clarissa awakens and rings before ye return, I'll just send Rose with the message that I sent ye out early for some shopping. How does that sound? Sir Thomas arrives early tomorrow, and no doubt, he will be wanting to spend some time with his family."

Cat thought swiftly. Henrietta also was to arrive at her town house sometime tomorrow. There was no question of Cat's explaining her masquerade to Clarissa or Lady Thomas. After having been their servant for three weeks, she had no doubt in her mind that if they guessed her identity, they would spoil whatever chance she had of being presented at Court and entering the glittering world of the *ton* out of pure spite. Even worse, Sir Thomas might recognize her, which she considered very likely. If Cat accepted Mrs. Congdon's idea, she could slip out of the house and disappear. Perhaps, she thought hopefully, they would never connect the disappearance of Cat Gryffyn with the appearance of Caitlyn Llewellyn. And if they did, how could they prove it? The gamble would be in disappearing before she was sure that her aunt had really arrived. The idea of being without a place to stay, alone and in London, was daunting, for she knew that once she slipped out the back door of Portman Square, there was no turning back.

"What do you say, Dear? Would you like that? The fresh air would cheer ye. And I could pack ye a bit of breakfast to take along. Come now, say you will do it. There won't be much time left after this," Mrs. Congdon added briskly. "The Court presentation is less than a month away, and after that is the first ball at Almack's. Ye'll have no more time during the Season. Will ye accept my offer?"

Cat looked down at the white silk stocking in her hand. If she did not take her chance now, there might be too many questions to answer later. She had gambled her life's happiness on this plan. Did she now lack the courage to continue? She thought of her prospects if Clarissa or Sir and Lady Thomas discovered her identity. Her reputation would be ruined forever among London society. If she meekly returned to her father, what then? A lifetime of captivity to an elderly husband and children on a remote estate, along with the dubious eventual freedom granted a dowager. Resolutely banishing her fears, she answered, "Yes."

Mrs. Congden looked surreptitiously over her shoulder at Alice and Jane, who were whispering together in the chimney corner. A burst of high giggles punctuated their conversation. Satisfied that they had heard nothing of her discussion with Cat, Mrs. Congdon whispered, "Come down around eight of the clock. That way, you will have three hours before you are wanted. I will put up a little cold snack for you to take. We all of us deserve a day out, even if some people seem to forget that," she sniffed.

"Thank you, Mrs. Congdon," Cat replied in a low voice. "I will enjoy the open air in the Park very much. May I be excused? I think I will take some rest while Rose is still out." With that, she took her workbasket and the still-unfinished stockings and departed the servants' hall via the dark backstairs toward her drafty little room.

Closing the door to any intrusion, she debated what she would wear. It would be foolish to go forth alone, dressed in Clarissa's pretty castoffs. She had no desire to attract male attention, as she surely would if she paraded in the Park unaccompanied, dressed as a lady. Better to wear one of the old grey frocks and take the cloak with her. In the back of her mind lingered the unwished-for possibility that she might be homeless tomorrow eve. If all went well, her aunt would receive her in her house by tomorrow afternoon, and the disappearance of Cat Gryffyn would be only a minor mystery, soon forgotten. And, she thought savagely, perhaps a great inconvenience for Clarissa at the very beginning of her Season! She lay down in the little bed, but sleep fled from her fast-closed eyes. Trepidation kept her awake even after Rose was safely home and snoring softly beside her. Only at the first grey of dawn did she fall into a fitful sleep.

Vere Courtenay Fairfax slept no better that night. The convoluted coils of intrigue in which he found himself willingly and unwillingly drawn were not conducive to restful evenings. The attentions that the Comte du Foix had paid Cat were dangerous, and Vere's own attempt to warn her of that danger had been lamentably unsuccessful. He savagely damned his inability to convey his real concern to her. Lord Carrington had further complicated matters by inviting him into the Government's confidence, thereby making him an active agent.

At any other time in his jaded life, the prospect of matching wits with one of Bonaparte's top spies might have appealed to his sense of adventure. Now he could only clearly perceive the increased danger that Cat was incurring in attracting an association with the Comte. Whether Montclair had any motives beyond personal lust were not clear to Fairfax, but even one motive was enough to assure his total destruction.

The dinner party had been rather dreary, as such things often were to Fairfax. Used to the worldly repartee of the finest society on the Continent, Fairfax found the preoccupations of London Society during the Season trivial and provincial. The Delafields were personally unknown to him, but Lord Carrington's recommendation had been sufficient to gain him the promised entry. He had immediately noted, on being shown up, the presence of the Comte du Foix with Clarissa and Lady Thomas. Fairfax had walked unobtrusively among the other guests until he had been close enough to the little group to overhear some of their conversation. It was frivolous to the point of boredom, and he gained no clue as to what the true activities of the Comte might be. Idly inspecting his opponent's appearance, Fairfax reasoned that such a turnout required money, much more than could be explained by Monsieur's claim of some profitable estates in Spain. Fairfax had traveled in Spain. He was quite sure the trans-Pyrenees did not hold lands wealthy enough to produce the disposable capital necessary to enable the Comte to live abroad in such style.

Although Lady Thomas had clearly seen Mr. Fairfax, she gave him no sign of recognition or invitation to join them. Fairfax felt nothing but relief at her snub. Save that Cat yet dwelt in Portman Square, he had no reason to seek their company. At their luncheon that day following his visit to Gentleman Jackson's establishment, Lord Carrington had as much as sworn Fairfax to preserve his anonymity. The mystery he had created as to his identity would now serve the Government's purpose as well as his own.

Just refrain from claiming his titles until this business was solved was all that Carrington had asked. Vere had shrugged. It suited his purpose for the present to leave unused the titles of Earl of Falconbridge and Count de Montferrato until he had won Cat's heart. There would be time enough, after she was his, to set things aright and reveal his identity.

"Your word on it, Fairfax," Carrington had asked, and Vere had agreed readily enough. "It may get a bit difficult socially," Carrington warned him, "but I don't think you care that much for what all those rich squires' daughters and their mamas up from the country might think. Do you?"

Vere had been tempted to reply, "Only one," but he held his tongue. Carrington was an honorable man, but he would use any tool that came to hand. Vere was already one. He did not want Cat to become another. Still, he mused, whatever Carrington did to blacken Vere's reputation, all in the course of honorable government service, could hardly be darker than what Vere had already done to himself. Together, they had set off to Portman Square, in hopes of sighting the Comte.

Lady Delafield, dressed in a filmy ivory silk and bedizened with pearls, bustled up to him. She found herself strangely uncomfortable in the presence of this tall, dark, saturnine figure, but Lord Carrington's reputation was impeccable, and his recommendation had the force of a command. She had placed Mr. Fairfax advantageously next to the Honorable Isabella Sinclair on the strength of it, although she now somewhat regretted giving the young and beautiful Isabella such a formidable partner. "Would you take the Honorable Miss Sinclair down to dinner?" she suggested after introductions had been made.

"Most certainly," answered Fairfax smoothly in a resonant voice with one of his slight smiles and intense glances that had reliably carried him into half the hearts of titled Europe. She cast one more anxious look upon the couple and then hurried off to see to the rest of her guests.

The dinner party had been pleasant enough. The food was well-prepared, and Vere's companion was most charming. A month ago, Vere might even have found himself considering her possibilities seriously. She had a worldly manner about her that belied her age. He could foresee the ripe sensuality with which she would blossom in a few years and the indifference to sentiment that would accompany it. Her conversation did not lack intelligence. Nonetheless, Fairfax found himself haunted by his recall of the quicksilver emotional interchanges he had had with Cat.

Putting a charming smile on his face, Vere turned to address a witticism from the Honorable Isabella. He rather ruefully admitted to himself, listening to her mannered chatter, which was crafted to flatter, that he would rather have had the challenge of Cat's defiant barbs hurled at him like weapons than Miss Sinclair's honeyed words, poured out by rote upon his male vanity.

He observed the Comte covertly. His smiling open countenance charmed his hostess and the elderly man on his left. Nothing of consequence was being said, as far as Vere could ascertain. Still, snippets of information passed in disjointed dinner conversation could be collected by a clever intelligence agent and grand plans thereby deduced. Eventually, the social currents would carry the Comte into the presence of government and army officials.

At last, the savory appeared, and the diners parted to congregate in the salon. Vere joined Montclair's dining companion, an elderly gout-ridden gentleman, in a brandy as he observed his quarry from the fringes of the group. The Comte was making good use of his fresh open good looks and Gallic charm. His murmured anecdotes were bringing guffaws from several of the red-faced lords who surrounded him.

Judging from their leering expressions, Montclair must be relating some racy sexual incidents. Vere could not but marvel at the lack of delicacy and taste of the average English gentleman, whose appreciation of the arts of love barely rose above the schoolboy stage. This explained why Vere spent little time in England after reaching his majority.

The thought that Cat might have been married off to one such filled Vere with horror and strengthened an evermore single-minded determination to claim her, marry her, possess her as soon as possible. He would have the first awakening of the passionate woman within the tempestuous schoolgirl. He knew that he could bring her from sleeping innocence to electrically charged sensuality without damaging her proud spirit. He thought again of the touch of her hand upon his lips, the warm smooth heat of her skin as he had pressed that brief kiss upon her white fingers. In so little must his huge desire be compassed! His preoccupation was making it difficult to follow the maunderings of his companion, who seemed to be recalling a long-ago foxhunt. Vere smiled expectantly at him and the old gentleman continued with his remembrances. Fortunately, for Vere's eroding sense of politeness, his host signaled the end of the dinner party.

No ball was to follow the dinner, so the guests departed in their carriages half an hour later. Waiting for his carriage to be brought around, Vere covertly studied Montclair. Although Vere could not distinctly hear the words being exchanged by the Comte and the small group of younger men who surrounded him, the tone of their ribald laughter suggested that this departure hardly marked the end of the Comte's evening. On impulse, Vere decided to follow him at a discreet distance. In keeping with his resolution of hiding his identity, he had ordered the smaller carriage for the evening and the third team of horses, usually reserved for the household staff's necessary errands. The order had resulted in quiet astonishment carefully covered with punctilious correctness, which was as near as his excellently trained staff would ever come to questioning one of Mr. Fairfax' s decisions. Thus doubly disguised in an equipage that would scarcely draw a second glance, Vere gave orders that his coachman should follow the Comte's landau at a leisurely pace. He then leaned back upon the rather inadequate cushions, his deceptively relaxed posture giving no hint of the excitement of the chase that began to thrill through his veins.

The carriages proceeded down Kingsway and turned on to the Strand. Vere leaned back in disgust and tipped his hat farther down, deepening the shadows that hid his face. It seemed that Montclair was in quest of amorous company, and his carriage joined a long procession of other carriages that rolled slowly down the Strand toward Haymarket Street and back toward Covent Garden and the theater districts where the nymphs of the pavement solicited their wares. From within the dim recesses, he watched as the parade of women passed by. Sometimes they knocked upon the carriage window, a painted, beribboned show. Barely moving, he raised a gloved hand in a gesture of refusal. From above, Charles, the coachman, spoke quietly. "Yer party's stopped ahead. Should I pull up too?" Vere thought briefly.

"No, continue driving. It will be easier to observe him when I pass by."

"Yes, Sir," replied Charles with alacrity and jogged the horses to quicken their pace imperceptibly. "On your left, Sir, we shall be passing them now," he murmured. Vere turned his head to observe his quarry. The Comte's elegant carriage was stopped, and Montclair himself was leaning out the window. Fairfax's distaste gave way first to shock and horror, then to anger. The woman standing outside the Comte's carriage, preparing to ascend, was dressed in periwinkle-colored satin, her deep red hair swept up upon her head, dropping about her face in ringlets. Fairfax's hard-raking stare soon revealed that the fetching creature of the evening shadows had only a passing resemblance to Cat. But that resemblance was enough to harden his suspicion of Montclair's dangerous interest in Cat. Would not he too recognize her once she appeared in Society? He would not scruple to ruin her. With a growing anger burning in his breast, he rapped quickly on the carriage roof. "Drive home," he said and settled back to meditate on how best to achieve the Comte's complete destruction.

HYDE PARK

Cat stood silently before the closed door and turned away. At ten in the evening! The kitchen maid's words reverberated within her mind. Climbing the area stairs, she thought of her choices with despairing clarity. She could return to Portman Square and await another chance to escape, perhaps rising early and slipping out while the others were yet abed. Could early morning London be more dangerous than evening London? Could she wait and take a chance of being sent to the milliner's within the next week? Every day counted now, as the Court Presentation, required to receive an invitation to the first ball at Almack's, was but weeks away. And she would need frocks, gloves, and shoes! With every seamstress in London engaged in sewing ball gowns and Court Presentation dresses, what would Cat do for a suitable wardrobe, essential if her plan of having a Season were to succeed?

There remained the problem of Sir Thomas, whose arrival was expected this morning at Portman Square. Cat had danced with Sir Thomas at the last county assembly, but it had not been a pleasant experience. Sir Thomas had contrived to appear a genial neighbor, but his pleasantries hid an over-familiar manner. On the pretense of being an "old neighbor and friend to her father," he had encircled her waist, patted her cheek and attempted to kiss her forehead, which Cat was sure was going to be a purposefully fumbled attempt that would have him maneuvering to kiss her lips. She had stood stock still, pinned against the sideboard, until a hail from one of his country friends had diverted his attention for the split second that it had taken Cat to duck under his arm and walk quickly and smoothly away.

She would have to remain here in the green park of Berkeley Square or somewhere like it until dark and damp drove her forth to mingle with the crowds that flowed in an eddying stream around the theaters and opera. At least she could rest her feet, eat the bit of bread, cheese, and fruit and save her strength for the later trial. The green enclosure of Berkeley Square was far too small to loiter for long. She would certainly attract attention.

Calmly, she thought of all possible places where she might spend seven or eight hours comfortably, yet unnoticed by the passing world. The best place for her purpose came to mind: Mrs. Congdon's suggestion of Hyde Park. It was conveniently located to Berkeley Square. As the day advanced toward evening, Cat could make her way towards Aunt Henrietta's along the neighboring expanses of Green Park. With all the Fashionable riding in Hyde Park, looking only at each other, she would be, in her plain grey, to all purposes invisible!

The idea was such a novelty that she might see and yet be unseen by the greater world at large that she resolved to walk there immediately. It might even be profitable for her future to watch covertly all those whom she must later encounter by the strict rules of the *ton*. Walking slowly, now that she had a plan and an entire sunny day to enjoy both the weather and the leisure that she had not had since she left home almost a month ago, she resolved to enjoy each fresh moment of the London scene with the novelty that it deserved. Suiting action to thought, she walked sedately down the street toward Park Lane, enjoying with judicious tranquillity both the mild, bright day and the imposing facades that lined her processional way. Unnoticed among the bustling throng, Roberts the footman furtively trailed her.

Upstairs in his bedroom in the elegant Park Lane town house, Vere sipped his breakfast tea from a brightly colored cup of Chinese ware. Last night's excursion had unfortunately produced no useful information for Lord Carrington. Vere would gladly have destroyed Montclair with as little conscience as a gardener destroys vermin, but that would not help the government's case in discovering the spy network that Montclair was without a doubt coordinating. Vere could, he reflected, continue to create a persona well-placed, but impecunious enough to be open to an offer of treason from the Comte du Foix. On the other hand, Montclair might move against Cat before Vere's plan had time to mature. It might be quicker to find how the Comte transmitted his information back to his masters on the Continent. If Vere could manage to discover that, he might be able to remove Montclair entirely and transmit completely different information designed by Carrington to mislead and ultimately ruin Boney's designs against England. He sipped his tea while watching the parade of people passing by his window on the street below.

The varied spectacle of late morning revealed young dandies on horseback, richly clad dowagers in open carriages, and young ladies accompanied by their maids sedately strolling along the Lane. All around them hurried men of affairs, footmen on errands, and purveyors of every kind of goods taking provisions to the great houses. Vere noted with interest a spirited pair of magnificently matched grey carriage horses harnessed to a light curricle of simple elegant lines. He put his quizzing glass to his eye to ascertain who was driving the splendid equipage. "Young Stanhope," he murmured to himself. "I wonder if he is so sprung to consider selling the entire rig? How did I miss acquiring such a splendid team? Apparently, I have been too distracted with other things to give due consideration to Tattersall's," he thought regretfully.

As the team swept off down the lane, his eye was caught by the slight figure in grey who had been walking on the other side of the street. The deep rich copper hair, coiled in a braid at her neck, and the delicately upturned profile could only be Cat's. Clarissa was nowhere in sight. What could Cat be doing here alone at such an hour? Belting his dressing gown more tightly about him, Vere stepped through the long French windows to the tiny balcony, mindless for once of the impropriety of his actions, and scanned the street after her.

She had crossed over farther down, with the clear intention of entering the Park. Vere stepped swiftly inside and rang for Stevens. "Quickly," he commanded. "Riding clothes. The buff breeches will do and the blue broadcloth coat. And the top boots, not the Hessians." He had already shed his dressing gown and now poured cold water from the ewer into the basin. "Now, Man," Vere snapped, catching sight of his startled valet's countenance in his shaving mirror as he reached for the sharp straight-edged steel razor. "I am in a particular hurry and have no time for superfluities. When you have done that, tell Charles to saddle my horse." He turned back to the mirror and began lathering his face. Stevens mumbled a brief, "Yes, Milord," and turned away in numb surprise. His lordship had been acting very strangely of late, but there was never any telling what the Quality might take it into their heads to do, and all in all, Stevens had no reason to complain, to himself or to other servants. Rapidly, he turned to obey.

The April morning was becoming as fresh and clear as anyone could wish. Even the clouds in the sky sparkled with the clear light that washed over the rich abundance of spring lavenders and pinks, with pale gold and green glowing from trees and flower beds. The light grey rain of the morning had burned off, and Cat walked with a lighter step toward Hyde Park. She had passed the point of no return, she thought. Or another one of them, she laughed to herself, her lips curving into the barest of smiles. After all, she had escaped an arranged marriage, maintained her masquerade as Cat Gryffyn, and would soon be safe at Aunt Henrietta's. Then she could send a note for her father. Of all the dangers of her meditated scheme, leaving her father without a word was her greatest regret. He was not young, she reminded herself again. He had always seemed so absorbed in the abstract that she felt that he had recognized her as a real creature only seldomly and would thus be calm about her disappearance. Could she really be so self-deceiving as to believe that? Was it not just an excuse for her unfilial actions? Even now, he might have taken to bed, frail in his grief. She must have Henrietta send to the country with news of her arrival in town. For the first time, she felt a tremor of guilt for her willful behavior.

Perhaps she should have waited until after the visit from Lord Falconbridge and pled her cause then, but she believed that he would not have listened to her. At this moment, her deepest feelings were fears for his health due to her unknown whereabouts. Which one was her father? Casting her eyes decorously down to hide her face, newly troubled by conflicting thoughts, she did not see Mr. Fairfax as he rode by her.

He had ridden his horse after her at a slow walk, reining in his impatience by great effort of will, but unable to conceal it from his horse, who persisted in trying to break into a jaunty trot. He trailed the slight figure in grey cotton woolsey for some hundred paces, but at last had to overtake her or become too obvious. She was walking, head bent, her gaze fixed on the ground. He judged that she would continue into the Park. Once past her, he kicked the willing gelding into a brisk trot toward the bridle paths of Rotten Row, where he could consider his strategy. She would almost surely walk toward the Serpentine, blending in with the nursemaids and governesses who were out with their young charges. If she lingered, he could keep an eye on her. The Row was crowded with many young fashionable riders with all degrees of skills and horses. It would be easy enough to fall in with a fellow and proceed at a sedate walk, discussing the latest gambling hell or the newest turnout. At that instant, his foxhunting after-dinner companion from yester-eve saluted him. Drawing up, he ambled alongside him, while discreetly assuring himself with quick glances that Cat was still in sight.

The rig that had caught his eye this morning flashed by on his right, driven by the Viscount, who looked rather the worse for wear after what had apparently been a long night. Fairfax gave a polite but curt good-bye to his erstwhile companion and wheeled the powerful horse to follow Stanhope. The Viscount, Vere noticed with satisfaction, was driving in Cat's direction. He spurred the horse to an easy canter with a quick pressure of his powerful thighs as he rode to overtake them.

Stanhope clucked the reins of the prancing greys desultorily. If he couldn't come up with the hundred pounds to meet his debts, he would have to give up the entire rig. The Comte du Foix was most insistent that he would consider taking the carriage and horses in lieu of the money, although they had set him back five times the amount of his debt. He could sell them, of course, but he doubted that he would get their full value at such short notice. The Comte du Foix had been most emphatic about his repayment date. No, either way, he was going to lose the horses and curricle, so he had been driving around the whole of the evening, making the most of what was soon to be a lost pleasure.

Stanhope heard the canter of a horse behind him, a flurry of hooves as its rider pulled up, then a lazy drawling voice that had all the force of a command. "Greetings, Viscount, you look all done in. My respects to you, Sir. Would you pull up your horses? I have a mind to inspect them more closely." Fearing at first to be greeted in the liquid accents of the Comte, Stanhope gratefully recognized the smiling face of the haughty and mysterious Mr. Fairfax, seen everywhere, but known, it seemed, by none.

"Oh, yes," he slurred, still somewhat intoxicated from his night of heavy drinking. "Met you at Jackson's after the mill. Damned shame. Not you," Stanhope hastily corrected himself. "That damned Black George. Lost my rig, I did," he waved his arm vaguely to embrace the handsome team and their equally handsome equipage. "Bet it against du Foix's hundred-pound wager. Last little ride," he murmured apologetically.

"Indeed," Vere replied, betraying no excitement with his tone. "How unfortunate for you. I was just remarking to myself what a fine team you have and how equally matched they are by the carriage. Are you thinking of selling?" he drawled, his tone conveying a well-bred lack of interest. Over the horses' heads, he could see Cat drifting between a harried red-faced woman and her many small children. Her look of deep reverie was hardly disturbed by the shouting of the nursemaid or the squeals of her charges. He stole another glance at her as she sat down on one of the benches that faced the carriage drive. She bowed her head, hiding her expression from him and the world.

"Oh, I will have to sell; there is no answer for it. But damned if I want to let it go cheap. Five hundred pounds at least," he muttered in a defeated tone.

"Really?" Fairfax politely intoned, his brows arched in mock surprise. "I am prepared to offer you six hundred for them, but if you have promised another buyer," he let the sentence trail off, waiting for his prey to come to the bait.

Stanhope blushed deeply. It was really damnable to be in this contemptible spot. "You see," he mumbled, "dashed if I don't need the funds by this afternoon. Bit of unpleasantness, but there you are." He smiled a sickly smile.

"And if I paid you the sum you requested today, could I take possession of the team and carriage?" Fairfax pounced with his offer. "How soon do you need the money?"

"By one o'clock. He's to call at my town lodgings. I was a pure damned fool," Stanhope blurted, misery choking his young voice. "And he is a blackguard of the deepest sort. He played me well," he laughed, bitterness suffusing his expression. "I was so foolish in my vanity. Anyone that self-deceived deserves to be rooked."

"Perhaps," rejoined Fairfax with a note of sympathy. "That, however, does not excuse the behavior of Monsieur Montclair. It is unfortunate that your lesson comes at such a high price, but it has been my experience that such lessons invariably do." Fairfax smiled a thin smile, his expression remote and inaccessible. "However, if you would sell your equipage to me, I would be much obliged. And in your debt," he offered as an added inducement.

Vere slackened the reins as he waited calmly for Stanhope's reply. He could still glimpse Cat between the swirls of the promenaders, seated on the bench, head bowed and hands folded. She seemed to have no intention of continuing her journey. He wondered if she were waiting for someone, but her posture of inward repose seemed to deny that. Beneath him, the black gelding shook his head and stamped his hoof, anxious to continue on into the park. He turned his gaze back to young Stanhope, whose befuddlement at the choice offered him was writ large upon his pallid features.

"If you wish more time to consider my offer, please go on with your cogitations. However, I intend to continue with my ride, so allow me to take my leave." Fairfax wheeled his horse about, preparing to ride deeper into the Park.

"Please hold," came the voice of Stanhope. "I regret that I have forgotten my manners. Your generosity is greatly appreciated, and I accept your offer with gratitude." He sat up straighter, attempting to gain a good deal more control of his voice and himself. "Shall we say noon at my lodgings? Six hundred pounds, I believe you said."

"Certainly," replied Vere. "And, if you don't mind, I would like to remain there when du Foix arrives to claim his wager. I am interested in how he takes his loss of the rig."

"Of course," replied Stanhope, relief showing in his eyes. "I am not a coward, Sir, but I would appreciate another person at the interview. One I could call friend," he added boldly. "The Comte du Foix is a greedy winner. I fear he will also be a dangerous loser."

"Indeed, that is my perception as well. I see you are not entirely without brains. It is experience you seem to lack. Will three hundred in notes and a draft on my bank be satisfactory?"

"Entirely satisfactory, Mr. Fairfax. My lodgings are located at Gower Street, Number 32. Will you take a bit of luncheon with me there?" he added hopefully.

"I am at your service, Viscount," replied Vere, bowing perfunctorily, as his horse tossed its head, eager to be on his way. He swung the powerful black gelding toward the West carriage drive and spurred him into an effortless canter.

Stanhope lingered another moment, reflecting on all that had passed. His troubled expression cleared, as reviewing his options, he decided that he had made the best of a bad bargain. Clucking to the two spirited greys of his team, he headed out toward Park Lane, towards his own lodgings and long-delayed sleep.

Vere reined in his horse after the long, smooth canter had taken him nearly to the gates where the North Carriage Drive meets Park Lane. He slowed his horse to a meditative walk and reversed his course, going back into the Park again. In all it had been a most fortunate occurrence. The turnout he had just purchased was exceptionally brilliant. He would not have scrupled to offer a thousand pounds, if necessary. Moreover, the situation also offered an opportunity to bait Montclair. A plan was slowly taking form in his mind. We like what seems most like ourselves. Vere thought that if he could present himself as a counterfeit similar to du Foix's own, he might gain his confidence. Or his enmity. As far as his observations could confirm, no one had achieved any intimacy beyond that smooth unrevealing politeness that marked all of Montclair's interactions.

He flicked his horse lightly into a trot. Cat might have left the bench and the Park while he had ridden the circuit. Allowing his horse to find the way, he intently scanned the crowds that ebbed and flowed upon the pathways of the Park.

Rounding the curve of the carriage drive, he pulled up on the reins, slowing his mount again to a walk. Between the passing figures of ladies and their chaperones, youths and their tutors, serving maids and footmen on their morning off, he saw Cat, seated erectly on her bench, her glance still bent downwards. Vere inwardly cursed his reckless desire. Had he not ridden off in pursuit on his horse, he might now be able to approach her. He should at least have taken a groom with him! Then he could have dismounted and thrown the reins to him. Deciding to ride home and return with his carriage, he gathered in the reins again, preparatory to setting the gelding into a trot. At that moment, a bawling female voice assaulted him from an approaching carriage.

"Mr. Fairfax, dear Sir! Hold up a moment. I want to talk to you!" The loud flat tones belonged to Lady Bullstrode, his fellow caller at Portman Square. He saw with a sinking heart that she was dressed conspicuously in yellow and purple, with a matching striped turban crowned with a nodding feather of amethyst. The costly elaboration of her open carriage with its two bright chestnut horses was attracting everyone's attention. Cat alone, of all the world, seemed unaware of the spectacle they were presenting.

Vere bowed in recognition to her ladyship, whose merry eyes above brightly rouged cheeks betrayed no sense other than pleasure at their chance encounter. "So nice to meet with you, Sir. A fine day," she bugled in loud tones, her accent overlaid with a faint quack of broad "a," which revealed her ancestry. "Enjoying your ride in the Park, eh?" she brayed, displaying large teeth in a wide grin.

"In truth, Lady Bullstrode, I was just regretting I did not bring my carriage."

"Well," she replied, with a small incongruous simper, bringing her carved Chinese fan to her eyes and rapidly waving it, "you are welcome to ride with me!"

Vere stiffened, momentarily caught off guard by the proposal and by the ludicrous absurdity of Lady Bullstrode's sudden impersonation of a debutante. Did the woman think that he might fancy her? Did she entertain hopes of his tender regard?

"In fact, the morning is so pleasant, I rather fancy to walk by the Serpentine, and having foolishly come out without my groom, I have no way to dispose of my horse. Had I taken my carriage, I might have left the horses with the coachman."

"Perhaps you would let me take custody of your horse. My groom could take him safely home." She looked at him shrewdly from beneath the bobbing ostrich plume.

Vere considered. He could return to his town house and then walk back, but time was of the essence. He needed to arrive at Viscount Stanhope's establishment in one hour. He also feared that Cat might leave the Park before he was able to return. Casting a surreptitious glance towards where he had last seen her, he was relieved to see that she still remained seated on her bench, seemingly oblivious to all traffic. Unbidden, he remembered Lord Carrington's recommendation to him.

His decision made, he smiled affably at Lady Bullstrode. "Your ladyship is most generous. If your groom will take my horse to Number 18 Park Lane, I shall be obliged."

SCANDALS

Vere walked briskly, without undue haste, toward where he had last seen Cat. The sparkling spring morning was flicked by a chilling breeze, which drove the flock of white clouds into a grey herd that threatened rain before afternoon. Ahead, his quarry, sitting demurely on the bench, pulled her cloak more closely about her with a slight shiver. Other people were getting up, leaving the benches and the walkways, in good advance of the certainty of a spring shower. Cat also looked up, her face registering dismay as she realized that she would have to leave her bench. So preoccupied was she with her own thoughts that she did not recognize Vere's approaching presence among the hurrying throngs until he stood before her.

Some yards before Vere reached her, his heartbeat felt enormous to him. He could not draw a deep quiet breath. Something in her expression slowed his last steps. What he did in these moments could never be undone. At this moment of vulnerability, he could win first her trust and then her love. A misstep and he might lose her for all time.

"Good morning, Miss Cat," he said quietly. "Are you enjoying your morning out? I hope you have, as it seems there is a change coming." The dark grey lowering clouds roiled together, blocking the bright sun, deepening the chill of the increasing breeze. He waited silently as her startled eyes took him in. A flash of despair mingled with fatigue shadowed her pretty features. She hid it quickly and contrived a look of disdain, even as she stood up to leave.

"Indeed, I have had a pleasant morning of unbothered solitude," she replied pointedly. "As you say, it appears it will rain, so allow me to take my leave." She drew her cloak more tightly about her as she stepped around him. However, the usual proud toss of her head was absent. She walked by with her eyes lowered, veiled by thick-fringed lashes.

"A truce, Miss Cat," he said softly, his voice as low and gentle as it had been when he talked to the maddened carriage horse on that road long ago. "I see you are in some distress. I am not a man of so little feeling to take advantage of a woman's misfortune. It is about to rain, and you are provided with no umbrella. It is no little walk from here to Portman Square. You perhaps have no money, or perhaps you have brought your entire fortune and are reluctant to spend it on a hackney coach to return there. Allow me to assist you in whatever way I can." He smiled briefly. "Even to the humble extent of hailing the coach. I am at your service."

Cat thought briefly. He stood easily before her, tall, subdued, restrained. The bright flame that burned in him was carefully banked, low, intense, still dangerous, but quiet, put to simple uses. No baiting words, none of those glances that rouged her cheek with rising blush, were present in his calm demeanor. Where was she to go? If this were not Sunday, she could linger at the shops until they closed. What then, with the evening darkness coming on?

"The storm is going to break over us even as we speak, Miss Cat." As if to punctuate his words, a great cold gust of wind swooped down on them, dragging at Cat's cloak.

"I've left the Thomases' without notice," she said impulsively. "I cannot return there, but my new mistress does not arrive till very late."

"My town house is very near here." At the startled rise of Cat's brows, he hurriedly continued. "I am appointed to meet someone within the hour elsewhere. You will be quite welcome and safe there in my absence. If upon my return, I may help you in any way, I shall be honored. If not, please allow me but to bid you adieu before you depart. If you wish, I shall escort you, but we must hurry if we are to avoid the storm."

The trees swayed in the gusty air; the damp rose from the earth beneath the roiling grey sky of clouds. Sharp as a pelted stone, the first spit of rain fell against their faces. She searched his face, looking for a decision there. There was none. The choice was hers alone, and he would abide by it. She gathered her cloak and skirts more firmly about her. She would not be thought the child by him. "I thank you for your offer, Sir, and the delicacy by which you made it. I accept your kind hospitality and will gladly thank you when I bid you adieu."

He looked steadily into the raised green eyes, the thrill of her returned gaze running deeply through him, betraying no ripple of its passing in his own expression. They stood there in silence, held motionless in each other's gaze, the rain falling unheeded upon them.

Then, mischievously, she smiled. "Well, Sir, as we are to be got quite wet whether we walk or run, I am prepared to maintain as brisk a pace as you can devise."

He turned toward the homeward path when a voice at his elbow interrupted. "Beggin' yer pardon, Sir, I have brought the carriage. I thought you might be needin' it." Cat stood still suddenly, staring at him with mingled disbelief and weary contempt. "How long have you been watching me, that your closed carriage," she spat the word with emphasis, "should suddenly appear to convey us?" Vere turned to the coachman. Behind him, the closed carriage waited. "From whence," he said, in tones of bone chilling icy command, "did you entertain the notion of bringing the carriage without my specific order?" The rain began to fall more softly, unheeded by either.

"Beggin' your pardon, Sir, it was 'er ladyship, Lady Bullstrode. She brought yer horse back with her groom and

said yer lordship had told 'er he wished for his carriage."
Charles bowed his head. He should not have obeyed her
cajolements. "She said I should nip around right quick, as it
looked like 'twer to rain. I'll take it back, if you prefer." He
bowed his head and stepped back, awaiting orders.

Vere turned to Cat, where she stood huddling on the path,
the grey rain falling on her grey cloak. "What is your pleasure,
Miss Cat? Will you accept hospitality and the fortunate
providence of Lady Bullstrode and step into the carriage, or
would you rather I leave you here in the rain and proceed
directly to my appointment? The choice is yours and all else.
You have my word on it."

She looked at him again. He was patiently awaiting her
decision. She hesitated. Doing her best to equal the same
calm spirit of his own inquiry, Cat replied, "Thank you for
your kindness. The carriage is most fortunate and welcome."

Vere signaled his groom to assist Cat into the carriage.
Vere entered after her and silently sat facing her, his serious
face now proof against her frank look, his heart wholly captive.

Skulking among the rain-darkened tree trunks of the Park,
one lone figure remained, his narrowed close-set eyes
following the two figures as they entered the carriage and
drove away. He reckoned that he knew them both well
enough, the pretty jade that was maid to the young Mistress
and that fancy buck who had come twice to call. Had he not
seen them by the stairs together only a week gone? Roberts
smiled a small, mean smile. Too proper to walk out with him,
a mere footman, was Miss Cat? But willing enough to go off
with a rich toff in his closed carriage, the draggle-tail slut.
Information like that was valuable to Roberts, and silence a
commodity bartered for gold . . . and other things. He would
slip back to the house before his absence could be noticed
and his whereabouts questioned. He would wait to sell his
information to the best buyer at the best price.

Mr. Fairfax hurried her up the stone stairs and through
the door. Once inside, he quickly took her cloak from her

shoulders, shaking off some of the water. A light-footed servant was immediately at hand to take it from him. "Send for some hot negus." He turned politely to Cat. "Will it please you to wait in the drawing room until I return? I regret that I must leave you for another engagement. May I order anything else for your comfort in my absence?"

"The drawing room will be perfectly suitable, thank you, Sir." She paused within the great marble-floored entry hall, with its tall narrow windows and its high coffered ceiling. Turning back to face him, she found him putting on a greatcoat against the weather.

"Jessup will show you to it and attend to any wants you might have during your stay. Your pardon, but I must take my leave."

"By all means. My thanks for your kindness. My apologies for any rudeness I may have shown you."

Mr. Fairfax bowed over her hand, and, for a long heart-stilled second, she thought that he might kiss her yet again. Her blood sang thinly in her ears, but he only murmured a good-bye and left her feeling curiously disappointed. The butler was standing quietly at her right elbow. "If you would care to follow me, Miss, I will show you up to the drawing room." She followed him silently up the airy curving stairway to the first floor. Opening a white-paneled door to her left, he bowed her in to a pleasant room of blue and ivory with a warm fire burning cheerfully in the marble-mantled fireplace. Upon a slender table by a chair placed invitingly near the fire were a slender carafe and a fluted glass on a tray. Jessup bowed to her.

"May I pour you a glass of negus, Miss?"

"Yes, thank you."

"I have ordered a cold collation. It can be brought if you wish."

"Please, that would be most welcome."

He bowed briefly and left the drawing room, closing the door after him with a discreet click. Taking up the glass of negus, Cat found herself alone in a room of pale-sheened blue silk-paneled walls. White silk draperies half hid tall French windows. The furniture, by Sheraton, was marked by straight and curved lines in elegant proportions. The marble mantle was bare of ornament, save for a graceful Wedgwood vase of Grecian design. She stepped closer to inspect it. Upon it, in white frieze, were several figures of men and women, holding branches and crowned with wreaths, standing before an altar. In vain, she puzzled her memory of myth to unravel the meaning.

The doors opened quietly, and the butler, with a footman and a tray, entered. Reluctantly, she turned from the vase. "Thank you."

"Will there be anything else you require? If you would like to choose a book from the library to read or anything else after your meal, I am ready to oblige."

"The vase upon the mantle. Is there a history to it?"

"Not that I know of, Miss. Is there anything else I can do?"

"No, that will be fine. I shall look forward to seeing the library."

"Very good, Miss." He signaled the footman, and they bowed out, leaving Cat once more alone in the calm and imposing room.

The silence and the formality of the great house were unsettling. Cat would have preferred the cheeriness of the servants' hall rather than to be standing in this cold, correct room. Everything in it bespoke of the wealth and taste of its owner, from the rich tones of the cherrywood furniture to the subtle blend of colors and textures. The white ceiling was adorned with a circular bas-relief from which a graceful candelabrum depended. About the walls were frosted-glass sconces with unlit beeswax candles.

She sat gratefully in the slender chair and helped herself to the platter of meats, fowl, cheese, bread, and fruit set before her. How long had it been since she had sat down to a meal by herself, waited on by servants in a quiet room! Strangely, she found herself missing the cheerful banter of Rose and

Agnes, of Mrs. Congdon and Mr. Arbuthnot. She wished herself more properly dressed. What could they be imagining belowstairs about her in her drab country servant's clothes!

She was, she reflected, between two worlds. The one belowstairs represented her childhood, so much of which she had spent with Old Bessie and the others. Her escape and masquerade as Cat Gryffyn were over. Soon she would take her rightful place in this glittering world of drawing rooms and dinners, theaters and balls. He held sway in this world, she thought with a slight wave of dizziness. In this world, he entertained important callers, visited in other elegant rooms, dined with jeweled ladies, was sought after and admired. Here, he exercised power and authority. It was in this world that she would surely meet him again.

In this world, he would possess her secret. Could he be trusted with it, or would he use it for his own advantage? With a trembling hand, she brought the slender crystal goblet of wine to her lips. During her time of service with the Thomas women, she had already learned of the jealous passions that underlay the brittle politeness of Society, the ruthless scheming for position hidden behind the frailty of a fan. How lethal to her hopes would be the secret of her identity! At the brink of her beginning, she suddenly wished herself back in the safety of Eldertree Manor.

The hot wine drink warmed the chill that had taken her limbs and brightened her heart's courage. She set the delicate glass down carefully upon the silver tray. Across the room, her own face, reflected in the gilt-framed mirror, returned her gaze. The rose flush of the wine painted her high cheekbones with delicate color. Her dark-fringed eyes with their straight unflinching stare bespoke a self-sufficiency that she was far from feeling. "But it doesn't matter what I think or feel," she thought wildly, "only what I look like." Her reflection, calm and unreadable, continued to stare back haughtily. Setting her mouth in a slightly curved smile, she lifted her chin in imperious disdain. "As I see myself now, so shall the world see me." Her reflection nodded in assent. "So shall he see me in the world." Calmer now, with new resolve and with some real appetite, she turned her attention to the tempting food set before her and ate the first good meal she had consumed since leaving home.

Roberts entered the areaway at Portman Square feeling disgruntled. He had gotten a considerable soaking on the way back from Hyde Park. He was assuredly late in returning. He had no idea how he could profit from the information about Cat. The gentleman in question could have him sent to Old Bailey for blackmail. He determined at least to tell Mr. Arbuthnot and have some revenge upon the slut. She could have a'cozied with him and still sold herself to the rich rake. If she thought that she could return here without paying, she was mistaken, although he really didn't think that she would be returning.

Stepping through the door into the kitchen, Roberts was greeted by Mrs. Congdon's angry stare. "Where have you been off to now, I'd like to know. Sir Thomas arrived this hour gone and you off and away beyond your time. Lucky Sir Thomas brought his own valet with him. Mr. Arbuthnot's in a fair fury for having to do your job. Is Cat Gryffyn with you? Miss Thomas is throwing a fit upstairs because Rose cannot do her hair properly."

Mrs. Congdon looked at him shrewdly. Roberts had given her the distinct impression that he had intended to accompany Cat, and yet he returned alone. "Cat has not returned. Something is 'as happened, and you know what it is. You'd better tell me. Mr. Arbuthnot is angry enough with you as it is. Tell me, and we will decide what to tell Mr. Arbuthnot."

Roberts was not very bright. He still felt that there would be some profit for him in all this sometime. He would let Mr. Arbuthnot handle the problem for now, he would wait, and he would watch. Something else might happen. Roberts told.

Mr. Arbuthnot was not worried. The suggestion of scandal was not too serious. It would reflect badly on the household of a young girl whose lady's maid had run off with one of the gentlemen callers. However, he saw no reason why that knowledge should become public. It would serve the gentleman's reputation no good either. Lady Thomas was entertaining a caller in the drawing room. Sir Thomas must be informed. He knocked deferentially on the door of the library.

Sir Thomas sighed as the butler finished the tale. It was his first morning, and here was another complication already. This Season for Clarissa was already ruinously expensive. Now another maid would have to be found at three times the salary, London rates. Nor did he want the slightest suggestion of impropriety. He wanted to get Clarissa married off, preferably to money. Nothing must stand in the way. "Very well, Mr. Arbuthnot," he said. "I will take care of everything. See to it that another suitable lady's maid is found." Now he would have to speak with his daughter. Lady Thomas would be better suited, but Clarissa had already sent downstairs twice in search for her maid. She would have to be told. Stiffly, he instructed Mr. Arbuthnot to have her fetched.

Clarissa stood and stared at him in unbelief. Cat had gone and would be replaced. No explanation was offered. She stamped her foot petulantly, tossing her hair in a pretty gesture of defiance. "Am I a child that I am to know nothing of these circumstances, which touch on me most nearly? Will I get another maid half as good in this short time?" Circumstance alone won from Clarissa the due praise that Cat had merited.

"You will have a London maid. They must be more acquainted with fashion than a country housemaid." He chucked her under the chin. "You shall have your heart's desire. Now run along and see your mama."

She looked at him sulkily, a slight pout on her Cupid's-bow mouth. He could not resist that look, she knew. "Is that all Mr. Arbuthnot knew?" she said in a whispery little voice.

"Now don't worry your pretty little head about it," he replied indulgently.

"Of course, Papa," she demurred, "But Mama must be told, should she not?"

"Certainly," he answered with relief. "Now run along and see her. You have been sent for several times already."

Clarissa walked with quickening steps towards the drawing room. With a savage push, she flung open the tall door, only to startle not only her mama, but also Lady Bullstrode.

"Excuse me, Lady Bullstrode, Mama, but I was sent to tell you from Papa that my maid, Cat Gryffyn, has disappeared, and I am to have another. Mr. Arbuthnot, who knows all about it, informed him."

"Hush, Child! I will not hear scandal broth in this room. Please forgive her, Lady Bullstrode. She is not wise in the ways of the world."

"Perhaps she should be sent from the room, then, while you interrogate Mr. Arbuthnot. Propriety must be maintained."

"You are, of course, quite correct, Lady Bullstrode. Clarissa, Dear, return to your room. You can attend to your embroidery. That's a good girl."

Covering her fury, Clarissa made a meek submission. "Yes, dearest Mama, of course I will." It would not do to alienate that fat cow, Lady Bullstrode, and forfeit her ticket to Almack's. Mama would tell her soon enough. Carefully closing the door, she paused noiselessly a moment, but the conversation did not resume, so she slipped quietly away, content to wait.

"Ring the bell, Lady Thomas!" Lady Bullstrode trumpeted. "You must be forceful in your own house. Quiz the servants at once! Let no irregularity remain unexamined!"

"You are so thoughtful," smiled Lady Thomas ingratiatingly as she pulled the bell rope. No matter how officious and dowdy the woman was, she had friends. It was so important to keep on her good side, no matter how interfering she was.

Mr. Arbuthnot entered. "It seems we have had some distress over one of the servants. Could you kindly tell me the details?" Lady Thomas demanded sternly.

Mr. Arbuthnot coughed discreetly. "It seems that Mrs. Congdon, unbeknownst to me or you, gave Cat Gryffyn leave to go out walking for a bit by herself this morning."

"A grievous act of insubordination, no doubt. You should reprimand Mrs. Congdon, Arbuthnot," Lady Bullstrode interrupted. "However, we do not want to hear every little detail. What has become of her? Where was she last seen?"

"Yes, Arbuthnot, where was she last seen? Has anything dreadful happened to the poor girl?"

Mr. Arbuthnot stared straight ahead to some spot behind Lady Thomas's left shoulder. "She was last seen, by Roberts, getting into a closed carriage in Hyde Park with a gentleman." Mr. Arbuthnot coughed discreetly behind his hand. "Roberts rather thinks he may recognize him as a gentleman who has called upon this house."

"Does he have a name, this 'gentleman'?" Lady Bullstrode asked peremptorily.

"Mr. Fairfax was the gentleman named."

"Send for the footman involved," imperiously commanded Lady Bullstrode to Lady Thomas. "We must interrogate him for ourselves!"

Lady Thomas waved her handkerchief weakly at the butler in mute assent, unconditionally surrendering to Lady Bullstrode's invasion the conquest of her domestic sovereignty. Roberts, cowed and sullen, was brought before the two women, while Mr. Arbuthnot remained in attendance.

"You are to tell us what you saw in that park."

"It was like I told Mr. Arbuthnot," Roberts said, eyes lowered, speaking to the floor. "I was in the Park, behind some trees, and I saw him come up and speak to her where she was a sittin' on the bench."

"So you were not with her then?" questioned Lady Bullstrode. "Had you met her earlier walking in the Park? Spoken with her?"

"No, your ladyship," he smiled, "She didn't see me."

"So you were spying then, were you? Peering from behind trees?"

"A person's as got a right to be among the trees of a public park of a Sunday morning," he said defensively.

"It is strange a fellow servant such as yourself would not go over and speak to another, especially as she was a pretty young girl as well."

"She did not fancy such a one as me," he smirked. "Her ambitions fly high, that one!"

"And how do you know that?" Lady Bullstrode snapped sharply. "Did she tell you?"

"No," he said. "One afternoon, I was in the dining room, laying the table for supper, and I heard her come down the front stairs, and directly after, I heard one of the gentlemen a'coming down after. And she makes to slip, 'cause I hear a little cry, and then I hears that Frenchman's voice. Doofwah. And they talk a bit."

"Do you remember of what?"

Roberts fidgeted. "Not rightly, but he says something like 'have a care,' and she says a word in his language in return. But then they are interrupted by Mr. Fairfax, who is a'clatterin' down the stair behind him."

"And where were you all this time?"

"A-standing inside the dining room door, your ladyship, out of sight."

"So if they could not see you, you could not see them. How do you know who came down?"

"He spoke to her and the Comte. I recognized his voice."

"So he spoke to both together?"

"No," Roberts' smile became a grin of remembrance. "He spoke first to the Frenchman, and after that he called out to Miss Cat and asked her to wait for him."

"And did she?"

"She did, your ladyship," he replied, relishing his tale of her humiliation. "Just in front of the backstairs door. I peeked through the dining room doors, and I saw Mr. Fairfax catch her up by the wrist, and whisper in her ear, and kiss her hand. So I followed her this morning to see what the drab was about!" His face had the malicious delight of a witch's pumpkin. "That afternoon, she said to him not to try to seduce her, threatened to scream, but she knows a gentleman what likes a challenge! She was willing enough to get in the carriage with the likes of him today. She knows right well the benefits of her service under him!"

"Oh," cried Lady Thomas. To have such a thing happen concerning a servant and a visitor in her house. If it got out, her reputation would be that of a brothel keeper. She turned fearfully to Lady Bullstrode. "Oh, what shall I do, Lady Bullstrode, against this misfortune?"

Lady Bullstrode looked at her, eyes narrowed, and tapped her fan against her gloved palm. "Mr. Fairfax seems intent on showing himself as the blackguard he is. I have been correct in my intuitions. He is a member of many racing clubs, and a habitué of low company in boxing salons. He was a wastrel at Oxford and worse. He has lived abroad for years. The rumors about his birth and breeding are many and uncomplimentary. You must close your doors to him, Lady Thomas!"

"Oh, yes, I will, Lady Bullstrode. Thank you for your advice."

"I shall look into this matter personally. Be assured that I will say nothing of this to anyone. Be sure that you do not either."

"No, of course not, Lady Bullstrode. Thank you, Lady Bullstrode."

Lady Bullstrode rose from her chair. "I shall bid you farewell now, Lady Thomas. See that you follow my instructions exactly. Clarissa's invitations depend on it." She swept from the room.

Lady Thomas sent a summons to Clarissa to join her in the drawing room. She would be made to see the importance of keeping silent, even if she had to tell her every sordid detail.

RETURNS

Vere quit the mews after overseeing the installation of his new horses and curricle in their new home. The encounter with the Comte had been polite and unpleasant. Vere did not think that he had furthered the government's case. However, the Comte's notice had been drawn, as was his intent. Nevertheless, he hurried to put the experience from his mind for the immediate present. Cat was well within his doors, and he wanted to see her. Vere could but conclude that Lady Leacock was to arrive at last, to take charge of their delicate passenger pigeon. How much had Sir Merlin told her? Would she interfere with the masquerade?

And even if she did not, the Season, a world of dinners and balls, was replete with rich young men, men younger and more innocently ardent than he. Had he come so far only to lose Cat to another, in front of all eyes? Jessup, the butler, awaited him in the hall and took his hat and greatcoat from him. "Is the young lady still within?" Vere asked, divesting himself of the garments. "Has she been made comfortable?"

"Yes, Sir," replied Jessup, "I have complied with your directions in every particular."

"Where is she now?" asked Vere, straightening his cravat before the mirror, running his hands through his rain-damp hair.

"She is in the library. She asked permission to choose a book, marveled at the comfort of the room, and begged leave to remain there. I hope that is satisfactory."

"Perfectly," replied Vere. "Leave her there for the moment. It has been a cold afternoon. I require a brandy and a change of clothes. See to it." He swung on his heel and mounted the stairs to his own room. Jessup hurried below to notify the valet of the master's return, motioned the footman to bear upward the decanter and glass, and sent the parlormaid to inform the young lady of the return of Mr. Fairfax.

In his dressing room, Vere quickly stripped off his white linen shirt and washed his face and body while Stevens laid out the coat of midnight blue, with silver buttons, and an elegant dove-grey waistcoat. The cool water on his brow did nothing to calm the heavy beating of his heart. That she was here in his house fairly shook him with anticipation. He knew that she never would have accepted his offer of help if she had not been at the end of her resources. Desperation was hardly the best recommendation, but here was his chance to undo all that had befallen previously between them since that first meeting on the road.

He stilled his breathing and sought to compose his mind. His eyes met his own level stare in the mirror. His face was closed, impassive. He smiled a smile of polite attention. The face before him reflected nothing of his inner turmoil. It was an expression devoid of passion, empty of emotion. She had seen quite enough of his feelings already. Drying himself with a towel, he turned to Stevens, who held fresh linen. With a practiced hand, Vere tied and smoothed the folds of a fresh cravat while Stevens waited, ready to help Vere into the grey waistcoat. Putting on the coat, Vere surveyed himself, noting with satisfaction how the quietly elegant lines set off his figure handsomely. With a steady hand, he poured a glass of brandy and drank it. The fiery liquid calmed his nerves. Speaking with a coolness that he did not feel, he dismissed his valet and left his bedroom, descending the curving stairwell with a deliberate pace, one that took a great deal of willpower to maintain.

The door of the library opened, and the parlormaid stepped out, bobbing a quick curtsey to her master. He nodded his head to her and entered the paneled library, then closed the door behind him. She stood in the light of the fading afternoon sun that shone feebly through the window, slowly turning the leaves of one of his recently purchased books. She looked up at the sound of the closing door and smiled graciously. His heart turned over in his chest, but he returned her smile with bland impersonal warmth. "I am glad to see you have found something to interest you while I have been away."

"Indeed, I have been admiring your library. You have a great selection of books, both old and new. It seems you are a most diligent and discerning scholar."

"I cannot take that much credit for the selection. The collection has been in the house for many years. I endeavor to update it with what may be worthy among our contemporary writers. I am gratified that my choices have met with your approval. May I ask which one that may be?"

"It is a work by Coleridge, 'Dejection: An Ode.' I picked up the book, and it fell open to this page. Is it perhaps a favorite of yours?"

"It is my favorite among this work," he replied with a show of indifference, turning away from her, picking up another volume from the table beside her. "I see you have also chosen the works of John Donne. You are to be congratulated on your choice. You show a most mature taste for one of your years. I would have expected most young ladies to have chosen Mrs. Radcliffe's *The Italian*." She blushed quickly, grateful that his back was turned. *The Italian* was one of her favorites. She had read it secretly, guiltily, beneath the beeches last summer. He put down the book and faced her.

Taking a careful breath, he said, "Is it not time we put aside certain fictions, Miss Cat? No daughter of a stablehand would be familiar with John Donne. Nor would she have spoken to me as you have." Her eyes widened, but she neither dropped her gaze nor turned away. He paused briefly, but she made him no answer. In as soothing and even a tone as he could manage in his present emotional state, he continued quietly, "I have no desire to pry from you a secret you wish to hold or to take advantage of your situation in any way. It is merely obvious that you are no lady's maid, although for unknown reasons you have been masquerading as one. I deduce that now your need for such subterfuge has ended. I must also assume that although you consented to accept my hospitality, you did so only because there was no other alternative. Knowing this, but without the impertinence to inquire more closely into your concerns, I ask: What I may do to assist you?"

Cat closed the book and sat gracefully upon one of the library's comfortable chairs. "Your tact and discretion are appreciated, Mr. Fairfax." She pronounced his name with some inner difficulty, as if, in addressing him so, she had obscurely acquiesced to some greater intimacy. "It is as you say. Unfortunately, I had to act earlier than I had intended. I did, in truth, find myself without a place of recourse for too many hours. The rain only compounded my difficulty."

"Then may I offer you the hospitality of my house for as long as you need it and the use of my horses and carriage for the continuance of your journey?"

She smiled at him. "How do you know I would not be taking your carriage for a five-day journey?" she said merrily, her eyes sparkling with the jest.

He went cold. What did she guess? He had met her at her aunt's. Did she deduce that he was already aware of her identity? Could she then be aware of his own? Perhaps she was not such an innocent after all, but a jade already wise in the ways of artifice. He looked at her again. Her hands were folded in her lap. Practiced composure to prevent any revelation of weakness? Perhaps her manner was only a display of high spirits and nervous bravado by a girl hardly out of the schoolroom.

Keeping his tone as bland as before, he bowed and replied, "If that is what you require, I will, of course, oblige." He watched her carefully as she framed her reply.

"I thank you, Mr. Fairfax. Fortunately, I do not require that. Your discretion is essential. Although I am young in years, I am not entirely insensible of the precariousness of my situation or the danger of my actions. Although I have but a short journey more to make, I cannot arrive before ten in the evening. I fear I will never accomplish it without your silence and your complicity."

"You shall have it and gladly. Having now established the conditions of our meeting and parting, may we not talk of pleasanter things? Is there any other amenity of my house I may offer you?"

She smiled and gestured for him to sit. "You must not neglect yourself in the offer of those amenities," she said. "I am curious about one thing. Can you tell me something of the Wedgwood vase on the mantelpiece in the drawing room?"

Involuntarily freezing at the question, he pretended that he had not seen her invitation and instead idly picked up the books and reshelved them. "Nothing," he said. "It was already part of the furnishing. I know nothing of its history." That was a lie; he knew too much of its history. He looked indifferently at the spine of the book in his hand: *The Poems of John Donne*. It was too near the matter. With a slight shiver, he put it away. He blinked. Turning back to Cat, he bowed again. "Your pardon. Perhaps you had not finished with the books. May I get them for you again?"

The silence between them was interrupted by a clamor that echoed up the stairs from the entry hall. They heard a few words, delivered in a bawling female voice, "Must speak with him . . . matter of great urgency . . . prevent a scandal . . ." and the murmured but unintelligible replies of Jessup. Frozen in place, Fairfax and Cat listened as a pair of light footsteps ascended the great stair. A soft knock came from the paneled door.

"Enter," said Fairfax grimly, placing his body between Cat and the entry. Jessup stood outside, his usually imperturbable countenance somewhat flushed. "I beg your pardon, Sir, to interrupt, but the intrusion cannot be helped." His eyes shifted hurriedly to Cat, who now stood behind Fairfax. "Lady Bullstrode is in the hall, and she insists on seeing you." He cleared his throat apologetically. "Something about a young lady and a scandal. I think you had better go."

A devil of a complication, thought Vere. Behind him, he heard Cat's sharp intake of breath. Would she swoon? That was all they needed, to be found here alone, by that gorgon, Lady Bullstrode, with a supine Cat unconscious upon his floor. Why Her Infernal Nuisance had not already followed Jessup up the stairs, he could not fathom. He turned, but Cat, although quite white, still stood upright, her shoulders squared, her head proudly lifted. Brave girl, he mentally congratulated her. She had mettle. He smiled at her reassuringly, but he knew too well the seriousness of their situation. The word *scandal* disturbed him. How much of the truth of Cat's identity did Lady Bullstrode know? Runaway servant girls were not grist for the rumor mills unless something else was involved.

His reputation was in danger only from the cutting comment it would excite among the Exquisites of the *ton*. Gentlemen took mistresses from the Opera, the theater, and discreetly from each other. They did not lower themselves with servants. Bad enough that she had been posing as one this past month. If she were known for whom she truly was, what explanation could he offer for her unchaperoned presence? For Cat, it would be a disaster. She would be ruined.

A selfish thought flashed like a meteor through his mind. He could end the masquerade right now. She would have to marry him to preserve her reputation. They could elope to Gretna Green that very evening. Presented with the alternative of discovery, she would have no choice. He searched her face. Her direct gaze met his without faltering. She stood ready to face the situation, although despair battled with pride upon her lovely troubled features.

He could not suggest it. He would not force her. He could not make her a bartered bride in such a dishonorable fashion. She would never forgive him; she would never love him. There must be a way out of this situation. Lady Bullstrode had sent the carriage, he remembered. Had he mistaken her, he wondered? He took her for merely an officious bore. Was Lady Bullstrode playing some other game, and if so, for whom?

By all means, he must protect Cat's secret. Deciding on a course of action, he smiled reassuringly at Cat. "It seems you must resume the masquerade for a while yet. Please remain here," he said courteously. "I am sure Lady Bullstrode is under a misapprehension." Turning to Jessup, he continued, "I will attend to Lady Bullstrode myself," and suiting action to words, he left the library, taking Jessup with him, and shut the door upon Cat.

Descending the curved stairs, with Jessup padding softly behind him, Fairfax saw Lady Bullstrode, her back to him, dressed in her walking dress of peculiarly unlovely shades of yellow and purple, closely examining one of the hall pictures through her lorgnette. He affixed a polite chilly smile on his face, but before he could address her, she, hearing his booted step upon the stairs, turned to him.

"Mr. Fairfax," she said, peering behind Jessup toward the upper hallway. "I am sorry to interrupt your afternoon this way, but I simply must speak with you. There is a scandal brewing, Sir, one to which you must put an immediate answer."

"And that is?" He replied politely, showing only well-bred surprise.

"The disappearance of one Cat Gryffyn, Miss Clarissa Thomas's lady's maid."

"Why apply to me?" Fairfax asked, his closed face revealing nothing.

"Because she was last seen entering your carriage," Lady Bullstrode answered.

"Indeed? By whom?" he inquired, his tone implying the utmost indifference.

"By the Thomases' footman, Roberts. I was paying a morning call to Lady Thomas, shortly after I left your town house, when the great hubble-bubble occurred. Clarissa herself burst in upon us with the news. A most unregulated young person." She frowned. "I could hardly avoid the knowledge. There is more."

"I see. Would you care to attend me in the drawing room? It is most ill-mannered of me to keep you standing in the hall."

Lady Bullstrode smiled widely. "Thank you, Mr. Fairfax. This is a most elegant town home. I would love to see some of the other rooms. I am sure you will be able to explain this situation to my satisfaction. Sir Thomas has just arrived from the country, but if I can ascertain the truth of this matter, perhaps he will not have to be involved." With careful courtesy, he led her up the marbled staircase to the drawing room.

"Well," said Lady Bullstrode, once she had been ushered into the pale blue drawing room, and the door had been shut behind them. "I must speak frankly, although it pains me to front you in your own house." Her glance roved about the room, taking in the tasteful decor with an approving eye. She snapped the lorgnette shut and dropped it into her reticule. "You are suspected of seducing Cat Gryffyn, Miss Thomas's lady's maid. You were seen together by the Thomases' footman twice, once some days ago in a familiar intimacy in the front hall and today in Hyde Park, where you were seen handing her into your carriage. I need not elucidate further on what the world may see in this. Do you have anything to say for yourself, Sir?"

Fairfax looked at her blankly, momentarily at a loss for words. The rain might explain the carriage. But the kiss! Damn and blast! It had been foolish to kiss her hand where anyone might have spied upon them and apparently had! Lord Carrington had as much as warned him then, but it had been too late. Now the conclusion was inescapable. The obvious interpretation of his actions was simple. He had proposed a tryst, and she had accepted. If she indeed had been only a serving girl or a light-skirts, it would have been a minor annoyance. He would have suffered a trifling drop in reputation. Taking a servant or a common drab as a mistress was *de classe* among the Corinthians of the *ton*, but he was far too fine a master with a four-in-hand to suffer social banishment. Had she been only that, he could have enjoyed her at his pleasure and set her up handsomely when his attentions inevitably waned.

However, Cat was neither of these things. Nor could he ever give her up. No, revelation and elopement were the only way out after this. Would she consent to such a thing? Lady Bullstrode could convince her of the precariousness of her position and the lack of honorable alternatives. And Cat's feelings on the matter? After hearing the sorry litany, she would hate him for his actions, which alone had brought her to such a dishonorable pass. He had proved himself everything she had accused him of being. His title would only add to the total of the damnation. He could say nothing in exculpation or defense. He looked bleakly at Lady Bullstrode across the unbroken silence, which assented to his guilt.

Still, she had referred to Cat as a lady's maid. She seemed unaware of Cat's identity. By continuing the masquerade boldly, he might yet salvage his plan, if he were willing to perjure himself. Selecting the properly correct and concerned manner of an English gentleman, he replied.

"Lady Bullstrode," he said smoothly, "I can understand the confusion that has resulted in your mind. However, there is a perfectly simple explanation. The maid in question comes from Foxearth, in the Welsh Marches. I have a connection," he paused briefly to emphasize the implication, "with the family whose tenant she was. That is why she allowed me to find her shelter from the rain. The meeting in the Park was quite accidental. It seems she had taken another post and consequently left the Thomases' quite abruptly. She was waiting on her appointment when the rain began. I merely offered her shelter after recognizing her and ascertaining her plight. There is nothing more to it. Whatever else the footman fancied he saw must be a lie."

"I am glad of it," Lady Bullstrode remarked, fixing him with an intense stare. He bore it unflinchingly, adopting a look of languid boredom. "Well," she continued briskly, "No doubt she could not endure her position at the Thomases'. Of course, she was quite wrong to go with you, but she certainly had little choice, save return to the Thomases'. However, I am sure a grand gentleman such as yourself would never seduce inexperienced maidservants or publicly embrace them in the hall. You should have come to me right away, dear Sir!" She transformed suddenly from a vengeful gorgon to a pouting flirt and laid her arm upon his with a knowing smile. "I can certainly help arrange for the poor little thing to get to her new position. Bring her to me, and we can scotch this scandal before it spreads any further. Those Thomas women have adders' tongues. I know she is here."

Fairfax rang for Jessup. "Do you wish to interview her privately? Or shall I acquaint her with your ladyship's generous offer?"

Lady Bullstrode thought. "No reason for you to leave your own drawing room, Mr. Fairfax. I can perfectly well interview her in your presence." Jessup appeared in the doorway.

"Please bring the young woman here," Vere said flatly. He watched with trepidation and curious hope as Jessup left the drawing room. Would Cat have the wit to resume the role of a runaway servant convincingly enough to persuade Lady Bullstrode?

Cat was already on her feet as Jessup entered the library. "Please follow me to the drawing room, Miss," he said kindly. "You are wanted by Lady Bullstrode." Cat felt apprehensive and perplexed. Now only hours from her goal, another obstacle appeared in the interfering form of Lady Bullstrode. How did she come by her knowledge? What use was her secret now? Being found alone, however innocently, with Mr. Fairfax in his town house must surely compromise her. There was no place to which she could flee under the watchful eyes of Jessup. She had no choice but to continue her masquerade. She bobbed a brief curtsey and followed him quietly out the door.

Shown into the drawing room, she saw them both, first Mr. Fairfax, leaning with easy grace upon the marble mantle. What had he said in explanation? The cold arrogance of his face revealed nothing. Lady Bullstrode sat on one of the pale blue silk armchairs, ludicrously overlaced in her walking dress of clashing shades. Cat saw that she had canary yellow walking boots on. She bowed her head to hide an involuntary smile, although she felt tired, wanting rest beneath her aunt's roof, not engagement in another battle of wits to gain a goal that constantly receded.

"My Girl," Lady Bullstrode said, "Mr. Fairfax has been very kind to you. However, you have been very remiss in your actions, accompanying him to his town house. Your whereabouts have become known and misconstrued. I cannot allow this situation to continue. You are to come with me at once. It will be much more seemly." She turned to Mr. Fairfax. "Do you have anything to add?"

"Yes," he replied, leaving his post at the mantle to stand behind Lady Bullstrode's chair. "Having heard your history," he said very deliberately, "Lady Bullstrode will of course honor the promise I made to see you on to your planned destination. You have only to inform her." His expression did not change, but his voice held a new emphasis. "She will on no account return you to the Thomases'." He smiled down at Lady Bullstrode, a flinty smile. "Am I not correct in this, Lady Bullstrode?"

"Of course you are," she replied with hearty jocularity. She stood. "Thank you, Mr. Fairfax. I hope I might count on you to come to my rout in May." She smiled at him demurely.

"Your ladyship's servant," he replied, bowing curtly to her. He looked at Cat and smiled an encouraging smile, but his eyes were serious. "Heaven help me," he thought, "I have done what I can."

Lady Bullstrode stood up.

"Come," she said. "You will accompany me in my carriage, and we shall see what is best to be done." She swept out of the room, leaving Cat and Fairfax to follow her.

"I told her nothing of your confidences to me," Fairfax whispered as Cat passed by him on her way out. "She yet believes you a lady's maid, running away from your post." Cat gave him a small, strained smile.

"Thank you for your efforts. You cannot be blamed for this misfortune," she said softly.

He felt pained, for indeed his was the entire blame. Would Lady Bullstrode recite the unfortunate sequence of events, showing his own part far too plainly?

"I regret I was not able to accomplish all that you charged me with, and that which I promised," he said aloud. "I have no doubt Lady Bullstrode will keep her word." He bowed deeply. "I wish you good fortune," he said, as he stood, hands clasped behind his back. It was all he could do to keep himself from gathering her to him and declaring himself to her; with the world well lost, at that moment.

"Thank you," she murmured in a tremulous voice. His coldness hurt her more than she thought possible, but given the situation, and his honor, perhaps, he could behave no other way. Resolutely, she would play out her bluff to her last card. "Goodbye," she said, lifting her head proudly, her back as straight as a young poplar tree. He bowed to her again, unable to craft a suitable reply from the many emotions he felt at that moment.

Taking his silence for farewell, she turned and followed Lady Bullstrode's receding figure down the curved stairwell to the front hall, where Jessup stood ready, waiting with her cloak. Outside, in the starless early evening, Lady Bullstrode's carriage waited. A footman scrambled down to open the door for them. Quickly, Cat was shepherded inside by the lady herself. In response to a sharp whistle, the horses broke into a smart trot.

Cat took a deep breath. "Thank you for your attentions," she began timidly. "It is very kind of you to help. Mr. Fairfax promised to see me on to my next position after his return. My employer does not reach London until late this evening, and I was waiting in the Park when the rain began. Mr. Fairfax kindly offered me shelter."

Lady Bullstrode looked at her shrewdly. "Mr. Fairfax explained that you were a tenant of the Fairfax family at Foxearth, I believe."

Cat felt herself drain of color. "Oh, aye," she murmured at last, "At Foxearth." Again, she saw herself standing with him in the street, repeating her bold lie of being a servant girl there. How could she have forgotten that Foxearth was owned by the Fairfax family, the family name of the Earls of Falconbridge? "Who is he?" she thought through the shock of realization. "What is he to Lord Falconbridge?"

"Well now, my Girl," Lady Bullstrode said. "Put all this behind you. Your secret is safe." She took Cat's hand and patted it reassuringly. "I know you are not a lady's maid. Knew it the first time I saw you in the Thomas drawing room. 'There's quality,' I said to myself. 'Something odd here.' It is a good thing I happened to be calling on the Thomases this morning. Now, who are you really, and how did you come to be in such an improper situation?"

Cat felt the heat of blood rising to her face. She did not want to explain everything from her flight from the arranged marriage with Lord Falconbridge to the present. As to how she came to be alone with Mr. Fairfax in his drawing room, she could hardly explain that to herself. She felt acutely embarrassed before this woman, who, although a figure of fun, was very formidable. She could make no answer that would not discredit her.

"Never mind," came the voice of Lady Bullstrode from the darkening carriage. "I can guess. A country girl hoping for a Season in London, rebelling at the choice of husband from among the local county beaux. No doubt counting on some relative here to sponsor you. Am I right?" she cawed. "The only real question is how did you come to be a lady's maid in the meantime?"

"Yes," replied Cat in a wretched voice. "You are right. It seemed a good idea at the time, but it did not work out as I had planned." She continued with an edited narration of the entire sequence of events. "I did not think . . . that is, I thought, and it seemed the only way. I see now I was wrong."

"Certainly you showed a sad lack of judgment," Lady Bullstrode replied severely. "It will never do, in Town, to play such pranks. Nor cultivate familiarity with such men as Mr. Fairfax. Youth does not excuse recklessness, especially in females. It is a harsh world in which we live and are judged. At least he did not guess your identity. You were, no doubt, safe enough from him in the servants' hall. You have been lucky, as well as clever." She smiled at Cat. "However, I was young once myself," she added in a lighter tone, "and I know what a London Season can be for a young lady. So, who is this relative upon whom all your hopes depend?"

"Lady Henrietta Leacock," said Cat faintly. "She arrives tonight at ten o'clock. I had no choice. Had I waited longer, I would have surely been found out when Sir Thomas arrived this morning."

"Well, you are quite lucky that I arrived. Lady Leacock is a good friend of mine." Lady Bullstrode pursed her lips and considered. "The Ladies Thomas will certainly try to make mischief, especially if they recognize you once you have entered Society. What is your real name, Girl?"

"Caitlyn, Caitlyn Llewellyn."

"No doubt, those who know you well will call you Cat. Well, Miss Cat Llewellyn, we shall have to establish your credentials immediately. You are coming home with me tonight, and I shall send to your aunt. I like your mettle, Girl, and I have a fancy to see you the White Ewe Lamb of the Season. You can rest easy, as we shall take care of everything. What you want is a proper supper and a long sleep."

The house felt empty to Vere. The vibrancy it had held was gone, and the dead stillness left behind had no tranquillity for him. After the departure of Lady Bullstrode, with Cat following meekly behind, he had returned to the library. The resonance of their passage there still rang in his senses. Still fresh in his mind were her graceful gestures as she laid aside the book. Again, he experienced the shiver of lightning he had felt as he recognized the books she had chosen. So young and so innocent, he would swear to it, yet familiar with the most sublime poems of passion in the English language, such a creature he would have. The sweet quiet intimacy that they had shared over the books gave a tantalizing view into wider dimensions of shared life. In addition, he must press his suit under the canny and probably disapproving eye of Lady Bullstrode. Such women judged by only one thing. Position. He was unable to use his. How did Cat judge? Sentiment. He hoped he had gone part way in reversing her judgment of him.

Now, at the government's behest and Carrington's connivance, he must embody all that was doubtful about himself, his lineage, and his sentiment. How could he contrive to win Cat honorably and yet continue his masquerade successfully? At least on her reappearance as a debutante, he could legitimately offer to her all the homage to which his esteem entitled her. He resolved to show her no more than an honorable courtship, curbing with a hard rein his mind's appetite, already turned toward those other pleasures of intimacy, in which he would initiate her as soon as the courtship was ended. Involuntarily, he looked at the Wedgwood vase and the *hieros gamos* it depicted. He sat up late that night reading, unable to sleep for impatience. Knowing that the game would begin soon in earnest, at three a.m., he left the house to visit some gaming hells where he might encounter the Comte du Foix.

APPEARANCES

Cat stretched luxuriously in her clean soft bed, snuggled deep under thick comforters, upon a plump goose-down mattress. The morning sun streamed gloriously through the tall windows. It must be nearly nine o'clock, she thought with a start. In her first confusion, she wondered why Rose had not awakened her, why had not Clarissa sent for her to be fetched? Then she recalled the events of the previous night. She was at Lady Bullstrode's town house. By the bed hung a long velvet rope. She had only to pull it, and a maid would be sent to her, with hot water to wash and tea. Part of her longed to lie abed a while longer, but excitement recalled her to her plan for the day. Her aunt would surely arrive with the carriage and sweep her away for shopping and fittings. She pulled the rope vigorously in her excitement. When the neat and silent maid entered, she found Cat already up, brushing her hair before the mirror. Twenty minutes later, she skipped light-footed down the stairs to the breakfast room, where Lady Bullstrode, already vividly gowned in mauve and blue, sipped tea from a china cup of Dutch blue-ware. "Well, my Girl, I see you keep country hours like me," she said approvingly.

Cat smiled. It would never have occurred to her to call rising at nine o'clock "country hours." "I am excited," she demurred. "My first real day in London. Will Aunt Henrietta be here soon?"

"If she is keeping Town hours, no. She won't arrive until after one o'clock. You would do well to learn patience. It does not do, in Town, to appear too eager. It marks you out as a rough, country lass, not worth a second glance. You must learn to cultivate a certain air. It makes 'em more eager. Now," she gestured towards the ornate flame mahogany sideboard behind them, "help yourself to some breakfast. I have already sent round to Mmsl. Du Sable to send over some suitable gowns at eleven o'clock. Your aunt will probably arrange for dressmakers, but you will need something right away, in the meantime. You must present your cards as soon as possible. Including a call on the Thomas ladies." Her dark eyes sparkled with mischief.

Cat paled noticeably, but her hand did not tremble as she put down her cup of fragrant tea.

"You must make a bold play, before any talk can be started." Lady Bullstrode reached out a comforting hand. "Both your aunt and I shall accompany you. Say nothing, and leave it all to me." She smiled broadly. Her expression became serious again. "But in the future, show no special recognition of Mr. Fairfax. You will meet him socially, of course. It cannot be helped. His vices do not bar him from general Society, and you are sure to meet him there. But his reputation with women is very bad, and his fortune at present is quite unknown. You look like a sensible girl. Not entertaining a fancy for him? You wouldn't ruin yourself over some romance of Mrs. Radcliffe's? Books is one thing, marriage is another." Her mouth curled in a small smile. "Oh, yes, I know what young girls are up to thinking these days, reading romantic nonsense like that woman writes. So did we, at your age. Take my words for gospel, Girl. In life, the sensible course is always the best. Find a young man your own age, with a good fortune and a good heart. One who wishes to marry. Handsome he may be, but a black rake like Mr. Fairfax can offer no good to a girl such as yourself."

Cat sipped her tea in silence, her expression carefully contrived to reveal nothing. Her heart protested against Lady Bullstrode's accusations most strenuously. She had detested him! She had known him for what he was in that first encounter! But yesterday, when she had been entirely at his mercy, he had shown a most delicate discretion, which had truly surprised her. She had not credited him with such sensitivity. However, Lady Bullstrode was a woman of the world, and Cat felt that she had already acted too much the child. Unbidden too came her memories of his kiss upon her finger, his breath in her ear. Mutely, she bobbed her head in agreement. It would be better to avoid Mr. Fairfax, much better.

At one o'clock that day, Cat sat demurely in Lady Bullstrode's drawing room, awaiting her Aunt Henrietta. Now Cat was charmingly dressed in neat white India muslin, flounced with eyelet white lace about cuffs and hem, and threaded with pale spring-green satin ribbons. Her shapely hands were gloved in white-netted mitts edged with fine lace, and beside her was a ruffled parasol, also white, with a carved ivory handle in the shape of a bird. Her long, heavy hair was coiled artfully up on her head, held with a tortoiseshell pin. A few long curls drooped upon her neck, showing her small, neat ears.

"You look every inch a debutante," Lady Bullstrode said with hearty approval.

Cat smiled with simple pleasure. "Thank you, Lady Bullstrode, for your kindness. I hope my aunt will approve."

"Oh she will; no need to worry about that. Don't worry about anything," she added. "Everything will be our secret."

The door opened. "Lady Henrietta Leacock," Lady Bullstrode's butler announced. He stood aside, and a tall woman entered. She had the height of Lady Bullstrode, but was far more slender. Her hair retained some of its famous gilt color, which had helped make her the leading Beauty in her day. Now she wore a quiet mauve gown edged with black braid, the badge of her widowhood. Her serene countenance quickly lit with joy upon seeing her niece.

"Caitlyn," she exclaimed, hurrying forward, her hand outstretched. "I should scold you, but I simply can't. I am so glad to see you. We have been so worried! How lucky you came to be in Lady Bullstrode's household! It's a good thing your father has given his permission for you to have a Season here with me. Your disobedience has caused no end of worry to that good man. What have you to say for yourself, Truant?"

"Oh, Aunt, I am truly sorry, but I could do no other." She looked at Lady Bullstrode surreptitiously. "I must live my own life and make my own decisions."

"If one of those decisions is to run away from responsibilities, I fear you are not ready to make decisions of your own. Did you have no thought for the embarrassment and anxiety you caused your father?"

"These modern young people," Lady Bullstrode laughed, as Henrietta sat by, mortified by her niece's and her own impertinence. "Bless me, I remember how we thought twenty years ago! I wager you she can find fortune and favor every bit as good as her papa can arrange. And a proper marriage to follow it."

"I certainly intend to keep an eye upon her to assure that this is the case." Henrietta smiled gently and reached for her niece's hand. "You must be obedient from now on." She patted her gently. "No more headstrong actions." A squeeze. "And no more elopements," she added significantly. Cat blushed. She fully intended to fall in love with an honorable man, one whom she could proudly present to relatives and friends. She would keep her distance from men of Mr. Fairfax's sort.

"Yes, Aunt Henrietta," she murmured. "I understand you perfectly. I shall give you no trouble." She added in eager tones, "I am so glad for this chance. I will not disappoint."

"That is good," Henrietta answered approvingly. "It is a censorious world, as Lady Bullstrode must have told you. We women must be very careful. Lady Bullstrode," she said, addressing that Worthy, "We have many matters of business to attend to, fabrics to select, frocks to order, cards to present. Thank you for your kindness, but I must beg your leave to depart."

"Of course, dear Friend. Only too glad to have been of help. But there is one thing you must do immediately. You must call on the Ladies Thomas this morning." She cast a reassuring glance at Cat, who sat by, whitely silent. "Near neighbors," she winked. "Quite imperative. Manners and precedence. Allow me to accompany you."

Henrietta sat stiffly still. "I had not thought of that." She thought a moment before continuing. "Certainly, Lady Bullstrode, if you think it that important. There have not been any irregularities, have there?"

"Nothing to speak of," replied Lady Bullstrode, laying a finger aside of her nose. "But it would be wise all the same."

"Then let us go," said Henrietta, arising gracefully from her chair. "Caitlyn, Dear, are you quite all right?"

"Yes, certainly, Aunt. Let us go. I am anxious to see Clarissa again. After all, we have not met since the Assembly Ball." She glanced quickly at Lady Bullstrode, who returned her glance with approval. All three left the drawing room and descended to where Lady Henrietta's carriage sat waiting in the street.

Lady Thomas squinted through her lorgnette at the card that her butler presented to her. "Lady Henrietta Leacock" it read. "I am not sure I know the lady," she mused aloud.

"She is accompanied by Lady Bullstrode," her butler added discreetly. He coughed. "And a young person. I think you might wish to interview them." Lady Thomas looked at him sharply, but his features revealed nothing. Nevertheless, there had been something in his tone.

"Very well. Tell them I am at home. Send to Clarissa to attend me."

"Very good, your ladyship."

Clarissa, in her dress of white with blue-sprigged flowers, sat graciously beside her mama, awaiting her new visitors. That tiresome Lady Bullstrode accompanied them. And it was important to please her. What importance the other two could command was unknown, but fixing her expression in a welcoming smile, she waited quietly. She gasped with astonishment as the three ladies entered. Beside her, her mama also uttered a smothered little cry, for shepherded in between the two elder ladies was none other than Cat Gryffyn! Before she could utter a word, she felt her mother's hand like a claw, grasping her wrist. Lady Bullstrode smiled broadly.

"Lady Thomas, Miss Thomas, allow me to present my dear friend, Lady Henrietta Leacock, and her niece Caitlyn Llewellyn. They just arrived yesterday for the Season." The newcomers bowed. "I believe you already know Miss Llewellyn," she squawked. "She is your neighbor."

"How thoughtful of you, Lady Bullstrode," Lady Thomas murmured, striving for composure. "Please be seated." She motioned towards her guests, trying not to stare at the young woman. She could only hope that Clarissa was not gawking at her like some country lass at a fair. She recovered herself swiftly. "But of course we know you, Miss Llewellyn. You are our neighbor at Eldertree Manor. We met but four months ago at the Assembly Christmas Ball. Surely you remember Caitlyn, Clarissa." She turned expectantly towards her daughter, one brow raised in emphasis.

"Of course," said Clarissa. "How lovely that you could come to London for the Season. You should have told us," she ventured. "We could have ridden down together."

"I would have liked that," replied Cat, reddening. "I did not know I was to go until the last minute," she added boldly.

"It was her father's doing," smoothly interrupted Henrietta. "He does not understand we ladies need time ahead to prepare our gowns for Court Presentation. However, my dear friend, Lady Bullstrode, has helped me engage the services of Madame La Croix to design Caitlyn's court dress."

"Oh yes," bellowed Lady Bullstrode. "Madame La Croix is the *modiste* of the year. I am sure Miss Cat will be well turned out." Her eyes narrowed as she looked shrewdly at the ladies' reactions to the name "Cat."

Clarissa hitched in a short breath while Lady Thomas busied herself with the tea that was being handed round. "Indeed," she replied. "Miss Cat is very fortunate. I engaged Madame La Croix's services by post last January. Clarissa had her final fitting just last week." She took a small sip of her tea and laid cup and saucer aside. "Madame La Croix was very flattering about it. She said she had never fitted a gown for one with such a slender, petite figure as Clarissa's. She proclaimed her the epitome of womanhood!"

"I am sure Miss Thomas will be very beautiful in it," said Lady Leacock, also setting aside her cup. "Miss Cat's greater height gives a certain elegance to whatever she wears, so she may wear the simplest frocks, but, of course, Madame La Croix is designing all her ball gowns."

Clarissa swallowed some more tea to hide her chagrin. She was to be the outstanding belle of the season. It was so important that she make a great marriage. Now Cat Llewellyn was here. Even Clarissa had to admit that Cat's beauty was superior to her own. But she possessed Cat's secret entire. Roberts had been most forthcoming to her. If Cat's prospective beaux were to know that story, they wouldn't be too anxious to dance with her or propose marriage. She smiled over the rim of her teacup at Cat, who nodded her head pleasantly to her in return.

Lady Bullstrode fixed upon them a hard and flinty stare and smiled a shark's wide-toothed smile. "No doubt, you will be quite friendly to each other, being from the same county. We think a lot of Miss Llewellyn here, and we think a lot about you! So I know it's always going to be a pleasure to see you." She withdrew two deckle-edged cream-colored folders from her reticule, spreading them like a fan upon the table. "Two vouchers to Almack's," she announced. "I would not want to hold the Ball if we were not to see your faces. Our invitations," she continued, "have never been rescinded." Lady Thomas blanched.

"Lady Bullstrode," she quavered, "I cannot adequately express my sentiments of admiration and devotion to yourself. It was most gracious of you to come by yourself and bring along your dear friend and," she added with a twinkle to Cat, "our near neighbor! I hope you shall visit us often, dear Child."

"Thank you, Lady Thomas. I should be delighted to visit you and Miss Thomas. I hope I shall see you at every ball." The rustling of her aunt's and Lady Bullstrode's skirts told her that their visit was over. Smiling, she rose to her feet, saluting both the Ladies Thomas. Clarissa stood by her mother, smiling pleasantly as their guests left.

Lady Bullstrode lingered briefly behind as Lady Leacock and her niece descended the stairs. "I have some news for you on that matter we discussed," she said portentously. "It seems the maid in question was homesick. Since she was a tenant of Foxearth, an estate of the Fairfax family, it seems she applied directly to Mr. Fairfax. Apparently, he merely returned her to Wales. Good day to you."

Silently, they stood together, listening as the footsteps of the departing guests dwindled and ceased at the closing of the heavy front door. "That vixen!" burst out Clarissa. "That scheming vixen. How dare she try to ruin my Season and make a fool of me! And play the light-skirts with Mr. Fairfax! Society shall know about this by the very first Ball!"

"Clarissa," her mother hissed. "Do you not see the danger in the course you pursue? Lady Bullstrode as much as warned us directly. She said tickets have never been rescinded; she didn't say she would not rescind them! This girl is a favorite of hers, but we know her secret, so she has to be nice to us. Lady Bullstrode will ruin us if we pass any slander, so cease

your complaints. Time is always the best teller of tales."
Together, they left the salon.

The rest of the day had been a long one for Cat and Aunt
Henrietta, even with its attendant excitements. Proceeding
at a bold pace, behind a swiftly trotting pair of matched black
carriage horses, they arrived first at the drapers, where, amid
a profusion of fabrics, they chose bolts of muslin, watered
silks, delicate lace, skeins of braid, ribbon, buttons, and other
trimmings handed round by eager salesclerks while their
purchases were borne away by attending servants. Passing
next on foot, they entered the milliner's, trying on bonnets,
for daywear, for rainwear, for paying calls, for church on
Sunday. They also bought feather and ribbon trims, silk
flowers and leaves, for twining evening garlands into Cat's
long thick hair. They crossed the street to the boot makers,
where they bought ball slippers of white with satin ribbons,
of green with velvet ribbons, walking shoes of supple leather,
half boots for riding, and soft doeskin slippers for the
bedchamber. Everywhere they went, they were accompanied
by the bright jumble of color and noise. Cat felt quite dizzy
at the plethora of choices she was to make and the strange
sensation of merely wanting as the only criterion for
possessing. "This is but a fraction of what we must buy,"
smiled Henrietta, when Cat declared fatigue after the glover's,
where they had bought several pairs of gloves: white kid ball
gloves, a pair of grey ones to go with her green and grey
spencer, several crocheted white "mitts," and a sturdy pair
of leather riding gloves. "We have but two weeks till Court
Presentation. Madame La Croix will begin measuring you
tomorrow. Unfortunately, we need more than she can make
now, so my dressmaker, Alice, will have to make you some
simple gowns for daily wear. Of course, we can't go out
evenings until we have the others."

"Your evening gowns would fit me very well, Aunt. They
hardly need any remaking and look nearly as elegant on me

as they do on you. I do so want to go out to the opera tonight. Could we not use this remedy?"

"My dear Child, the colors are all wrong for you, and the style is much too old. Remember, I am not only a woman of older years, I am also a widow. You must wear gowns of fresh color that suit your age. You have come all this way to have a Season, and you have no idea of the work and subterfuge it entails! You cannot afford to look dowdy if you want to attract a rich young lord. They can afford to be supercilious in their choice, even in the case of a rich dowry. I am determined you shall be the debutante of the Season, and nobody will see you looking less than perfect and poised. Therefore, with the exception of the Thomases, which will serve some purpose—of allowing them to underestimate you—no one will see you until we are ready. It will give you some time to get some of the excitement of London out of your gestures. You cannot seem to be too much of a child at seventeen."

Arriving back at Berkeley Square, after hours of shopping on Bond Street, with myriad purchases, with the remainder to be sent, Cat longed for rest and quiet. She felt that she had been through so many states of strong emotion and turmoil that she could not experience one single new thing more. Unfortunately, Aunt Henrietta had something to say. Cat could see it in the determined way she had taken off her hat, ordered tea, and dismissed the maids with the packages, to be carried upstairs and exclaimed over later.

"Caitlyn, we must speak. I have had a letter from your father. I admit to being puzzled by some of what it says, but I shall of course be glad to bring you out into Society. Your father has enclosed a quite generous cheque, and there will be more whenever needed. I also have an enclosure that he directed me to give to you." She held out several sealed sheets of paper to Cat, inscribed with her father's clear handwriting in address on the outside. Quickly, Cat took the letter and unsealed it with trepidation, wondering what it should contain.

My darling Daughter,

I will not censure you for what you have done, though you should have thought beforehand of the dread of uncertainty your acts must have created, as well as the danger to yourself. It saddens me that you did not feel you could trust me with your concerns. I love you dearly as the daughter of your mother, as well as my own. Remembering your mother, you should know that I would never hurt you in such a way as to compel you to marry against your will. The proposed union between yourself and the Earl of Falconbridge was never more than anything but a proposal. Certainly, the advantage of uniting the lands of Foxearth and Eldertree Manor cannot be lost upon you, as it was not upon your mother and me when the proposal was first made. I should have thought nothing of it after all these years, if a post from Lord Falconbridge himself had not arrived reminding me of it. I felt honor bound at least to entertain his proposals. It was never my intention to force you to honor them.

However, here I must confess that in the present imbroglio, I have played a shabby part. By not being frank, it seems that, between my Self and Bessie, this allowed you to believe your intended was my old friend, the previous Earl of Falconbridge, when in truth it was his son, the Viscount de Montferrato. When his father died, he inherited the titles and wrote to me of the old promise. I had known him when but a youth, and thought well of him. It was but a sadly misleading jest on my part not to be forthright.

Young Lord Falconbridge has been to see me since. I told him you were currently in London with your aunt for the Season and apologized for the ill timing, saying nothing of your actual behavior. He was most gentlemanly, taking full responsibility for the unfortunate confusion. I cannot say if he suspects aught of your absence, as his advising letter was quite specific on his date of arrival. Nevertheless, he would still like to meet you when you return from London, as he remains firm in his wishes to offer marriage to you.

I realize you have every right to choose your own husband, and should your choice fall on another, as long as he is suitable, I will have no recourse but to agree to the nuptials. However, it is to be understood you will take no action without first seeking my opinion. You are yet young in the ways of the world, and your heart, though honorable, may not be the best judge of husbands. Rank and wealth must also be considered.

The new Earl of Falconbridge possesses both in abundance, more than enough to compensate for the differences of age and experience. Despite the age difference, I believe him to have a mind and heart that will well accord with your own. On speaking with him at some length, he has demonstrated he has every quality you may prize in a man: forthrightness, courage, intellect, and sensitivity. Nevertheless, it is your own head and heart that must ultimately decide. Therefore, I must ask that before you promise yourself to another suitor, you first do Lord Falconbridge the courtesy of listening to his proposal.

I shall be coming to London for the Derby. Until that time, remember you are under the guardianship of your Aunt Henrietta and be advised by her in all things.

Your loving Father

Cat refolded the letter, relieved and troubled at the same time. Her father had acknowledged her desire to have a Season in London, but she must still return afterwards to refuse Lord Falconbridge in person. She had no scruple about running away rather than refusing an old man. How much more she now dreaded facing a young one. Marriage to an old Lord Falconbridge was inconceivable. In retrospect, it would have been a small but disagreeable task to reject him. A young Lord Falconbridge might have been a different matter. "And," she thought in a sudden epiphany of recognition, "now he is also Count de Montferrato." All her fervid dreams aroused by her imaginings while reading *The Italian* came rushing back. In the meantime, the glittering world of London and the *ton* stretched before her imagination. She would use this period of enforced waiting to quiz her aunt on everybody whom she would encounter, everywhere she should go. When she appeared, she would be no unrehearsed, young, simple schoolgirl with a great fortune and an open heart, but a polished woman, fully in command of herself, one to inspire rivalry among the highest of the *ton*. Cat smiled to herself. The despised *poseur*, Mr. Fairfax, would be reduced to one man among many, his impertinence to importuning. Her aunt was looking at her kindly, her curiosity politely masked.

"Dear Aunt," Cat said gaily, "I am to have a Season after all. Father trusts us both in all things. He is coming down for the races, but until then, you are to be my guardian and guide. And as I cannot go out until Madame La Croix finishes some of my gowns, let us have tea, and do tell me everything I need to know for my presentation at Court and all else besides."

Vere returned home to a grey mist of rain pearling the dawn light until the rising gold of the sun blazed through, presenting him with a day entirely of his own choosing. Cat was gone, withdrawn behind that feminine curtain that presages the reemergence of the schoolgirl as the poised woman of the evening star. Fresh youthful beauty, innocent and still unshaped, had its own charms. Had he been another man or even in his first youth, he might have married only so. Being witness, however painfully and unwillingly, to his own parents' marriage and having been so often a third member of many others since attaining his majority, he had no immediate desire to marry. Nor did he ever fall in love.

Nonetheless, he was his mother's child after all, and the passion of love that sang in her blood called darkly through his own. He had few morals about easing the body's lusts, but he had never misled himself that he did it for love. He would not willingly try that wounding again.

To marry as the Earl of Falconbridge was a different matter. He had meant to make a marriage of mere convenience to a wealthy brood mare who would enlarge his lands and bear in due time the requisite "heir and a spare." Now, in love as he was, he could bear no passionless union of convenience to some colorless country heiress, flaccid, vapid, insipid. Now, the possibility that she with whom he would share his life and his fortune could have desire and vitality to match his own possessed his imagination. In such a union, might he find redemption of soul and spirit? He had seen in Cat a brave and bright companion, as she tamed the horses beside him, the wild March winds whipping at her long braided hair.

Where there was spirit, there must be the soul's desire. She knew the words, the language, for who could not, who read John Donne? Was she somewhere within the cloistered corridors of her mind aware of that potential of desire, which reaches to the root of the soul, that tree of good and evil? Never had he thought to dare that dangerous Eden again. She was his choice, of both heart and head, by a happy fate. Could he make himself her choice?

Undressing and then wrapping himself in his dressing gown, he rang for Stevens. Vere bathed and shaved, then attended to some private papers in his study. There were matters that he needed to look over, thoughts to order. Lord Carrington expected a report later that morning. Vere's courtship of Cat would have to take second place for now. Nevertheless, Vere penned first a courteous, but forthright, request to Lord Carrington to obtain for him an invitation to the first ball at Almack's that followed the Court presentation of the Season's debutantes. Then, seizing another sheet of foolscap, he began to enumerate, while it was still fresh in his mind, what he knew of Monsieur Lucien Montclair, the so-called Comte du Foix.

CONVERSATIONS

Cat stood as quietly as she knew how while all around her fluttered the minions of Madame La Croix. Darting here and there, like so many hummingbirds, they circled around, taking a tuck here, placing a pin there in the white silk presentation dress, while Madame La Croix stood by approvingly, sometimes clapping her hands to point out a missed pleat in the train, sometimes speaking brightly to Henrietta and Lady Bullstrode, who sat by approvingly.

"Pearls is the best," Lady Bullstrode said. "Just the thing for a young girl. Looks fresh and innocent."

"*Oui*," agreed Madame La Croix, bobbing her head energetically. "So young, so unspoiled. Pearls are exactly right for such purity."

"I had rather preferred diamonds," sniffed Henrietta. "Among all that white, diamonds make a girl stand out."

"Plenty of time for that." Lady Bullstrode fanned herself complacently. "Pearls says one thing, diamonds another. Surely, you don't want her taken for a woman of the *demimonde*. Nor do you wish to attract those only interested in fortune."

Henrietta agreed reluctantly. Cat looked more a young queen than an untried princess. She could wear diamonds with the careless assurance of her own birthright. She had to concur with Lady Bullstrode that due to Cat's extreme inexperience with most society, Cat should not be thrust into deep water right away.

Madame La Croix clapped her hands briskly. "*Fini,*" she called to the seamstresses, who reached out with skilled fingers to help Cat out of the now fitted gown. "There will be one more fitting after the seamstresses have finished. Return early next week. You shall see how lovely you will be."

Cat stepped down gratefully, while all around her the fitters took up her train and slipped the nearly finished gown over her head, careful of the delicate lace and her artful coiffure. They buttoned her into her moss-green poplin dress, carefully retying the satin sash beneath the modest bodice. Putting on their shawls and bonnets, the three exited the shop.

"How do you like it, Dear?" inquired Henrietta.

"Very much," replied Cat. "Except it seems designed for one who is just out of the schoolroom."

"And so you still are," Lady Leacock said. "And I would not put you in harm's way with a dress that beckoned to all our *roués*. Marriage is your goal. Anyone seeing you thus will know what is expected. You do not yet have the experience to tell an honest affection from a seduction."

"Is that so great a danger, Aunt?" Cat asked. "By your words, I would believe there are wolves running loose in the ballrooms, such is the danger of my being carried off."

Henrietta sighed. "I do not mean to impute your reputation or good sense in this, my Child. The young are headstrong and ignorant about the world, not to mention about themselves. You have lived a very secluded life. You have great spirit, but no experience. Moreover, you are passionate. I fear you may make an ill-advised marriage out of misplaced, misunderstood sentiment. If you were poor, there would be less danger, but you are very rich, and every out-of-pocket rake will take notice. They are wolves to women, devouring happiness, health, wealth, and reputation. I merely wish to protect you in every way I can."

Lady Bullstrode nodded her head in approval. "Being women, our world is very circumscribed. A good marriage can widen it, but a bad one can destroy utterly all hopes of happiness. Once the mistake is made, it cannot be undone. Men are allowed many more failings than we, and we must often overlook those failings. Such is life. We must have a good eye out for our own happiness, and that can be compassed by a man of property and honor who will fulfill his contract. Love comes of solid values. Remember that in these next months."

ACQUAINTANCES

C at held her back uncompromisingly straight. She did not even touch the cushions of the open carriage. She remained as aloof as possible from the languishing softness of Clarissa's posture as they were driven towards Hyde Park under the flinty gaze of Lady Thomas, who was seated opposite them. The Four-In-Hand Club, led by the Prince of Wales himself, was to drive round the Ring that afternoon, and all the *ton* would be there to witness it. Lady Thomas had extended an invitation to Cat and her aunt to accompany them three days ago, and Cat's aunt had accepted on her behalf. Henrietta had no wish to brave the crowds and noise, for either herself or her horses, but it would do well for Cat to be seen by the *haut monde*. The vividness of her niece's coloring seen beside the pale gold and ivory of Clarissa would draw attention to them both from every quarter. Refusing Cat's demur with an uncharacteristic brusqueness, Henrietta summoned her maid and perused Cat's wardrobe, then chose an outfit that would highlight Cat's resolute charms in spite of the inevitable contrast with Clarissa's rounded soft femininity.

Dressed in an afternoon dress of white percale and a spring-green spencer, Cat observed the passing throngs from under modestly lowered eyelids while Clarissa chattered on about what they were to view.

"It is the most exclusive society among the dandies in London. Only the best drivers are admitted. The Prince is, of course, a member, as is Lord Barrymore, who has a really dreadful reputation," Clarissa murmured with a toss of her shining curls at her own daring knowledge. Narrowing her eyes, she looked at Cat while adding in dulcet tones, "I believe our preserver of the road, Mr. Fairfax, is also to drive." Cat curled her fingers upon the carriage sill, but did not flinch under Clarissa's insolent look. "He is said to have great mastery. It is a shame he is not eligible."

Cat turned her gaze outward into the gathering throngs. She had no wish to front Clarissa's malicious little barbs. Although they both had to pretend that none of the events of the preceding month had happened, the knowledge was there. Clarissa continued to remind Cat by such little pricks and jabs to Cat's pride that she had not forgotten.

"I see you have better things to mind," Clarissa added sharply, noting that Cat's attention was somewhere else.

Annoyed by the constant surreptitious warfare of words, Cat turned her green gaze on Clarissa. Determined to finish the sordid little contest at that very instant, Cat's words died, and her fury choked her throat. The Comte du Foix, impeccable in shades of grey and blue, accompanied by Colonel Percy, resplendent in his red coat, approached their carriage. Clarissa was not slow to interpret the object of Cat's attention. Flicking open her fan, Clarrisa arranged the drapery of her blue and white floral shawl to better advantage, revealing more of her rounded white arm. Lady Thomas, her vulture's stare alerted by her daughter's coquetry, raised her lorgnette to her eyes and turned her head as the handsome riders passed by.

"Le Comte du Foix," Lady Thomas called, as he drew up to the carriage. "A pleasure to see you again."

"Lady Thomas," he said politely, turning his horse to accompany their carriage as his companion looked appreciatively at the cargo of beauty that it contained. "Surely the pleasure must be all mine, one which, if you will allow me, I will share with Colonel Percy." He bowed slightly in the direction of the red-faced man, whose bemused look was entirely taken up by the young ladies. "I believe you know Lady Thomas, and her daughter, Miss Thomas. Allow me to present to you . . ." he paused in his recitation, with a conspirator's smile. "I fear I am unacquainted with your companion, Lady Thomas. May I request an introduction?"

Clarissa, her blue eyes upon the Comte and the Colonel, smiled prettily from behind her fan. Cat, less skilled in the arts of flirtation, blushed when she found the Comte's eyes levelly meeting her own. Lady Thomas curled her lip in disdain. How vexing that the Llewellyn girl was with them. Lady Thomas did not intend to see her own child play second best to that one!

"Miss Caitlyn Llewellyn," Lady Thomas replied shortly. "Our neighbor, in Town for the Season."

"A pleasure to make your acquaintance, Miss Llewellyn," the Comte smiled. "I hope you are enjoying your stay."

"I am indeed. Each day brings a new experience, more delightful than the last."

"Alas, I am too forward then. I should have met you on the last day of your Season. Colonel Percy, can you bear to be presented today, knowing that tomorrow you shall be superseded by a greater delight?" Cat blushed and looked away.

Lady Thomas noted Cat's discomfiture. The girl was a graceless bumpkin after all, she thought triumphantly. "Our neighbor," she said, her voice tinged with the faintest disapprobation, "has never been to Town before," dismissing Cat as an artless child scarce worth a second glance. The Colonel smiled politely at her and bestowed another interested look upon Clarissa, who flashed a brief look from behind her fan.

"Most honored to see you again."

"Colonel Percy," smiled Clarissa, with a quick sideways glance into his handsome, but vacuous, face, "the honor must be entirely mine."

Cat sat stiffly in the carriage, feeling herself a clumsy rustic in comparison to Clarissa's flattering femininity. She could not even summon one lucid sentence, but sat dumbly while Clarissa stole the initiative. Cat wished that she had never embarked on so dangerous a course, which seemed likely to bring her only shame and embarrassment. Nothing was as she had envisioned it. She sat in silence as Clarissa prattled teasingly on, contriving to show the charms of her person to good advantage, letting her shawl slip to reveal the rounded lushness of her figure to the Comte and the Colonel, to whom she directed all her smiles.

"Your companion is most voluble," commented du Foix to Cat, who had not ventured another syllable against the torrent of Clarissa's laughing chatter. "Your artful impersonation of Silence enhances the contrast between you and your cheerful companion. By economy of effort, you out-do your fair rival. Swept away by your friend's animation, the Colonel, a man most sensible of feminine charms, yet casts an interested glance in your direction. Your unmoved beauty is a beacon to us adventurers, lured too often upon the rocks of boredom by such siren songs."

"Your words are as fair as your looks, my lord, and I am greatly indebted by your kindness to a mere country girl."

"Oh, you are more than that, *n'ecst-ce pas?* You need not fear, your secrets are safe with me."

Intruding upon their conversation, Lady Thomas called out loudly, "The procession has begun. Look there, the Prince is leading with his team of white horses." Cat turned toward the direction that Lady Thomas indicted. A long line of coaches, each with four horses, was parading in splendor. She counted fourteen handsomely drawn equipages, the first driven by the Prince of Wales himself, whose showy team of four white horses drew every eye. Hard behind him followed a team of matched greys driven, she was informed in an excited whisper from Clarissa, by the notorious Lord Barrymore. His team pranced in the traces, tossing their long rich manes at each expert crack of the whip that reverberated over their heads like gunshot. Each team was a superb example of horseflesh, driven with great skill by the most notable Corinthians of the *ton*. A high-perch phaeton drawn by high-stepping black horses, in somber contrast to the foregoing teams, caught her eye. Their fluid grace and powerful docility, driven by a man garbed in midnight black, was the antithesis of the flamboyant styles and turnouts of the Earl of Barrymore and the Prince. The driver's economy of technique showed, to Cat's critically trained eye, the better skill.

'Twas some seconds before the familiarity of his proud profile revealed his name to her mind. Mr. Fairfax, so fully in command of so much power with such insouciant grace, left her breathless with admiration. No longer aware of the conversations around her, Cat watched as the teams, having completed their first circuit of parade, quickened their pace. Fairfax's team needed but the touch of the whip to shift into a trot.

As the Prince in the lead carriage swung round again, he whipped his team into a canter, and the other carriages in line followed suit. The thunder of their passing overwhelmed all conversation. Through the raised dust, Cat saw the matchless symmetry of Fairfax's sable team, whose smooth-gaited action appeared effortless, as did their driver's control. It was as if the reins were a living extension of his will, so responsive to his lightest touch were the horses.

The line of elegant equipages slowed to a walk upon completing the last circuit and drove out of the park through the Cumberland Gate to Edgeware Road. "They shall, no doubt, drive to some coachman's inn at Paddington, where they can indulge in drink after such thirsty, dusty work. I do not understand your noble Englishman's enthusiasm for aping the modes of the laboring classes," remarked the Comte.

Cat did not vouchsafe a reply to his peevish comment, so caught up was she in her admiration of Mr. Fairfax's elegantly displayed skill. She felt drawn and challenged by his mastery over his team, by his powerful command of the spirited horses, which meshed their will to his own. With such mastery over horseflesh, what skill would he bring to love's bower? Did he seek to drive her to his pleasure as he did the four he now held in hand, to slow or speed in their paces as he desired? Even in her inexperience, she knew by his first look that he would ride her as man rode a woman. Seeing his prowess, so spectacularly on show, she knew in her heart that her young girl's wildness would be no barrier to his ultimate, passionate conquest of her body and soul.

Mortified by the tenor of her own thoughts, as well as her rudeness to the Comte, she quickly sought a suitable rejoinder. "We as a country have always prided ourselves on our horsemanship, Sir. No doubt things are done differently in France."

"Very differently indeed," rejoined the Comte, with a small smile. "Perhaps someday we may discuss our different methods of harness and control. Your servant, Madame, Mesdemoiselles."

He saluted the company and rode off with the reluctant Colonel Percy in tow. His last remark lingered uneasily in Cat's mind. Mr. Fairfax had unsettled her indeed, if innocent comments provoked such wayward thoughts. Such speculation must be firmly put away. No young lady of gentle breeding could admit in any way to such an interest in a man, especially a man of such disreputable character. She turned her full attention to Clarissa's empty chatter. Clarissa was most gratified by her appreciative audience and preened over her field of conquest.

PREPARATIONS

"**U**p, Cat," called her aunt gaily, as she swept into the room ahead of the maid, who bore a large unwieldy cloth bundle. "We must rehearse for the Court Presentation!"

"Rehearse? Now? I am barely awake. Let me at least have my breakfast."

"I would not have you too full for the lacing." Behind her, the maid spread out the bundle that she had been carrying. Caitlyn saw that it was a set of hoops and a heavy brocade gown.

"My own Presentation dress; terribly out of fashion now, but all very well for you to rehearse in. It is no easy thing to be graceful while wearing court dress, and any mistake will be noticed and commented on. You will do well to accustom yourself to moving while wearing this, well before the Presentation date. We have a great deal of work to do, if you are to be ready!"

The maid fitted the wide hoops about Cat's waist. They bowed out from the hip, adding nearly four feet to her figure. Moving in them was rather like walking within a large bell. "Take a turn about the room," Henrietta suggested. Cat did. The hoops swayed violently.

"As I feared. You really are a country girl, and your stride is much too masculine. You are not climbing over styles to find lost sheep; you are being presented to the Queen. Again, slowly."

181

Cat stepped forward again, but the hoop still moved. She tried again with slower steps, with the addition that at every step, she came to a full stop, rendering her progress across the floor awkward and broken.

"Curtsey," ordered her aunt. Cat bent her leg and made a token curtsey, while the hoop rocked upward in a sharp angled thrust.

"No, no, no!" Henrietta clapped her hands. "Remember to keep the hoops level. Do not pitch forward when you curtsey. Sink straight down. Again!"

Cat complied. Keeping her back straight, she sank down toward the floor on her flexed knees. Riding had given her strength, but here were muscles that she never she knew that she had, crying in pain!

"Deeper," ordered Henrietta. Cat did her best to comply, but fell on her hands.

"That will never do!' cried Henrietta. "You must also hold up your head," she chided. "Watch me!" Lady Leacock executed a deep curtsey, almost touching the floor, her head held high, and her eyes never leaving Cat's face. "My curtsey was remarked upon by all present," she recalled happily. "It was one of the reasons I was acclaimed the reigning Beauty of the Season. I cannot accept anything less for you. Here," she motioned to her maid, "this will help you keep your head up." Taking something unseen, she pinned it to Cat's high collar.

"What is it?" Cat looked down, trying to see what was pinned there. "Ouch! That hurts! What is it?"

"A sprig of holly. I assure you that it is the best reminder! Now hold your head up and try again. Glide," she commanded her niece. "There must be no rocking motion to your skirts. Slowly! Good; continue!"

Cat felt the prick of the holly upon her chin. Lifting her head, she continued her slow circuit around the room, aware always of the slightest motion of the treacherous hoops. "Float," called her aunt. "You are a white cloud, floating in the sky. Smoothly. No hurry. Steady. Do not screw up your face in such a way! You look like you are lifting a sack of grain! Smile, yes, that's good!"

Feeling as if she were being tortured, Cat walked slowly about the room again. "Are we done?" she asked.

"We have just begun," Henrietta said before she walked through the bedroom door to the other end of the hall. "I shall be the Queen. Walk to me, slowly. When you arrive, curtsey! Now, slowly, slowly! Smile! Too fast! Move with stateliness! Float like a cloud! Good, good. Curtsey! Deeper! Again!"

Cat, repeating the same motions in endless circles, in the ridiculous hoop, wished that she had never conceived her foolish scheme. Her knees ached from practicing her curtsey, and more than once, she had fallen in a heap, the despised hoop rocking up to show her underskirts. Henrietta had transformed herself into a merciless tyrant, and Cat feared that the pricking holly had drawn blood! Still, she could feel that the hoop was swaying less with each step now, and on several occasions, her aunt had cried, "Good!" She advanced down the hall again, her head lifted, the hoop steady, even while every muscle in her body threatened to cramp, with a sweet smile fixed firmly on her face.

"Excellent, my Dear. You have made a good beginning! We shall have some breakfast and continue our practice. This afternoon, we shall rehearse backing out! We have but five days!"

"Five days!" Cat quailed inwardly. No doubt, her aunt intended to drill Cat all day for five days. The holly pricked Cat's chin. Lifting her head, taking a careful breath, she calmed her emotions and took a firm step forward. The hoop barely swayed.

"Good," cried Lady Leacock. "Proceed."

Much later, with aching muscles, Cat sat down to the breakfast tray. Her legs were as stiff as if she had ridden all day. She ate slowly, to prolong the few minutes of rest she had been granted in what would be a very long, very tedious, span of days.

PRESENTATIONS

"Today is the day," thought Cat a week later, opening her eyes to a bright ray of sunshine streaming through the filmy curtain into her pale yellow and ivory-colored bedroom. A soft knock told her that the maids were outside with hot water for the bath. "Come in," she called gaily. Behind them bustled Aunt Henrietta.

"We must hurry," Henrietta said, waving the maids through to the dressing room. "Already the morning wanes. We have but six hours to get ready. Hurry, hurry, child. You are not dressing to pick onions in your kitchen garden this morning!"

Cat laughed as she threw the bedcovers off and got out of the tall four-posted bed. "Is it that great an event that we must begin so early? The Presentation is not until five."

"My Dear, we must arrive before that! We must be there a seemly time beforehand! Besides, are you not curious as to your fellows? Seeing your rivals is half the battle," Henrietta said gaily. "Up, now, and wash yourself and your hair. I have brought some lavender to scent your bath. As soon as your hair is dry, we must begin to arrange your coiffure." She touched the long heavy braid with her hand. "It will try our ingenuity to dress it fashionably. Why is your father so opposed to cutting it? He specifically instructed me to leave it long."

"I do not know," said Cat, whose first request, to trim her unfashionably long hair, had been firmly denied by her aunt.

"We shall turn it to our advantage, then," laughed Aunt Henrietta brightly. "What I have in mind will take two hours alone to arrange. When it is done, you shall be the most beautiful of all!"

Cat unbuttoned her nightgown, slipped it quickly over her head, and handed it to the maid, who stood near to receive it. Cat stepped gingerly into the large tub. The water was pleasantly warm and fragrant. She sat down gratefully, then quickly slid down, submerged her upper torso and head, and soaked her wide-floating hair. Sitting back up, she took one of the large sponges and a small cake of soap to wash her legs. Henrietta herself took the other sponge and began to wash Cat's neck and back while the other maid began to work lather into her hair.

"This is so exciting for me, dear Niece. It has been nearly twenty years since I had the excitement of a Season. I love my son Arthur, but it is not quite the same with a boy. The excitement of balls and theaters, riding in the Park, the racing at Newcastle and Derby week. The gowns and the suppers! It is a Wonder!"

"Riding in the Park?" Cat said, her hand, clutching the soap, stopped suddenly, poised upon her smooth skin, right above her heart. "Does that mean I can have a horse?"

"I don't see why not," agreed her aunt amiably. "Your father has certainly sent more than enough funds. I wish Mr. Sanford were here to advise me. He looks after all the horses at the estate. I am afraid I didn't listen to him very carefully when he explained his choices to me." She smiled ruefully. "I shall send for him!" she added brightly.

"I can choose my own horse," Cat replied, sitting up violently in her tub of water, splashing one of the maids in her excitement. "Tell me I can go tomorrow!"

"Tomorrow!" exclaimed Henrietta. "As soon as that! Not the day after that?" she said teasingly, handing Cat her dropped sponge.

"Oh, yes," laughed Cat. "I cannot imagine being presented at Court can be as exciting as that will be! I shall be perfectly composed today!"

"I hope that you will be," Henrietta said gently. "A Season should be fun, of course, but do not forget what is important! Begin well tonight!" The undermaid took the ewer, filled it with warm water from the large pail, and poured the water over Cat's head and hair, rinsing the soap.

"More," laughed Cat, wiping the rivulets of soap from her face and eyes. The maid poured another pitcher full.

"Good," said Henrietta, standing back from the tub. "One more, I think. Then use the scented rosemary water for the final rinse. It will give it extra shine."

"'Rosemary for remembrance,'" quoted Cat. "I hope you are not intent on making an Ophelia of me, Aunt."

"Oh, Dear, no," replied her aunt, a little puzzled by her comment, "but that is a good point. They will certainly remember you. Now stand up so we can rinse you off."

An hour and a half later, Cat sat in front of her mirror at her dressing table, watching as the hairdresser behind her worked deftly at coiling and pinning the many-sized braids of her hair. She had been sitting straight and still in her silk wrapper for such a long time, she thought. When the woman first began braiding her hair, she had begun to worry that she was going to look like some wild Indian from America! However, one by one, the woman tucked and wove the braids into place. As Cat watched apprehensively, an elaborately simple coiffure of intertwined braids formed a Greco-Romano arrangement, swept back off her face to the sides of her head, where the several small braids were interwoven to form an intricate French roll to which the larger longer braid was then coiled in a heavy figure eight and fastened to the back of her head, leaving her lovely neck bare to the nape.

The maid stepped away and brought Cat a smaller hand mirror so that she could see the coiffure from all angles. Smiling with delight, Cat studied its deceptively simple elegance. She looked like a young goddess with burnished hair, softly glowing with copper highlights. Her lovely throat, like an alabaster pillar, was fully exposed, showing the strong curve of her jawline and the gentle roundness of her chin.

"I have just the earrings for you," Lady Leacock said. She set a velvet box down upon the dressing table before Cat. Cat opened it a bit clumsily, fumbling the clasp in her excitement. Until she had seen herself in the new hairstyle, she did not really believe all their preparations were real. Now, staring at her own face, she saw a young woman of restrained and proud beauty, cool and distant. She smiled, tentatively, and was glad that she looked a bit more like her old self. Yet her old self was transmuted, in an exotic way. She looked down at the now-opened box. Inside was a pair of earrings, each made of a single baroque pearl, set in gold filigree, depending from small scallop shells.

"Here, let me help you," Henrietta said. She took the earrings from the box and put them in Cat's delicate, small ears.

"What about yourself, dear Aunt? Should you not be getting ready? Surely you are coming with me?"

"Yes, Dear. However, before you begin dressing, you must eat a little something first. There will be nothing to eat until after the Presentation. I would not have you feel faint. Anne, bring Miss Llewellyn a tray in her room. Eat slowly, Dear, but do eat. You promised to follow my advice in all things. I am going to prepare myself. When I come back, we will finish with you."

Aunt Henrietta swept off to her room, leaving Cat, finally released from sitting, to get up, to stride quickly around the room, and to feel the weight of her luxuriant hair pulling her head back with its heaviness, giving her the mien and posture of a young queen.

In the corner stood the dressmaker's mannequin with the beautiful white dress upon it. Made of white shantung silk, its lovely scalloped bodice bared shoulders and arms. Cunningly attached upon the short puffed sleeves were nets of lustrous pearls. The same conceit was worked into an intricate embroidery upon fine tulle that fell invisibly over the skirt, as well as another design of pearls sewn upon the hem itself. Formed into a pattern of lace at the neckline, they coolly touched her skin when she had her final fitting, highlighting the milky whiteness of her delicately rounded décolletage. Obediently, she turned to the simple meal set out before her and endeavored to eat, although she discovered, much to her surprise, that she had no appetite.

The two ladies, bundled in their wraps as much to protect their finery as to guard against the slight chill that remained in the air, joined the other carriages in procession to St. James's Palace. A goodly crowd had gathered to watch the arriving debutantes and their friends. Leaving their wraps in the carriage, the two women got out and were escorted into the Palace to the Drawing Room. There were dozens of other young women already there, a rainbow of brightly colored gowns topped by nodding white plumes, like so many clouds. When Cat entered, dressed all in white, there was a sudden silence. Cat was disconcerted as she faced so many stares. "Aunt," she whispered behind her fan "They are all in colors. Why am I all in white?"

Henrietta smiled. "Why, to be different. You shall be remembered, I assure you."

"But surely, I would be just as noticeable in a dress such as those!" All about them, there were girls in beautifully colored dresses. One brunette with the darkly fashionable coloring of the time was strikingly turned out in a gown of midnight-blue and silver. The jewels in her hair flashed like small stars.

"That is the Honorable Lucinda Mortimer. Very noble, but with the mind of a six-day-old chick. She is already pledged to the Marquis of Beaumont. Her parents have played it very canny. He has done no more than look at her. A good thing, too, because he has some sense, even if she does not. Do you see that girl over there?" Aunt Henrietta indicated a fair-haired girl in a rose-colored gown, trimmed with silk roses of a deeper hue about the bodice and hem. She was so slight that she seemed overwhelmed by the elaborate conceit of her dress. "Arabella Hamilton, the last of the Hamilton girls. If all else fails, she can marry her cousin, young Lord Middlesex. He is nearly as colorless as she is."

"Aunt, I think I see Clarissa and Lady Thomas. Over there," Cat whispered, nodding her head slightly in their direction. Her aunt looked in the direction that Cat had indicated. Although the crush of people was growing larger, she could clearly see Clarissa and her mother. She was dressed in sky blue with golden sunbursts worked in gold thread on her short puffed sleeves and down the skirt. Small blue and gilt-enameled stars were woven into her shining curls. She was as beautiful as a spring sky.

"I am not sure being dressed all in white is to my best advantage."

"Do not worry, my dear Niece. Do you remember what I told you?"

"Of course. We wait here until we are summoned to the Presence Chamber. Then I enter through the door, approach Her Majesty, curtsey, and kiss the Queen's hand. Then I back out, taking care not to stumble, the train carried over my left arm. You have rehearsed me enough in this."

"I hope so," her aunt declared fervently. "All the World will know within a day what happens here! You will be wonderful! Are you feeling all right?"

Cat, whom the excitement was finally beginning to effect, nodded with a surety that she was not feeling. "I am fine," she replied, but she worried to herself. Would her headdress of three white feathers stay in place? Would she fall down while making the deep required curtsey, or would she somehow trip over her train when she backed out? With effort, she thrust such thoughts from her mind and concentrated on the other girls, noting the details of their richly colored dresses, hoping that she was not being stared at and talked about, yet knowing that she was.

"Oh, it is beginning," Henrietta whispered in Cat's ear, as she pointed out with her fan a pompous, elaborately dressed gentleman in front of the door, list in hand. "That is the Lord Chamberlain. He will announce the presentees' names, and each girl will then be admitted to the Presence Chamber. Once inside, you must let down your train. A Lord in Waiting will announce you to Her Majesty. Do you remember what to do next?"

"Yes, Dear Aunt. I must curtsey to Her Majesty, kiss the Queen's hand, curtsey once again to Her Majesty, and back out."

"And you must also nod to other members of the Royal Family present. And there may be a number of them," she smiled. "Do not forget any!"

"Are there so many, then?" Cat lightly asked.

"Yes, Dear, but there is only likely to be the Prince of Wales and one or two of the Princesses in attendance today. It would be a rare state occasion if all were assembled!"

"How will I know them? It seems impossible."

"You will see. Trust yourself."

The crowd slowly thinned, but the wait seemed interminable. Cat judged that nearly half the room had been presented by now. How disappointing, she thought, looking at the remaining colorful throng. No matter how vivid their dresses and coloring, they must all look alike to Her Majesty after such a number had passed in presentation. Few indeed could hope to be singled out or remembered! If it were not for all the trouble that she had put everyone to, Cat would just as lief go home to a good soak in hot water and enjoy scones and tea afterward with a good book. At least as an officially presented debutante, she could now attend the balls, the theater and the opera. Perhaps they could go tomorrow evening. With that happy thought in her mind, Cat heard her own name being called.

"Miss Caitlyn Llewellyn," intoned the Lord Chamberlain. Cat looked around quickly at her aunt, who nodded her head and smiled with encouragement and pride.

With her train draped over her left arm, Caitlyn walked through the indicated door. Once within, she let down her train, which was spread out immediately by Lords in Waiting. Slowly, with grace, as she had rehearsed it, she moved forward to the figures at the far end of the room.

As she drew nearer, she saw that the Queen was very much like anyone's grandparent, kindly and a bit tired. With elegant precision, Cat made her first curtsey to the Queen. Cat kissed the offered hand as she curtsied so deeply as to be almost kneeling. Rising slowly, her eyes upon the Queen, Cat heard the Queen say, "All the swans belong to the King, you know, M'dear." There was a polite susurrus of laughter all around. Rising, Cat met the insolent stare of a dissipated man of around forty years of age, lavishly dressed in velvet and gold lace. As she did so, she blushed prettily and curtseyed again. She recognized the Prince of Wales, of whom Aunt Henrietta had had much to say. Backing out slowly, she kept her eyes fixed upon the Queen, hardly daring to breathe until she was again in the now familiar anteroom.

With a faint rustling, her Aunt Henrietta swept up to her. "Was it quite awesome?" she inquired. "Never mind that now. We shall take a turn about the Drawing Room first. We should congratulate The Honorable Lucinda Mortimer and her mother. There she is, over there with her intended, the Marquis of Beaumont! Look! There is Lady Bullstode, accompanied by the Marquis of Bradbury. I believe she is bringing him over to pay his respects!"

The next day, Cat sat restlessly inside her aunt's carriage as they moved slowly through the crowded streets on their way to Tattersall's Corner, *haut* London's horse market. "I am sure we should have gotten here much earlier. At home, all the best buys are to be made by ten o'clock. After that, there is nothing left but the hacks and the spavined."

Her aunt laughed and put a calming hand upon her arm. "Dear Cat, this is London. I assure you nobody is out at that hour but the grooms and the daughters of Paphos going home from a long night's work. As it is, it is but three. We shall be horribly early and, I fear, dreadfully conspicuous."

"I shall be very businesslike, Aunt. I have bargained before. Besides, see with what care I have chosen my clothes." She had indeed dressed quietly, in a rich cream dress and brown pelisse, with sturdy but elegant half boots. Her hair, dressed with woven braids, was caught up by a neat little hat of forest green.

Henrietta smiled. "Well, if we are conspicuous, you are dressed with exceptionally good taste, and it will do us well to be noticed. If you wish to speak in confidence, simply spread your fan and speak from behind it *sotto voce*. It is a wonderful tactic to use when we must venture forth into Man's world."

As Henrietta predicted, the sale had not even begun, although there were quite a few small crowds of gentlemen moving from horse dealer to horse dealer. Others were inspecting hooves or teeth while eager grooms held the animals in position. Out in the ring, a bay cob trotted in a circle on a lunge lead.

"Hurry," Cat said, grabbing her aunt's wrist as soon as their carriage slowed to a halting roll.

"Cat," Henrietta replied sharply. "You will not act in such a childish manner. You are not five, and this is not a Christmas treat. We are looking for a serviceable lady's mount for you to ride in the Park."

"Serviceable mount be damned," Cat nearly said. Shocked by her own vehement reaction against her aunt's intention, Cat thought more calmly, "That's what you think. That is not what I intend to have." She said, "Oh please, Aunt, let me just choose my own, as you promised." She snapped open her fan and murmured "I will give you an entertaining lecture on what is really going on while I look for a good horse." She laughed. Henrietta snapped open her fan in answer. In good spirits and feeling well agreed, the two stepped down into the dust, straw, sawdust, and crowds that were Tattersall's Corner on auction day.

George Augustus Frederick, Baron of Renfrew, Earl of Chester, Earl of Carrick, Duke of Rothesey, Duke of Cornwall, and Prince of Wales, watched lazily as the two females wandered about, inspecting the horses shown by the dealers, pausing awhile to gawk and giggle beneath their fans and then walk on. In that, they showed more sense than did several of the men who were actually talking to the dealers. As he continued to watch, he further noted that they spent the longest time eyeing the horses standing in the pens or being put through their paces on the lunge leads by experienced horse trainers. With the younger woman shepherding the elder, they never stopped for an elaborate address from a dealer with flashy but unsound horseflesh, no matter how enticingly ingratiating his description. Instead, they seemed to be gravitating in their circular perambulations to Tweedmuir's stalls, where the best horseflesh was generally to be found, along with the keenest eyes in finding it. Could this be a female who actually understood the art of horse buying? He sauntered nearer, his companions following him, the better to hear what transpired.

About an hour had passed since they had first alighted from the carriage. Cat had amused her aunt, as promised, by describing all the faults in the horses on display and how the ignorant buyers were being gulled or mislead. Henrietta laughed at the self-defeating assumption of knowledge by the unfortunate men who were being so rudely tricked.

"And are you sure that you cannot be fooled, as these have been?"

"You cannot be fooled if you keep your mind on your intent. I know well what I am looking for and will know it when I see it." Her eyes swept the various rings, judging the spirit of the animals by their gaits, how they held their heads, a spirited flick of the tail, or the white of a rolled eye, a flattened ear.

"There," she said, "that one entering the ring now, the strawberry-roan. I've had my eye on him since we entered."

"What about this sweet little mare here, Miss," wheedled a wizened vendor at the stall next to them. He held the reins of a fine-boned gentle chestnut mare of about fourteen hands. "Just the thing for a young lady like yourself to ride in the Park of a Sunday morning."

"If I were a young lady of about five and still on leading reins," Cat replied imperiously. "That mare is at least sixteen years on, broken in wind, and weak in the fetlocks. Pretty she may be, but a ride on my nursery hobby-horse would have more spirit and speed!"

"Well said," the Prince of Wales murmured to his attendants. "You are my advisor on horseflesh, Fairfax. Does she know what she speaks?"

Vere looked briefly at the proffered little mare. He had been watching Cat with quiet pleasure all morning, feeling almost in a state of grace from the largesse of being able to regard her unobserved so tenderly. "Oh, indeed, she is quite correct in her judgment. So much so, I wonder if she will not outbid you on the horse you desire. She has had her eye on that strawberry roan you covet this past half-hour. See how she watches him in the ring. She will bid for him."

"Perhaps we can put her off him. Come, what are the horse's faults?"

Fairfax regarded the roan. "He fights for his head; see there how he pulls against the line. Now he speeds to a gallop. He will try to bolt with his rider." The dealer signaled the trainer to bring the horse over. As he seized the halter, the horse reared, trying to pull free. "That horse will challenge any rider for dominance. Only the very skillful should try to handle him, Your Royal Highness."

"And I suppose that only includes yourself, Fairfax. Your skill is too well-known for you to have to boast of it."

"Your Royal Highness draws his own conclusions. Do you intend to bid?"

"Perhaps we should inform the young lady of the deficiencies of her choice," he said. Together, the Prince and Fairfax followed the two women to the enclosure in Tattersall's indoor ring.

When the roan was brought in, Cat stood patiently by as the dealer extolled the horse. She knew that the tiresome recitation was necessary for business, but she was determined on this horse and was anxious for the bidding to begin. Her irritation surfaced as a drawling fool standing just behind her spoke.

"Such a horse is not for you. He will fight for his head and bolt with you. Surely a less troublesome mount would suit you better."

Without taking her glance off the dealer, she replied shortly, "Sir, I am well able to handle this mount. He is spirited merely and can be trained by a good rider to his paces, but he must have the run of his heels. If it were not well-known that the men here are gentlemen, I would think that you were trying to frighten away a young woman who is also a competing bidder." Behind her, there was a collective gasp. Even her aunt turned pale and dropped a quick apologetic curtsey. Cat was far too interested in the clean strong configuration of the horse before her even to notice for some minutes that the dealer was standing quietly looking at them.

Finally, aware of the unnatural silence, she turned and looked behind her. Coloring with astonishment, she saw first Mr. Fairfax. He was looking at her with an inscrutable expression. Then she blushed a deeper rose on seeing the Prince of Wales, the man to whom she had so impertinently replied. She made a quick and graceful curtsey in amends.

"The King's Swan," he said loudly. "Brave as well as beautiful. You are correct, Fairfax. Only the very skillful should try to ride this mount. Let us continue." He sauntered away.

Cat's face blanched at the audacity of his words. She looked at Mr. Fairfax with a cold and killing eye. His lips were bloodless, pressed closely together. He bowed to her and turned away sharply. Everybody was staring at them now. Wordlessly, she turned back to the dealer, who, obviously relieved, opened the bidding.

Vere, his face a thundercloud, strode after the Prince. Georgy Porgy had lost none of the execrable self-centeredness that had marked his youth and middle years. Now Cat would think that Vere had been abusing herself and her reputation to the Prince for his own coarse amusement. He had the most cursed luck.

"Well, my Dear!" exclaimed her aunt rapturously from behind her fan. "The Prince actually spoke to you. By tomorrow, everyone will know you as the King's Swan. How fortunate you thought to come here. You must of course buy this horse!"

STRATEGIES

Dessed in a rich brown riding habit, Cat waited impatiently as the groom tried to cinch the oiled leather strap of the saddle about the restless roan's belly. She would have preferred to do it herself, but the coachman was most insistent.

"It's not yer place to do it, Miss Llewellyn. Her ladyship would never forgive us if something 'twer to go wrong."

"I could have done it better myself in half the time." She stepped up to pat Jupiter's great head, calming him with some apple slices. The groom quickly finished his business and took the reins, preparatory to leading her horse over to the mounting block. Cat hated the elaborate ceremony of life in Town. It was so pompous and inefficient! Left to herself, she would have arrived in the Park a quarter of an hour gone! With determined dignity, which hid her haste well, Cat accepted the groom's assistance in adjusting her stirrup. As soon as he had finished and stepped back, she loosed the reins a trifle, and with a light flick of her whip proceeded at a brisk trot out of the stable mews and towards Hyde Park, leaving the groom to scramble after her as quickly as he could.

She was pleased with the big horse. He had spirit and speed, and the brilliance of his roan coat made them an unmistakable pair. She was determined to set London on its ear with demonstrations of her horsemanship. No demure debutante she, she would throw a challenge to all the *haut monde* of London. Only the boldest and the best could attempt to win her. Her dear aunt was a shockingly bad horsewoman and so would know nothing of her plan at all.

The gates of the Park drew near. The brilliant, soft, spring afternoon had brought out every kind of rider and carriage. The North Carriage Lane was jammed with vehicles, and Ladies Mile was thick with riders: mothers with children on ponies and fat husbands on sturdy cobs. It was vexing. Jupiter snorted with impatience as she reined in. There was no room for a mad gallop here, not even a brisk canter. She bit her lip in disappointment.

She would ride on Rotten Row. The dandies showed off their horseflesh there, and she knew herself to be impeccable when mounted. Her groom had caught up with her, following slightly behind and to her left as the horses picked their way among the slower moving riders. As she passed a stopped carriage, the slender gentleman dressed in grey conversing there looked at her briefly before again returning his attentive smiling gaze to the handsome older woman in the fashionable landau. Shortly thereafter, with many gallant protestations of devotion, he turned his smooth-gaited grey toward the Row.

Vere Courtenay Fairfax found some brief surcease from his impatience and desire in exercising the tall black gelding in the Park. And the Park was an excellent place to observe the Comte du Foix. Like most people of Fashion, he was seen frequently there. Unlike the others, his purposes were wider and more dangerous than mere social jockeying. From his investigations of the low dives and various hells the Comte was known to frequent, Vere deduced that funds were ever his weak point. The paymaster system Napoleon's agents had created was very ingenious, but it kept the agents-in-place on a very tight leash. In an operation like this, thought Vere, the resignation of Fouché, Napoleon's spymaster, was a tactical disaster. Details and suggestions for exploitation of that blunder were already before Lord Carrington and those who were in his confidence. Fairfax thought that he might have one idea how the Comte was making up the deficit in his funds. Reaching the end of the Row in a lazy canter, he wheeled the black and trotted back toward the Ladies Mile. Cat reined in her impatient horse as she observed the Row. As much as she longed to spur to a gallop, there were too many people proceeding at a decorous trot. To overrun them would be horridly ill-mannered, even though some small demon inside her thrilled to do it. Still, she might manage a canter, if she found space enough in the traffic. Clicking her tongue lightly, she set heels into her willing steed, and with great eagerness, her horse set off in a spirited trot. Behind her, the Comte followed at a discreet walk.

Vere saw her coming long before she was cognizant of him. The beautiful coat of the strawberry roan shone whitely in the nimbus of sunlight. Putting himself and his horse to an even stricter discipline, he rode steadily, stonefaced, towards her. No expression or gesture could be allowed to suggest that he knew her. She could never acknowledge his previous acquaintance in public, nor would she want to, he thought, again wincing at the malice of the Prince's words yesterday.

Steadily, the distance between their paths closed. She sat proudly straight upon her tall horse, manifesting the power and control of a pagan queen. Boudicca would face the Romans thus, he mused, though not riding sidesaddle. She spurred her horse to a powerful canter. Unwilled, but not unwanted, came the thought of Cat galloping toward that dawn fence, thighs spread, knees tight about the great horse's ribs. How they must have soared, yoked in power. His heart in flight, his face a mask, he joined them in imagination, bonded and became the ridden as she passed him by in a flurry of hooves, her young face alight with life and passion.

She saw him ahead of her, approaching at a disciplined trot, his strict control a mockery of his dangerous sensual nature. Challenged by his show of indifference, she resolved that he would take note of her, publicly become her helpless admirer, and that with him thus reduced to an abject state, she might pay him back in like coin for the humiliation that he had made her feel. Assuming her haughtiest expression, practiced for hours before the mirror last evening, she flicked Jupiter into an easy rocking canter. Nearer she came and nearer, fully aware of the stares of the young dandies, now fastened solely on her. She fixed her eyes on some middle distance, hotly aware of him as they drew abreast: the proud insolence of his control, the power in him that fused man and beast and made them one. Her heartbeat matched their hoofbeats until she felt that she might sway in the saddle, then she had passed him by and was gone. She reined Jupiter in as she drew abreast of a gouty old man, a friend of her aunt's. She recognized him with a gracious smile and, accompanied again by the groom, sedately rode by his side while he clucked over her youth and beauty and became the object of envy of every young buck there.

The Comte du Foix rode deliberately towards Vere and sketched a polite salute. He had watched them both with a bland smile that revealed nothing of his conclusions. Keeping his face carefully pleasant, he said with reluctant regret, "Monsieur Fairfax, I have unfinished business with you. Might you spare me a moment?"

Fairfax drew rein with interest. He had been stalking the Comte with the hope of just such an opportunity. Betraying nothing of his excitement, he selected a tone of great hauteur and replied loftily, "I do not recall any unfinished business between us, but I am curious enough to spare you a moment."

"You have examined me closely on several occasions. Your attentions, Sir, verge on the impertinent. I have, in fact, taken offense."

"Indeed, Comte du Foix," Fairfax murmured. "Please enlighten me as to this offense."

"In your pursuit of my habits," the Comte said in a sneering tone of deliberate emphasis, "you must surely have noticed my favorite color is grey."

Vere made no reply, but merely sat and looked at the Comte with a steady gaze that revealed nothing of his thinking. The Comte du Foix continued.

"You deprived me of my prize. Those horses and carriage were to be mine, and your interference deprived me of them."

"I merely made him a better offer," Vere replied. "I fancied them myself."

"It was a debt of honor," the Comte continued, "in which you had no right to interfere."

"Oh, but I did," Vere interjected smoothly. "The debt owed was to be paid in money or with the equipage. I merely made it possible for him to pay in money, rather than the turnout you wanted. I regret the disappointment," he said in a tone that betrayed no regret at all.

"Nevertheless, I desire the team and their carriage. I am prepared to dispute you for their possession."

"And how do you determine to do that?" Vere inquired languidly, hoping deliberate insolence was a goad to this man.

The Comte looked at him carefully. Fairfax was a dangerous enemy, and it would not do to underestimate him. The Comte smiled knowingly, sure in the knowledge that Fairfax had underestimated him. Choosing a tone that barely concealed chill contempt, he replied, "As the original wager was a sporting one, and I have heard you are a man of sport, I propose another wager of the same sort."

"Another dubious challenger with heavy odds? I think not, Comte du Foix, your . . . luck is too well-known."

The Comte remained unruffled, despite the insult. "I propose something more particular between us," he said smoothly. "As I take your possession of my equipage as a personal insult, I suggest we settle this with a boxing match. I have heard that you are well-known at the Academy of Monsieur Jackson."

"I have boxed there," Vere replied coolly. "What is your proposal?"

The Comte smiled lazily, a cat with cream on his whiskers. "Simply this, a match between us at the Fives Court in which the last man standing wins."

Fairfax looked steadily at du Foix. "Agreed. Have your seconds contact Lord Carleton."

Cat walked demurely down to the drawing room. Freshly gowned after her afternoon ride, her white muslin dress with its pale-green embroidered flounces emphasized her blooming youth. However, something new had entered her eyes and expression. The full drama of her headstrong desires began to show itself. From within came the low voices of women in conversation. Henrietta's visitor must be Lady Bullstrode again. Cat sighed. A little of her ladyship went a long way. No doubt, she had some more advice. Cat opened the door, resigning herself to endure more well-meant homilies.

The two women paused in mid-sentence as Cat entered. Lady Bullstrode was dressed, for once, in comparative moderation. Her grey and green gown was uncharacteristically subdued. She set her cup down with a flourish and smiled brightly at Cat. "Our Hunting Diana returns," she said with a smile. "I was telling your aunt that it seems you are following in the footsteps of Her Grace, the Duchess of Devonshire."

Aunt Henrietta smiled and patted the settee beside her, indicating that Cat should sit. "Lady Bullstrode reports that your performance in the Park was greatly admired by the *beau monde*. You are becoming an object of universal scrutiny."

"I had no object save that of enjoying my horse," demurred Cat, her eyes studiously examining the worked flowers on the carpet beneath her feet.

Lady Bullstrode gave her a hard calculating look as Cat continued to avoid her eyes. "I see you have decided to play a more spirited game than originally intended. I suppose it is inevitable, being who you are. You will not be content to merely sit and be beautiful. Well, Her Grace was very much like you when she came to town. At seventeen, she married His Grace, the Duke of Devonshire, and has been a notable light of Society ever since. You could do worse than to imitate her."

"I am not imitating anyone," Cat said softly. "I am just being myself."

"And that can be very dangerous indeed," smiled Henrietta. "You cannot know the perils attendant on such a course, but I see we shall have no choice in the matter. Very well. Remember you have given your pledge to be guided by me. Are you prepared to honor it, or am I to send you home immediately?"

"Of course I will keep my word. It was just a short canter in the Park. I do not understand why you are making such a mare's nest of this. What did I do that was so wrong?"

Lady Bullstrode smiled, a hard, tight, little smile. "My Dear Child, there are two kinds of women who come to us for the Season. The first are gentle well-bred young ladies who are content to watch sedately from the sidelines, to display their charms passively at ball and dinner, sweet children of tender years and uncomplicated desires. Their quiet modesty is no challenge to the lord who seeks a tractable wife. They will nearly always make a match if their beauty and dowry be sufficient. As to what will happen later, that is unknown, but most return to the country and bear at their lord's pleasure what he will."

"The second kind," Lady Leacock continued, "are both headstrong and youthful. They play their many admirers off one against another. They are always noted, wherever they are. They are bold without being vulgar, masterful without being shrewish, and imperious, all without losing their feminine nature. It is a very difficult game to play successfully." Lady Leacock sighed and put down her cup. "But as you are determined to play this game, I see nothing to it but to help you as much as possible with it."

"All this," Cat exclaimed, the flush of color rising prettily to her cheeks in pique, "because of one ride in the Park? How came you to decide all this from that?"

"Hush, Child, do not take offense," rejoined Lady Bullstrode. "I saw you in the Park, as did everyone else. I know you will not be content to play the passive doll, awaiting your Fate. You are determined to play a high hand, and we," she smiled broadly, her conspiratorial glance taking in Henrietta as well, "are going to help stack the deck!"

Cat looked from one to the other. Both ladies were smiling at her now. How amusing would they find her plan to humiliate Mr. Fairfax? That idea she would hold close to herself. Helping herself to a cup of tea, she smiled at them in return. "And just how do you intend to do that?" she asked them with a sweet smile that fooled no one.

From the Park, Vere Courtenay Fairfax rode through London's crowed streets to Jackson's Boxing Academy on Old Bond Street. He looked forward to engaging the Comte at last. The encounter had put his blood up, and a little sparring practice would be a relief from the tensions of these past days. Inside, he was greeted by a swirl of the raucous uncomplicated laughter of men engaged in sporting wagers. Signaling to an attendant, he headed toward the changing room. As he stripped off his coat and shirt, he called over his shoulder, "See if Mr. Jackson is at leisure to attend me."

"As it happens, I am right here, Mr. Fairfax," Jackson's hoarse loud voice boomed. "Been wondering when you would show. Have something here you might be very interested in."

Fairfax turned to him. Jackson was holding a betting book in his hand. "An interesting and profitable wager of which you wish to inform me? I am most obliged if you will set down my name. Are the odds very favorable?"

"So far, the betting is running five to one, which is favorable enough. Are you not a bit curious as to who might be the Fancy's White-Haired Boy?"

"Most certainly," Vere replied. "Might it not be young Thomas Cribb, whom you have promised to me as a sparring partner?"

"As to that matter, I have sent for him immediately. Ye'll get fine work out o' him today, no doubt. No, in this matter, it is yourself whom the odds favor. Against our favorite French Comte. The book has been circulating for several days. I wondered when you were going to appear."

Vere's expression hardened. "As well you should wonder. As do I. We only agreed on the match this morning. What is your idea on this?"

Jackson rubbed his hands together. "There is some mischief being planned, I've no doubt. 'Twas begun by some hanger-on friend of du Foix, Mr. Ranulph, younger son of Baron Carmody. I don't like the look of it, Mr. Fairfax."

Vere was standing stripped to his breeches. He held out his hands for the attendant to lace up the mauleys. "Have you seen him box, Jackson?"

Jackson wrinkled his brow in thought. "I cannot say that I have, although it seems he sparred here once or twice. Quick but slender. Not the strength you've got," he said, looking with approval at Vere's powerful back, wide shoulders, and long well-muscled arms. "'Tis a pity you are a gentleman," Jackson continued with a broad wink. "I could put you in the ring myself and make a right good sum of it too! I suspect him of some trick. I just cannot fathom what it is."

"Never mind it, then," Vere said. "Just show me this Thomas Cribb, and let's put him to some honest work."

Jackson grinned at Vere, his eyes sparkling with wolfish glee. "'Twill be some honest work for you, Mr. Fairfax, to put Tom Cribb away. He's going to be England's champion, you mark my words. Even the Prince has come down to watch him. Come along now, and I'll introduce you two."

The human buzz barely abated as Vere and Tom Cribb entered the ring. If anything, it grew greater when it became generally known that Cribb's sparring opponent was Vere Courtenay Fairfax. "I don't like the smell o' this," Jackson mumbled to himself. Why a book on a fight before one of the main participants had even agreed to it? He watched with a critical eye as the two men sparred lightly with each other, testing their strengths, taking each other's measure. Certainly, Fairfax could match Cribb for strength. Fairfax had a quick elegance in landing a punch, but Cribb was built like a bull and could take a great deal of punishment without being leveled, still returning blow for blow, battering his opponent from close in.

Droplets of sweat shone on Vere's body as he circled Cribb, looking for a weakness. Cribb had blocked Vere's lefts twice with Mendoza's guard. Vere had barely slipped Cribb's right crosses, and Vere's upper-cut had failed to find the target, being warded off by Cribb's powerful forearms. Cribb then rallied with a quick down-cut. Moving quickly, Vere stepped inside the circle of the other's defense, feinted a body blow, and then landed a gravedigger left. It rocked Tom's head back, but did not drop him. Lunging forward, exceptionally quickly for a man of his blocky build, Cribb rallied with a one-two and aimed a blow deep into Vere's stomach, one that Vere was only partially successful at deflecting. It took the wind out of him, and he aimed his cross-cut with less accuracy, achieving only a glancing hit to Cribb's jaw. Cribb bored in with a straight right, forcing Vere to mill on the retreat. Jackson looked at his watch. They had been sparring for near thirty minutes. He signaled for a break and climbed into the ring, where Vere sat.

"A pretty fair piece of work," Jackson noted judiciously. "You still have power and speed, but I can see you've not had a worthy opponent for a while. Too much time in silken combat, eh?" he laughed.

Vere took a long drink of water. "Sometimes the one is worse than the other," he said ruefully. "I believe I prefer a dance with Tom Cribb to an elegant ball with all the ladies of the *ton*. Less harrowing to the nerves."

Jackson looked at him shrewdly. "Do you mean to tell me you may have finally lost your heart to some fair Angelic at Almack's?" He stared at Fairfax a minute more, while the other man toweled the sweat off his naked upper body. "I do believe you have," he pronounced with a laugh. "This is cause for celebration." He waved over one of his ring handlers. "A bottle of my finest and two glasses."

Vere looked at him with annoyance. "This is no time to play the fool, Jackson. I think we must suspect some trickery on the part of our friend the Comte du Foix. I am not happy about that last punch. I should have blocked it. Save the wine until later. I want another round." Tossing his towel over the ropes, Vere stood and signaled to Cribb that he was ready to resume.

"If that's the way you want it, Mr. Fairfax, Tom Cribb will oblige." Jackson stood and climbed out of ring. "Keep close, you are too open. Tom!" he called "Go straight for him. Make him work." He sat down and signaled for an ale as he watched Tom Cribb wade into his distinguished patron, while Fairfax parried as many blows as he could, his powerful frame rocking against the shock, his quick hands reaching suddenly inside Cribb's defense to hit him with a left to the side of the head, a right uppercut to the jaw.

Tom staggered, but did not fall. A smaller man like du Foix would be counted out already, Jackson mused. What was Fairfax up to? "Block it, block it," he cried again, as Cribb bore in, his punch landing squarely in Fairfax's midsection, knocking his wind out and staggering him on his feet. Fairfax recovered enough to check Cribb's next hit, a powerful right aimed again at his sternum. Fairfax followed it with two body blows of his own, slamming Cribb backwards. Unfazed, Cribb circled around, searching out Fairfax's weakness, seeking again to get inside his guard. Vere was breathing heavily, watching warily as Cribb circled. With sudden speed, drawing on his reserves of strength, Vere quickly stepped inside his opponent's defensive zone and landed two quick powerful jabs to the head before Cribb's heavy right fist caught him on the jaw, making him stagger, but not dropping him. Feeling the effect, Vere gathered to himself all of the energy he had left. Keeping low and guarded, Vere rained upon the thicker, younger man a series of hard, quick jabs to face and midsection, followed with a hard left muzzler that rocked Cribb on his feet, but failed to level him.

Shining now with sweat, the two men circled each other, looking for a definitive opportunity. Jackson could see that Fairfax was tiring. His great height was not an advantage against the more compact Cribb, once Cribb got inside the other's defenses. However, such was the power of Vere's punches that any other man would have been counted out long ago. Cribb came back at Fairfax with a one-two. Vere stepped back and shot a straight-armed right to Cribb's ribs. Cribb shifted and cut away, but not fast enough to avoid it altogether. Countering, he landed a winder that drove Fairfax to his knees.

Judging Fairfax exercised enough, Jackson signaled for the end of the contest. In a hearty voice, he cried, "That's enough time for you both; you will not bring each other down this day." Signaling the ring attendants to bring towels for the fighters, he continued, "I want you both in my back room for a glass. I would have a private word with you." Thus pronouncing, he went into his parlor to ponder the vexing question of why the Comte was encouraging such odds against himself and what trickery he was plotting.

Later, Jackson, Vere and Cribb sat quietly ensconced in comfortable chairs around several glasses of excellent claret. Neither looked too much the worse for wear, although Jackson suspected that each might be moving a little more cautiously than usual.

Looking at Vere with a shrewd eye, Jackson commenced, "Mr. Fairfax, I suspect this upcoming match. The Comte is planning some trickery, mark my words. What are the terms of the wager?"

"Most simple, Mr. Jackson. The last man standing wins."

"So du Foix has something in mind that makes him think he can drop you. And you are not an easy man to knock down, eh, Tom?"

"No, Sir," Tom replied with a grin. "I did my best, I nearly had you, and I may have had you yet," he added impishly, "if Mr. Jackson here hadn't intervened."

"Well, there will be no intervention in our bout," Vere replied grimly. "So the Comte du Foix believes he can both knock me down and lay me out. Now why does he believe that, I wonder?"

"How much time do we have until the bout?" Jackson asked.

"The date has not been set, but I believe du Foix will request it for sometime after next week's ball at Almack's. If he is looking for a bride with money, I doubt he wants any damage to his pretty face."

"That gives us time to work. If you are right, he will want to wear the mauleys. No need to pickle your knuckles and spoil your gentleman's fine hands," Jackson laughed. "You need to practice your blocking. I would bet he intends to go after your center and keep hitting until you fall. Although how he intends to do that and keep out of your reach, I cannot fathom. I foresee you will be spending a great deal more of your precious time here, Mr. Fairfax."

Vere laughed. "That will suit me well, Mr. Jackson."

"Then drink up, Mr. Fairfax. 'Tis the last spirit you will have for a while." He watched thoughtfully while Vere drained the glass. "A question for you, Mr. Fairfax. Do you dance?"

THE OPERA

Cat paced in the hallway, awaiting her Aunt Henrietta's descent. They were going to the opera! They would share Lady Bullstrode's box, up in the fourth tier, just to the right and above Mrs. Fitzherbert's box, where the Prince of Wales was generally in attendance. It was an excellent location from which to observe three-fourths of the *ton* and to be observed. Cat paused in her restless round to observe herself in the mirror.

Tonight, her other self wore silver-colored satin. Her coiled and curled hair fell in one lone lock across her forehead, partially veiling her left eye as it hung down by her left cheek, all held in place by a single large pearl-headed pin, which matched the lustrous sheen of her dress and her teardrop pearl earrings. She stared at herself, more alabaster statue than living girl, in the silvery depths of the mirror. "Who?" she thought.

"You look like the Queen of the Night herself!" Lady Leacock exclaimed from the stairway behind Cat. "What a coup this will be. Your dress perfectly matches the opera! Everybody is sure to take note."

"*The Magic Flute* is one of my favorite operas, Aunt, but surely you must know that the Queen of the Night is the villain of the piece!"

"Oh, nobody will pay any attention to the plot! Do not fear any meaning to the allusion! It will be enough that they connect you with the title. There are still a few Royal Dukes available!" she smiled.

"Dear Aunt!" Cat interjected hastily, "I am quite sure I am not attracted to any Royal Duke in the least and would have you put it out of your mind immediately!"

"Well perhaps not a Royal Duke," Lady Leacock mused, "but another Duke mayhap would be acceptable. Certainly no one lower than an Earl!"

Thinking on Mr. Fairfax, Cat laughingly said, "I quite agree: no one lower than an Earl."

"Well, we should see quite a few of them on display tonight. The opera is another great hunting ground, where all the world passes to view itself. You have already been noted several times. Tonight, they will all see you, and you will see them, so that you may pick and choose among them before you meet at Almack's. I have the opera glasses. Let us depart."

Vere sat a bit stiffly in his carriage on the way to the opera. *The Magic Flute* was being sung, and it was his favorite opera for many reasons, not all of them musical. Still, he thought that he would have, on the whole, rather stayed home in a comfortable armchair and read after his hot bath. The sparring with Cribb had been the least of his aches, he thought ruefully. It was the "dancing" lesson with Jackson that had really strained him.

"He's gong to come at you from some unexpected direction. Maybe ducking and weaving, coming in from low," Jackson had said. "You have to be ready to pivot and twist as well as block. And move about too, quick like. He'll not come at you like yon stolid ox that wades right in and stays until he's knocked out. Now, again."

Prinny had sent Vere a ticket to Mrs. Fitzherbert's box. Maybe he had been ashamed of his behavior at Tattersall's. More than likely, he had hugely enjoyed Vere's discomfiture and sent him the ticket in malicious thanks for the amusement Vere had provided. That would be more like Prinny. Nevertheless, despite the occasional infamy of being known as one of the Prince's set, Vere quite enjoyed the view from that box and fully intended on employing it.

Fairfax was satisfied that whatever the sartorial excesses of his erstwhile companions in the box, he was soberly dressed as an impeccable gentleman. The new, severely tailored coat of midnight blue bath superfine magnificently set off the whiteness of his linen, his neckerchief elegantly tied in the Waterfall pattern. Among the gaudy dandies, he could pass almost unnoticed, yet be instantly perceived by those of taste, distinction, or power. His opposition would mark him well. Certainly, all hope of infiltration was lost. The oblique struggle was accomplishing what direct action could not, hindering Montclair's operations, while allowing Carrington time to investigate and entrap Montclair with all his spies and accomplices. He would probably be here tonight. Fairfax smiled a ruthless smile. He hoped there would be a further encounter.

"Well, Dear, what do you think?" Lady Leacock inquired of her niece after they had settled themselves in Lady Bullstrode's box. All around them, the four tiered rows of boxes displayed their glittering occupants. Beautiful women in brightly colored gowns, sparkling with jewels, bloomed lavishly like so many orchids. Beside them, handsome men, white-haired fathers, and portly husbands came and went, bringing champagne, flattery, and gossip. Fans flashed, and young debutantes leaned close to their chaperones and whispered hopes, dreams, and fancies. Cat perused the scene before her with the avidity and the wonder of all her seventeen years. "They are all so beautiful, dear Aunt. How can I hope to compete!"

Lady Leacock laughed. "And they are all known so well. You have the advantage of novelty, and you are very beautiful. They will all be looking at you tonight."

On the other side of Henrietta, Lady Bullstrode bowed and smiled. "I believe there are your neighbors, the Thomas ladies. Over on the King's side, the fourth tier, to your left," she said as she sketched a salute with her fan. "We would do well to keep on friendly terms with them."

Cat, looking where she was directed, nodded and smiled. Clarissa was dressed in pink silk, her shining golden curls wound with silk rosebuds.

"How jejune," sniffed Lady Bullstrode, "much the safest course. She will certainly be no competition to you. Alaster," she called to her servant, "Please go to yonder box with my compliments and invite those two ladies to visit us at their convenience. That," she said with a smile to Henrietta and Cat, "will keep the gossips at bay." She followed the ensuing drama carefully through her opera glasses, nodding and saluting their effusive response across the distance that separated them.

Below them, in Mrs. Fitzherbert's box, Vere strove to keep boredom and sleep at bay while he waited for the overture. Prinny was there, with a large noisy party. Lady Jersey, encountered just outside the box, had been obnoxiously officious. "You have been too long absent from our company, Mr. Fairfax!" she had scolded, fluttering her lashes behind her carved Chinese fan. "Are the ladies of the Continent so fascinating, then, that you should desert poor us?"

"Your ladyship knows all," Vere said shortly, not caring.

"Ha, Fairfax!" called the Prince of Wales, overhearing the exchange. "We invite you for your delicious insolence, and you never disappoint!" He laughed uproariously at Lady Jersey's discomfiture as Lady Jersey departed in a huff for her own box.

Obviously, the rumors Vere had heard on the Continent of the two being on the outs and Lady Jersey's desperate attempts to regain her position were true.

"Have you broken any horses since our last meeting, or have you been too busy dodging the embraces of young Tom Cribb? I've already got my name down in the book."

"On which side, Your Royal Highness?" Vere inquired with chill politeness.

His Royal Highness, George, the Prince of Wales, ignored him. He was intent upon viewing the boxes through his opera glasses. "I don't see the King's Swan here tonight. I am disappointed," he said aloud.

"Perhaps she is in Lady Bullstrode's box," Mrs. Fitzherbert snapped. "Is it worse, I wonder, or better, to be deprived of seeing either your King's Swan or Lady Bullstrode?"

"No doubt Her Grace, the Duchess of Devonshire, could tell you," Prinny replied absently. "There she is, at her box, third at the end of the row opposite. George is with her."

"Oh yes," Mrs. Fitzherbert laughed mirthlessly, looking at them across the horseshoe shaped tier of boxes. "Your favorite, Beau Brummell. The insinuating little monkey."

Vere looked with more interest through his glasses. Georgiana, the Duchess of Devonshire, had always been a favorite of his. He looked forward to greeting her later in her box. He realized with a start that Cat was indeed very like Georgiana. Cat would be here tonight without a doubt. His blood stirred with desire.

From above, Lady Leacock whispered to Cat. "Do you see the woman below, in the third box from the end of the second tier? That is Her Grace, the Duchess of Devonshire. The comparisons made between you are inevitable." She looked more intently. "I do believe she is saluting us! What a very great honor!"

Beside her, Lady Bullstrode chuckled. "I believe we will be invited to join them during the intermission. Even Her Grace is anxious to see this new paradigm, all the more because you recall to her her own youth!"

Alaster knocked, and the two Ladies Thomas entered. Lady Bullstrode welcomed them with effusive kindness and watched with benign, unblinking eye as the two ladies saluted one another. The young ladies greeted each other with all the appearance of that friendship shown by neighbors who meet far from home.

"Lady Bullstrode, Lady Leacock, what a pleasure to see you again. Such an evening! How lovely you all look!"

"Yes," smiled Clarissa, glancing around at all in turn without looking directly at Cat. "It is so exciting to see the world *en masse*. I do so long to meet them at the Ball!

"You probably shall," Lady Bullstrode smiled amiably. "You two must have a lot of stories to trade. Leave us to our own gossip."

"You looked quite lovely in your Presentation gown," Cat said impulsively. "I felt so colorless in my own."

"You are too kind," replied Clarissa. "I vow not one of us could compare with your impact. We hear you are called the King's Swan."

"I wish I were not," Cat confessed. "I am not pleased to be bandied about." She blushed, remembering the Prince's words at Tattersall's. What lascivious things, what thoughts of desire had Mr. Fairfax spoken, to cause that humiliating ribald jest? Within, where she could not mention, even to herself, she felt a powerful throb of desire.

Clarissa's mouth became a round "o," until she remembered to shut it. The chit did not wish to be talked about or noticed! What simple-minded fool was this? However, she knew that Cat might have real reasons to fear being talked about. What had passed between her and Mr. Fairfax? For all anybody knew, she might still be in clandestine contact with him. Resolving her strategy instantly, Clarissa laughed and said, "Pay them no attention; it is all small-minded pettiness. I know who you truly are. Continue to be yourself."

The veiled threat was not lost on Cat. "I know what you truly are also," she thought grimly. Outwardly, she smiled sweetly at Clarissa. "This is so very different from our small country assemblies. Being noticed by the world can be useful for many things and being unnoticed that much the worse for it. Would you not agree?"

"Oh indeed," said Clarissa, aware of the many eyes turned toward their box, clearly perceiving Cat's hidden meaning. "I prefer to be noticed, and thus I come to the opera. Lady

Bullstrode's box is nicely placed for observing, as well as being observed. Do you see any friends?"

"Truly, I have not been looking, though I know so few as yet. And you?"

Clarissa scanned the tiers intently. "I do think I see the Comte du Foix in that last box in the fourth tier. He is with a woman. How disappointing," she pouted.

"Perhaps he is there with a friend."

Clarissa continued to stare at the box. "Another man has entered. He is kissing the woman! Now he turns to the Comte. They embrace. You were right, Cat! He has exited the box. Perhaps he goes for champagne. I should ask Mama for ices!"

"Perhaps he will call on your box," Cat suggested, tired of Clarissa and her mama. "I do not have the pleasure of his intimate acquaintance," she said, "but by your account, he is reckoned a most charming man."

"Indeed, we should go," Clarissa agreed with alacrity, gathering her fan and reticule. Her mama had already reached the same conclusion. She rose and saluted both the older ladies. She said, seeing Cat, "I wish you great joy in your Season. I hope we shall see you often." She smoothed her skirts and hair, and, smiling benevolently at Clarissa, ushered her out of the box.

"How tiresome," Cat lamented once they were gone. "Are we to salute them at every event?"

"As much as is politic for neighbors and friends," answered Lady Bullstrode. There was a discreet knock on the door. Alaster let in a liveried footman who carried a note addressed to Lady Bullstrode. "Please give Her Grace our compliments and say we will attend her at the intermission," she said to the footman, whereon Alaster showed him out of the box. "We are to visit the Duchess of Devonshire at the conclusion of Act I. You will like the Duchess. Everyone does. And I suspect she will like you."

Below them, on stage, there was a rustling of anticipation, as the lights went down and the curtain come up on *The Magic Flute*, even as the undimmed society buzz went on as before. In the darkness, Cat forgot the Duchess and the Thomas women in the rising tide of music.

Cat, wrapped in the beauty of the voices and inundated by the haunting words and harmonies of Papageno's and Pamina's aria, whose sentiments spoke so nearly to her own, had no desire for the gaudy carnival that continued all around them.

From the box of Madame Reynard, in the fourth tier at the advantageous end point, Lucien Montclair, the Comte du Foix, watched intently from a posture of complete indifference as his unhurried, steady gaze found, each in turn, the players in his little game.

Fairfax slipped noiselessly out of the Fitzherbert box. Prinny and his friends were gossiping and paid no attention to the business on the stage. Her Grace was a lover of music; Fairfax could properly hear the music from her box and in better company too. It also occurred to him with a stab of heightened pleasure that if Cat were here in Lady Bullstrode's box, he would be able to observe her. With no appearance of haste, Vere strode to the Duchess's door. The footman posted there took Fairfax's card and passed within. Immediately, there was a laughing trill, and the door reopened.

"Peregrine," said a low vibrant voice from within, using her fond code name for him. "You have been too long away from us. George, give place to our wanderer."

"Don't move, Brummell," Vere contradicted her, smiling at the remembered affectionate name. "Your pardon, Your Grace, but I can just as easily hear the music from here," and he sat himself down in the darkened corner of the box to enjoy the music in quiet pleasure, unobserved by the glittering spectators while his ardent glance sought Cat.

"You can be the most annoying *connoisseur*, Vere, and you are always so perfectly justified. Now we will be quiet also in deference to your superior taste."

Vere smiled in acknowledgment to Her Grace's comment. She was a bit light-minded, but she had good sense generally and an even better heart. Thirteen years ago, she had been the one bright light in his darkness. She had been kind, and she had understood. On her left, George Brummell, already the supreme arbiter of men's fashion and complete ruler of the *ton*, nodded to Vere, as much an acknowledgment to Vere's tailor as to Vere himself, no doubt. He had met Brummell when the latter was but a newly commissioned officer in the Hussars. Vere found Brummell's impudence engaging and his meticulousness amusing. Brummell, to his credit, was not slow to recognize and even envy Vere's casual elegance. As much as two men of very differing temperament and experience could be friends, they were such.

From where he sat in shadow, Vere turned his dark-eyed gaze upward to where Cat was sitting. She was a veritable vision, so white and silver, sitting almost within her own glow. The soft sheen of the satin and the glow of her pearls made her a divine visitation from some happier world, he thought. In front of him, the Duchess whispered to Brummell. "Is not that the King's Swan in Lady Bullstrode's box? She of whom we hear so much?"

"Indeed," drawled Brummell, seeking her with his opera glasses. "Also known as the Hunting Diana. No doubt, some fool will soon suggest Queen of the Night."

"And what would be your suggestion?"

"I will have no suggestion until I meet the young lady."

"Then that is already accomplished, for they shall be visiting us as soon as this act ends. I expect to be impressed with your eloquence, Brummell."

"How can I say anything so wonderful, Your Grace, when she is but a shade of yourself? I cannot be more eloquent to the copy than the original and you have said that I have failed so far to impress."

Inside his shadowed darkness, Vere burnt with his own exquisite torment. If he stayed, the Duchess would surely introduce them. Such an introduction would allow him to approach her socially in front of all the *ton*. Not even Lady Bullstrode would dare to cut him when he was under the Duchess's patronage or within sight and hearing of Beau Brummell. Signaling to the attendant, Vere requested a glass of the vintage champagne from the bottle open on the table.

Vere would have trusted his nerves with pistols at ten paces, but he was not sure that he could speak three words to Cat when he faced her. Slowly sipping the light, dry vintage, he studied her face, which was transformed by the rapture of the music beyond mere beauty to a reflection of all that the soul longs for that is pure and high upon this mortal plane. He felt as if he had never loved her until this moment, and he resolved in that moment that somehow she should know of his feelings.

The intermission at the end of the first act brought much bustling in the tiered boxes. A great many visitations were occurring. The two ladies exited in the general rush, not noticing in their hurry that Mr. Fairfax was also a visitor to the Duchess's box. Cat followed nervously behind them. She was to meet Her Grace and Mr. Brummell, the ultimate arbiter of fashion. A set-down from him was a thing no person in Society could hope to survive. Breathing carefully to calm herself, Cat tried to avoid being crushed in the press of people. Nevertheless, she was aware of the many admiring glances that she was drawing. Proudly lifting her head and squaring her shoulders, she looked neither to the right nor the left, but imperiously through the figures that thronged her way, and concentrated upon how she would curtsey to Her Grace. Ahead, Lady Bullstrode and Lady Leacock had paused at the door of the third box. A bewigged, red-liveried footman opened it for them. "Lady Bullstrode, Lady Leacock, Miss Caitlyn Llewellyn," he announced.

From within came a low voice of dulcet tones, "Please come in, we have heard so much of you."

Cat had the immediate impression of warm eyes, a welcoming smile, a pale complexion rouged by a hectic flush. Beside this elegant woman stood a slender man with red-gold hair and an engaging and mischievous smile. Behind them both stood Mr. Fairfax, the dark angel sent to reeve her soul away. Gravely, while the others looked on, Cat bent her neck gracefully, dropping to a precise and steady curtsey. "Your Grace. An honor," she said, glad to avoid Mr. Fairfax's obsidian stare, which, like that of the basilisk, put her in mortal peril.

"I can see why you are taking the town by storm, my Dear. The King's Swan and the Hunting Diana," the Duchess said kindly. "How do you feel about being the belle of the Season?"

"I like it very much," Cat answered dishonestly. "Although it seems," she added daringly, directing a quick look at Fairfax where he stood at his ease behind the Duchess, "that one must suffer gladly the fools who make one the object of speculation. I mean," she continued quickly, "that I hope no one will add to me the sobriquet of 'Queen of the Night.'" The Duchess and Brummell exchanged a quick look.

"You have my sympathy," Brummell bowed, "and my full support."

"So you have already felt the gusty winds that blow 'round the Season's Favorite. So did I when I was your age. May I present to you Mr. Fairfax, a most dear friend of mine?" Georgiana, Duchess of Devonshire, smiled toward the tall saturnine man behind her.

"A pleasure," Lady Leacock replied for both of them.

"Lady Bullstrode, Lady Leacock, Mr. Fairfax."

"Your servant." He bowed to them both.

"Miss Llewellyn, Mr. Fairfax."

With faultless decorum, Vere stepped from the shadows and made her a courtly bow. "Miss Llewellyn," he said and no more.

"Mr. Fairfax," she replied softly.

The Duchess graciously indicated that they might sit, and the three visitors settled themselves in the vacant chairs arranged around the box. The red-liveried footman passed around glasses of sparkling champagne. Cat found herself advantageously placed between the Duchess on one hand and the Beau on the other. Lady Leacock sat on the other side of the Duchess, while Lady Bullstrode, uncharacteristically silent, sat grimly beside her. Behind the Beau, in the back, out of the direct line of sight, Mr. Fairfax sat with unstudied grace. She felt his eyes upon her, but was helpless to avoid his gaze.

Mr. Brummell looked idly through his opera glasses at the chattering crowds that filled the boxes. "They are all no doubt comparing the two of you. What do you suppose they are saying, Miss Llewelyn?"

"To be compared in any way to the Duchess must flatter me, Mr. Brummell. I imagine they say that as the Duchess married a Duke at the end of her Season, her imitation must be content with nothing less than an Earl."

"Is rank all that impresses you, Miss Llewellyn?"

"Indeed no, Mr. Brummell," she replied with energy, "A fine gentleman of noble heart must always have recommendation." Then, laughingly, she added, "but surely an Earl may have such qualities as well."

"You are clever in your flattery, Miss Llewellyn. Can you fault our new paradigm, Fairfax?"

"As I agree with her words, I find no fault in them."

"Now you have quite surprised us," the Duchess commented. "Fairfax agrees with no one, unless it be to turn their folly onto themselves."

"I shall take your Grace's warning seriously and seek to amend myself beforehand by being disagreeable, lest I commit to folly all unknowing," Cat replied, feeling the sudden heat that blushed her cheeks with a quick-blooming rose.

"The second act is about to begin, Caitlyn. We have trespassed upon her Grace's good nature long enough," Lady Leacock interjected. "We must return to our box."

"Please stay with us," Her Grace said. "We shall be quiet. Mr. Fairfax has commanded us to silence during the arias, and I have seen with what delight Miss Llewellyn has listened to the performance."

The lights grew dim again, sparing Cat's reply. That Mr. Fairfax should enjoy the opera enough to command silence from the Duchess did not totally surprise her. She remembered the books in his library and the poem she had found that seemed a window into his secret soul. She did not feel that she could remain in the intimacy of his presence. "Your Grace's pardon, but I would prefer to return to Lady Bullstrode's box. Such grand company as yourselves makes it most difficult to surrender completely to the music." She rose quickly to go, and Lady Leacock, surprised by Cat's words, rose with her.

Her Grace looked at Cat quizzically. "Go then, by all means, Child. We keep no prisoners here, though Mr. Fairfax is a stern jailer to all our gossip."

"Only while the music plays, Your Grace."

Cat hurriedly left the box, trailed by her puzzled aunt and a silent Lady Bullstrode. Her Grace turned to Mr. Fairfax, interrogation written large upon her face, but Vere closed his eyes against her and let other visions take her place.

From above, Clarissa observed the little drama in the Duchess's box. Few words had passed between Cat and Mr. Fairfax, Clarissa noted, but she saw how he watched her and had seen the nervous color that came and went upon Cat's cheeks when he addressed her. Beside her in the box, momentarily forgotten, the Comte du Foix spoke to her in sweetly persuasive tones.

"What do you see, Mademoiselle, that you stare so hard through your glasses? It must be very amusing. Surely you can tell me."

Clarissa glanced at her mother. Lady Thomas was in animated and loud conversation with Monsieur and Madame Reynard. Clarissa doubted that her mother would overhear. Some sense of caution prevailed, though, for she merely replied, "I wonder if there is not some sort of understanding between the King's Swan and Mr. Fairfax."

"On what basis do you draw your conclusions?" the Comte asked with interest.

"I have never seen two people so unwilling to be in each other's company."

"So, as they show no interest in each other, you assume they must have an understanding in private? Truly, the way a woman's mind works must always compel amazement."

"Or perhaps I have information that you lack," Clarissa said saucily.

"Your words interest me very much," Montclair replied, as the curtain went up.

Roberts sat alone at one of the back tables in the Horse and Groom and slowly sipped his pint of porter in perplexity. Several evenings ago, on letting that Frenchy Count out of 'er ladyship's box, the Comte had slipped Roberts a shilling, inquired as to his night off, and murmured an invitation to meet him at this same pub, with a promise of more money to come. Sitting alone, Roberts now wondered whether the Comte had only been toying with him, as suchlike were oft wont to do with servants. His puzzlement was soon brought to an end, when the Comte himself, muffled in a black greatcoat and hat, slipped into a chair in front of him. Following him, the landlord set down two pints from a tray and disappeared behind his crowded, noisy bar.

"It is good of you to keep our rendezvous, Monsieur," the Comte said, his sly grey eyes darting rapidly around the room. No one was watching them. Indeed, most eyes were turned to the exceptionally buxom and quick-tongued sportive serving wench whose round replies to some drunkards were producing much laughter and knowing winks. "You have mentioned this to no one?" he inquired softly, his eyes hard and watchful behind his purposefully pleasant expression.

"No one, and I thank you," said Roberts, taking a long swallow from his porter. "What service can I render yer lordship?" he asked, his eyes agleam with the sudden promise of wealth, which the Comte had indolently made by producing several guineas and laying them out upon the table in front of him.

"I have heard from a good source that your talent for watching things is very well-developed," du Foix said silkily. "You are also in a position to perhaps overhear other things. I would like to buy the service of these talents."

Roberts sipped his porter and nodded once. Pleased by this acceptance, the Comte continued. "For a price, I hope that you might also be counted on to relay messages. There would be no danger to you, and it would even be an agreeable task, as one of your correspondents would be a pretty, young French girl in service to another establishment. Might I hope that we have an agreement?"

In response, Roberts reached boldly across and scooped up the guineas. The Comte watched with narrowed eyes and a little smile upon his lips. "*C'est bon.* There will be more to that by and by. You travel with your mistress and Miss Thomas upon their calls and errands?"

"Yes," said Roberts eagerly, taking another long swallow of the porter. Du Foix signaled the barman for two more, which were brought by the saucy serving wench, whom the Comte vouchsafed not even a glance, although Roberts smacked his lips and grinned at her. She set the two mugs down with a toss of her black curls and scooped up the coins from the table without even glancing at du Foix.

"I seek information, Monsieur," du Foix said softly. "Information that you may come across in carrying out your duties and information that may be passed to you to be passed to me. Are we of accord?"

"I'll do nothing against my mistress," said Roberts sulkily. "It would be worth my place to betray 'er ladyship or Sir Thomas. Yer lordship cannot expect me to betray my livelihood." Roberts sat silently, waiting du Foix's reply, with the Comte's guineas still in his pocket.

"*D'accord*," smiled the Comte, "but of course. It concerns another lady altogether. If you can call her a lady," he added maliciously, his tone lewdly conspiratorial as he leaned closer across the table, inclining towards Roberts. "I mean Miss Llewellyn, lately of your acquaintance as Cat Gryffyn."

Roberts' eyes sparkled with malice. So, this Frog had a score to settle with high and mighty Miss Cat as well! There was money in it for himself, as well as revenge. Roberts did not even bother to think twice. "What is yer lordship's desire? I am at yer service."

Briefly, the Comte outlined his requirements. "I am most interested in every detail of Miss Llewellyn's social engagements and her wardrobe. I wish you to report every detail you observe or overhear from her ladyship or Miss Thomas. In addition, there is a seamstress at Madame La Croix's who may report to you. I know that all the fashionable debutantes this season are having their gowns made there. It is most important I know these things as soon as you hear them."

Roberts thought. Ladies' tittle-tattle about gowns and such was easier to come by than to avoid, and it would be a pleasure to speak to any of the saucy wenches who sewed for Madame La Croix. A practical objection to the scheme entered his mind. "How do I communicate this information to you?" More to the point, how would he be paid?

The Comte du Foix raised an eyebrow in appreciation of the question. Roberts had a practical cunning that pleased du Foix. "It is better that we do not meet after this, for both your safety and my own. Look for an urchin whom I shall send. He will station himself outside Portman Square every morning. He will offer to sweep the steps for a penny. You may communicate your information to him."

"And the money to be paid me?" Roberts inquired.

"Return here to the Horse and Groom each night you have off. Sit alone at this table. Order porter. Someone will join you. He will give you the money."

"How will I know this gentleman, then? I am not risking any danger."

"He will wear a red ribbon in the buttonhole of his coat and address you as 'Johnson.' Have we an agreement?"

"Yes," replied Roberts, who picked up his porter and gulped it all down. When he put down his mug, the Comte was gone.

THE BALL

"We are nearly there, my Dear. Are you quite composed?" asked Henrietta. Beside her, Cat sat up straighter and looked out the carriage window as they approached the imposing building with the wide staircase and white portico.

Cat felt quite breathless. Her heart was beating as rapidly as if she had been running. In spite of her trepidation, she contrived a sweet smile for her aunt and replied in a low musical voice, "Of course, dear Aunt, though I must own some excitement in attending my first London ball."

Henrietta returned the smile, glancing fondly at her niece, who looked lovely, arrayed in a high-waisted pale Eau de Nile green gown of the finest watered silk. Her wrap, a delicate French lace difficult to obtain these days, draped her bare shoulders. Her slender legs were encased in white silk stockings and showed the fine turn of her ankles. Her graceful feet wore white velvet slippers.

Henrietta's own maid had spent an hour winding Cat's long hair into a deceptively simple Grecian arrangement threaded with lustrous pearls. Pearl-drop earrings hung from her delicate ears. Her lovely columnar throat and décolletage were bare of ornament, displaying the flawless beauty of her rose-tinged ivory skin. Long white kid gloves encased her slender arms, and she carried a Chinese fan of carved white ivory.

"My Dear, you shall be the most beautiful girl there. I vow every buck and lord in the room will be lining up to dance with you." She took her niece's hand in her own and murmured, "Courage."

Cat hardly heard her aunt's words. The blood pounded in Cat's ears. She felt faint as the footman handed her down from the smart carriage. She searched with gloved hand in her reticule, which hung by a ribbon from her wrist, for the smelling salts her aunt had put there. Dear Henrietta, so understanding. Until this minute, she had felt adequate for whatever challenge life had to offer her, but the prospect of facing all of London society at once reduced her to an unusual timidity.

Sternly, she addressed herself in thought, "Do not be so missish! You are both learned and brave. You can ride better than any of these fragile debutantes and most probably better than most of their gentlemen! Your person is far from unattractive, as the unwelcome attentions of Mr. Fairfax have demonstrated, and there are sure to be real gentlemen among the men here! Now enjoy yourself." Silently delivering herself of this homily, she accompanied her aunt up the broad staircase into Almack's.

"I say," said one buck upon seeing them enter, "Who is that divinity over there? She has the exact expression of a hunting Diana!"

"Where?" answered his companion, one Sir George Whitby, who fixed his quizzing glass and surveyed the room. "Jove! You mean the young beauty by the matron in mauve just inside the door? I say, she is a topper! Puts your little blonde back in the schoolroom where she belongs, what?"

"Not precisely back in the schoolroom," said the other, a rotund squire dressed in ornate style with a gold waistcoat and a coat of bright blue superfine, sliding his eyes toward where Clarissa Thomas stood with her formidable mama. Clarissa had come in the lightest of translucent blue voile over a white shift that she had dampened down to cling more seductively to her rounded hips and bosom.

"A ripe one, that one, for all her youth, but this other—" drawled Sir George, peering sharply through the quizzing glass, "Dam'me she's a blue ribbon, not a golightly."

"Where have you been hiding?" languidly drawled Lord Melton, whose ragged countenance betrayed his years of dissipation. "That is the King's Swan, also truly named the Hunting Diana by some. She looks too resolute for me. I prefer an easier female."

They were not the only two who remarked upon the entrance of Cat and her aunt. A faint rustle of whispers went all around the ballroom as the two women entered the hall. Even the Thomas women became aware of Henrietta and Cat's entrance. Until this moment, Clarissa had been holding court, unchallenged and alone, to all the most eligible men in the room. Clarissa's eyes darkened with anger as her rival advanced to where Lady Sefton and the Duchess of Suffolk were greeting the arrivals.

"Mama," she hissed, "I cannot believe she has the impudence to show her face among all Society here after her shameful behavior! Her deceitful imposture and licentious flirtation with Mr. Fairfax make her unworthy of any decent company!"

"Hush now, Clarissa," her mother whispered. "Would you have everyone hear you? It would be our reputation spoiled by initiating vicious gossip. Let us see if she does not betray her own low nature!"

Her ladyship gazed at her daughter with some apprehension. Her spoiled arrogance might be overlooked in a small assembly, but it could not pass here in London. She regretted that Clarissa had resorted to such tricks as dampening her underskirt. It too much resembled the habits of the Fashionable Impures. Nevertheless, Lady Thomas could see that many admiring glances had followed their entry, and Clarissa had scored several notable successes among her suitors. Nevertheless, it was vexing to see how much attention the Llewellyn girl was attracting.

At the far end of the hall, Vere Courtenay Fairfax languidly inspected the cuffs of his dark coat. "Do you not think Weston overdid these cuffs a bit?" he asked Lord Carleton idly. "I am not sure I approve of this fashionable excess."

"If the Beau is wearing those cuffs this Season, I do not understand why you should cavil at them, Falconbridge."

"My dear friend, I asked you specifically not to address me by my title. There are arrangements that would be upset if my true identity were to be revealed."

"Up to some tricks, are you?" asked Carleton wickedly. "Or are too many mamas on the hunt for a rich bridegroom for their daughters, eh? What game are you playing?"

"Carlton, if my request to you as a gentleman is not enough for your silence, and you persist in making insulting intimations, I will have to consider our friendship ended. Beyond that, I may have to call you out."

"Now, Fairfax, there is no need to be hasty, you know. No disrespect intended, none at all. Trust in my discretion."

"I would ask you to show some," rejoined Vere curtly.

Carleton looked around the ballroom, noting the arrivals. "There's Lady Bullstrode, over there in the turban. Gets more eccentric every Season, what?" he exclaimed, looking a second time at the outlandish figure of Lady Bullstrode, gowned in a combination of purple and red silks. She half-turned and revealed Cat to Carleton's appraising glance. "I say, who is that gorgeous gel in the green? Can't say I've seen anything so heart-stopping since Siddons suckled the asp in *Cleopatra*!"

Vere looked toward the group that Lord Carleton had indicated. Standing a little apart, radiant in her finery, stood Cat Llewellyn, already the acknowledged belle of the ball. "You should really leave the gaming tables once in a while, Carleton. That is the Season's reigning beauty. I need to pay my respects. Do excuse me."

"So you already know the filly? Eh, Falconbridge, er, I mean Fairfax. Dam'me, I believe you know every lovely woman in Europe. I never thought to see the day when you were on the dangle for the matrimonial sweeps. Now, now," he said hastily, "I won't be revealing your imposture, though blast if I can understand why you want to hide your identity from anyone. As Lord Falconbridge, you have the edge over every eligible buck in the room."

Fairfax glanced down at his shorter companion with a haughty look mixed with pique. "I warn you, Carleton. I have my reasons. You are trying my patience."

"No, no, Fairfax, consider it done, though I am cursed if I can figure it out. Look sharp, there's that blasted French count standing partner to your mystery gel for the first dance. Something damned suspicious about that frog."

Vere's lip curled in disdain. "I couldn't agree with you more, Carleton."

"He's sent his second, Monsieur Reynard, to arrange the bout at the Fives Court. He asked if we would agree to the wearing of the mauleys. No doubt, he fears your strength and hopes to win some advantage thus."

"Who is holding the ring?"

"Jackson is, of course. Reynard looked as if he would object to that, but Gentleman Jackson's reputation is too well-known to be repudiated."

"Good," replied Fairfax, as he looked intently at the dancers. "I think I will go over there, where I can keep a better eye on them." Fairfax sauntered off across the room. His tall elegant figure in severe black and faultless white drew the eyes of many of the mamas and their charges. A fine figure of a man, he could not hide with his leisured gait his vibrant masculine strength. Beside him, the tulips in their velvets, embroideries, and colors looked ineffectual and weedy. Whatever game Fairfax was playing, it was sure to be dangerous to somebody.

Cat found herself beginning to enjoy the ball. When she had first entered with Henrietta, she had felt wretchedly self-conscious. The self-confidence she felt on horseback had all but disappeared. Most of the other debutantes were in pinks, blues, or whites. The dress that she had chosen for herself seemed quite ill-suited for this occasion. Her doubts had been but little dispelled by the effusive greetings of Ladies Sefton and Suffolk. Henrietta had been quite pleased by their words. "My Dear, you are made!" she whispered. "They are never this kindly out of politeness. You are the official belle of the evening!"

Cat remained quite uncomfortable while Lady Bullstrode again claimed their attention. Her ladyship presented such a spectacle in her clashing reds and purples, speaking in a voice so piercingly loud as to be heard over even the musicians, that Cat longed to slip out the door unnoticed. Nevertheless, she allowed herself to be chosen as part of the figure of the first dance set. Now, just as she was feeling her most wretched, a quiet masculine voice spoke at her elbow.

"Mademoiselle, it is my pleasure to be your partner in this dance."

Raising her eyes, Cat saw that the speaker was Monsieur Montclair, the Comte du Foix. He was standing very quietly in front of her, his face expressing nothing other than the most correct interest in her reply.

"*Oui, Monsieur le Comte du Foix. Enchanté,*" Cat replied, offering him her hand. He held it lightly and gravely as they took their places in the beginning steps of the dance.

"You need not be so formal, Mademoiselle. I have been in your country for several years now and am much charmed by its informality of manner," the Count admonished.

"Some of my countrymen are much too informal in manners. I find your correctness to be very refreshing," Cat responded.

"I am equally refreshed by your beauty, Mademoiselle Cat." The stately music proceeded and he saluted her gravely.

Cat tried to maintain an equal dignity, but could not refrain from smiling at her handsome partner, who indicated his pleasure by his courtly bow. She returned it with a curtsey of great grace, catching even more admirers among the *ton*, who stood observing the dancers.

"Have you been in our country long?" Cat asked the Comte, as they stepped forward in the first figure.

"I arrived shortly after the Terror began. I, along with many others of my countrymen, was lucky to escape with my life. You cannot imagine, Miss Llewellyn, the memories of the survivors. Imagine yourself at a ball such as this. Each invitee must have lost a family member to le guillotine. The women wear cropped hair and thin red ribbons about their necks. By such celebration we vanquish the Terror."

"I am sorry," Cat murmured, "I did not mean to recall you to such memories."

The Comte smiled a bright smile. "Do not fret yourself, Mademoiselle. Having seen such death, we look on life with new eyes, eyes that must always welcome beauty such as you bring."

"*Merci*," Cat replied, smiling in her turn, touched by his travails. "You have great courage."

"No more than yourself," replied the Comte lightly. "You also have the courage to create a new life. Is that not so?" Seeing her sudden confusion, he pressed her fingers reassuringly. "I am a keeper of secrets." She gave him a grateful look, which he returned with a slight bow, "and I am a keeper of friends."

Excitement rouged her cheeks with high color. "I hope we may be so," she stated boldly.

Vere had no mistaken ideas about the pretty scene before him. Lucien Montclair, the so-called Comte du Foix, might pass for a gentleman here at Almack's and be seen in all the fashionable places, but Fairfax knew of his less respectable haunts as well: the gaming hells, the money lenders, and the scum who gathered dockside on the Thames.

Fairfax leaned negligently against the wall, his eyes seeming to droop in weariness, but in reality following the two of them intently through the courtly measures of the dance. Cat appeared dangerously taken in by the scoundrel, even to the point of flirting with him, a thing that she had never done with Vere. Watching her face as she looked up at the slender blonde Comte through lowered lashes, Fairfax clenched his vermeil snuffbox in his fist so tightly that his knuckles went white.

"I say, Old Boy, that's one of Jacobi's better works. Do you mean to break it?" Carleton's voice broke in on Fairfax's solitary thoughts.

Startled out of his unpleasant reverie, Vere relaxed his grip. "Thank you, Carleton," Vere said smoothly, his voice betraying none of the inner turmoil that besieged him. "May I offer you some? It contains a receipt of my own, and I fancy it is a superior blend."

"Most obliged, Sir. I shall avail myself of your offer." He helped himself to a pinch and added in a lower voice, "Your fair beauty is at leisure. You'd better catch her for this next dance before somebody else does."

"Exactly my thinking," Fairfax replied, closing the box with a snap and striding quickly across the floor.

Cat sat very straight upon a slender chair beside her aunt. Her eyes sparkled even as she strove to fan herself languidly with her fan, as all the other young debutantes were doing. Still, it was difficult to hide her excitement. The dance with the Comte had been charming. She found herself recalling with great pleasure each delightful measure every time their hands or eyes met. So lost in her reverie was she that she was not aware of Mr. Fairfax standing before her.

"May I have this next dance, Miss Llewellyn?" Mr. Fairfax asked gravely, bowing as he did so.

His sudden appearance took Cat by surprise, although ever since their formal introduction at the opera, she had been expecting him. They had not been alone since Lady Bullstrode had found her at his town house. Curious to further test her impressions of him and remembering her plan to humble his pride, Cat made a swift decision. Heedless of the disapproval that she might generate from Lady Bullstrode or her aunt, she coolly answered, "The much-admired Mr. Fairfax. To what do I owe your special favor?"

"Like every other man here, I am drawn by your beauty. Unlike the others, I had the wit to recognize it immediately. Surely, you cannot hold against me circumstances that were not entirely my fault. May we begin again?"

Cat concealed her sudden pleasure even while suspecting that his smooth answer only disguised his vile intent. She hesitated, irresolute about the wisdom of continuing her scheme. The musicians struck up a few tentative notes.

"The dance, Miss Llewellyn," he said patiently, without a hint of a smile, "Will you stand up with me?" Cat looked around her, but no one had overheard their conversation. She had made no other commitments.

Boldly she replied, "Certainly, Sir, I will dance with you, but I beg you to remember where we are. I shall entertain none of your rude jests." It was as close as she could come to censuring him for the Prince of Wales's rude remark at Tattersall's.

He led her to a place in the figure. "You mistake me, Miss Llewellyn. I intend no disrespect."

He made her a graceful bow as the music began, and she returned it with an equally graceful curtsey. When their turn came, he took her hand in his strong fingers and walked her through the line between the other dancers. She felt the heat of him through her gloved palms. As they circled within the figure of the dance, she felt his intense gaze upon her, as searing hot as fire over her face and breasts. She wished that she had worn a higher-necked gown, knowing where the glance of his lascivious eyes rested when she made her curtsey.

"Do not stare at me so," she whispered as they crossed diagonally, "I find it most unpleasant."

"Can a sunflower resist the sun?" he asked, smiling at her as they met and took up their positions opposite each other again.

She was acutely aware of him as he stood across from her. His powerful figure displayed so well in the black coat, his head lifted proudly in his white stock, and his long legs so beautifully delineated by the tight white breeches produced an uncomfortable heat in her own limbs. She actually felt faint and worried that she might disgrace herself by swooning.

Each couple in the figure stepped in turn to the center, and their gentlemen took the ladies' hands. Each lady then pirouetted about her partner as he stood in the middle and turned around with her. Cat felt the gentle yet firm grip of Mr. Fairfax's long fingers upon her own. She was close enough to him to smell his scent of leather, fresh linen, and bay rum, to feel the heat of his physical presence as he looked down at her face. His expression was carefully composed, but he could not disguise the intensity of his desire, which shone in his brilliant dark eyes. She lowered the gaze of her own green eyes, unable to bear his fierce glance, fully aware of his ardor in her every nerve ending.

The measure drew to an end. Each couple walked arm in arm through the final figure, a promenade. She could feel the hard muscle of his arm beneath the smooth weave of his superfine black broadcloth sleeve. Into her mind, unbidden, came the memory of his strong wrists and graceful hands taming the plunging carriage horse on the road on the day they first met. She trembled involuntarily and leaned briefly upon his strength.

"It is very hot in here," she said to excuse herself.

Instantly solicitous, Vere asked, "Would you like to take some refreshment upon the balcony? The cooler air will doubtless refresh you."

Without thinking, she agreed, "I believe some cooler air would do me good. The candles have heated the room up greatly. A small glass of orgeat would be most welcome."

Deftly, he escorted her through the crowds. Several couples among small gatherings of dowagers and aged gentleman were already present in the cool dimness of the outdoor verandah. Scarcely believing his good fortune, he led her to the most secluded spot, motioning to one of the footmen bearing trays of refreshments. Carefully, he placed a glass in her hand, gently curling her white-gloved fingers around the stem. Her pallor was alarming. "Would you sit?" he murmured as she swayed against him and nearly spilled her glass. Quickly, he took it from her nerveless fingers, and putting a firm supporting arm about her slender waist, he half carried, half walked her, leaning against him, to a chair near the railing.

Cat was mortified by her sudden weakness. Mr. Fairfax's close physical proximity had unnerved her. His merest touch sent rivers of fire flooding up her body. Even the feel of his hand upon her own brought longings for the touch of his lips upon her face, his fingers running through her hair with passion.

She half sank gratefully into the chair that he offered her. Behind her closed eyes, she could still see him, his fine chiseled features, his lean long body, in his austere black. She longed to feel the length of his tall straight body against her own, to feel his arms enfold about her, pulling her tightly against him. She was appalled at the physical intensity of her unexpected feelings toward him.

"I am no better than he is," she thought. "I am a low-bred licentious light-skirts to be thinking such thoughts! To desire a man only physically, without respect for his character, is to prostitute one's soul!" Her position was becoming increasingly dangerous. One more touch and she felt that she would go up in flame like tinder.

Vere sat down beside her. He was confused as to what action he might take. With her eyes closed, he could study her face as much as he wished. She looked feverish to him, the rising flush tingeing her skin with delicate color from the sweet curving rise of her young breasts to the faint flush upon her throat and cheeks. Never in his life had he desired more to set a kiss upon those full, tender lips, her closed eyes, and her shining russet curls.

He knew that if once he yielded to the impulse, he would not, could not, stop until he had possessed her fully. To feel her trembling body beneath his own, eagerly submitting to his passion, was his desire, one that almost made him groan aloud in the agony of his need.

Her eyelids fluttered, and he drew back from his position of mere inches from her to a more relaxed pose. She opened her eyes and stared at him,

"Are you feeling quite well, Miss Llewellyn? May I offer you a sip of orgeat? The heat in a ballroom can be quite upsetting to the more delicate ladies."

"I am perfectly fine, thank you," she managed to reply. "It must have been, as you say, the heat of the ballroom." She looked at him sharply, trying to detect any barb or mockery, but his bland expression revealed nothing. "I regret making such a fool of myself. I am quite better now. We should return, lest anyone remark upon our absence."

"Certainly, Miss Llewellyn," he replied gravely, inwardly damning the ridiculous formality he was compelled to use. He wanted to draw her slender figure to him and whisper her name as he ran his hands over her skin.

He stood and offered his arm to her. She took it with great reluctance, he fancied, and walked with her eyes averted. At least she did not hurl accusations of impropriety at him. He was grateful that her usual ability to read his mind seemed to have deserted her.

Halfway across the verandah, they met up with Lady Bullstrode and her companion. Cat felt unusually grateful. Lady Bullstrode would provide a cover of respectability for Cat's presence with Mr. Fairfax on the darkened balcony. "My Dear," Lady Bullstrode cried, sighting Cat. "You are exquisite tonight! Are you having a wonderful evening?"

"Yes, Lady Bullstrode," Cat replied with an effort at brightness. "Everyone has been so kind."

Lady Bullstrode's companion struck a light from his tinderbox, which revealed his face.

"Carrington!" exclaimed Mr. Fairfax. "I didn't know you were back in Town."

"Indeed I am, Fairfax," he replied as the sweet odor of burning tobacco filled the air. "Lucky coincidence meeting you here. Could I possibly have a word with you?" His serious expression was instantly understood by Vere.

"Of course, Lord Carrington. Ladies, could you possibly excuse us?" Fairfax said, bowing equally in the directions of Lady Bullstrode and Cat.

"Of course, gentlemen. Do run along," Lady Bullstrode replied. "We ladies know how necessary business can be, even if you must insist on being so tiresome at a ball. I will take Miss Llewellyn back to the hall," she added. Taking Cat's arm in her own, she swept Cat majestically back to the ballroom.

Reflectively, Lord Carrington stared after them. "Among all the Town tabbies, Lady Bullstrode contrives to show the most sense. I hope you have enjoyed the ball because I don't foresee your returning to it. Your information has been quite useful, and we are both wanted in Whitehall. My carriage is waiting. We must depart immediately."

As Cat and Lady Bullstrode approached the double doors that led back into the lighted ballroom, Lady Bullstrode addressed her charge in stern tones.

"Miss Llewellyn, you have been reckless beyond all sense! What possessed you to leave the ballroom alone with a libertine, such as Mr. Fairfax? That you even accepted an invitation to dance with him is damaging enough. No doubt, everyone remarked upon your departure with him. What have you to say for yourself?"

"I am sorry, Lady Bullstrode. I thought that having been introduced to him in the Duchess's company would make him an acceptable dance partner. I found myself quite faint from the heat of the ballroom. I wished merely to take the air and have some refreshment to revive myself. Would you rather I fainted amidst the company?" She watched from under lowered lashes as to how Lady Bullstrode would accept this facile reply.

"When an unmarried girl, Georgiana brought no disgrace upon herself by fainting on the dance floor," Lady Bullstrode said pointedly. "The Duchess of Devonshire is now a married woman. Her position in Society is high, which puts at risk those that would dare spread calumny. If she invites Mr. Fairfax to her box, she confers on him the respectability of her rank. You, on the other hand, are but a young and single woman, possessed of great fortune, but no great rank. Some would delight in seeing you brought low by scandal. I shall forgive you on account of your youth and inexperience, but I trust that such shall not happen again. Because of your tender years, even to be alone in his company is to be suspect. Luckily for you, I happened upon you. When we return, no one will dare question your absence. However, in the future, confine yourself to dances only with those who are beyond reproach. Young women who have spent time in the company of Mr. Fairfax are not well-regarded for future wives and mothers."

Cat nodded dumbly, glad that Lady Bullstrode had said no worse. Cat's plan to humble Mr. Fairfax was too dangerous to herself, and she was fortunate it was ended almost before it began.

RIVALS

"Cat, there is a letter here for you from Sir Merlin," Lady Leacock said over breakfast. The two ladies were helping themselves from the elegant serving platters upon the walnut sideboard. Cat had an omelet, a slice of bread, and a dab of strawberry preserves.

"Thank you, Aunt Henrietta," Cat replied. Cat sipped from her cup of hot fragrant tea. She felt the weight of it in her hand. "It is very long. I hope nothing is wrong!" With some trepidation, she broke the wax seal and tore the flap open. A folded enclosure in unfamiliar script fell out. Scanning her father's note, she read:

> *My Dear Daughter,*
> *I have sent you the enclosed at the behest of Lord Falconbridge. He asked me if he might address you by letter, as he is unable yet to do so in person. As he has reaffirmed his commitment to offer for you, I see no harm in it. I hope you will treat his missive with the consideration that it deserves.*
> *Your devoted Father*

"What is it, Dear? Not bad news, I hope?"

"I know not what to make of it," said Cat in a puzzled voice. "It is an enclosure from Lord Falconbridge."

"And just who is Lord Falconbridge?"

"The man my father wishes me to marry," Cat replied helplessly. "I ran away the day I was to meet him."

"So consequently, you know nothing of him?" Aunt Henrietta inquired, sipping her tea.

"Only that he owns the next estate over, Foxearth, has resided abroad for many years, and my father recommends him to me."

"Are you not curious as to what Lord Falconbridge has to say? If you are not, I most certainly am. Do open the letter."

Cat hesitated, unwilling to read the letter in her aunt's presence. Her feelings at the ball had left her confused and disquieted. At least here was an honorable suitor, one for whom she experienced no disturbing feelings, no untoward thoughts.

As if reading her mind, her Aunt Henrietta stood. "If you wish solitude to peruse your letter, I quite understand. I have an engagement to be fitted for a new gown an hour hence and must prepare. If you wish to confide in me, I shall be happy to listen when I return. Remember, if you go riding, to take a groom." Placing a gentle kiss on Cat's forehead, Henrietta left the room.

Still amazed, Cat hardly noticed her aunt's departure. The letter lay whitely on the dining table before her. A clatter informed her that the footman had come to clear the room. Resolutely, but with trepidation, she picked up the letter as if it were a truly dangerous object and bore it off to the morning room, where she might read it in peace.

> *Dear Miss Llewellyn,*
>
> *I have applied to your father to forward this to you. As I am unable, as of yet, to pay my addresses to you in person, I have taken this to remedy. I hope you are well and enjoying the London Season. Your father informs me that you are the reigning sensation. Please accept my congratulations and my own admiration, although it must necessarily come from afar. I regret that upon my arrival, you had already gone.*
>
> *As beautiful as is the portrait I have seen of you, it can not do justice to the living original. I have been informed*

that you are as intelligent as you are beautiful. Such a combination, so rarely met with, in one of your years, or indeed, anywhere, compels me to make my addresses even from the disadvantage of distance and invisibility.

I cannot pretend to offer you the same innocent heart you yourself possess. Yet I know myself at last to be capable of love and devotion, and I cherish the hope that you may in time meet me and consent to listen to my proposals. I shall endeavor to give you full knowledge of my character, that there may be honesty between us in this beginning.

Cat put down the letter in wonder and guilt. "Honesty between us in this beginning." Certainly, she had been dishonest with him. She had fled rather than face him. Her feelings for Mr. Fairfax belied an "innocent heart." Was she so lost to sense, were her sensibilities already so corrupted, that she could not look on him with composure, although aware of his character? With a tremulous hand, she picked up the letter again.

As you may know, I have lived abroad for many years, traveling often between Italy, France, Austria, and England. Upon inheriting my father's titles, I determined to take up residence at Foxearth as an English gentleman. My father had many years ago proposed to Sir Merlin that we join our estates by our marriage. Your father was in accord. Thus, I wrote to Sir Merlin to advise him of my proposed return and the old promise.

It was no mere mercenary motive with which I wrote. I had been kept informed by my father, through the agency of Sir Merlin's correspondence, of your many accomplishments, thorough education, and your beauty. For such qualities alone, I would have offered for you. Since my arrival here, it increasingly has been my hope that we would find in each other a congeniality of soul and spirit that would lead naturally to marriage.

You cannot know how ardently I desire to present my addresses in person. I fear that you will lose your heart to another before I am able to stand in your presence. This chance I must leave to the weavings of Fate.

I would welcome your conversation, even one borne upon as thin a hope as mere sheets of paper. We might talk of books or discuss horses, for I hear you are a notable horsewoman. If naught else to you, I yet remain your near neighbor and your sincere admirer. I would be much more to you than that, if you would but allow me to present my addresses.

Your most sincere admirer,
Lord Falconbridge

If you consent to write to me, you may send the letter to Mr. Isaiah Groatsworth, my factor in London, at 17 Holborn Street. He will see that your letter is forwarded to me.

Cat put down the letter. She hardly knew what to make of it. Reading it again only increased her puzzlement. Should she reply? Her father had made her promise that no matter what occurred, she would marry no one without his consent and without first at least hearing Lord Falconbridge's proposals. By his letter, Lord Falconbridge seemed a perfectly affable and charming man. She felt hotly embarrassed by her childish rudeness. Perhaps by an exchange of letters, she would not have to face him if she ultimately declined his offer.

What reply could she make to a letter such as his? He had invited her to correspond with him as his neighbor. He invited her to talk of books. There seemed little harm in that. Perhaps she should show the letter to Henrietta for her opinion of the matter. Deciding to ride in the Park after all, she rang for her maid and sent a request that the groom saddle Jupiter and prepare to accompany her.

Cat rode at her usual brisk pace, but she was, behind her carefully composed face, perplexed withal. Certainly Lord Falconbridge's letter, if perhaps peculiar, had no other fault or lack. Why therefore was she so reluctant to reply? Was it that she feared him to be hideous, deformed in some open or even secret way? Her father had assured her of his suitability in fortune, age, and temperament. Surely, he could not then be one of nature's deformities. His letter was well-written. The phrase "You cannot know how ardently I desire to present my addresses in person" haunted her. Why did it yield to her mind's eye only the memories of the frank, sensual gaze of Mr. Fairfax, that brief touch of his lips upon her trembling hand? Was she so lost to her better nature that it engendered in her only feelings that she blushed to remember? Had she lost her heart to another, or had she truly lost her soul? She remembered Lady Bullstrode's words only too well: "Find a young man your own age, with a good fortune and a good heart. One who wishes to marry. Handsome he may be, but a black rake like Mr. Fairfax can offer no good to a girl such as yourself." Lord Falconbridge was older, it was true, but he wished to marry, had a good fortune, and was offering for her sight unseen. Perhaps understanding that she had feared to meet him, he was offering her this chance to know him before she must actually face him. Did not the Church teach that it was better to marry than to burn? For she was decidedly in danger of fire from her ungovernable feelings for Mr. Fairfax. She must show the letter to Henrietta before she composed her reply. Having resolved her difficulty temporarily, she cantered Jupiter several times from Ladies Mile to Rotten Row and through the North Carriage Drive, drawing the eyes of several viscounts, two noble earls, and an exceedingly wealthy duke who had just buried his wife.

She arrived home just as Lady Leacock was unpinning her hat and directing her maid Hillis to unpack her new ball gown immediately and hang it up. "So," Lady Leacock smiled at Cat, "Have you read the letter? What does it say? Do you intend to write back?"

"I hardly know what it says, Aunt Henrietta. I have no experience to judge a matter such as this, nor can I frame a suitable reply. Dear Aunt, I do not know what to think!"

"Bring the letter to me, Child, and we can read it together. Then we can decide how you wish to reply to it."

Cat fetched the letter from where she had left it, on her own writing table. What could it mean? Her feelings were a turmoil. Fear and excitement mixed uneasily together. Established in her new life at her Aunt Henrietta's, Cat had felt, for the first time, fully in command of herself. Now, here was the literary intrusion of a person who represented that loss of the freedom that had been achieved with so much difficulty. His words, so gently persuasive, represented another threat altogether, and it was not the threat of him alone, but of every other man of the *ton*, indeed the world. Besides his professed sentiments, how did he really see their life together? Was she just to be a pretty toy, a jewel to display, worth all the more for her accomplishments along with her property?

She knew, as every young girl must know, that happiness in marriage was unreliable, yet that all a well-bred woman could aspire to was nothing more than marriage. How much did any woman know of a man's character before she married him? Would she even know as much as this should she meet someone at a dinner, ball, or play? How could she know their feelings, when she knew so little about her own?

"Aunt Henrietta," she said upon returning, "did you love your husband? How did you know you loved him? I am so confused."

Lady Leacock smiled gently. "It must have been quite a letter to bring all this on! I thought that you had no hesitations yesterday. What has changed overnight?"

"It is simply that I do not know how to respond. I have never before been addressed so in my life. He proposes marriage. He wishes me to learn to know him through letters until he can meet me. Why does this feel so much more intimate than meeting him at a supper or a ball? It is perfectly all right when men are all your admirers, but what happens when you find yourself becoming one of theirs!"

"Indeed, is that all it is?" her aunt said teasingly. "Lord Falconbridge must write an uncommon letter, to set you mind to such strange fancies!"

"I am loath to speak intimately to a man sight unseen."

"Let me read the letter and then pronounce." Henrietta held out her hand, and Cat shyly handed over the letter.

"Honesty in this beginning," Cat thought. Was letting her aunt read the letter another betrayal of honesty? How difficult everything was becoming! Cat had run away from a man well-qualified to be her husband, only to find herself becoming shamefully entangled in feelings for a man unfit and unwilling to be any decent woman's husband, although she had no doubt that many a "decent" woman had found Mr. Fairfax attractive. Her Grace, the Duchess of Devonshire, was proof of that. Cat felt the sudden thrill of her nerves as she remembered his face looking down upon hers during the dance. What could Lord Falconbridge offer to erase these longings but a heart open to love and a good fortune? She covertly watched her aunt, but Henrietta's expression gave away nothing.

Finally Henrietta laid the letter aside and smiled at her niece. "Cat, what is it that you wish from this Season? It is to get married, is it not?"

"Yes. No. I don't know," Cat replied wretchedly. "I just did not want to get married to some unknown man and settle down next door and have a life of only children and country balls for the next twenty years!"

"Does it not occur to you that should your Season be successful, that is exactly what will happen anyway? Save you may be settled a long way off from your home and your father. The sole object of a Season is to get married. The advantage is that you will at least know a great deal about your suitor: his fortune, his social standing, and his appearance. Nevertheless, a man courting a rich heiress may hide much about himself, even so. A happy marriage, no matter what we do, is very much a matter of chance. I was very fortunate in my marriage to Charles. We had similar temperaments and sentiments. Our shared society only enlarged our mutual tastes. It would seem that Lord Falconbridge is aware of these facts and wishes to acquaint you thoroughly with his character. I see it as a very considerate gesture made by a man of most discriminating feeling. I should be very intrigued, if I were you."

"Then you would recommend that I reply to his letter?"

"By all means. If it is a question of his appearance, request of him a miniature! Surely he cannot take umbrage at that!"

Caitlyn smiled. "Will you help me write the letter? My father very strongly recommends the match, but I want to marry for love."

"Love often comes after marriage," Henrietta said gently, "and sometimes it is all the stronger for it. By his letter, it seems that he is already in love with you. Yes, I will help you compose your letter."

DESIRES

Vere took a long swallow of water and wiped the sweat from his eyes. Jackson sat contentedly, watching him with a judicious, approving eye. "You are doing better, Mr. Fairfax. You nearly had the stick out of my hand." He thumped the floor with the stout oak stave for emphasis. "I only touched you twice."

"Either one of those hits, had they been done with full force, would have brought me down; something that you forbore from saying, but which nonetheless makes our work futile if I cannot remedy it. Again, if you please."

Jackson eyed Fairfax critically. The punishment was beginning to take its toll. Jackson did not like the look of some of those bruises. "I would not have you injured before you even step into the ring. At least we have discovered the most critical angles. We'll take it again, but slower. I would have you learn this as if 'twer second nature. Are you ready?"

Vere stood still in the center of the ring, watching warily as Jackson circled. Suddenly, the man brought the staff down low and then up toward Vere's ribs. Twisting quickly, Vere knocked it aside with a heavy upward blow of his forearm. Stepping in quickly, he struck at Jackson's midsection. The later tried to avoid the punch, but it caught him soundly in the ribs, causing him to grunt with pain. His eyes closed with the shock. "Jackson, I'm sorry. Are you badly hurt?"

Jackson gingerly touched his aching side. "Not broken this time," he said laughing. "Good thing, I don't want to have your training interrupted. But that was well-placed, well-placed. I'm beginning to think you may survive this contest after all. Maybe even win! Another round, Mr. Fairfax? Mayhap I was a mite too slow that time."

Vere looked at him again. "Yes, another round."

On the sidelines, the odds went from five to one to eight to one. Mr. Ranulph looked worriedly on as the two continued to spar in this peculiar way. The Comte would not be pleased, he thought. Mr. Ranulph took his leave as quietly as he could, without addressing anyone. He quit Jackson's establishment to report to the Comte on the decidedly peculiar training that his opponent was undergoing.

An hour later, Fairfax and Jackson tossed their towels to the ring handlers and, after dressing, repaired to the private salon for a confidential chat over glasses of wine. "You are getting quicker with your hands, Mr. Fairfax, Sir, and your endurance is improving. But if he hits you with strength, I am afraid he might lay you down."

"That is if he hits me at all, Mr. Jackson. With a little more training, I might remain unscathed and triumph over all. With your help."

"With enough time, that could be a true statement, Mr. Fairfax, but I think we'll need a bit more time than we are likely to get. When is the bout?"

"In two weeks. It will give either of us but short time to recover until the racing begins at Newcastle."

"A fortnight might be barely enough to train you thoroughly. I would we had double that at least."

"We are lucky to have as much as this," Vere said somberly as he sipped the wine. "I will return early tomorrow morning. It is a wonder I remember my own house," he said, grinning suddenly. "What else would you have me do?"

"Well," said Jackson hesitantly, "you might run, just to keep your wind good."

"Run?" Fairfax laughed. "Your methods are the most improbable! For that, I am thinking I will have to take myself to the country!"

"I don't think so, Mr. Fairfax. I have a friend with an indoor riding ring for training horses out in Camdentown. I think he might be persuaded to close it to all but one customer if the price were right."

"And, no doubt, I am prepared to offer him the right price," Vere smiled a mirthless smile. "And when do I box against Tom Cribb again? It is a boxing match I am preparing for, is it not?"

"Will tomorrow, after our trip to Camdentown, be soon enough to suit you?"

"Nothing has been soon enough to suit me," Fairfax replied with rare bitterness, "but, for lack of alternatives, it will do. But I would this business were over." Thus spoken, he rose. He took his coat, hat, and stick, then headed homeward in his carriage.

Arriving back at last, while the sun yet lingered in the sky, having blessed everyone but himself, it seemed, with a light-filled, warm day and a gentle evening, he handed his things to Jessup. Hard by on the sideboard, he noticed a folded missive, written in a distinct and graceful hand. Hardly daring to give his hopes credence, he ordered a cold collation and strong coffee to be sent up to the library. Walking with a lighter step, he had loosened his cravat before even reaching his room and quickly washed and changed, not waiting for hot water to be brought.

The fading red of the sunset filled the library, where the tall candles had already been lit. Sitting in the companion chair to the one that Cat had graced only weeks before, Vere meditatively sipped his coffee while he regarded the unopened missive that lay on the table. He had eaten of the cold repast of beef, ragouts, squab, and Stilton, not so much from hunger, but from the knowledge that he must eat if he wished to keep up his strength. The presence and promise of the letter before him made all lesser, grosser appetites vanish. How frail the *barque* that must carry all the freight of his hopes. He picked it up, and with steady hand commending his fate to whatever gods would have it, he unsealed the epistle.

> *The Right Honourable Lord Falconbridge,*
>
> *I am sensible to the great compliment you pay to me. My father has recommended you to me, and it is his wish as well as yours that I give to your proposals due consideration.*
>
> *Your letter was most unexpected, but I have no reason to doubt that the sentiments you avowed were honestly felt. I am honored to be the object of your interest. I would very much like to know something of your character and your tastes, what beliefs most strongly guide you, what hopes you cherish.*
>
> *I am young and inexperienced in the ways of the world. Your considerate attention shows a nobility of feeling that must be pleasing to anyone of gentle breeding. You know far more of me than I do of you, and my first wish would be to hear of your life, what events have transpired, what has shaped your youth and directed your path to this present.*
>
> *I regret that I cannot meet you in person. However, I am willing to become acquainted with you when circumstances allow. Perhaps, if it seems meet to you, you might send me a miniature of yourself, as in this again you have the advantage over me.*
>
> *Above all things, I should like to hear of your journeys through Italy, France, and Austria. Eldertree Manor and its environs are all I have known until I came to London. That which is novel must always intrigue.*
>
> *Sincerely yours,*
> *Caitlyn Llewellyn*

He read it twice, thrice three times. It encouraged more than it discouraged. He thought that he detected a finer hand in it than Cat's. Lady Leacock must have helped her write it, for it most subtly implied that he would have to compete for her as much as any other eligible bachelor during the Season. She was not to be overwhelmed with passion; that was the message that she had conveyed, he decided. Her request for a miniature disquieted him. How could he put her off and yet have her continue to write?

From the writing desk, he took several sheets of London's best hot-pressed paper. Pouring another cup of coffee, he sat before them, his mind empty of words. He wished to write that which would sear the paper. Instead, he must write a travelogue, those favorite topics of maiden aunts and spinster sisters. At least he had Cat's entire attention, unlike any other venue where he was likely to meet her. Seizing the pen, he began to write.

Dear Miss Llewellyn,

You have honored me by your request, and I will do all in my power to oblige. Of my early youth, I had a gentleman's schooling. If I was not entirely sensible to its benefit at the time, I hope I may be excused on that universal theme of youth. Young men are not often noted for the evenness of their temperaments, and if I write here that I was less of a serious scholar than I have since become, I hope you may forgive me. I may honestly say that I have a love for literature and music, which I treasure, and I indulge that love whenever I may avail myself of the opportunity.

I enjoy sport, essential for the English gentleman, so it seems. I am accounted a good rider, a capital shot, and a day spent in the saddle is never tedious to me. I would very much like to accompany you sometime, as your skill with horses has been made known to me. In taste and talent, I would venture that we are similar.

You have made known a wish to be told of the foreign countries I have visited. Should you consent to my proposal, I would be happy to show you all those places and more besides, whatever you fancy requires. As perhaps your father told you, I possess several estates abroad, so you must not fear that your life would be circumscribed by your childhood's environs.

You have challenged me to write of the countries that I have visited. The beauty of each is great, but so varied that only an impartial eye could judge which is most beautiful. In the order of what I write I must own a partial eye, and describe first to you, if you permit, my home in Tuscany, which I dare to hope one day will be yours as well. Until that time, I hope that the enclosure that follows will satisfy your request.

Alas, at this time I cannot gratify you with a miniature of myself. At Foxearth, there are none more recent than my nineteenth year. Although I am not a fair man, neither am I so dark as to be a Caliban. In this invisibility, I can only beg you to remember the final happiness of Psyche and Eros. I promise that you shall indeed behold me before a marriage is accomplished.

Your obedient servant,
Lord Falconbridge

The candle burned low before Vere recalled to himself that he had yet another long day to spend with Jackson and his friend in Camdentown. He put down his quill and hastily reread the enclosure describing his home and travels. He could not afford to wonder. He was too deeply involved to turn back. In his deep weariness, he longed for an end to the masquerade between himself and Cat. How he yearned to doff his mask of bastard and rake, to claim her as Lord Falconbridge, her honorable intended. It was as Mr. Fairfax, wastrel, libertine, and presumed bastard that he had lived his life in England. Now he was pledged to continue in that role until Montclair was foiled, even as Vere most wished to commence his own redemption. How many lives had Vere's selfish indifference destroyed? Would Cat be touched and tainted by him even if she acceded to the lawful intimacy he so intensely desired? Better, much better, to face Montclair than this. Snuffing the candle, Vere left his sealed letter upon the table and walked wearily towards the stairs and his bedchamber. Between now and the match with the Comte du Foix, Vere would indeed be invisible to her.

*   *   *

Cat cantered once more around the circuit. It was good to be out of stuffy drawing rooms, away from the shops, even free of the attendant conversations that accompanied the elaborate dinners that presaged the glittering balls. Cat found that even these amusements were beginning to pale. Jupiter was a fine horse, and Cat was well-aware of the picture that they made together. The Park was simply too well-known. There was no challenge riding there. Even the people were all the same. It had been exciting, she admitted, to be taken up by the Duchess and driven in her carriage. Cat was regularly saluted on her rides by a duke, two marquises, and seven earls, along with uncounted viscounts and barons, not to mention several wealthy knights and commoners, who could not be discounted because their fortunes were above ten thousand pounds a year!

Reflecting on such admirers, Cat did not feel inclined more for one than another, although most were pleasant enough in manners and face. She rather liked young Leighton, Viscount Roehampton, but as the Earl, his father, was still young and vigorous, this would not be the most promising match. By far the best, by the standards of the *ton*, was Henry, Marquis of Bradbury. He was not that old, and he had not wasted his estates, so she should have a respectable settlement and always be afforded a good turnout. However, his oldest son was four years older than she was, and should the Marquis die untimely, she would have very little future or fortune as a dowager marquise. Despite a great deal of fluttering among the mamas and the chaperones, Cat did not think much of her prospects if married to Bradbury. None of the others had fired her enthusiasm, certainly not as she had hoped when she was still back in Wales. They either seemed too staid, as if milk and water diluted their blood, or as empty in their self-importance as the strutting roosters in her kitchen garden.

Only one man had really caught her eye, and that had occurred against her will and despite her better judgment. Try as she might to prevent it, the feelings of her wild self would make themselves known, and she could not pretend otherwise. Even to see Mr. Fairfax was to be drawn into some new airless realm, where translated from common clay to some more ethereal state, she breathed and lived pure fire. He was not here, she decided finally, slowing Jupiter to a trot and then a walk. She had not even glimpsed him in nearly a week. How pallid seemed all the admiration and envy that she was exciting, with him not here to witness it and be jealous. Perhaps he did not care that much anyway. Was he a man who could give his heart to a woman? Perhaps he used all women only for carnal satisfaction. A shiver ran through her as she thought of all of his dangerous passion, so coldly employed, so capable of producing ruinous conflagration in herself. Worse, she knew that she was willing to become a sacrifice on the pyre.

Behind her, she heard the jangle of carriage harness, the brisk trotting of a lively team, the approach of a carriage, and her aunt's voice calling to Cat. "Caitlyn, we are on the way to the shops on Bond Street. The Royal Exhibition opens tomorrow, and I need to retrim my hat. Join us. You need something new. You can have the groom lead Jupiter home."

Bored by the further prospects of the Park, Caitlyn assented and entered the open carriage.

"You are very handsome on that horse," said Lady Bullstrode, who sat beside Henrietta. "Quite the talk of the Season you both are. Henrietta believes that several offers will be made soon. Do you have a favorite?"

Cat blushed. She had a favorite, but could hardly own him, even to herself. She searched her mind among those to whom she had been presented, with whom she had danced, or with whom she had held insipid little conversations. "No one who seems really eligible, but I rather like Piers Leighton."

"But you know his situation is not of the best," Henrietta added anxiously. "He has a pretty face and agreeable manners, but his fortune is not the highest, and though his prospects are good, they are not outstanding. Is there no one else you might fancy?"

Cat sighed. She had hoped to evade such questioning. Ever since the opera and the ball, she had spent all her time in the mad social whirl of the Season. She had been invited to all the best parties. The Duchess of Devonshire herself had presented her to several earls and a duke. They had all been of exceptional politeness and were unfailingly proper in their manners and address, kind and attentive. However, she could hardly recall who each one was. None stirred her imagination or her passion. As dangerous as the latter emotion was, she knew that she would not marry without consulting it.

"I have met so many of them, dear Aunt. They are all agreeable and acceptable. How can I tell which one is better than his peers?"

"Waiting for your heart to speak?" Lady Bullstrode inquired shrewdly. "That is a very dangerous game, for it gives sensibility rule over sense, and that can lead to grave regrets in time. I understand that you have another suitor, though, one we have not met!"

Cat blushed a deeper rose. Did her aunt and Lady Bullstrode suspect her feelings for Mr. Fairfax? Did their eyes see something in his conduct that she did not? Ever since Cat's formal entrance into Society, Mr. Fairfax had been extremely circumspect in public. At Almack's, only his eyes spoke the truth of his desire, and that truth he had spoken to her alone.

"It is your intended, Lord Falconbridge," Lady Leacock exclaimed impatiently. "What of him? I told Lady Bullstrode of your exchange of letters. What do you make of him?"

Cat dropped her eyes. "I wish you would not mention him as my 'intended.' Intended by my father, perhaps, but not by me. I am not sure what to make of his letters."

That was true. Falconbridge drew nearer through his correspondence. Cat could not but admire the clarity of his mind, the discrimination of his taste, the delicacy of his sentiment. He had been most gentlemanly at putting her at her ease. Indeed, she looked forward to his future missives. He had faithfully complied with her request and written in detail and in excellent style of the many places to which he had traveled. She read with wonder his description of his villa in Tuscany. She fancied that she caught something of the true man beneath his polite correctness as he described its rooms and grounds. Certainly, here was someone capable of love. If he loved his estates so well, would he love his wife with less devotion?

"He seems a most proper and interesting man. I would that I had a picture of him."

"Looks is not everything," Lady Bullstrode declared. "He is, no doubt, handsome enough. I knew his father and mother in the old days. Old Lord Falconbridge was very personable, and the Countess was a fine, striking woman."

"Have you ever seen him, Lady Bullstrode? Please do tell me."

Lady Bullstrode gave her a long, considering look. "I saw him when he was in his twenties, a dark youth who took after his mother, but tall and long-boned like his father. He was accounted very dashing in those days, but made no offers to anyone, which spoilt the hopes of more than one young debutante, though this spared the fears of their mamas. He can by no means be past his prime today."

"Thank you, Lady Bullstrode. It is enough to content me for the present." Cat rode in silence for the remainder of the way, while the other two ladies chatted about bonnet trimmings and various laces. Lord Falconbridge was assuming substance in Cat's mind, a dark cavalier to rival the black Mr. Fairfax. That night she wrote.

> *The Right Honourable Lord Falconbridge,*
> *Your kindness in gratifying my wish to hear of foreign lands is very much appreciated. The moving way in which you write of your home must convince me of the capacity of your heart. I feel that there is a similarity of temperament between us. Your letters have been so kind that I would there might be a meeting between us before the end of the Season. I will meet you, in any case, on my return to Eldertree.*

She put down her pen in wonder. He would be seen. Somewhere now he existed, going about estate business, riding, visiting, engaged in all the country pursuits. His lively mind, experienced as he was by his extensive travels, could not be satisfied with mere country topics. His letters to her gave a view of the depth and breadth of his interests. Here was one in whose society she would never feel dull. Knowing this, she wondered about his feelings. Was he capable of that breadth of emotion for which she longed? Looking back over the correspondence, she decided that he had been plain about his hopes in that respect.

What indeed were hers? She certainly had had excitement enough in her Season. If it were her purpose to meet all the rich and eligible bachelors in Society and to have them at her feet, she had achieved that. Was it her purpose to marry any one of them? With a sigh, she knew that it was not. She did not think that the passage of time would make the duke more attractive, or create a passion for the marquis. More dangerously, time's passage was not lessening that flame of desire within her own traitorous body, which made her search out the crowds for a glimpse of Mr. Fairfax's face. If only she possessed a picture of Lord Falconbridge, perhaps her indecision might be resolved. She wanted an honorable love. Why could she not find in marriage to Lord Falconbridge the fulfillment of the desires she felt for Mr. Fairfax? Could not Lord Falconbridge overcome the image of her oppressor? His writing made plain that he possessed deep passion. Putting pen to paper, she wrote.

> *I appreciate the sentiments you have expressed. Indeed no one I have met with among the* ton *has expressed a sensibility so near my own, nor has he excited in me a similar feeling. I feel we have a great commonality of interests and views, which, I have been told, makes a secure foundation for mutual regard. I look forward with pleasure to meeting you at last.*
>
> *I too would make a match with someone who would share my sentiments, with whom I could find a companion of both mind and spirit. I would further hope that the gentler tenderness and regard that can flower between a man and a woman be present as well.*

Quickly taking all her courage, she dipped the pen in ink and wrote two further daring lines.

> *Of all those I have met during the Season, you have shown the greatest likeness to the first qualification. Do not think me forward if I write that perhaps our meeting will tell whether the second qualification may be met as well.*
>
> *Most sincerely,*
> *Caitlyn Llewellyn*

There was so much else that she could write to him, so much more she wanted to know. What was proper? She wondered whether indeed she had shown grave impropriety by penning those last lines. She put her pen down, resolutely sealed the letter, and rang for her maid. Tomorrow was the exhibition at the Royal Academy. She and Lady Leacock would be part of the Duchess's party. Cat had decided to wear the white and green stripped *bazeen* frock. It would set off her hair and eyes very nicely, she thought sleepily. No doubt, not even the august position of the Duchess could keep all of Cat's suitors away. Cat slipped gratefully between the sheets that her maid had just turned down. Burying her face deeply into the soft feather pillow, she wondered what Lord Falconbridge looked like. "Dark," Lady Bullstrode had said. Did he have eyes like Mr. Fairfax's? Would he look at her in the same way? Certainly not, she decided, for one seemed all goodness, the other capable of the most reprehensible of actions. The sable quiet lulled her senses, and shortly she fell asleep.

In her dream, the towers of Foxearth were visible through the trees, and Cat was riding, riding on Meteor. Something tenebrous pursued her, and the trees of the park, once dappled with sun and shadow, became still, somber, and dead. She was on foot, walking on a childhood path that had become overgrown, choked with grass. Ahead, a shadowed figure waited in a clearing. Stepping into the clearing, she saw that it gave a view to the pastures and lawns beyond. The rich green of the lands of Foxearth stretched in every direction. She knew then that the unknown man beside her was Lord Falconbridge. He gave her his hand, and together they stepped out into the sunlight. Turning to him in her joy, she saw instead Mr. Fairfax. He drew her to him, pinioning her arms so that she could not struggle. She felt his kiss on her lips and his full length against her suddenly naked body. Fiercely, she threw herself against him, fighting to embrace him against his restraint, and awoke suddenly, tangled in the bed linens, shaken from the intensity of her dream and what it so clearly revealed.

At that instant, it had all became blindingly clear. Mr. Fairfax was Lord Falconbridge's bastard brother. Who else could he be? Clarrisa's envenomed words made sense to her now. Fairfax was the Falconbridge family name. That was what Clarissa had said Lady Bullstrode had told her mama.

Lady Bullstrode herself had warned Cat against Mr. Fairfax. Yet despite everything, Cat admitted that she desired him and longed for his touch. And she was intended for his brother. Were they alike, the brothers? she wondered. Had they the same nature, the same family resemblance? How could she marry the one while desiring the other? She lay awake, unable to return to sleep until the dawn began its slow, silvery appearance.

"It is a perfect May morning," declared Lady Leacock as they bowled through St. James's Park in the Duchess of Devonshire's carriage some hours later. "And you look like the Queen of the May! Our own 'Primavera.' Did you choose that dress out of respect for the day?"

"No, Aunt," Cat replied distractedly. "I thought it made my hair and eyes look exceptionally good." She turned her gaze outward, while inwardly she was examining the new thoughts and sensations that her dream had brought so violently to her consciousness. All of Society seemed to be in attendance. She bowed and smiled to the many people who greeted her as they drove by. She saw Piers Leighton ahead, but she turned away to address a remark to Lady Leacock and the Duchess. To see him now, after her most immodest dream, was more than she could bear. Perversely, she desired more than anything to see Mr. Fairfax. Nonetheless, despite all her watchfulness, he did not appear.

The crush outside was great, but the Duchess and her party passed through easily. Once inside the great hall of the Royal Academy, all of Cat's usual delight returned. Cat enjoyed paintings and was determined to be pleased. Mr. Fairfax had vanished from Society as suddenly as a stage Mephistopheles. Even her feelings from her too vivid dream were fading. It was easier to banish them in the common-sense light of day. Ahead of her, the Duchess greeted Mr. Brummell. Cat suddenly wondered what the Duchess really felt. Certainly, she spent much of her time apart from the company of the Duke. Looking at her laughing face, Cat judged the Duchess to be a happy woman. Perhaps they were right. If one were married properly to a rich man, happiness could be found within one's situation, without regard to the personal characteristics of the partner. A rich man who would be anxious to indulge his wife might be a better match than a poor one, whose early youthful affection might grow dim with time and age, turning the marriage later to a tyranny of disappointment. The proposal of Lord Falconbridge, looked at in that light, might indeed be her wisest, best choice. She sought fruitlessly in the gallery of her own mind for a face to give him, to replace the dark visage of Mr. Fairfax, who so haunted its corridors.

She walked sedately down the long galleries, behind the other ladies, looking at landscapes and portraits. She liked the landscapes best, fanciful renderings of ancient scenes, of fantastical and foreign places. The portraits held her, for as she searched each painted feature, she wondered whether she might pick out some feature to stand for her unseen suitor and perhaps savior, Lord Falconbridge.

She passed by one picture that had drawn a small knot of dandies about it. She paused briefly to look, imagining that it would be a sporting scene of racing horses. Instead, she saw that it was a picture of a boxing match, shocking and fascinating at the same time. It rendered in faithful detail the shouting, drunken crowd, the sweat and blood of the contestants. Pausing to look again, she heard part of the conversation of two of the young bucks viewing it.

"Have you got your name down in the book?" asked the first.

"Oh, yes, entered in last Friday, before it closed. Would not miss it."

"Who do you favor?"

"Why, Fairfax, of course. Odds have gone to eight to one, and I've been to see him train."

Cat was caught unprepared by this mention of his name. She lingered, hoping to overhear more. Perhaps this would explain why she had not seen him recently.

"Do you think he can take him, then?"

"I cannot say, I have never seen the Comte du Foix box. But Fairfax is a powerful fighter, and du Foix is a much smaller man. I am going with the odds."

"I am betting against them. The only rule is that the last man standing wins. I think the Comte is going to be that man."

"Then you must know something I do not. Have you seen him fight?"

"Once," his companion answered. "Would you care for a side bet? First claret to du Foix, for example?"

"Come, Sir!" exclaimed the other. "They are wearing mauleys. What makes you think blood will be drawn?" The first merely smiled.

"Damme no. You have inside information, I'd swear it in court, but I will hold with my original bet."

The two strolled off, while Cat reexamined the painting. Mr. Fairfax would be in a ring like the one she beheld. She studied the two figures, their painted naked flesh, and the detailed muscles of their arms and chests. Her mind's image of Mr. Fairfax so brought her to breathlessness again. Far ahead of her, Lady Leacock, Lady Bullstrode, and the Duchess had paused and were looking around for Cat. Tearing herself away from the strange brutal painting, with its implicit savagery and its animal grace, Cat hurried towards them, smiling brightly with a gaiety that hid her tumultuous feelings.

"You must try not to get lost, Caitlyn," her aunt scolded. "You were not speaking with anyone unchaperoned, were you?"

"No, Aunt. I was struck by the strange barbarity of one of the pictures. I was unable to detach my gaze from it."

"No doubt, it was the one of the fighters. Men are such brutes," the Duchess interjected. "Even among gentlemen, it is now thought an accomplishment to knock another down. I loathe physical brutality." She turned away from her companions. A troubled look came over her face. She walked quickly toward the other end of the gallery.

Lady Bullstrode and Lady Leacock said nothing to each other, although a quick indecipherable look passed between them. Cat wondered whether the Duchess was worried about Mr. Fairfax. Was there a greater tenderness between them than was outwardly apparent? Marriage became ominous of other darker emotions and betrayals that she had not considered before. Walking after the older ladies, Cat resolved to control as much of her future and wealth as she could, for as long as she could. She would accept no offer unless her conditions were met. One of those conditions was the slaking of the passion that ran riot in her youthful body, awoken now from childhood sleep, aroused against her will, and hungry to be filled. Silently, she accompanied the older ladies as they observed each picture in turn, the gaiety quite gone out of their little group.

Upon their departure, the Duchess turned and said, "I am giving a masquerade ball before the Derby. I do hope you will come. Invitations will be sent out within the week."

Although the last thing that Cat wanted was another masquerade, her aunt answered for both of them. "Such an agreeable entertainment. We shall be delighted to attend."

THE CONTEST

"Are you ready, Mr. Fairfax, Sir?" The boy asked anxiously. Vere Courtenay Fairfax extended his hands for the mauleys. Beyond the dressing room, he could hear the raucous babbling of the crowd that had come to watch the contest. He stood quite motionless while the boy attended to him. Fairfax allowed his attention to wander freely. In a minute, he would need to concentrate, but for now, he relaxed, knowing that he had done everything he could do to prepare for this moment. Jackson suddenly appeared at his side, walked around him, examined him critically, and checked the lacing.

"You'll do," Jackson said finally, nodding to the attendant. "Anything you want to ask me? Last words?" he inquired, a wicked smile on his face.

"I only wish to begin," Vere smiled a chilling, ferocious smile. "Is Montclair ready?"

"He is," Jackson said. "He'll come at you quickly when he does come. He might take some time to get your measure, but when he does, he will move fast."

"Have you witnessed him fight?" Vere inquired.

"Nay, I could not. They trusted me not and barred me from entering. But I have heard things. We were wise to train as we did. I fear that his supporters have deliberately encouraged long odds from the beginning. All the better for them if they win by an 'upset.' "

"They shall not win," Vere said calmly.

"Aye," replied Jackson, "I think we may take them. Watch him for tricks; I do not trust him at all. If he starts losing, he will try to blind you, anything to neutralize your strength and aid his speed."

"Then let us begin," Vere said gravely and walked out to the ring.

The large area of the Fives Court was packed with men of every sort. Young dandies, aristocrats, and people of fashion accompanied by their servants mingled with red-coated officers, gambler's runners, and fighters, all excited and aroused by blood sport. Many of the crowd obviously had begun drinking hours earlier, and some would not outlast the fighters. The atmosphere was noisy with drink and high spirits, but once inside the ring, Vere heard none of it. His entire attention was concentrated on the immediate area in which he stood and on his opponent.

Monsieur Montclair, the Comte du Foix, was a slender, but well-muscled, man. He was laughing with his handlers, calling jokes and jibes into the crowd. They were clearly on his side. "What crowd does not love the underdog?" Vere thought bitterly. If they knew, would they be any different? Vere realized that Montclair's agents had placed many of the bets in the book, and Montclair stood to gain a percentage of each one if his was the victory. It was rumored that the book was worth in excess of sixty thousand pounds, not including side bets that would be called out during the successive rounds. That money would be employed to drive a spear straight through England's heart, in service to Montclair's master across the water. Carrington's spies had reported that Bonaparte had bent his envious eyes toward the green shores of England. The treaty would soon collapse, and then only the sea and the King's Navy would stand between Englishmen and the Ogre of Corsica. To what use was Montclair intending to put his winnings? Well, there would be no winnings, Vere thought grimly. He would be the last man standing.

The handlers were weighing Montclair in. "Twelve stone," called out the man. Vere stepped up. "Thirteen stone even," the man announced to the crowd. The odds against the Comte were eight to one on the first round.

Tom Cribb led Fairfax to his corner. "Aye," he whispered, "you have the advantage of height, weight, and reach, so he will have to use his speed to get inside your guard and pummel you from close in. Strike hard, and strike first."

Jackson strode out into the middle of the ring, and the noise of the crowd increased. Shouting to make himself heard over all the voices, he announced: "The fight between Lucien Montclair, the Comte du Foix, and Mr. Vere Courtenay Fairfax will commence immediately. The rules are as follows. A round will last until a man is knocked down. The participants will have thirty seconds to come up to scratch after a knockdown. The fight will be over when one of them fails to come up to the mark at the call of 'time.'" The mob roared its approval. Vere and Montclair squared up. Jackson looked first to Montclair, then Fairfax. "Are you ready?" Montclair gave a little bow of assent. Fairfax nodded. Raising his arm, Jackson brought it down and stepped aside. "Begin," he bellowed.

The two opponents circled each other warily, feinting punches, testing each other's reactions. Montclair smiled tauntingly. "You are quicker than I imagined, Monsieur," he said, after he ducked Fairfax's first down-cut. "But you must do better." Moving with lightening speed, Montclair then ducked under Fairfax's guard and struck at him, but Fairfax slipped it, pivoting left. Montclair achieved merely a glancing blow upon Fairfax's cheek. The Comte danced quickly out of the way, but not fast enough, as Vere's following upper-cuts caught the Comte first on the jaw, then upon the cheekbone. Montclair staggered, but did not fall, and a new hard look came into his eyes.

Darting in low, du Foix bore in, dodging underneath Vere's guard and planting two good rib roasters before Vere's short-armed left again slammed into Montclair's cheekbone, knocking him down. Montclair sprung to his feet. Dancing backwards, he endeavored to draw Fairfax by a feint to the left, followed by a right jab to his jaw. Again, Vere slipped it, boring in with a quick one-two to the Comte's midsection, followed by a powerful crosscut to the head. Montclair blocked the second, but misjudged his distance, returning with a hard muzzler that barely clipped his opponent's jaw. Vere returned with a straight-arm left, which floored the Comte. The round ended with Fairfax the clear winner. Among the crowd, the gamblers' legs were calling odds of ten to one.

In the crowd, Lord Carleton stood with Lords Sefton and Alvanely, both ardent followers of the Fancy.

"He shows well," Sefton said to Alvanley, nodding toward Fairfax. "He means to aim to the head and overpower him in the shortest time. Will he do it?"

"I have it on good authority that du Foix has bet a considerable fortune on his own behalf that he will not only draw first blood, but also win by a knockdown."

"Will he, indeed? He seems to be getting much the worst of it."

Round two began with Montclair ducking and weaving, fighting shy of Fairfax's long reach. Twice he dodged under Vere's guard, but Fairfax blocked the Comte's blows with Harmer's guard and again struck at Montclair's head, planting a facer that left a large ugly bruise beneath Montclair's right eye. Boring in, Fairfax hit du Foix again with a hard right, but Montclair retreated, without countering, earning him the hisses of the crowd. Pursuing the Comte, Fairfax stepped in and delivered a left down-cut, but Montclair rallied and landed several powerful body blows before Mr. Fairfax stepped in with a powerful stomacher that dropped du Foix to his knees.

In his corner, Cribb attended to Fairfax, held the water bottle, and whispered strategy in his ear. "You must take some of that shine out of him, Mr. Fairfax. He looks to dance forever, like some girl who is queen of the ball. He's quick, all right. Get him against the ropes and batter him until the spring is taken out of his skips. Odds say he will not outlast the sixth round."

Time was called, and the fighters came to the mark. The swelling from the bruise already disfigured the Comte's pretty face. Fairfax could see the anger in Montclair's eyes.

In round three, Fairfax took the offensive again, hammering back Montclair's defenses, following him closely and landing three out of four hits, despite du Foix's shifting and dodging. Du Foix rallied with a straight right and a one-two, but failed to stop Fairfax, who pursued du Foix, knocking aside his guard and felling him with a gravedigger's left that laid him out again. Odds were called ten to one, and the round was unanimously judged Mr. Fairfax's.

In his corner, Vere sipped some water. Du Foix was getting the worst of it, and two more rounds like this one would see an end to it. Beside him, Tom Cribb murmured, "Even though that last round was yours, du Foix's agents took all the bets offered. Mr. Jackson thinks this is the round where whatever trickery he has planned will be revealed." The timekeepers called time again, and both men took their mark.

Montclair was not yet winded, but the terrible punishment Fairfax had given him was beginning to tell. His handsome face was now disfigured by ugly swelling; still, he managed to slip and counter many of Fairfax's punches, dancing outside Fairfax's long reach and using his smaller size to dodge under Fairfax's guard to plant short body blows. None was sufficient to bring Vere down or even weaken his stamina. The longer the fight went on, the more severe the disadvantage would be to Montclair. Judging that the best way to bring out his weakness would be to make him lose his temper, Vere decided to smoke him a bit.

Closing with terrible swiftness, Vere knocked aside Montclair's guard and planted a hard right cross to his body, driving him to his knees. Vere followed this with a left-handed rib roaster, which caught Montclair as he fell. "I do not think you will be leading any dance figures at Almack's in the near future," Vere gloated over his fallen opponent. "Without your pretty looks, I would surmise your London career to be quite ended."

The anger in Montclair's eyes was palpable as Vere's foe clambered to his feet and came to scratch. "It will be your turn soon enough," Montclair said. He feinted left at Fairfax's guard. Stepping in to parry the blow, Fairfax was caught by surprise as Montclair kicked high with his right foot, striking Fairfax square in the left eye, drawing blood and closing it altogether. A collective gasp arose from the crowd, followed by a chorus of boos, hisses, and catcalls. Montclair wheeled and kicked again, straight to Fairfax's middle, taking the wind out of him and knocking him to the ground. Time was called, and Gentleman Jackson motioned the combatants' seconds into the ring for a hurried conference, as Cribb attended to Vere's eye, lancing the flesh around it to reduce the swelling while the side bets for first blood were settled. From his corner, Montclair called over to Fairfax. "It is quite probable that you will be the one to be absent from our next entertainments."

Meanwhile, Cribb fussed around Vere. "Are you all right, Sir? Never in my years have I seen a dirtier trick. Jackson will rule against him, I am sure."

"I think not," said Vere, watching the conference between the seconds. "We agreed to 'the last man standing.' I made no other stipulations. He is within his rights."

The worried look that Jackson passed to Vere confirmed his belief even before it was announced. Waving his arms for quiet, Jackson spoke. "Since 'twas the principals' agreement that the last man standing should be the winner, and since no other conditions were put on the fight, it is the judgment of this ring that the Comte du Foix's use of *le sabot* in no way constitutes a foul. Fighters, take your mark."

Vere stood to the mark. Montclair smiled a nasty smile. He immediately kicked high, but Vere, in a reflexive motion, pivoted away and downblocked the kick with his forearm. Montclair danced away, spun, and came at Vere again with a scissors kick that first took him in the throat, and then hit him in the chest. Vere fell, but at the end of the count was again at the mark. Du Foix closed again, kicking at Vere's face and middle. Vere retreated, blocking and countering where he could, but Montclair kept well out of his reach, nullifying all Vere's attempts to regain the offensive. Montclair ducked Vere's downcut and kicked, catching Vere in the throat again and felling him onto the canvas. The fifth round went to Montclair, and odds were four to one for du Foix.

"Well, I did not expect that to happen," said Lord Sefton, ruefully paying over the money he had lost by betting that du Foix would be out by the end of the fifth round. "Stand to lose a packet on this. Perhaps I should bet the new odds." He rolled his eyes to where the gambler's legs were taking bets for du Foix among the eager crowd.

"Wouldn't if I were you," Carleton drawled.

"Indeed?" questioned Lord Alvanley. "Are you sure of your man, or is it just friendship that advises you?"

"He has trained with Jackson for just such an eventuality," Carleton replied. "I will lay you a side wager, if you like."

Alvanley looked to Fairfax's corner, where Tom Cribb held a basin wherein Vere spat a great quantity of blood from his injured throat. "Doesn't seem that training did much good," Alvanley observed. "I'll take your side bet and your money too. Four to one is being cried. Will that suit?" They shook on it, and Carleton, looking at Fairfax's battered countenance, hoped that his faith was not misplaced.

"Can ye see, Mr. Fairfax? Will ye continue?" Cribb asked as the timekeepers prepared to call "time."

"I can see well enough," Fairfax muttered. "As I have his measure now, this drubbing was not entirely to my disadvantage." Doggedly, he came up to scratch, but he feigned a greater weakness than he actually felt. If Montclair believed him nearly beaten, he might grow careless in his attempt to finish him off, and Fairfax's strategy depended on the Comte's repetition of his fearsome scissors kick.

At the call of "begin," the two fighters came to the mark. Both showed the results of their contest, du Foix with his swollen and lopsided face, and Fairfax with his left eye a blood-filled ruin, with deep cut marks around the socket where it had been drained. They circled each other cautiously, Fairfax fighting long, du Foix dancing out of reach. Suddenly, Montclair struck at Vere with a high kick aimed at his injured eye. Vere deflected it outward with his forearm and reached inside du Foix's guard to strike a hard muzzler upon his already swollen jaw. This blow leveled the Comte by its sheer force. Du Foix rose before time, and Fairfax struck at him again, clipping him at the ear.

"His distance is all wrong," muttered Alvanley to Sefton. "Fairfax can't win unless he fights close in, for he won't be able to land a long 'un."

"If Vere's superior reach is neutralized, du Foix will fold him up like paper. Never thought I'd live to see the day when a Frenchie fighting *à la savate* would beat an English gentleman in an English ring."

In the ring, du Foix narrowed his eyes, surveying Fairfax, who stood guarded and waiting for his opponent's offensive. It came quickly as du Foix kicked repeatedly, forcing Vere to mill on the retreat, driving him around the ring. To his credit, Fairfax blocked many of du Foix's blows with the same outward cut of his forearm, but several got through, opening the cut over Vere's eye, which bled freely. He failed to block another, and the Comte kicked him hard in the stomach, dropping him yet again.

The crowd screeched its disapproval at du Foix and called for an end to the fight, but Jackson stolidly held the ring while Fairfax rose to his feet just before time. Montclair was walking around the ring, sardonically acknowledging the hisses and boos of the crowd, while Fairfax stood still in the middle of the ring, waiting for the next attack, with, it appeared, no more animation than an ox led to the slaughter. The Comte turned and came to scratch where his opponent awaited him.

"You have fought well enough," du Foix sneered. "In the eyes of your countrymen, you are perhaps the winner, according to what they believe the rules should be. But if this new age we live in teaches us anything, it is that the old rules no longer apply, and we new men may live by rules of our own choosing." So saying, he kicked again, the same dangerous scissors kick with which he had so punished Vere before.

This time Fairfax was ready for him. Turning sideways and blocking the kick upward with his left arm, he threw Montclair off balance. Stepping in, Fairfax hit Montclair with a churchwarden's right as he fell, followed by a straight left, which drove him down full length upon the floor. There was a hush as the timekeeper counted out the thirty seconds. At the end of it, du Foix was still stretched out senseless, though the roar that resounded through the Fives Court was enough to wake the dead.

Afterwards, all was motion and noise as du Foix's seconds came to carry him off and bring him to consciousness. Cribb helped Fairfax out of the ring, and later Jackson came back to fuss over him like a hen with but one chick.

"Here's some raw meat for that eye. 'Twill be swollen something awful for a few days and bloody for a week or more. Hold still!" Jackson commanded as the surgeon leaned over to examine Fairfax. "We will have to stitch that cut up first. It looks to be split nearly to the bone. You'll be no pretty sight at Almack's for a while."

Tom Cribb handed Vere a glass of strong spirits. "Ye can drink to your heart's content now, Mr. Fairfax, and per'aps ye'd better. This will sting no little bit. On my life, 'tis the bloodiest, finest mill ever fought by two gentleman at the Fives Court. And all for a coach and pair."

Vere tried to speak, but Montclair's blow to Vere's throat had taken his voice, and even swallowing was extremely painful.

"Nay, Tom," replied Jackson. "'Twas for the honor and glory of England that Mr. Fairfax fought. It's war, Sir! Addington's government declared war on France today. I am right proud of you, Mr. Fairfax, and proud to have had a part in your training, as you should be too, young Tom. 'Twill be your turn soon. Do your part as well, and England shall shine in your glory! Give me a hand, and send for Lord Carleton. Mr. Fairfax needs his bed more than anything else now."

Surrendering to their helping hands, Vere closed his eyes and let himself be dressed and bundled off in his carriage to his home, where he slept a full four and twenty hours without awakening.

"Shall we see you at the Duchess's masquerade ball?" asked Lady Thomas to Lady Leacock later that same day as they sipped tea in Lady Thomas's pale blue drawing room.

"Indeed, yes," replied Lady Leacock. "We are expecting several offers of marriage to be tendered at the ball."

"How fortunate for Miss Llewellyn," Lady Thomas said with a small smile. "Miss Thomas has already received several, and I expect several more before the end of the Season." She forbore to add that she considered few of them first-rate. Colonel Percy offered the best name, but in exchange demanded a ruinous settlement. "I am sure I don't know whom Clarissa favors most. These young things never tell us, do they?"

"I believe I may interpret my niece's heart," Lady Leacock said with satisfaction. "She appears to favor her father's choice, the Earl of Falconbridge, our near neighbor. It is the wish of their families that they be joined. He has written her some pretty letters. Although she has not spoken openly, I believe that her fancy is captured and that there will be an announcement at the end of the Season."

"He is the Lord of Foxearth?" Lady Thomas inquired. "A rich estate indeed."

"Nor is that the extent of his holdings," Lady Leacock continued with satisfaction. "He has several more estates and coal mines as well. His wealth is considerable."

"I wish you joy," enthused Lady Thomas, inwardly seething. Could not such a prize be somehow detached by Clarissa's wiles? The scandal scotched by Lady Bullstrode might now be resurrected to the Thomases' benefit. "More tea, Lady Leacock? Pray, what are you wearing to the ball?"

Roberts stepped out the great front door of Portman Square. A young ragamuffin with shrewd eyes older than his years ran up to meet him. "Sweep yer steps, Guv'ner?" he inquired. Roberts looked quickly around, but no one was observing them. "Tell your master that while serving tea, I heard it from Lady Leacock to Lady Thomas that Miss Llewellyn is wearing a shepherdess costume with a fox mask to the ball. 'Tis being made at Madame La Croix's establishment," he said in a quick whisper, then raising his voice, he said loudly, for the sake of Mr. Arbuthnot or any other passersby who might take an interest, "Be off with you, we need no such help here." The boy, with a saucy grin, said, "Thanks fer yer help Guv'ner," and ran off. Relieved, Roberts stepped back inside and closed the door.

BAL MASQUE

Cat stood irritably while around her, Madame's seamstresses completed the last fittings on her shepherdess costume for the Duchess of Devonshire's masked ball. "This is excessively silly," Cat complained to Lady Leacock while looking at herself in the billowing skirt and the sequined embroidered bodice in the mirror before her. "What shepherdess could tend her sheep in this dress? Even the hat is preposterous." She looked with dismay at the flat little hat fetchingly perched at an angle upon her long tumbled curls. "What use is this for a *bal masque?* I am obviously myself, and I look ridiculous!"

"*Non, non,*" murmured Madame La Croix as she tied a whimsical fox mask over Cat's face. "It is a *bon mot, n'est-ce pas?* A joke," she said brightly as she stepped back to give Cat and her aunt the full effect.

"It is delightful," Lady Leacock beamed. "Very fetching, don't you think so, my Dear?"

Cat surveyed herself through the eyeholes of the mask. The face in front of her was slyly flirtatious, the mouth turned drolly up in a little smile that suggested hidden laughter. "Are you not afraid I will be labeled a vixen by the *ton?* Foxes have such a reputation for being fast."

"And being clever," replied Lady Leacock, who was looking at herself in a gilded bird's mask. "You will be very much noticed and talked about in that costume."

"My dear Aunt Henrietta," Cat replied with patience. "I am already noticed and talked about. I thought the object of a masquerade was to be disguised as someone other than oneself."

"And so you shall be, in that costume. They may speculate, but they cannot know, unless you take off your mask."

"And my hair, what about that?"

"My Dear! The Duchess herself has hair colored very like, as do Lady Atherton and the Honorable Sarah Rochford. I think that it suits you very well. Besides, this is the last big ball before the racing season starts. I cannot believe that no one will offer for you after this ball. It is most mysterious that you have not had any offers yet!"

"Perhaps I have not been enthusiastic enough," Cat muttered, laying the mask aside and signaling to Madame La Croix's minions to remove the costume.

"Do not speak so. Your conduct has been above reproach and quite seemly. I am quite sure that you will have at least one offer made at the ball! A masquerade ball makes a suitor much bolder."

"But the purpose is to be unrecognized!" exclaimed Cat, picking up the pretty fox mask and holding it in front of her face again.

"Oh, one who truly cares about you will penetrate any disguise!" laughed Aunt Henrietta. "Will that not serve as a test for any true suitor?"

Cat stared at herself in the mirror. The fox face looked back, sly with a secret laughter. "Yes, I think you may be right," she replied.

"Good!" Henrietta clapped her hands. "We shall take this. Wrap it up."

"Very good." Madame La Croix bowed and beckoned to one of the pretty seamstresses. "There is some work that needs to be done yet on the hem," the girl said hesitantly.

"Very well," said Lady Leacock. "Finish the work, and see that it is done no later than Thursday. Her Grace's ball is Friday."

"*Oui*," murmured the young woman. "It will be finished in time."

"But of course," added Madame La Croix smoothly. "We never disappoint a client."

The two ladies left the shop. Lady Leacock was pleased, but Cat felt rebellious and sulky. Her aunt would be sure that everyone in the *ton* knew the secret of her disguise unless she could contrive to obtain another costume, unbeknownst to Henrietta. It would be quite droll, she thought, to be a "Fair Unknown," to see who might be sincerely interested in her and not just her wealth. No doubt, she could obtain a modest dress and mask at one of the other shops in Bond Street. The Venezia came immediately to mind. Stepping into the carriage with her aunt, she settled it quietly to herself.

"Lady Bullstrode has invited us to tea. You are not too fatigued, are you?"

"I am perfectly fine, thank you. Tea with Lady Bullstrode would be welcome." The gossip would be interesting. So little actually happened to women that gossip was almost the only item of interest. Tomorrow would be enough time to achieve her plan of an alternate costume.

Lady Bullstrode was effusive and sparkled with excitement. "Are you ready for the Duchess of Devonshire's masked ball?" she beamed, pouring them each a cup of tea from her fine white china teapot that was decorated in tiny figures of orange and red. To Cat, she appeared costumed already, in a dark green and white gown, decorated with rows of red rosettes and topped by a large green turban, complete with a nodding red feather that punctuated every statement.

"Such news!" Lady Bullstrode trumpeted, her face fairly bursting with the information. "There was a perfectly dreadful *melée* at the Fives Court. I heard it from Lady Sefton, who had it from Lord Sefton himself, who was there! Monsieur Montclair, the Comte du Foix, and that horrid Mr. Fairfax fought each other, and both received severe damage. It was, according to Lady Sefton, a very bloody fight indeed."

"Do tell!" said Henrietta, sipping her tea. "What was the outcome of the matter?"

Cat put her cup down suddenly to conceal the trembling of her hand. Her mind was assaulted with a rush of images: the compelling and brutal painting at the Exhibition, the jesting words of the dandies viewing it, the touch of Mr. Fairfax's lips upon her hand, the strange bitter smile that passed over his coldly handsome face afterward, and the suave and pleasant words of the Comte as he danced with her at Almack's. Lady Bullstrode was continuing with her narrative.

"It seems that it was a bet over horses and a curricle. The Comte du Foix swore he had won them, but Mr. Fairfax, fancying them himself, had bought them from their owner, Viscount Stanhope, who was sprung, you see, and was going to give them to the Comte in lieu of the money he had lost on a wager. So, the Comte du Foix challenged Mr. Fairfax for a bout at the Fives Court. My Dears, everybody was there!"

"But this is nothing new." Lady Leacock rejoined serenely. "Gentlemen often settle wagers there. What was so different about this?"

"The ferocity!" Lady Bulltrode dropped her voice portentously. "Even with the gloves on, there was blood drawn. The Comte du Foix fought with his feet, as well as his fists! It was dreadful!"

Cat could not bring herself to speak, afraid that the emotions sweeping through her would give her away. Picking the teacup up with a steadier hand, she drank up the burning liquid in quick sips.

"And the outcome?" Lady Leacock inquired calmly.

"Oh, Mr. Fairfax won. Lady Sefton said that Lord Sefton had never seen anything like it for bravery. But Mr. Fairfax was taken away quite cut up. I doubt we shall see him again before the end of the Season." Cat set down her cup wordlessly. Lady Bullstrode immediately filled it with tea. "What are you wearing to Her Grace's masquerade ball?"

Cat put the refilled cup to her lips and sipped sparingly of the hot tea. Lady Leacock filled the silence with a description of Cat's shepherdess costume. "And we have another surprise," she said, smiling at Cat. "Sir Merlin is coming to London tomorrow with Meteor! He is running him in the Derby, where he is greatly favored to win! Is that not wonderful, Cat?"

"Oh, indeed," said Cat abstractedly. On another occasion, she might have objected to being told nothing of her father's arrival, but her disappointment contested with her horror about the fate of Mr. Fairfax. A pang of regret stole through her heart, even as she knew that this was the least difficult and most sensible end to her dangerous dilemma. She, remembering all of their few short minutes alone, could not help wondering, with regret, whether he might not be a better man than was generally credited. Now, she found it very hard to believe either the veracity of her own first impressions and experiences or what she had been told of him.

Arriving home, she immediately saw a letter on the sideboard, addressed to her in the now familiar hand of Lord Falconbridge. She hardly had time to pick it up when she saw her father, Sir Merlin himself, descending the wide white staircase in front of her.

"Caitlyn!" he cried, his arms opening forth in embrace as he approached her. "You have been a very vexing child to do such a thing! I should take a riding crop to you, but I am so glad to see you, and you are so lovely, I cannot do anything but give you the warmest of embraces and thank God I see you again."

Cat flew into his arms and kissed his cheek as he caught her in his strong embrace. "Oh, Father, I am so glad to see you. I will never do such a thing again. I promise."

"Well, let me look at you! You are a fine grownup woman now. How many suitors should I expect to be calling on me?" he jested.

Cat appealed to Lady Leacock with her eyes. "Dear Brother," Henrietta said, "The entire list of the contestants in the running has not been posted. I do believe your favorite, Lord Falconbridge, is one of them."

Cat colored. It was true. His letters had made him seem far more eligible than she had first thought, but his close connection to Mr. Fairfax was most uncomfortable. If she married Lord Falconbridge, she would never be able to bear seeing Mr. Fairfax again. Taking a bold tone, she answered back. "Lord Falconbridge might be my favorite, if I were to catch even a glimpse of him. He has remained quite hidden."

"Well, I have brought a friend of yours with me," Sir Merlin said cheerfully. "Meteor has come in a boxvan all the way. Have you not heard he is favored in the Derby? Do you wish to come and see him, or have you gotten too missish?"

"Of course. Let me just change into something more suitable." With a quick kiss, she left them and hurried up to her room, leaving the letter on her dressing table, where she could read it later.

She nearly forgot it that night in all the excitement of the arrivals. She had grown fond of Lord Falconbridge's letters, against her original inclinations, even as she found herself hopelessly desiring a glimpse of his scapegrace brother. Now both were invisible to her. Tearing open the seal, she read.

My very dearest Miss Llewellyn,

The business that has kept me away from you is nearly done. On the eve of a difficult completion, I find my thoughts turning to you more than to anything else. I hope this business does not keep me away from you longer than it already has. When I first began it, I thought 'twould soon be ended, and if it were anything but what it is, I would turn away from it now to go to you.

In part, I welcomed it because I have feared the moment of meeting you. A coward part of me would have put off that time yet a little more, even while I know delay can serve only to enhance my rivals' power. Having read once, twice, thrice, and more times the final lines of your last letter, I know I must see you and give answer to your questions in person. I have a great fear, not unfounded, that you will be disappointed upon seeing me.

Yet I am willing, nay eager to risk all. I therefore hope to see you in London as soon as circumstances permit. Please believe my heart is truly thine, more than my own.

Lord Falconbridge

Cat drew a deep breath. Her maid must have posted her last letter for her. Cat wondered why had she not destroyed it after the shocking revelation of her dream.

The next morning, Cat dressed in a very plain white frock and a bonnet more notable for what it concealed than what it revealed. Thus attired, she most unusually took her maid in the closed carriage. Unremarked by any of the fashionable world, they alighted at the Venezia at the most unfashionable hour of ten-thirty in the morning. With little ceremony and few words, she bought a plain black-lace veil and mask, with a traditional Venetian tricorn, much out of fashion these fifteen years, which gave all the more reason to suppose it a complete disguise. Her maid dispensed the requisite coin to the elderly shopkeeper, and both of them reentered the carriage and drove away.

At 18 Park Lane, Vere Courtenay Fairfax paused briefly in his restless perambulations to regard his battered visage. The swelling had gone down, but the bruising remained, an ugly yellow and mottled purple. The black stitches around his eye were still in place and could not be removed until the week following, or so the surgeon had said. It was a face to frighten a brigand, and the eye patch that the doctor had tactfully recommended he wear hardly improved matters.

Rumor had it that Montclair was utterly ruined in fortune and had fled. This gave Vere some satisfaction. Montclair would not be able to pursue Cat or any other scheme, but, then, neither would Vere. Vere had indeed become a Caliban, he thought regretfully, unable to show his face. A stray thought niggled at his mind, something about a party that Georgiana was giving. The invitation had arrived before the contest at the Fives Court, and he had laid it aside with barely a glance. Now, with sudden inspiration, he hurried to his study, where he had left it upon his desk. Eagerly he perused it again, and seating himself, he seized a sheet of writing paper and penned a courteous reply to her Grace, requesting one favor. Then he rang for his valet.

The night of the ball, Lady Leacock, swathed in veils and a turban like a Pasha's wife, knocked discreetly on Cat's door. "Are you ready yet?" she asked anxiously. "We shall be late in making our entry if we delay much longer."

Cat's young whey-faced maid opened the door quickly. Cat stood before her, fetchingly gowned in the shepherdess costume, holding the fox mask in her hands. "Oh, do run along without me, Aunt Henrietta! If we make our entry together, no one will be fooled as to my identity. Let me come separately in a hackney and allow them all to guess. Please say yes, dear Aunt!"

Henrietta looked fondly at her niece. It would do no harm to indulge her in this. She had it on good authority that both the young Lords Leighton and Atherton would offer for Caitlyn as soon as Sir Merlin would receive them. The Marquis of Bradbury was rumored to be in the running as well. It would do no harm. "Very well," she said benignly. "Only do not arrive too late."

"I shan't," said Cat. "I shall arrive within the hour. There will still be plenty of time to dance before supper."

"If you so desire," Lady Leacock smiled indulgently and, giving her niece one final kiss, withdrew, trailing her multicolored scarves behind her.

"Quickly," said Cat as she watched from her window as the carriage departed. "Help me off with this. In five minutes, no more, I wish to be dressed and ready to leave." With capable fingers, aided by Cat's own hurried desire, the maid helped Cat out of the beautiful shepherdess's costume and quickly buttoned her into a plain green gown, one of those that she had worn during her first days at Lady Leacock's, and since discarded for the more elaborate creations of the fashionable *modiste.* Putting on veil, mask, and hat, she studied herself briefly. She was merely a slender unknown. Satisfied, she hurried down the steps, clutching the Duchess's invitation, and out the front door, where the unremarkable hackney coach waited.

The Duchess had every reason to be satisfied with the ball. Attended by Brummell, who, by custom, never assumed a mask, she looked with pleasure at the bright throng that filed her ballroom.

"I do believe that is Lady Jersey over there, costumed as a milkmaid. I thought that you said this was to be a masquerade, Your Grace?" he inquired in his pleasant drawl.

"You are too bad, George," she said with a giggle. "There are many here I do not recognize."

"Isn't that the point of a masquerade, Your Grace?"

"But after I do not recognize them, I want to know who they are."

"Then allow me to point them out to you. That woman there," he looked again through his glass, "I believe it is a woman, ah yes, Lady Bullstrode in fact, in that purple domino. She has carried on that disguise very successfully for nigh twenty years or more. Where is the King's Swan tonight? I have heard that she was to come as a vixen dressed in a shepherdess costume: 'Hide fox and all after.' I do not believe I have seen her yet."

The Duchess giggled again. "She is coming later. Lady Leacock said she wishes to make her entrance unannounced and unaccompanied, to remain unknown until the unmasking."

"Indeed," Brummell drawled. "How very sporting of her, to try to give us something to wonder about." His eyes swept the room again, scrutinizing each fair unknown. His eyes fell on a slight graceful figure in a rather unmodish costume who was standing quietly among several other young ladies. "I will wager you a guinea I spy her first."

He looked at the Duchess, but she appeared not to have heard him. Her attention was elsewhere. She was looking at a tall figure of a man, cloaked and hooded in black, with a white mask of the Apollo Belvedere upon his face. "Please have me announced," he said in a hoarse voice that barely rose above a whisper. The Duchess took the proffered card from his white-gloved hand and handed it wordlessly to the footman.

In a loud voice, the footman announced, "The Earl of Falconbridge and Count of Montferrato." Below, the dancers seemed to pause in their colorful whirl, and a few whispers went through the crowd among the mamas of the eligible debutantes, but most continued in their pleasures, unmindful of the new arrival.

Cat sat down suddenly upon one of the vacant chairs that lined the wall, grateful for the black mask that hid her from all eyes. She watched the Earl as he saluted the Duchess and made his silent way around the dance floor, the beautiful expressionless mask viewing the dancers and the wallflowers with blank impartiality. She dropped her gaze as in his perambulation he slowly approached. Mercifully, she was asked to dance by a red-faced gentleman of little acquaintance and no accomplishment. He whisked her away in a strenuous reel. She hoped that her anonymity would be protected among the more gorgeously gowned dancers on the floor.

Although her partner had little accomplishment in dancing, her own grace made her a popular partner at once. She had barely returned to her place when a young grenadier promptly requested her hand. She was whirled away into a lively schottische and had no leisure time to speculate on the further activities of the dark figure of Lord Falconbridge. He was standing slightly apart from the rest of the crowd, inspecting the dancers from behind his ideally beautiful but disquieting mask. He watched as the pretty, slender masque in green was returned to her place, only to be invited again out to the floor where another dance was beginning. Bowing courteously to a plump dowager standing beside him, he inquired in a barely audible voice if she would favor him with this dance. Too surprised by the invitation to think of refusal, the dowager allowed him to lead her out to a place in the line.

Cat found herself greatly enjoying the ball. With no need to choose her partners based solely on their eligibility, she found that her naturally high spirits soared. Her grace and liveliness were commented upon by more than one member of the company. Moving gracefully through the measured steps of the Touchstone, she found herself unexpectedly partnered with the tall masked figure announced as Lord Falconbridge.

With elegant precision, he made a respectful bow to her and lightly took her hand as he walked her down the aisle formed by the other dancers. His mask hid all trace of his face. Curious to hear his voice, Cat sought for a suitable remark. As they saluted and parted from each other at the top of the figure, Lord Falconbridge whispered, "Your servant" in a hoarse tone barely audible over the music and released her hand. Curiosity piqued her, and she watched him covertly as they circled with their next partners. His severe correctness betrayed nothing of his humanity, and she was glad when the dance ended with no other passage between them. So that was the man I almost considered marrying, she thought in relief, looking back again at the tall black-garbed figure. How fortunate that I have been saved from all that coldness!

If she were done with him, however, it seemed that he was not done with her. The musicians next struck up a lively gallop, and her strange suitor stood before her, bowed again, and petitioned her with his hand outstretched and but one word, "please," spoken again in that low unnatural tone. Meaning fully to refuse him, Cat changed her mind. He surely must be unaware of her identity. From the corner of her eye, she had seen Lady Leacock and Lady Bullstrode talking in animated and intimate conversation, staring furtively at the door. If they were not aware of her presence at the ball, how could he be so? Deciding that this was an opportunity to learn something of his actual being, as forbidding as her first impression of him had been, she nodded a gesture of assent and allowed him to lead her on to the dance floor.

The light pressure of his hand upon hers, as they joined the whirling dance in rapid circle, was protective without being oppressive. Contrary to the strange somberness of his mask, with its combination of deep sable clothing and pallid but unmoved ideal beauty, he was as lively a dancer as the young dandies who spun around at an ever maddening pace to the loud shrieks of their breathless partners. Quite grateful at the dance's end to be led to the sidelines, Cat accepted with gratitude a chair beside him.

"You are a most energetic partner," she murmured. "Thank you for the honor of the dance."

"The honor is all mine," he replied in that curiously husky voice. "You are breathless. May I get you some refreshment?"

"Please," she replied in turn, grateful for the respite. He rose and bowed to her, and she watched him covertly as he walked across the ballroom. He was intercepted several times, she noticed. The Duchess herself approached him first. Cat could not hear what she was saying, but the expression of concern was evident on her face. She tentatively reached her hand up toward the blank white mask, but he shook his head slightly, took her hand in his and, after bowing over it, continued on his way. The next encounter made her heart start within her bosom. Lady Leacock and Lady Bullstrode next approached him. "They must be telling him that I am expected," Cat thought with a shudder. His posture was courteous, but only perfunctorily attentive. He looked beyond them, directly to where she was sitting, as if to confirm that she yet awaited his return.

"How curious it is," Cat thought. "Could he have guessed my identity? I cannot believe it possible. Perhaps I can use this opportunity to test his character. A man who writes of love to one woman may be quite different while conversing with another." Excusing himself to the Ladies Bullstrode and Leacock and procuring a lemonade, he directed his steps again toward her. Cat waited with great composure, knowing that he could have in no way penetrated her disguise. It was merely an interesting coincidence that had provided her with an unparalleled opportunity to assess this man whom her relations were so eager to foist upon her. His letters had been intriguing, she admitted, but she had not been prepared for the rather fearsome reality of his actual presence.

He stood in front of her, bowing slightly and offering her the lemonade. She took it graciously from his white-gloved outstretched hand, and with a simple gesture invited him to sit beside her. He assented with a single nod of his head. They sat in unbroken silence for some minutes. Such taciturnity was not promising, she thought. However, his letters had been filled with lively turns of phrase and wide-ranging thoughts. Perhaps speaking pained him. Cat thought that his voice had suffered an injury. Turning brightly to her silent mysterious partner, she asked.

"Forgive me for being forward, but I cannot help noticing your voice. I hope that you have not suffered a grievous hurt?"

He bowed slightly in acknowledgment. "You are perceptive. I have had a slight injury, which I hope will soon mend."

"Are you enjoying the ball? It must be difficult to be compelled to silence around so much gaiety."

"Yes," he replied, "though silence in no way detracts from my enjoyment."

"Indeed, I would think conversation was one of the principle enjoyments of a ball."

"The company of so much beauty must be accounted the first," he replied so softly she could barely hear him. "To be compelled to enjoy it in silence is a stricture I must bear." What could he mean, she wondered? Nothing of her face showed from beneath the mask. Save for the plump woman he had partnered in the Touchstone, she had been his only partner. "Indeed, I dare not show my face among such beauty," she replied saucily.

"But not for reasons of beauty," he replied, "for I am convinced you are the most beautiful woman here."

"You are too forward," she said quickly with some anger. How could he, after writing such letters to her, be dancing and flirting with some perfect unknown? Her disappointment was sharper than she realized. First, she had suffered the impossibility of Mr. Fairfax and now the betrayal of Lord Falconbridge. It was too much.

"Pray forgive me," Lord Falconbridge whispered again in husky tones. "Have I made a mistake?" His tone held a note of question. "I thought you to be Miss Llewellyn. If I am mistaken, I regret revealing myself to you thus." Nevertheless, he made no move to rise.

Cat was taken aback. How could he have penetrated her disguise? Even her Aunt Henrietta and Lady Bullstrode were unaware of her presence, for they were still awaiting her entry. Unwilling to reveal herself to him, but fairly puzzled as to how he had concluded that she was indeed Caitlyn Llewellyn, whom he had never met, she decided to quiz him.

"I must be flattered indeed to be mistaken for the King's Swan," she ventured boldly, "but unmasked, my Lord, you would see we are nothing like."

"I cannot believe that," he replied, "for you have her very grace, liveliness of temper, and air of charm. Indeed, unless she were to appear beside you, I would not believe that you are not her."

"You are much mistaken," Cat replied, deeply flustered. How could he claim to recognize her? He had never set eyes on her. "You have not looked on your lady with much knowledge to be so mistaken."

"In fact, she has never been formally introduced to me as Lord Falconbridge. When I arrived from the Continent to meet her, she was already gone to London. We have spoken truly only in letters. Nonetheless, I feel that I know her as well or better than any other woman of my acquaintance. Seeing her so often in my mind's eye, I feel certain that I would recognize her anywhere."

"So you picked a masquerade ball to make your first introduction? How very singular! Are you then an eccentric?" she added daringly.

He bowed to her again, hidden behind the idealized, frozen beauty of his mask. "It is not eccentricity, but necessity that demands it. Forgive me if I speak to one beautiful woman of my love for another, even though nothing short of unmasking would convince me that you are not her. I have spoken truly to her through our correspondence. If I were to tell you the best of my life is centered so firmly around her letters as to make them the hope and polestar of my existence, I trust that you would believe me to be in all earnestness. In my letters, I promised her that she would find me no Caliban, but an accident has put a lie to that promise for the present. Yet so desirous am I to see her finally in front of me that I could not wait for more sober judgment to counsel continued delay, but rather availed myself of this first opportunity, poor masquerade that it is. You must understand that I fear that she might surrender her heart to another before I can offer my claim."

Cat was touched by the evident ardor in his voice, low and roughened as it was. She looked into his masked face. A black gauze lining made both eyeholes disturbingly blank, with no semblance of true feature upon which to fasten her imaginings. How touchingly he presented his plea. Her heart went out to him. How plainly he had stated his hopes on paper, with what delicacy of feeling he had sought to ease her fears and to court her. Now he feared all his patience was for naught. How wretched and cowardly she felt at her continued deception.

"No one who has received your words could fail to care for you," she murmured almost inaudibly. "I do not think your lady has been carried off by an unworthy attraction," she continued, blushing as she spoke, knowing her sinful desire for Mr. Fairfax, brother to this man.

"Even if she had," he whispered, leaning close to her, "I would hear it from her own lips, that I could in turn plead my case, for I have waited so long to be in her presence. My own maladroit beginning has caused the delay, nor can I be sure my attempted amends have achieved their purpose. Braving my fears and counting upon the generosity of her spirit for forgiveness, I had hoped to find her here. Yet, if you do not lie, it seems I must wait a little longer. Perhaps," he continued, "it is better to let time go by. I fear that she could not yet bear my unmasked face."

"If she truly loves you, love's eye shall see truly."

"Then, my lady, the unmasking is at hand. I am prepared to hazard all, if you will but show your unmasked face to me. You have been the Muse to my better self, calling me forth from a hell of bitter memories and black regret. Judge me as you will, oh Terpsichore, for you have tuned my heart to love." He reached out gently, touching the mask upon her face.

Cat stood suddenly in her own confusion, even before she was aware of it herself. "Please do not bother to rise. I wish you good fortune with your lady. I am not her whom you seek. She must be of a braver stamp than I. I have engaged your conversation too long. I feel I must take a turn about the ballroom." She fled, in the general direction of the supper room.

Vere Courtenay Fairfax, Earl of Falconbridge and Count of Montferrato, started after her. His way was blocked by a sudden swirl of high-spirited young tulips calling loudly for a rigadoon while the rest of the ballroom suddenly began a general exodus towards the supper room.

Pushing his way forward, he found himself confronted by a pretty mask dressed as Columbine. "Lord Falconbridge," she offered in trilling tones, "although your costume shows you no Harlequin, yet I presume upon you, as we are near neighbors. I hope I may intrigue you to find me out. I see that you have not yet found out your intended, Miss Llewellyn. We hear that tonight she comes in the mask of a vixen. Did you know of her previous masquerade as my lady's maid or her dalliance with that well-known rake, Mr. Fairfax?"

With effort, he had disciplined his fury at this check in his course. Now he did not bother to discipline his words. "I found you out long ago. I advise you to marry the first man who will have you, Miss Thomas, before your attempts to blacken Miss Llewellyn's reputation are generally known throughout Society, something I can easily arrange. I know the truth of the matter between Miss Llewellyn and Mr. Fairfax. You do not. Your hypocrisies do not blind me, and I shall take great pleasure in revealing them for what they are. Hasten to marry before the unmasking, Miss Thomas. Good night to you." Searching the crowd for Cat, he pushed brusquely past Clarissa, leaving her standing in open-mouthed dismay, staring after him.

Cat paused only briefly to look back in her flight. He meant to follow her. Even while the crowd around the sumptuously laden buffet supper thickened, she did not feel that she could evade him for long. Looking desperately around, she sought an escape. The darkness of the gardens that lay beyond the bright circle of light cast by the ballroom offered the only shelter. Stepping gratefully between couples, she sought the edge of the light on the terrace.

She felt her elbow being grasped in painful hold. *"Mademoiselle,"* whispered a faintly familiar voice in her ear. "If you wish to evade detection, you must come with me." Before she could recover from her surprise at thus being addressed, the mysterious stranger stepped from the shadows, forcing her away from the brightly lit windows and beyond the terraces into the darkened gardens. She tried to turn her head to catch a glimpse of her abductor. She opened her mouth to scream, but he covered it cruelly with his gloved hand and wrenched her arm behind her, forcing it up in a painful hold. Again, the harsh voice whispered in her ear. "I shall break it if you do not hurry your pace." He jerked her arm up farther, suddenly intensifying the pain. He pushed her quickly, forcing her to stumble through the garden's dark walkways, towards a small postern gate. Beyond it, she could see a shabby horse and carriage. "You needn't fear that I am an agent of Lord Falconbridge," her captor hissed. "I have something much more interesting in mind." They reached the postern gate. He unceremoniously bundled her through it and inside the small closed carriage. With a crack of the whip, the horse sprang into a quick trot, and they swiftly vanished.

Fairfax reached the supper room, but his intense eye saw no Cat revealed among the diners. Over the noise, he heard the Duchess's footman announce from within the ballroom, "Miss Caitlyn Llewellyn." Unbelieving, he remained caught by indecision. Determined, he stepped quickly through the large doors onto the shadowed terraces. Strolling couples looked at him curiously. The silence of the gardens beyond answered him with an ominous darkness.

Returning to the supper room, he strode his way with haste through the crowd. There on the steps by the entrance to the Ballroom stood an auburn-haired woman in a pretty blue and white shepherdess costume wearing a droll fox mask. About her clustered Lady Leacock, Lady Bullstrode, and several of the most eligible beaux of the *ton*. He watched as the young woman trilled a delighted laugh and, placing her arm coquettishly within that of the Marquis of Bradbury, strolled toward the supper room.

Refusing to believe that he could have been mistaken about his Fair Unknown and with an ever-growing apprehension, he forced his way towards where the woman announced as Miss Llewellyn was holding court. Before he could reach her, Sir Merlin Llewellyn intercepted him. The old man was breathless and distraught.

"Falconbridge. I am glad I found you. Meteor has been stolen. I stepped out to the mews to see him before going to bed and found only an empty stall. I fear this is not the whole of it."

"You are right," Fairfax whispered. "There is more. It is imperative that you immediately remove Miss Llewellyn from this assembly. I also fear a greater plot in progress." He thought quickly. "It would be helpful if we could speak with her first away from the guests. Do not alarm her. I will ask Her Grace for the use of a private room somewhere out of the way." Turning to Lady Leacock, who had just joined them, he said, "I have requested a private interview with Miss Llewellyn. Would you accompany Sir Merlin and aid him with your persuasions? Bring her to the great staircase." He swiftly made his purposeful way to where the Duchess was standing in lively conversation with Beau Brummell and Lord Carrington.

"Your Grace," he said, his voice a low, painful rasp, "could you put a private room at my disposal? I desire to speak to Miss Llewellyn *tête à tête*."

"Indeed?" Her Grace said archly, smiling beneath her white and gold half mask. "Have you something to propose to her?" Turning to Brummell, she laughed and laid a gentle white-gloved hand on his impeccable sleeve. "You owe me a guinea, Sir!" Turning to Falconbridge, she said, "Moulton will show you up to the Blue Room."

George Brummell took up his quizzing glass. "Demned if I believe it!" he exclaimed *sotto voce* to Lord Carrington.

"Falconbridge, would you present me to your Fair Lovely unmasked, as I have not yet had the privilege?" Lord Carrington inquired blandly.

The blank mask revealed nothing. After some seconds' thought, Vere said, "Good of you to think of it. Come with me, Carrington," and walked quickly to where a rather sizable group was now standing.

The rufous-haired shepherdess was herself herded between Sir Merlin on her right and the Ladies Leacock and Bullstrode on her left. As Vere approached, he heard Lady Bullstrode say in her confiding bellow, "My dear Lord Bradbury, Miss Llewellyn extends her regrets. It seems long-standing family business must take precedence over even you. Please excuse us for the moment." Moulton made the group a quick bow and silently led the little party up the Grand Staircase.

CAPTIVE

The cab pulled up short, in a dark and stinking street, in front of a stable door. "Out," the man growled while shoving Cat in front of him, as he jumped down. The driver cracked the whip again, and the horses' hoofs clattered loudly in the dank, chill air. The man seized her again, but Cat was ready for him. Swiftly raising her leg, she kicked back viciously with her heel. There was a satisfying crunch as her foot connected to the kneecap, but he did not release his hold on her. Giving an enraged cry, he spun her about. Raising his hand, he slapped her a back-handed blow. She slumped with the force of it. As he caught her, he put the fingers of one hand about her neck and squeezed. Everything spun out into darkness. Picking her motionless body up in his arms, he brought her over the threshold of a mean little building. The lower floor was a dark and filthy stable, and the upper floor was barely more than a loft room, dark and crudely furnished.

* * *

"Miss Llewellyn," Lord Falconbridge rasped, "I must insist that you take off your mask." The woman in front of him looked first at Lady Leacock and then at Sir Merlin with frightened eyes.

"Do it, Child. It will be all right," Sir Merlin said encouragingly.

"Take it off now," Falconbridge whispered implacably. "We shall do it if you do not."

Lady Leacock gave an astonished cry at the implied brutality. "I am not sure I like your tone, Sir!" she answered haughtily.

"Then you do it, Sister," Lord Merlin replied for Falconbridge, catching his urgency. "Quickly!"

Lady Leacock remained motionless in shock. Lady Bullstrode stepped behind the pretty shepherdess and deftly untied the fox mask. The pallid young woman revealed thereby was definitely not Caitlyn Llewellyn. Fairfax drew in a ragged breath. He recognized her as the light-skirts whom du Foix had picked up after the Delafields' dinner. "Where is she?" he said harshly. "What has he done with her?"

"I don't know," she cried, hanging her head.

"What is happening?" cried Lady Leacock in distress. "Where is Caitlyn?"

"Lady Bullstrode," Lord Carrington spoke. "Please help Lady Leacock to a seat. She is fainting. Sir Merlin, pray you attend her. Leave the young woman with us. Falconbridge, who do you mean by 'he'?"

"Du Foix," Falconbridge whispered. "He had this planned long before. How could I have been so blind?"

"Not as blind as you were meant to be," Carrington replied grimly.

Falconbridge turned back to the red-haired girl who was blubbering softly in fear. "How was the contact made?" he inquired harshly. Her sobs only increased. Seizing her shoulders in a strong grip, he faced her to him. "No one here will harm you. Every moment counts. Where did he contact you? How did you get the dress?"

Her snuffling decreased as she stole glances at the watchful, waiting faces. "I'm afraid," she said softly. "He threatened me. He said he would cut me up in pieces if I told. He's horrible."

"You are safe for the present," Lord Carrington said. "We will protect you from him, but we must know everything that has happened tonight."

The young woman looked around at the serious men and the two women on the settee, distress in every line of the younger one's face. She shrank from the immobile blankness of the masked Lord Falconbridge, found reassurance in the avuncular countenance of Lord Carrington.

"He picked me up at King's Street in a hackney coach tonight. The contact is always the same. I am to stand at the corner of King's Street and Covent Garden at noon each day. A hackney coach, always driven by the same driver, will drive by slowly. I go up to the window and rap on the glass. If the passenger waves me off, I am to return to the same corner by five of the clock that evening. Tonight, he told me only that I was to go to a big party, and I should have a good time for myself, with plenty of swell toffs to dance with. I might even find myself set up permanently if I played my part right," she whispered. "He took me to the back door of a shop where a woman helped me into this gown. Then we drove to a little gate that let into the gardens. He told me only that I should have a good time, but to dance and eat without removing the mask. He then gave me a blue domino to put on over my costume, and we entered through the gardens. He said that it was such a large party that no one would question our presence. As we were dancing, he suddenly pulled me from the figure and took me into the gardens. He told me to reenter the party and take off my domino, where I should have myself announced as Miss Caitlyn Llewellyn. I know nothing else."

"When was this arranged?" Falconbridge whispered, the agony of his anxiety adding menace to his tone.

"A week ago."

"Was anything else said tonight?"

She fell silent as she strove to remember. "Not to me," she said at last. "But he did say something to the driver. He said, 'If anyone asks at the Ring, I'm at home.' And the driver says, 'How will I know who he is?' Then Montclair says, 'It won't matter; he will know you.' That's all I remember."

"Where is the Ring?"

"I don't know. I never heard of it."

"Not much to go on," Lord Falconbridge said quietly, looking at Caitlyn's distraught family huddled on the settee. "Can you add anything, Carrington?"

"As it happens, we have been keeping a watch on Montclair and his associates for a while. After the fight, he was taken first to the house of his opera-loving friends, the Reynards. After a week, he disappeared. We think he repaired to a small house in the East End near Seven Dials, rented by one John Stokes. If he was being nursed there, he slipped our observers sometime last week. We think he's still in the area, though. The man who tended him may still be there."

"It's a thin chance, but one I must take," Falconbridge said. "There is no time to lose. Where is this house?"

"It is two doors down on Gravers' Lane. Gravers' Lane is off Churchwarden Street, nearest to Colliers' Court. A man needs to watch his back in that part of town. Let me go with you."

"No. This is better done alone. I'd rather you helped Sir Merlin and Lady Leacock get 'Miss Llewellyn' away from the ball before the Diamond Squad realizes what has happened. They must not find out that the real Miss Lewellyn has been abducted and that they have welcomed a daughter of Paphos to their bosom in her stead. There must be no gap in perception. They must simply be allowed to think that Miss Llewellyn, in company of her family, departed the ball early. Sir Merlin, if the Marquis of Bradbury approaches you with a request for a private meeting to ask for her hand, put him off. Say my interview tonight upset her so much that you had to bundle her home." Falconbridge removed his mask and read the shock on their faces. He smiled pitilessly. "Lord Carrington, can you obtain me a horse and a weapon?"

*   *   *

Consciousness came back with a burst of panic as Cat opened her eyes in the gloom onto the whitewashed brick archway above her. The harsh scent of hay was in her nostrils, along with stronger stable smells. She struggled to sit up and found her arms tied by the wrists to rings set into the stone wall. Her ankles were bound to the legs of the table on which she was lying. She could feel her hair, loosened from its pins, spread out over her shoulders and down her back. Looking around, she saw that she was inside an empty stall. Candles burned from various positions around the dark chamber, creating a stark contrast of light and shadow. Across the way, a nervous horse stamped and wickered. She could not blame him. All those candles, burning near so much straw, brought her to near-panic. The horse stamped with his hoof and neighed loudly. "Meteor?" she said, half-believing that she had fallen into some frightening dream. A trumpeting neigh answered. She pulled against her bonds with all her strength. They would not give; not a dream, then. "Meteor," she called loudly.

From the dark shadows came the incongruous sound of slow applause. "Congratulations," a black-hooded figure said, stepping into her field of vision. "Your skill with horses cannot be denied. I am sure the same must be said for the rest of your charms." He reached down with his riding crop and drew it slowly along her arms to her face, then down her neck and, like a lingering insolent hand, caressingly across her breast, down her belly to her cleft. "You notice perhaps you are a bit chilly? Alas, I had to remove your charming frock. I have left you your shift, for the present."

"Who are you? What is going on? Release me at once!"

"Ah, Mademoiselle, you do not recognize me. I have had a little accident since last we danced. Allow me to formally introduce myself." He threw the black domino carelessly over the hayrack. "I am Lucien Montclair, the Comte du Foix.

My intimates call me Luce. And we are going to be very intimate indeed." He drew a limping step nearer to her.

"What do you want?" she cried bravely, knowing with an ever-growing terror exactly what he wanted.

"Miss Llewellyn," he said deliberately with a sneer. "You are not that innocent. Were you fleeing from the mysterious Lord Falconbridge or to him? You were most devious, dear Cat." With an unhurried motion, he ripped the thin India muslin of her shift from the neck to her navel. "As you changed your disguise, unbeknownst to anyone, including me, I had to modify my plan accordingly. But extemporizing is part of the spice of the game." He leaned over to kiss her. Cat spat full in his face. He struck her a sudden vicious cut with his crop across her breast. "You are a spiteful little cat. I shall enjoy humbling you. But first your silence must be compelled." He took his linen cravat from around his neck and tied it tightly about her mouth, gagging her cruelly. "I feared at first I had been misinformed as to your costume. Such pains by the seamstress to replicate the original, and all in vain. You do not arrive. With your double in duplicate costume, covered by a blue domino, I search the ballroom. I was even about to abandon my vigil. Of course, when I saw the man announced as Lord Falconbridge, rumored to be the favored suitor to Miss Llewellyn, pay special attention to the modest Venetian mask, the deduction that the King's Swan was thus disguised followed naturally. Again, the clever vixen had given them all the slip. Were you on your way to a rendezvous with him when I so happily intercepted you? Never mind answering. Fortunately, I was close to the terrace doors when I saw you head toward the supper room. I whispered to my accomplice. *Très bon*, the prepared decoy, the expected Miss Llewellyn appears at the front door as the unknown Miss Llewellyn slips out the back. I must admit I found it very droll to replace a virgin with a trollop! Did I just save your virginity for myself? Were you planning a tryst all along within the darkened gardens? The poor man, how he must have suffered, unable as he was to court you, choosing a masquerade because it was his first opportunity! Perhaps you prefer the wastrel rake. Clarissa was very forthcoming on your history one night at the opera."

Cat struggled against her bonds, but with no success. Lucien sat down beside her. Grasping her head between his two palms, he held her immobile. Leaning over, he brushed his lips up the side of her face and over her fast-shut eyes, inhaling the scent of her tumbled hair. "You are delicious," he whispered in her ear, inserting his tongue and nibbling on her earlobe, "I shall eat and drink my fill of you."

Very delicately, he reached over and spread the torn edges of her thin shift, exposing her naked breasts. The cold had hardened her nipples, and he ran his fingers over them, squeezing them gently between thumb and forefinger. "Do you like it?" he crooned to her. "Shall I find out?" he whispered hotly as he drew her shift further up her legs, trailing one questing finger lightly up her thigh.

*   *   *

"Lord Carrington, can you obtain me a horse and a weapon?"

"I can do better than that. Lady Bullstrode, will you be so kind as to accompany 'Miss Llewellyn' and her family home?" Lord Carrington said over his shoulder. "Come with me, Falconbridge; I have both sword and pistols in my carriage. Never travel without 'em. One of the Coldstream guards can lend you his horse. It's a good'un, and he'll want it back, so try not to lose it." Carrington walked quickly with Vere, once again masked, and followed him down the stairs and through the hall, out to the front door, where Carrington signaled for his carriage. "Ask Mr. Ramsey to join me, please," Carrington told a footman. "He's in the ballroom with Brummell, no doubt."

Lord Carrington's coach arrived at the same time as Mr. Ramsey. "Leo, I want you to give Lord Falconbridge your horse. He'll do his utmost, but we can't promise anything. Understand?"

"Yes, Sir," Ramsey replied. "You'll find he's spirited on a calvary charge. Hope you are a good rider, Sir."

"Lord Falconbridge is the best. Follow me to my carriage. Where is your horse, Ramsey?"

"Duke's courtyard, Sir!"

"Meet my carriage at the corner." Together Fairfax and Carrington entered the coach, while Ramsey hurried back towards the porte cochère and the stables beyond.

Vere took off his white gloves and the Apollo mask, tossing them on the seat opposite. "I am glad to be finished with masquerades at last." His voice was so soft as to be difficult to hear. "What do you know about this place and its resident?"

"Very little. We know him as John Stokes, but he uses many names: Jack Stark, James Simon, and John Ball. He seems to be a messenger of Montclair's. Has a few beggarly horses and hackneys, rents 'em out as a jobber. We think when he's working, it's just cover to receive messages from his informants on the streets. Dried up fellow, very small, face brown and wrinkled, like a walnut."

"Did you say one of his names was John Ball?" Vere inquired after several thoughtful minutes.

"Yes. Do you make something out of it?"

"It is curious that this illiterate ruffian takes the name of a fourteenth-century English revolutionary priest as an alias. I suspect the sly hand of Montclair in this name. Like most things about the duplicitous Comte, it probably has several layers.

"Graver's Lane is in a bad bit of the Wen, you know. Worse, in its way, than dockside Thames. Here is a pistol that you will appreciate, by Manton. And a good sword." He held it out by the scabbard, and Fairfax belted it on. "It's a good possibility that he has got not only Miss Llewellyn, but also Sir Merlin's stallion as well. He was sure to win the Derby. If he is scratched, it's an open field. Guess who has a dark horse entered at 40 to 1? The Comte's opera friend, Monsieur Reynard."

Fairfax finished belting the sword and stowing the pistols. "No doubt, he meant to race Meteor himself. There are ways of altering a horse's color. We have consistently underestimated the man," he said, his voice sinking to a bare whisper. He shook his head.

"Perhaps," Carrington said. "But it's my thought that he has underestimated you."

"I have the horse, Sir." Outside the carriage stood Ramsey and the horse.

"I need another coat. Let me have your coachman's coat and cloak," Vere requested. The exchange was made, and Fairfax, looking even more like a highwayman, swung up onto the high-strung, eager horse and spurred it into a canter.

"Falconbridge!" Lord Carrington called out after him, "We need him alive!" The echo of the clattering hoofbeats soon faded in the still night air. "I ought to send a squadron after him," Carrington thought, "but a squadron would be noticed. No one can know this secret."

*   *   *

Montclair was setting up something just outside the range of Cat's sight. "Sacraments, my Dear Girl," he said with a purr as he arranged things. "Every virgin deserves a wedding night celebrated with all the appropriate rites. I'm afraid you won't be enjoying the wine, but other pleasures will be yours." He slid his ungloved hand up her belly to her breasts, caressing her skin with his palm. "You asked why you were here. For several reasons. The scent of your frock calms that demon stallion, but that is rather an unexpected bonus. I had not considered how difficult the horse would be to contain. As the King's Swan, you are the most magnificent social prize of the Season. For beauty, grace, and, no doubt, purity, you are desirable in your own right. How could I pass up such a woman, especially one red-haired, green-eyed, spirited, one born for the devil? A sacrificial victim of such rare quality was its own goal. Of course, that you were the sacrosanct beloved of Lord Falconbridge made it all the better. Or mayhap, passionate being who you are, you had already decided upon the surrender of your innocence for yourself? Now, as in all your life, again the choice is made for you. How will he feel when you are muddied beyond redemption? But then, you will also be dead, so I imagine, in the end, he will be sorry. Do I scare you? I assure you that the terror is part of the pleasure."

Singing a bit of a tune to himself, he poured red wine into a silver chalice. "Spoils from the old regime. From Notre Dame, in fact. While Robespierre conducted his tribunals, we pillaged at will. Is it not interesting how the theme of wine and blood is important in so many of man's religions? The Maenads tore Dionysus to pieces, mad on wine; wine becomes blood in the Last Supper." He took a long drink from the bottle. "Wine is usually an adequate symbolic substitute, but it is not sufficient by itself this time, my Dear. We shall have real blood for this ceremony. Yours, actually. It may hurt a little, but I assure you, in time, the pain and the pleasure will be interchangeable." He downed the rest of the wine. Delicately, he uncorked a smaller bottle. "Holy oil," he smirked, "used to anoint kings and bishops. And virgins on their wedding night. How little you suspect of the world. Did you accept *Die Zauberflöte* as merely a pleasant fiction, or did you, hoping to believe in its reality, fail to surmise its inverse? I saw you that night, my dear Miss Llewellyn, so captivated by the music and the sentiment that I determined to have your sweetest flower then, and now, *voilà*, you are here. I assure you that both the Light and the Dark are equally real. Certain of our gentlemen's clubs, if you could witness them, would testify to these realities. But which gentlemen belong to which reality? The man you secretly treasure, for example, which is he?"

He leaned over her, as she struggled against the bonds that held her fast. "Such a pretty mouth. Too bad I cannot kiss you upon it." His hands stroked her naked breasts softly and slowly. "But you have other treasures, other lips."

*   *   *

Vere galloped the horse through the now mostly empty and black streets. The hooves struck flashes from the cobbles, although once inside the crowded warrens of the poor in the East Side, the narrow lanes were as often of mud, dotted with dark heaps of dank, foul-smelling offal. At one corner, he even surprised a sow and her farrow that had been rooting in the garbage. They fled with indignant squeals. A few shadowy figures flitted through the gloom, but here most folk were already abed. The dark street gave way to an open court. Just beyond it, he could see Churchwarden's Street, and the quiet, deserted Graver's Lane. The second house was dark and shuttered.

Without knocking, Vere pushed upon the door, and when it failed to yield, he kicked it in. Stepping inside, pistol drawn, he was met with only empty quiet. Striking a light from his tinderbox, Vere lit a half-burned tallow candle on the table and searched the small mean rooms, looking for any clue to Montclair's whereabouts. The table was bare of paper, pen, or books. The bed was nothing but a thin mattress covered with a few dirty blankets. There was no food in any of the cupboards, save for a stale end of bread.

No creature comforts, he noted. No reason to spend any more time here than necessary when not sleeping. Where would a man be then when not at home? If he were a spy, most likely somewhere in public, where he could be contacted. According to the bit of Haymarket ware currently in Sir Merlin's custody tonight, he should be at the Ring. "If anyone asks at the Ring . . ." Montclair had intimated that the man would recognize Stokes.

There had to be more to Montclair's safety precautions than that. The name of John Ball, with all its sinister associations, must be a recognition code between Montclair's intimates, most especially those dedicated to the overthrow of King and government. If only Vere knew where the Ring was located. Probably anywhere within the twisting alleyways of East London.

His heart sank at the impossible task of locating one unknown public house among thousands in the rat's trails of the slums. To ride about inquiring would waste precious time. Chances were that the Ring was not the true name. Montclair would never convey uncoded information, even within his own operation it seemed. He could be looking for the Circle, the Circus, or the Chime.

He stopped. Memory insisted. "John Ball." The rising of the peasants under Wat Tyler had been coordinated by that single sentence "John Ball hath rungen thy bell." *Hath rungen thy bell.* For "Ring" substitute "Bell." He had passed a public house not far back called The Bell and Bottle.

At last, he had the beginnings of a plan. Rushing out of the dark empty house, he seized the reins of his horse. Flinging himself into the saddle, he galloped back toward the larger streets, away from the sinister waiting darkness of the blind maze that concealed Montclair and his captive Cat.

*   *   *

Cat lay motionless in an agony of anger and shame. Beside her, Montclair had placed the chalice filled with wine on a tray with what looked like a communion wafer and a sinister dagger. "You are to be my altar, my dear Miss Llewellyn. My altar, my bride, and my sacrifice," he said when he placed those objects there. "The truly holy rites," he continued with a laugh that chilled her with rills of fright, "are always those of the body." Noting her expression, he laughed. "Oh, you are still a virgin, at least for the moment. Such an exquisite distillation of innocence and lust will take some time to prepare and quaff." He drew his finger lightly over her face, wound her unbound hair in his hand. "To think how many have wanted you. Would any one of them imagine how I will take you? Could you even begin to imagine what awaits you? Poor little Cat. Your life is over before it is even begun. Did you realize how short life's little masquerade would be before the hour of midnight tolled?" Turning from her, he picked up a silver bell and rang it three times.

∗   ∗   ∗

Dismounting even before his horse had come to a full stop, Vere pushed through the doorway into The Bell and Bottle. It was a low-ceilinged, dark place, with a couple of silent carters drinking their ale, a few dispirited prostitutes weary of soliciting customers, and one lone man, his face brown and deeply lined, drinking alone at a table.

Boldly, Vere strode up to him and sat down. He addressed him without any preliminaries. "I need to see Montclair at home. There's been trouble. If your name is John Ball, tell me where he is," he growled.

"If my name is John Ball," the little man replied truculently, "what's the rest?"

Vere reached out and pulled the man toward him across the table until his lips were by his ear. "Hath rungen thy bell," he rasped. To emphasize his point, Vere drew his pistol and laid it on the table.

Stokes, code-named John Ball, looked at him nervously. The stranger's face this close was enough to frighten the devil himself, with his one baleful eye glaring, the other hidden by a black patch from which radiated evil looking lines of black stitches. The pistol, pointed at him, gleamed dangerously from the dirty table.

"He's in the stables, off of Mitre's Court." The dark man picked up the pistol and drew back the hammer. "Two streets back," Stokes gabbled in fear. The grim ruffian put two guineas down on the table.

"You never saw me," he growled and left as abruptly as he had come.

*   *   *

Cat looked up at Montclair with wild fury and despair, straining against the ropes that bound her. The clear vibration of the silver bell was just dying away. She watched in a near swoon as he picked up a sword and made strange passes about the room and over her body. He laid it aside in the black shadows that menaced from the dark corners. When Montclair touched her forehead with the holy oil, she was overwhelmed by its suffocating scent, sweet and musky, smelling of attar of roses. His two fingers touched the hollow in her neck, and next the sternum between her breasts. His touch grew bolder and more sensual as his hand moved down, now at the slight roundness of her taut belly. She closed her eyes against his next touch, helpless to prevent either it or her own tears.

His last caress was a loathsome abomination. No doubt, the depth of shame he intended for her was beyond everything she had experienced thus far. He would do more than despoil her. He would pollute her beyond forgetting. His taunting words had made that very clear. Her tears flowed unchecked across her face as she flung herself against the unyielding bonds. Love and passion, the forbidden territories of her most secret hopes and dreams, had become grotesque nightmares of depravity and death. Through her tears, she saw by his rapacious expression how her fear was adding to his pleasure, how her humiliation fed the perverted eroticism of his acts.

Hardening her heart in anger, banishing shame along with hope, resolving to deny him what she could, she steeled herself for the next outrage with a hatred that consumed every other emotion. She stared at him with contempt as he elevated the chalice.

He took the dagger in his other hand and immersed the blade in the wine. Using the tip of the dagger, he then drew symbols with the wine upon her breasts and belly. As she stared at him with defiance, he drained the wine from the chalice. Slowly he bent over her, and, catching her bound wrists in a light touch, he began to kiss her, first her forehead, next her rich spreading hair, then the delicate whorl of her shell-white ear.

She felt his hot breath upon her and thrust from her all thoughts and memory. She felt his hands and lips upon her skin, traveling down her body like greedy flies on a hot summer day. She felt her own desperate desire to shrink away from him and held herself against it, refusing to give him the satisfaction of feeling her powerless revulsion. She felt far away from herself, bounding away upward as a kite sails aloft on a March day. His hands were on her spread thighs; his lips were upon her belly. As his lips touched her abdomen on their southward way, she felt the darkness rush in and hoped for death in its dark folds.

*   *   *

The heavy stable door was barred from within. Vere looked quickly upward, seeking any means of entrance. There was a small dirty window from which some faint light shown. If he could ride his horse beneath it and stand in the stirrups, he might be able to hoist himself into it. Rapidly remounting, he positioned the nervous steed beneath the window. Standing up in the stirrups, he could see that the window was too far above his head. Could he control this horse well enough to allow him to stand on its back? He spoke gently to the horse, stroking its neck with a calming hand while keeping the reins relaxed. The horse sidled as he put one knee on the saddle, but he pulled up on the reins, and it stood still. Gingerly, he brought the other knee up until he was kneeling on the saddle. The horse twitched its ears, but remained still. Reaching up, Vere touched the wood of the rough-framed window and, moving slowly, using the crude sill for support, gradually stood upright. Quickly, he boosted himself through the opening and found himself in a dark musty area that seemed to be a sleeping chamber. Moving quietly, drawing his pistol, he stole toward the little door and the stairs beyond.

The sight below horrified him. Cat lay limp and bound, nearly stripped naked, upon a table. Montclair, his back toward Fairfax, stood at its foot, between her bared spread legs. Anger left no room for despair. Cocking the hammer of his pistol, he stepped out of the shadowed room. Below him, in one of the stalls, a horse screamed and began to kick the boards. Using the noise for cover, he trod swiftly down the few stairs. Before Montclair could turn, the cold steel of the gun touched the back of his head.

"Step away from her."

Montclair stood quite still for the several seconds it took him to button his clothes. "Always the unwelcome Mr. Fairfax," he called over his shoulder. "You have a habit of showing up at the most inconvenient moments." The pistol probed then withdrew.

"Now," Fairfax commanded.

Montclair stepped back. He turned and faced his adversary. Vere's pistol was pointed straight at his heart. "You do not shoot me," he drawled. "Most men would, even the most consummate gentleman. But you are not on this errand for yourself only, are you, though this is what you have desired all along."

"Explain your meaning," Vere said, the pistol still pointed unwaveringly at Montclair's heart.

"You would have killed me immediately if you had not to do your master's bidding. Had you come but ten minutes later, you would have been too late. I admit I did not expect you," Montclair sniffed, with a faint smile. "You are far more clever than I believed. I regret I have underestimated you and your friends considerably. I almost laughed aloud when you tried to engage my attentions one afternoon at Portman Square and betrayed your interest in *la chatte*. 'Pursuits in common,' I believe you said. Did you seriously think I would believe you were interested in the Thomas girl? You have wanted our pretty captive for the same reasons I do, although I believe you are rather unimaginative in your desires. We are more alike than you will admit. Neither of us values women, for example. When they have served our purpose, *voilà*, they are dispensed with. You see I have followed your career on the Continent. I knew who you really are. How much amusement your assumption of my ignorance has provided. As it does now. Tell me the truth, if I were not here and you found her like this, piquantly prepared but yet untouched, how long would she so remain? If I were still master of the situation, I would gladly offer you the pleasure of what was left, before I killed you both."

Rage loosed its lead and Vere struck him hard with the butt end of the pistol. Montclair crumpled to the dirty straw.

Dropping the pistol, he bent to where Cat lay, her eyes closed, her body limp and motionless. Using the dagger, he cut her bonds, untied the cruel gag upon her mouth and picked her up, cradling her to him in a wild fervency of anguish before finally feeling her stir in his arms. He swept off his borrowed cloak, wrapping her in it, covering her near nakedness. Laying her down on some soft clean hay, he chaffed her hands and feet against the chill, seeing the raw red welts where the cruel ropes had cut into her skin. He felt her move, heard her sudden cry. Rising quickly, he gathered her to him. Her eyes opened and gazed deeply into his face, with incomprehension. "You," she murmured, blushing a deep crimson, but he put his finger gently against her lips as her eyes widened in horror. He felt the prick of cold steel on the back of his neck.

Behind him, Montclair, blood running down his forehead from the blow that Fairfax had struck him, stood, sword in hand, his foot on Vere's dropped pistol.

"So I have netted two birds with one cast," Montclair smiled. "The King's Swan and that arrogant and proud peacock, her lover, Mr. Fairfax," he sneered. "Your passion has again betrayed you and its object. Alas, the time now is too short to do full justice to the possibilities of a double sacrifice. Put her down.

Cat clung to Fairfax, blocking his sword arm. Montclair reached out and pulled Cat to him by her hair, holding her against him with his arm about her chest, the sword pointed at her throat. "Throw down your sword," he motioned. "Do you imagine I am a patriot?" he drawled, his voice full of contempt. "Do you think I admire the revolution or our new leader, Consul Bonaparte? I am interested only in the slaughter that he will inaugurate, that river of blood that will characterize our new terrible age, one that will be shaped and governed by such as I."

As Fairfax moved as if to obey, Cat, the sword still at her throat, kicked at Montclair's injured knee. The sudden intense pain caught him unaware. His grip loosened, Cat struck the arm that held the blade.

Seeing Cat safely away, Vere drew his saber and slashed at Montclair. Cold steel rattled on steel as Montclair met Vere's thrust. Driven by a white-hot rage, Fairfax slashed repeatedly at the Comte, riposting and parrying every return, driving Montclair back by his mere fury. Retreating past the burning candles, Montclair suddenly kicked one over. The straw started to burn, and the flames spread quickly. A sheet of flame billowed up between the contestants. Seizing his opportunity, Montclair ran in a limping gait toward the freedom of the barred doors.

The great stallion screamed in fear within his stall. Cat, fallen against a bale of straw, paralyzed at first by the savage contest between the Comte and Fairfax, shook off her strange lethargy. The fire leaped in spiraling sheets of bright orange, cutting them off from escape. Fairfax paused, sword in hand, as he watched the Comte vanish on the other side of the flames. Bending to retreive his pistol, Vere then plunged through the burning barrier after him.

"Meteor!" she cried. "We must take him!" The great stallion was rearing and neighing in his stall as the flames raced everywhere at once, turning the old stone and wooden building into a roaring hell of burning crimson. Ahead of her, obscured by the thickening smoke, Mr. Fairfax was pushing against the closed barn door. Dimly, she could hear another horse screaming. "Meteor!" she called again, entering the box stall. He struck out savagely with his hooves. Her voice could not calm him. Knowing what she must do, she quickly dropped the cloak and stepped out of the torn and ruined shift. As she did, Mr. Fairfax looked back over his shoulder and saw her, her total nakedness fully revealed. For a few seconds, her eyes met his unblinkingly. The horror of the evening had shredded all conventional boundaries. Her nakedness meant nothing to her but the salvation of the panicking stallion. She stepped into the smoldering stall with the torn shift, dodging between falling clumps of burning hay. Calling in a strong voice that the stallion could identify, she evaded his iron-shod hooves as she threw the twisted garment about his eyes and led him from the stall.

Vere pushed at the barn doors. They yielded, but would not open. Montclair was gone. Beyond the stout oak boards, he could hear the terrified neighing of Ramsey's cavalry horse. Montclair had probably tried to mount it, and when it had resisted, he most likely had tied the reins to the doors, making the horse a terrified living obstacle to escape. The maddened whinnying of Meteor was probably a contributing factor. Vere turned briefly to see what could be done and saw Cat, her naked slim white body, paused in the act of dropping her shift. He knew what she meant to do, and his heart was caught by her purposeful courage. Not wanting to, yet compelled, he looked with awe upon her shining beauty, her complete self-possession terrible in its truth and resolution. For an eternity of seconds, he gazed upon her, seeing in that long unblinking moment only the courage and purity of her soul.

Using his saber to slash through the leather reins that held the two doors closed from the outside, he pushed them open and turned back in to the bellowing blaze. Cat, choking on the smoke, tried to lead the skittish stallion toward the open door. Sparks and burning bits of straw fell all around them. Vere caught up both the faltering Cat and the lead of the stallion's halter, leading them both quickly out of the burning stable. As they won the safety of the dark court, he was glad to see Ramsey's horse standing ten feet away. The flames would soon bring others, and he had no desire to be caught here. Montclair was on foot, but he knew these back alleyways far better than Vere could hope to. Above all, he must get Cat back safely.

She stood huddled and pale beside Meteor, wrapped again in the coachman's black cloak. Shock had taken effect. He lifted her onto the saddle. Swinging up on the tall sorrel, Vere gathered her to him, and tying Meteor's lead to the saddle, he set spurs to his mount. They galloped off, flames shooting upward into the dark sky as people opened their doors, and a rising babble swelled to a roar.

Cat clung to Mr. Fairfax, feeling the warmth of his arms, the strong bulk of his body, protecting hers as they raced through the dark unfamiliar streets. She did not know where she was or where they were going, but she did not care. All that she had known before as reality had burned away like a painted paper screen, leaving only this dreamlike flight on horseback with the man she had feared to desire, who had saved her from Hell and the Devil. She knew only the dark of the endless streets, the rushing blackness of the wind, the loud echoing beat of the horses' hooves, and the heat of his body as he held her, close and warm, treasured and defended against all the terrors of the night.

They clattered up to a darkened house. Dimly, Cat recognized her aunt's home in Berkeley Square. Dismounting, Mr. Fairfax gently lifted her from the saddle and quickly carried her down the areaway steps before they could be observed. He rapped upon the door, but watchers waiting opened it even before his fist had finished touching the paneled wood. Drawing Cat and Fairfax in, the women immediately took Cat from him, guiding her between them upstairs. Sir Merlin and the coachman saw to the horses. Carrington alone seemed to have time for Fairfax. Vere paced back and forth, unable to sit, the taut excitement of the evening still thrilling his veins, making rest impossible.

"I lost him," he cried hoarsely. "I was a fool."

"Don't talk, Falconbridge, especially like that. You did a damn fine job. We will catch him at the ports. Never mind. He'll try to get back to France. England is hostile territory for him now. If he had succeeded, and he very nearly did, we might have been invaded within the year. Don't fret. It will be fine."

"I'll kill him for what he did." Vere stopped speaking abruptly. No one could ever know what had transpired that evening. He owed Cat so much; he could repay that little, at least. How many more might be party to the terrible secret? "What about the other?" he croaked, his voice all but gone.

Carrington helped himself to a glass of brandy from the dining room sideboard and handed it to Fairfax. "With Montclair fled, we can release her to wherever she wants to go. You go home, and get some sleep. I will take care of the rest. Take Leo's horse. I'll explain later."

"Caitlyn," he whispered.

"Later," said Lord Carrington, firmly guiding him out.

Fairfax shrugged off Carrington's insistent arm. "When I hear how she does," he scowled his voice a whisper. "Not till then."

Soft hands bore Caitlyn along. Unresisting, she swayed against their warmth as they guided her down quiet familiar halls toward the sanctuary of rest within her own bed. With calm efficiency, they took the dark cloak from her. Without asking about her condition, they gently washed her, put salve on her bruised flesh, and a soft clean shift over her nakedness. The sheets of her bed were cool and soft. She lay silently, tearless, as they kissed her gently upon her forehead and snuffed the candles. In the soothing dark, she heard the rustling of their skirts, the quiet click of the door being shut. Only then did she move, burying her face in the pillow until all the helpless tears were shed.

RESOLUTION

Vere slept. He awoke unrefreshed. The events of the previous night were still too painfully clear. The bright cheerful sunlight of the fresh spring morning could not change his black thoughts. What could he do, what could he say to her now? He only knew that the masquerade was utterly finished, that he had risked everything, but that the outcome was as uncertain as ever.

Coffee was brought, and still in his dressing gown, he wrote his last painstaking report for Lord Carrington. His mind kept returning to Cat. What was she thinking, what could he say to her now? Would she even be willing to see him, or would the awful events between them frustrate for all time the hopes that he had so long cherished? He longed to ride over to Berkeley Square, to hold her again in his arms and never let her go, but it was far too soon. She needed time to recover from the shocks of that night. Would she ever consent to see him again? Despair washed the very colors from the day.

Cat woke as the first light filtered into her room. The fear that had slipped from her with sleep returned in the confusion of awakening within her own bed. The tumbled images of the Comte du Foix, of Mr. Fairfax, of her own nakedness amidst the blaze brought her to trembling tears. Huddling under the covers, she shut her eyes and willed herself back into a troubled and uneasy sleep. She woke hours later, when the sun stood at nearly noon. With a heavy heart, unwilling to face her aunt or her father, she rang for the maid.

She ate her makeshift breakfast silently, alone in her dressing room. No one had intruded upon her solitude. She forced herself to take a few bites. She had no appetite and finally pushed her plate aside. For a long time, she sat motionless, staring out towards the long French windows, until her trembling grew so great that she bowed her head and cried. The silent maid bore away the tray and soon returned with hot water and the very worried Lady Leacock, who helped the sobbing girl gently into the tub, where she washed her and then led her back to bed.

"How does she?" Sir Merlin asked his sister. Henrietta smiled a strained smile.

"As well as can be expected, Brother! You cannot expect a gently bred girl like Caitlyn to go through something so awful and be unscathed by it the next day. Only time can heal her now."

Sir Merlin paced his sister's drawing room. "If I had not allowed her to be so headstrong, this would never have happened. I can never forgive myself."

"You are not to blame, Merlin," she replied, laying a hand on his arm. "She is young. She will surely heal, in time."

"I wish I could believe that," he said brokenly. "I had thought this Season would make her happy. I shall never forgive myself for any of it. How could I have let the situation continue, knowing what I knew? I should have brought her back to Eldertree Manor in the beginning. Yet how could I forgive myself if I persuaded her to marry against her will?"

"Brother, Brother, I do not understand what you could have known. You ramble. That is all past mending now. We must consider Caitlyn's welfare."

"What about the Derby?" he said suddenly. "Meteor runs. If she does not attend, it will look very strange. But how can I ask her to appear?"

"We women are stronger than you may imagine. I will talk to her tonight. I will accompany you, in any case. Do not fret. See to Meteor. I will care for Caitlyn."

Sir Merlin left the house, but Lady Leacock lingered in the drawing room, waiting until Caitlyn's personal maid summoned her again. After putting her distraught young niece back to bed and watching over her until sleep at last reclaimed her, Lady Leacock sat silently in her elegant house, praying that the healing might begin.

Vere instructed his coachman to drive him to Lord Carrington's. He had instructed his groom to take Ramsey's tall sorrel there. A combination of honey, spirits, and tea had soothed his throat, and his voice had somewhat recovered its timbre. His temper, however, was questionable. His despairing uncertainty about Cat was counterbalanced by his consuming anger towards Lucien Montclair, Lord Carrington, and himself. He should have ignored his orders. He had acted the part of the greenest dandy on the Grand Strut, and Cat had paid the price of it all. These thoughts succeeded each other unendingly for the length of the journey. Entering Lord Carrington's town house, he gave his hat and stick to Bentworth with a curt, "He's expecting me." Taking the steps two at a time, Vere Courtenay Fairfax, Earl of Falconbridge, hid from the knowledge that perhaps there was no action that he could take in the matters nearest to his heart and soul.

Carrington heard him coming. Stepping out of his study, he called, "Come in. Do you have your report? I am interested in your analysis. Fine job of tracking him in the field, by the way. Don't blame yourself for letting him get away. I should have let you go back last night. You were right about him. Fact is, I let him get away."

"What do you mean?"

"This morning, I instructed my coachman to drop the soiled dove of last evening wherever she chose. Given her fear of him, I imagined she would keep well clear of Montclair and his associates. He must have been watching for her, though. You suspected as much, I know, and I doubted you. I should have sent her to the country, somewhere safe. We found her again, after he had found her first."

"Where?"

"Near the gateway to Mitre's Court. I sent a squadron down there anyway. With the fire and commotion, a few soldiers would just be part of the fun. They discovered her there or what was left of her. Poor thing. We owed her better. I have alerted all the ports, but it's thin."

"Let me help."

Carrington laid a consoling hand on Fairfax's sleeve. "Go home. Rest and heal. You have something more important to attend to."

Vere shrugged off the older man's hand with irritation. "I will not be cosseted, Carrington. It is not my injuries, nor even the King's, that concern me now. Let me find him for you."

"You have done enough, Falconbridge. There is another who needs you more," he replied.

"I wonder," said Vere moodily. "Give me work. You need me."

"No."

Cat awoke. The slant of the light told her that it was nearly time for tea. She sat up suddenly, weary of lying abed, knowing that sleep had nothing more to give her. Her thoughts would not come to order, but flew in every direction at once. Those of her ordeal at the hands of du Foix were both blank and over-bright. The terror of the event could not be encompassed altogether in mere memory. The worst nightmare, of her awful helplessness, gradually abated as she began to feel safe again in her house. She could, with effort, put those memories briefly away from her, gaining strength from remembering how even in her terror, she had defied and denied Montclair.

However, those memories of Mr. Fairfax hurtled down from dizzying space, a vulture crew, and tore at her, demanding to be fed. She could not put aside his face bending over hers, his strong arms, and his hands cradling her to him. She could never ever forget the looks that they exchanged with the world burning down all around them and all convention with it. Nor could she forget the mad ride, naked through the night, as if in a wild dream, as they rode body to body in a pounding gallop with the echo of hoofbeats, assuring her it was all real. Beyond that, before her mind and her self had been ripped from that far-remembered dream that she had once called Reality, was the memory of her strange, fleeting, bittersweet encounter with the masked man she had come to know as Lord Falconbridge. Lord Falconbridge had been in love with a young innocent. That child who might have loved him was dead. The gulf between the untouched girl and the one who stood before the mirror now was unbridgeable. It was too late for them. Between his last words and her present self stood the fiery destruction.

Too sharp was the contrast between Lord Falconbridge's blank and perfect mask of beauty, his cultured taste and decorous manners, and the memory of last night. How could mere words, on paper or even spoken, compare to the look on Mr. Fairfax's face, so intense, so savage, with his passion so deeply revealed in every harsh and furrowed line? The recall of that emotion brought a swelling of joy to her breast, with the desire to hold him in turn, cling closely to him and claim him for her own. She was ceded by soul to Vere Courtenay Fairfax.

With tentative fingers, she picked up a brush and began to brush her long hair. She had felt his fingers in it as he caught her up. His passion had been the antithesis of the Comte's frozen cruelty. How different had been the feeling in that single gesture. She could not believe that he would not come to her again. She did not know what she would say to him. Behind her, the door silently opened. She saw Lady Leacock reflected in the mirror.

"Let me help you," she said. She came quietly into the room.

"I do not know if anyone can," Cat replied bleakly. "I only know that I cannot pretend that I am the same girl I was before last night. I am quite—" she began, but burst into floods of despairing tears, unable to say the word that hovered unsounded in her mind.

Lady Leacock gathered her weeping niece securely into her arms and held her as she wept, shedding tempests of tears that gradually slowed to brief sobs and long silences. What had happened to her niece during that terrible dark night? Vile things had been done to women by men throughout the centuries, and women had survived and borne their scars and gone on, even to happiness. What part did Lord Falconbridge play in all this? He was the only man in whom Caitlyn had shown any genuine interest, as Henrietta had confided to Lady Bullstrode. She had watched Caitlyn throughout the Season. Her accomplished dash and her piquant sweetness, universally admired, remained, withal, impersonal. Could Lord Falconbridge have withdrawn his offer of marriage? No, that was quite impossible. She had seen his face in that early morning, drawn and weary, hope briefly winning its battle with a torment of soul as his one-eyed gaze sought her face for news. In that moment, she saw that he suffered as greatly for Caitlyn's pain as she did herself. He would never forsake her. If Caitlyn were crying for him, he would soon dry her tears himself. Of the other events, time would heal, and words could soothe. Now, neither of them had any. She cradled her sobbing niece gently in her arms, rocking her as she had when she was a very little girl.

A long time later, Cat finally lay silently in her aunt's arms, reluctant ever to release herself from this timeless safety. "I don't want to see anyone," she whispered. "How can I face them now, with everyone knowing of my disappearance?" She could not go on. What du Foix had done to her was known only to herself, du Foix, and Mr. Fairfax. At one point, during those mad and cleansing fire-filled moments, it had ceased to matter to either Cat or Mr. Fairfax.

Henrietta stroked her hair gently. "Do not worry, Catkin," she spoke, remembering suddenly what her long-dead sister-in-law had cooed to her just-born. "Nobody knows that you were ever absent from the ball." She felt Cat start in her arms. "In fact, a shepherdess in a fox mask was seen arriving late and leaving soon thereafter, in the company of Sir Merlin and myself. No one knows what really happened. As far as the World is concerned, you left the ball far too early last night, after meeting with Lord Falconbridge, and they are all the more eager to see you at the Derby. Besides, they have more to speculate about than your possible offer of marriage from Lord Falconbridge. Clarissa Thomas eloped with Colonel Percy last night! It must be a love match, as it can scarcely be called financially advantageous for either one. I hear that the groom was half-cut at the ball, which perhaps explains the impulsive nature of the match. It is all the buzz this morning. It seems they left for Gretna Green so suddenly that Percy had to beg some hundred guineas from his commanding officer for the post chaise! He never seemed to be especially favored by her. What could have occurred to precipitate a marriage to a man of such meager prospects? Had you any idea of this beforehand?"

Cat withdrew herself from her aunt's embrace and stared at herself and her aunt, reflected dimly in the mirror. Her own face was wan, tear-streaked, and red. Across her breasts was a streak of crueler red, where du Foix's crop had broken the skin. Despairingly, but dry-eyed, all her tears shed, she raised her bruised and torn wrists.

"How can you talk of such witless events at this time? Are you blind? Is your heart deaf to feeling, your sense dumb to plain speaking, that you entertain me with such tittle-tattle?"

Lady Leacock rose from her place beside Cat, stood behind her, and began to brush the long tumbled hair, making a better job of it than had Cat's few poor attempts. "My Love, I seek only to distract your mind. Brooding can do you no good. It was a frightening experience, but you must be glad it was no worse. Your life has been interrupted in its course, but not overthrown. Dwell not on this past, but be resolute, and take up your future, for there lies your chance of returning happiness." She strode over to the wardrobe and searched among Cat's gowns hanging there. "For the race, you must certainly wear this high-necked jockey's jacket of moss green, with the very becoming matching hat *à la Hussar*. You also have those very nice new gloves sent to you by the Duchess in her signature color, Devonshire brown. They will go admirably. For a frock, I suggest the *bazeen* with the green stripes. Since you have a horse running, I see no reason why not to be daring and carry the theme in your dress. How many of the other debutantes have a father running a horse? It will be your last triumphal appearance of the Season. You shall be boldly different, as always. The race to offer for you will be of greater interest than the horse race itself!"

Cat's face showed alarm. She had not considered this possibility. She was fully resigned to resuming her role as the King's Swan for a short time, but only as a display from a distance, protected and hedged about by her relations. Being seen, she would bear, but speak, she could not. Still, a horse race with its crowds and noise was not a natural venue for the intimacy that might lead to a proposal. It would be easy to contrive never to be alone, to avoid conversation, to forestall any proffered declarations of affection.

"Aunt," she said carefully, "I am not in the least interested in marrying any one of the men I have met here. Even if last evening had never happened, I do not think I would have concluded my Season by accepting a marriage offer. In that respect, I am afraid my Season has been a failure. If any suitor approaches, help me away. They may address Father, but I will not speak with them." To herself, she wondered if that were a lie. Last night's events stood immutable, a torch burning between what now existed and what might have been.

Lady Leacock contrived to hide her expression of surprise. Had she been mistaken about Caitlyn's regard for

Lord Falconbridge? "I am very disappointed for you, but I believe that you are correct in choosing to have the right man or none. If there is none to win your love this year, you will be all the more eagerly sought after next Season."

"I am not sure if I shall want another Season," she murmured, watching her aunt pin her hair in a chignon at the nape of her neck. She saw her kiss her and felt the brief press of lips on the top of her head.

"Things may look very different to you in time," Lady Leacock said gently. "We will of course make our excuses for you at the race if you feel too overwhelmed to attend. Your father will be disappointed, but no one will dare question your absence."

"Openly, do you mean?" Cat said sharply, watching her aunt, who, back turned, was pulling out a pale-blue *batiste* gown trimmed with white eyelet edging from the wardrobe.

Her aunt met her level stare with one of her own. "Perhaps," Henrietta replied. "There is always that chance. It is your decision to make."

Cat continued her silence. Her aunt helped her off with her dressing gown and buttoned her into the pretty frock. A nicely ruffled high collar concealed her throat and pretty openwork mitts with a lace at the cuffs hid the other physical signs of her ordeal. Did she see anything written on her own face to betray her secret shame? Looking at herself carefully, she remembered her last fierce resolve to deny du Foix what she could. She could deny him the wreck of her life, in time. She lifted her head and smiled, observing this new, unknown woman in the mirror. Today, she would deny him the prize of her spectacular Season. She would parade in untamed triumph before them all, at the last the prize untaken, untouched by any. None could possibly guess that she was but a painted player queen. "Of course I shall go. Your suggestions for my wardrobe are just the thing."

"I know all this seems unbearable to you, but it is just for one week more."

"Where is Father?" Cat asked, after a short pause. "I have not seen him since. . . ." She let the sentence trail off, again hotly aware of all that had happened.

"He is in the stable with Meteor," Henrietta said brusquely. For the first time, a little flame of anger burned within, as she thought how Sir Merlin might have prevented all this by a little attention to his young daughter. He had left her alone to her own devices for far too long. In all honesty, she was not free of blame either. She should have taken a hand with the girl earlier. Could any care have foreseen this? She had been shocked at her niece's abduction and far too grateful for her return alive to question overmuch into the circumstances of that terrible night. Still, she wondered and feared. No one had said anything to her, least of all Mr. Fairfax, who had brought her back. The closed and somber faces of Lord Carrington and Lady Bullstrode forbade all inquiry, and she had not the courage to approach the other. At the end of a long night, her brother had finally told her something. It made very little sense. All about Meteor and the coming race, an attempted forced elopement by an impecunious émigré, fortunately thwarted by Mr. Fairfax, whose identity had finally been revealed. That he was the Earl of Falconbridge had astonished her. As to what had passed between her niece and him, she had not the temerity to ask.

"Of course," Cat said flatly. "Meteor has been considerably abused. I wonder if he will be steady enough to run." She smiled wearily. "But run we must, it seems." A tear slid down her cheek.

"I shall go down there and get him myself," spoke Henrietta angrily. "He should be here with you, not with some horse."

Cat smiled at her aunt's display of bad temper, even if it were in her favor. "Do not send for him. I am quite capable of running this course for myself. I intend to return to Eldertree Manor directly after the race. I am sure Father will wish it as well."

Henrietta looked at her niece doubtfully. Was she as strong as she pretended? She could only speculate on the events of that night. She knew with certainty that Mr. Fairfax, now revealed as Lord Falconbridge, was not the villain of the piece. What Cat knew, she could only guess.

"Tea will be in a few minutes, if you wish to join me downstairs. Do you feel well enough?"

"Yes, Aunt, I am perfectly well. Go ahead, and I will join you shortly. I shall be fine." Her smile had a brittle brightness, fragile as shattered glass.

Henrietta cast one doubtful, curious look her way and then left the room quietly, leaving Cat alone once more. Caitlyn sat, still before the mirror, looking at herself as if she had never seen herself before. Who was this stranger, her face a lovely marble mask, who had she become, and what were her feelings, her wishes? Cat only knew that she wished to leave London as soon as possible. The lonely enclosed Eldertree Manor seemed like a vanished Eden that she had foolishly fled long ago, when she was just a child, and too young to know better. Now it offered her shelter and rest in a comforting solitude. She would not have to face anyone once she returned there.

Except Lord Falconbridge. Did he know what had happened to her after she had fled him for the darkened gardens and her fateful encounter with du Foix? Her aunt had said that no one suspected her true absence. Nor had her aunt questioned Cat on her shocking condition after her return. Mr. Fairfax had never been mentioned. Why? How had she been seen leaving the ball? Had they discovered her ruse, recovered the unused costume in time, thus availed themselves of a duplicate, and thereby avoided the certain scandal? How had Mr. Fairfax become involved? He had an established enmity for du Foix. How had he found her? Perhaps as an enemy of du Foix, he had discovered the plot. Mr. Fairfax too had once desired her, and desired her still. She had seen the emotion in his face, had felt it in his arms as he held her against him. With his desire, she was safe. Her heart turned toward him in helpless longing. Even if he were to court her, her father would never permit a union. Nor was it likely that he was a marriage-minded man. Cat realized that she did not care. She wished that he had just kept riding, carrying them both far from this conventional and censorious world to one of their own making.

LAST MASQUE

Vere and Carrington sipped their sherry in silence. Carrington's final words left no room for argument. Nevertheless, Vere paced, piqued by a vague disquiet that he should be doing something, if only for the relief of action, for his thoughts of Cat were an agony of torment for her well-being and an unremitting self-reproach.

"It was all my fault," Vere burst out, turning suddenly upon the elder man, who sat at his ease in one of the library's armchairs. "I have bungled this from the beginning. If not for me. . . ." He tossed back the sherry and put down the glass. If not for his entire wasted life, he should have said. So many careless years could not be excused. He had been Nemesis incubating, and Cat had been the price paid. He felt a sudden grievous sorrow, piercing the heart within his breast, and a sudden start of tears, banished with his wounded youth long years ago, surprising him now. Turning abruptly, he walked away to stare out the window until he felt some recovery of perspective and a clearing of vision.

"Do you believe in Fate?" the older man said meditatively. "I rather do. Or more likely an interweaving of lives like strands of a carpet. Or polyphony. Like Montclair, you had a dubious past, which could be exploited to advantage. Curious, isn't it, that he knew of you? Interesting also that you volunteered your services. Your connections were impeccable. I had them checked." He smiled a sleepy smile that had nothing defenseless about it. "We had suspected du Foix already. His connections seemed unusual, even for a French *émigré*. Your offer was very opportune for me."

"Opportune for you?"

"Yes," Carrington frowned into the distance and settled back as one meaning to give a lengthy testimony. "I needed evidence to convince some of the cabinet. I hadn't an operative for du Foix's level. Nor is such a man easy to find in any case. You were a perfect match. You have handled yourself commendably. Perhaps in the future, you might consider a position with the government."

"You already suspected him!"

"Yes," Carrington replied.

"So you let me make a cake of myself, coming to you first as I did with my suspicions when you had already investigated the matter."

"And found damn little for our pains! We could see something was going on, we identified a few of the players, but not a ripple of other information betrayed what plot was being forwarded by the mechanism!"

"You could have let me know!"

"We liked you better as an unknowing agent. What we call a blindman. You were really quite resourceful."

"Resourceful," Vere repeated bitterly. He was too aware of the truth of Montclair's taunts to be comforted by the word, feeling again the pain that by his actions, he had brought Cat there to that place. "Self-absorbed, you mean. I was so sure I could defeat him, I was careless of everything but my own vanity." Which I selfishly mistook for love, he thought bitterly. "By my acquaintance, I put Miss Llewellyn in danger," he said.

"You are not to blame yourself for what happened with Miss Llewellyn!" Lord Carrington exclaimed.

"Then who am I to blame?" he asked sardonically. "You?"

"Perhaps. I did not properly assess the risk."

"To Miss Llewellyn?"

"To you both. I suspected that du Foix might recognize

you. Some of their operatives have shown great familiarity with our upper circles. I thought you would be more convincing if you were not aware of either of our suspicions."

"You used us for bait?" he inquired politely, the coldness of his tone adding menace. "I shall expect to see you on Wimbledon Common on the hour and day of my choosing. I shall bring the pistols."

"Reflect, Falconbridge! I was wrong to abuse you in such a manner, but you were both audacious and competent. Had you expressed any doubts to me, I would have informed you immediately. I myself saw no danger to her in your actions. Nor did my other agent feel it necessary to take further steps."

"Other agent?"

Carrington poured two more glasses of sherry. "Yes," he smiled as he sipped. "I have another operative quite as good as you."

"Who may that be?" Vere inquired politely. "Young Ramsey, perhaps?"

Carrington laughed heartily. "Ramsey certainly favors something of your style," he chuckled, "but no, it is not Leo. This agent's chief value is never to be suspected, able to be an intelligence gatherer of nearly unlimited access, within certain spheres. Not possessed with your skill with a sword, I freely admit, but adept in other areas."

"Perhaps you will favor me with an introduction."

"Nothing could be easier," Carrington chuckled. His face grew serious again. "I had no wish to pry into your private affairs, but I was given to understand that you were affianced to Miss Llewellyn. Your behavior in public was satisfactorily circumspect, so I intuited that no evil would come from the connection and saw no further reason to warn you away. Misinformation was laid in certain quarters to further confuse Society as to your identity. I erroneously believed that you had come to a previous agreement with Miss Llewellyn and had an understanding that included the period of your work for me. To make doubly sure, I had an agent-in-place watch her from the moment she left the Thomases until her appearance at the masquerade ball. Like you, I thought Montclair had been defeated after the match at the Fives Court. I greatly underestimated his tenacity and his resourcefulness. What happened at the ball could have only been prevented by me, not you."

Carrington took a long sip of the sherry and stood, his back to Vere, facing out toward the window. "Some of what we knew of him was just too evil to credit," Carrington said at last. "Rumor, an unsound informant, connected Montclair with a fraternity that pursued the example of Madame de Montespan. I thought it a variant of our own Hell Fire Club. I was very much mistaken; it was very much worse. I believe that he would have taken Miss Llewellyn in any case." He turned to face Fairfax again. "Against the Mad, Rationality has little defense. I cannot plead ignorance to you, and stupidity is no excuse. If you wish me to meet you, I am at your service."

Vere finished his sherry in silence. He could not erase the guilt in his own heart with a duel, and it was small comfort that Lord Carrington shared it. "Who is this agent of whom you speak so highly? I admit that in all my memory, I cannot recall a particular face or name a candidate for your agent."

Carrington smiled. "Can you not?" he said with a chuckle. "I am very gratified. But you have had nothing to eat in all this time. Perhaps you would take a light luncheon with me? Nothing formal, some cold meats, cheese, fresh fruit. I would be very much obliged!"

"Thank you, Carrington, I will."

"Capital! I was counting on it." He smiled as he pulled the bell rope. "I hope you won't mind if another joins us."

"Not at all," rejoined Vere politely.

They repaired to the small salon where presently there was a soft knock on the door. "Come in," Lord Carrington said.

A tall woman, quietly dressed in the muted colors of matrons or servants, entered, bearing a tray of savories and tea. There was something familiar about her that Vere could not quite place.

"Thank you," Lord Carrington said, "please join us."

Vere watched in perplexity as the quiet woman poured out the cups. Lady Carrington, perpetually ailing, was living in a retired fashion on Carrington's northern estate. The woman before him had a quiet grace, a stateliness that did not agree with his first assessment that she was Lord Carrington's housekeeper. Nor did it seem probable that Carrington would invite his housekeeper to dine with them. Vere stole another glance at her. Was she then his mistress? Though no longer young, she displayed a serene beauty, based as much upon experience as on the strong planes of her face.

Feeling his look, a slight smile curved her lips, as she continued with steady hand to pour out the tea. If she were aware of his speculations, she was merely amused by them. Lord Carrington took the cup from her hand. There was an intimate familiarity about his gesture, which confirmed rather than denied Vere's suspicions. Carrington made no attempt to interrupt the silence or explain the woman in any way.

"Will you take sugar, Lord Falconbridge?" she asked him. Her voice, low and musical, had just a touch of a Scots accent. He looked at her again sharply. Her eyes were lowered, but her smile had broadened, and she was struggling to hide her laughter. Carrington was looking at him now, his own smile breaking loose of its confines, to spread merriment across his face.

"Foxed," he pronounced with satisfaction. "You haven't guessed yet."

"Well, Sir, what do you have to say for yourself?" said the woman in a familiar voice.

He turned in puzzlement, then wonderment, to Lord Carrington. "She is. . . ?" He let the question rest, half-answered, because it was replaced by certainty.

"Lord Falconbridge," cawed Lady Bullstrode in her usual accent, "Your servant, Sir!"

"Lady Bullstrode," he spoke aloud in half-wondering tones. "You are much changed. I regret if my lack of recognition may have given offense."

Lady Bullstrode lowered her voice to a gracious and melodious level. "I am quite pleased and flattered that I have managed to deceive your powers of observation. I have found out that among both men and woman, a change of appearance may be completely realized by brightly colored and ridiculous clothes, generous applications of paint, and a loud and insistent bellow. Very few people scrutinize the obvious more closely. This allows me to go unrecognized in many places, even among the *ton*. I was once an actress, before my marriage."

"And a very good one. She has been invaluable in that way," beamed Lord Carrington. "She's been able to ferret out more on the information to which your investigations led us." He picked up cup and saucer of tea and handed it to Fairfax. "1797," he murmured reflectively, "mutiny at Spithead. Bad rations caused it, and it was the Devil's work to end it. Montclair was going to cause another. He had wormed his way into the confidence of Lord Marston, Quartermaster General for the fleet. Under his aegis, he would supply beef and bread to the Royal Navy. I imagine that the operation would be quite legitimate while Napoleon built his invasion fleet. Once that was ready, he planned to substitute rotten beef and weevily bread and pocket the difference as well. When the men mutinied, Bonaparte's invasion fleet would swoop down upon us like a cormorant on a fish. Clever, but not clever enough. Between your shadowing of Montclair and Lady Bullstrode's dramatic talent for disguise, we were able to discover the plot and prevent its implementation."

"I am more than willing to testify to Lady Bullstrode's aptitude for disguise. Where have your talents taken you, if I may inquire?"

"Oh, I may impersonate a lady's maid or a tradeswoman to infiltrate the servants' hall. Servants often overhear important things." She smiled. "Such as Lord Marston's contract with the navy and Montclair. His lordship's scruples are not all they should be regarding money."

"As soon as we had all the pieces in place," Carrington continued, "we were able to circumvent its implementation. With Montclair fled, we have arrested most of his cohorts. The danger has ceased, for the present."

"But he is still at large, and the war has just begun."

"Yes, that is so."

"There is nothing to prevent him from making another attempt, I suppose."

"No," agreed Lord Carrington.

"Nor is anything preventing me from hunting him down and killing him."

Carrington and Bullstrode exchanged looks.

"Nothing?" questioned Lady Bullstrode. "What of your marriage to Miss Llewellyn?"

"That is over."

"I am sorry to hear of it," Lady Bullstrode drawled. "Miss Llewellyn was quite taken by you, despite all our attempts at the contrary."

"What?"

Lady Bullstrode, unperturbed, continued. "I knew all about it from the beginning. Sir Merlin wrote to me and asked me to assist Miss Llewellyn in scaling the heights of the fashionable world. He also wrote of your proposed engagement. Matters were complicated when you volunteered to assist Lord Carrington. That day in the Park, I thought it would do no harm for you to experience each other's company for a bit. There might not be opportunity later. I attended to the Thomases to prevent the beginnings of any *crim. con.* Happily, I was there when Roberts made his accusations. I must apologize for my part in blackening your reputation in the course of duty. However, so sure was I of her attraction to you, I fancied my words, rather than discouraging her, would only fan the flames of her interest. I should not give up yet, if I were you."

*   *   *

The banners floated brightly over the voluble and excited crowd. The gay colors of the ladies' gowns and hats competed with the bright spring itself. The scene was a jumble of horses and carriages, footmen and grooms, betting touts, ladies calling gaily to one another, gentlemen discussing in serious hushed tones the odds for this horse or that jockey.

Down in the stables, Sir Merlin watched uncertainly as the groom curried Meteor. The horse stamped nervously and showed the whites of his eye. He was off his feed, shying at any movement. Sir Merlin considered scratching him. It was doubtful that he would make a good showing. It should be enough that he had gotten both horse and Caitlyn back. He blinked as he thought how close he had been to losing her forever. If Meteor was in such a state, what could be said of his daughter?

That awful night, Falconbridge had wordlessly handed her over to the ministrations of the women, and Lord Carrington had sent Merlin out to see to the horses. Sir Merlin had not had time thereafter to speak of her to Vere. In the end, after he had sent Falconbridge away, Lord Carrington himself had given Merlin a version of the events, reassuring him of Cat's ultimate well-being. Sir Merlin doubted that now.

She had come to him last evening and very calmly requested that they return to Eldertree directly after the race. She had appeared perfectly composed, but something lively and innocent had been removed from her, as if she were but a shade of her former gay and laughing self. Would it come back, that sweet girlish manner, or would she remain the subdued and lifeless girl whom they had returned to him?

"He's not going to be easy to ride, let alone race," the jockey commented. "I am not sure that I can even get a saddle on him. Look at the lather he is in." Merlin inspected Meteor closely. There was a faint shine of sweat all over the fine red coat.

"Curry him down," Merlin said curtly. "We have to scratch."

"Where is your father, Caitlyn?" Lady Leacock asked, surveying the swirling excited crowds. "I do not see him here. I hate to sit here alone without him."

"Yes," replied Cat, "I fully agree. He must be down at the stables. Shall we go there?"

Lady Leacock cast a concerned look upon her niece. Cat's expression was devoid of any feeling, but her fingers were interlaced tightly in her lap.

"Yes, I think we should. We would be out of this crowd." She signaled her coachman, and their carriage began to move slowly again through the throng towards the stables. Ordinarily, she would have used the open carriage, but, in consideration of Caitlyn, she had chosen to arrive in the closed. Nevertheless, the horses would soon be recognized, and she had no wish to expose Caitlyn to her circle of admirers.

They found Sir Merlin standing morosely by his jockey at Meteor's stall. "We are going to scratch him," he said in lieu of greeting. He handed Caitlyn down and kissed her on the cheek. Her demeanor did not match the brave flourish of her costume. "You look lovely, my Dear. Do you wish to stay and watch the race anyway?" She slipped quietly from his embrace and wordlessly approached Meteor. He reached out his long velvet nose to her questing hand.

"Poor dear," she crooned in a low voice, almost to herself. "It was frightful, I know. But you can run." She drew close to him, putting her arms about his neck. "It's almost over," she whispered. "Run now, and you never need run again. You shall have green fields and red colts and the peace of the western wind." She stroked the long mane as he nibbled at her collar. "I would like to see you beat them all," she said softly as she patted his glistening coat. Meteor's ears twitched at her voice. "We are a fine pair, you and I. Let's beat them all, for today." Her voice broke with a sob, and small tears trembled in her eyes. Meteor nuzzled her hair, blowing gently into her ear. She clung to him and his warm safe strength as her trembling increased. He whickered gently, and she wiped her eyes. "It's all right," she said finally, turning to face her astonished relations. "He will run now."

Her father eagerly escorted them both into the enclosure. The view was good, and they were away from the hurley-burley of the general populace.

In front of them, the horses with their gaily dressed jockeys were being put into place, Meteor among them. She watched him critically. Although Meteor was definitely skittish, she was glad to see that he was not rearing or kicking like some. The jockey seemed to have him under firm control. He had the place of least advantage, the outside rail. Meteor's distinctive coat shown burnished red in the strong sunshine as he pranced in position. She heard the shot of the starting gun, the thunder of hooves, and the multi-throated cry of the crowd as the race began.

Halfway around, four horses led the rest, among them Meteor, running close to the inside pack, a length behind a dark brown horse. They pounded into the turn, and Meteor, still gaining, trailed the leaders by half a length. The field was strung out, but the same four still dominated. Through her opera glasses, Cat saw the little jockey loosen the reins and lay on the whip. The great horse lengthened his stride and pulled out from the closely packed leaders, gaining ground with every stride: a half length, a whole length, two from the nearest horse as they came out of the turn and into the stretch. He ran as if he had wings upon his feet, opening his lead until he crossed the finish line five full lengths ahead of his nearest competitor. Well had he represented the great sire of his line; "Eclipse first, the rest nowhere!"

The shouts dinned in her ear, and the delirious sportsmen surged toward her father and herself, eager to offer congratulations and toasts.

Caught in a sudden eddy of empty space, she saw him coming towards her as if from a dream. Among all the frolicking, rejoicing crowd: Sir Merlin throwing his arms about Lady Leacock with a whoop, the bettors congratulating each other and boasting of their winnings, the losers counting their bankrolls, he strode purposefully, undeterred by the noise, as if from his own world stepping through the door into hers. His face, made more severe by the black eye patch, had an intent ferocity.

He was coming for her, and she longed to run and meet him. Around her, the press of happy winners were congratulating her father and offering toasts. Henrietta accepted their compliments for Cat, who stood wordlessly by, in a mixed agony of desire and fear. What he said to her here could never be recalled, nor could her answer. Whatever was said would change her world irrevocably, forever. Her aunt had taken her arm. They were moving toward whence he came. He stepped through a little crowd of sportsmen. She saw her old antagonist, the Prince of Wales, and his companion, the Beau, part in surprise as he passed by them. She would have welcomed the Prince's rude jests or the Beau's disdain rather than face the fire of Mr. Fairfax's look.

Desperately, she clutched Lady Leacock's arm. The shameful memories of their last meeting brought a heated flush to her face, swiftly departing, leaving her pallid and cold. He alone knew the truth of her present masquerade. She felt more naked here among the *beau monde* than she had in the burning stable. Then his protecting strength had comforted her. Now she saw his desire in the purposeful way he strode toward her, claiming her soul. For a heartbeat of time, she longed to enfold herself in his embrace, to pull his long hard body close to her, denying family, honor, and fortune for the sake of the passion that ran in rivers of fire through her veins. Swiftly, sense overtook madness. Her father would never permit a marriage, even if Mr. Fairfax were to offer it. Their union had been sealed by fire, outside the bounds of Society's rule. She trembled on the verge of the great chasm of her intent. If she had the courage to be his mistress, would she have the courage to bear a dishonored life alone if he grew tired of her? Cold sense swiftly succeeded passion's heat. "Please," she whispered to Lady Leacock, avoiding his ardent gaze, "take me home."

He saw her through the crowd, and the people around him became no more than insubstantial wraiths, parting like swirling mist, offering a clear path to where she stood. His desire was a lodestone that drew him inexorably forward. With no thought but to claim her here and now before her family and all the *haut monde*, he stepped forward from the clamoring crowd. The joy he held within himself trembled and broke with her look. White-faced, faltering, she looked away, and Lady Leacock, in swift defense of her fainting niece, hurried her toward their carriage. She had given him the cut direct, and all London witnessed his humiliation. He heard their voices, but paid no heed to their words, only stood blinded by the brightness lost.

Lord Carrington laid a comforting hand upon his sleeve. "Not now, not here," he said quietly. "Live to fight another day." Fairfax allowed Carrington to guide him back into the crowd, toward the raucous laughter of the sportsmen who neither knew nor cared of his personal life, but pressed upon him great foaming glasses of champagne, an unlikely *Lethe*, welcomed as an alternative to his personal darkness.

"Alvanley has a book down at Brook's, doesn't he?" inquired Prinny to the Beau as he stared after first one then the other of the departing figures. "Is he 'for' or 'against'?"

"Oh, 'for,' of course," replied Brummell who had observed it all through his quizzing glass.

"Doesn't look very promising. It appears he has come a cropper finally," the Prince laughed, cocking an eyebrow toward where Fairfax stood.

"Alvanley lost considerable blunt to Carleton on the fight at the Fives," Brummell sniffed. "And, of course, we both know of his skills as a rider. I am sure on consideration, if Your Royal Highness subscribes to the book, you will choose the winning side."

UNMASKED

The last trunk had been strapped shut. The wardrobe had been emptied of all but her traveling clothes. Tomorrow, she and her father would leave London. There were no plans to follow the world of Society on to the gaiety of Brighton or Bath.

She herself would withdraw into retirement. Immured again in the green fastness of Wales, she would forget and be forgotten. She might eventually marry some comfortable, stolid country squire with whom she might pass her life free of this piercing pain. The only barrier to her complete peace was Lord Falconbridge. Somehow, she must finish that as well. She could never marry him now. How could she lay within his embrace when behind her closed eyes she saw only his brother? It would be best if she gave him her refusal as soon as possible. With her life in ruins about her, it was hard not to mourn what might have been, if her ungovernable foolishness had not betrayed her at the last. With despairing resolve she took her pen and wrote briefly.

The Right Honourable Lord Falconbridge
   The Season has ended. I intend to leave with my father,
Sir Merlin, for my home at Eldertree Manor. I will be glad
to give you my answer there.

                        Sincerely,
                  Caitlyn Llewellyn

She folded and sealed the letter before she had time to rethink her action. Decisively, she rang for her maid. Addressing it to Lord Falconbridge's factor in London, she handed it to the waiting woman. "Please see that this is delivered tomorrow." The maid curtseyed in reply, and Cat left her room for downstairs, her aunt, and tea. She felt a headache coming on and was glad for the excuse to cut the evening short and dine alone in the salon, where through the half-drawn curtains, pale as a pearl in the sunset sky, Venus shone upon her solitary supper.

Of the journey home, she noted little, her mind being tuned to an inward landscape. No distance could separate her soul from the shattering events of that night. Seeking to calm herself for the approaching meeting with Lord Falconbridge, whose unexpected appearance at the *bal masque* had released such a confusion of feelings within her, she could not avoid the overwhelming flood of images that followed. The humiliating degrading attentions of du Foix, who, while failing to complete his vile ravishment of her body, had still defiled her innocence and destroyed her youthful dream of presenting herself to the man she loved as pure, a bud yet unfurled, her softness awakening to the first touch of the long-awaited lover. She knew that something in her had longed for earthy surrender, not as a helpless captive, but willingly united in passion with a man. The images of the three men harried her thoughts: du Foix, all the more demonic for the angelic countenance he bore; Lord Falconbridge, the unknown possibility who might have been the resolution between the conflict of desire and duty, and finally and always, the memory of Mr. Fairfax, his strong arms gathering her to him, his hard body sheltering her in the ecstasy of their mad ride from the burning hell of her shame. To the passion in his touch, she would gladly have surrendered what was left of her innocence. Instead, she had shown herself a coward, false to everything that she held true, when she had turned away from him at the Derby.

In her decision to reject Lord Falconbridge, she strove to regain some sense of personal honor. Lord Falconbridge, for all his consideration, could not understand or forgive the stain on her soul that du Foix had put there. Nor would she keep it there, content to remain a whore and lie in the arms of a wealthy man while desiring his brother. Only Mr. Fairfax, who knew everything, who had been with her through the test of fire, could know her for what she was and yet desire her.

During the week following her arrival back at Eldertree Manor, Caitlyn regained something of her former mien, but the household knew that she was troubled. She spoke gently to all, but confided in none. Since returning to Eldertree Manor, Caitlyn had wrapped herself in a quiet solitude that kept everyone hovering uncertainly at its edges.

One day, she sat idly beneath the great oak tree beside the merrily running little stream. An opened book lay face up beside her on the grass, but she had long since lost interest in its words. Her afternoon solitude was interrupted by Bessie. As the old servant hesitated, Caitlyn smiled, as if to herself, and requested Bessie to sit with her.

"Bessie, tell me something."

"If I can, Miss," Bessie replied nervously. No one had held as much as a conversation with the young mistress since her return.

"That girl," Cat began. "That serving maid who killed herself in her abandonment—why did he deny her and her babe—how can men do such things?"

Sudden tears came to Bessie's eyes. She was the cause of this after all. Somehow, Caitlyn must have learned of the involvement by her betrothed in that old scandal of despair and death. How happy Sir Merlin had been when his daughter had begun to favor the arranged marriage after all, how deeply discouraging this last week had been for all of them. So this was the answer to the mysterious reluctance to entertain his proposals in London and her precipitous flight home to Wales! Bessie would put it right.

"He never knew. He would have made provision for her and the babe at the estate, but she killed herself before he found out. He was in London. She knew he would never marry her, and mad for love of him, she would not take joy in bearing his baby. 'Twas a terrible waste of what might yet have been a happy life."

"Thank you, Bessie," Cat said and turned away in dismissal, looking into the dancing rills of the flowing stream. What would she have done in that situation? The baby would not have prevented the girl from making a marriage, and she would have had a child to love, even if she no longer had its father. Caitlyn knew herself at last. Come what may, she would choose whatever love would allow her of him. She would choose even a brief happiness, were it offered again. Her love was stronger than her shame. If he yet desired her, she would find a way to him.

"Your pardon, Miss, but your father desires to see you."

"What about, Bessie?"

"'Tis not for me to say. You had better see Sir Merlin in his office."

With thoughtful steps, Cat walked slowly toward the great house, wrapped in afternoon shadows. Entering through the arched front door, Cat crossed the silent hallway to her father's little study.

Sir Merlin rose to greet her from behind his desk, which was heaped with papers and books. "Caitlyn, you have a visitor in the library," he said without preliminary. "You do not have to see him if you do not wish it. He will return another time if you so desire."

Cat felt the suffusing heat that flushed her cheeks, then drained away again, leaving her pallid as marble. It could not be he, he whom she both wished and feared. It must be Lord Falconbridge, come at last to claim his answer. Yet her father's manner, so strangely watchful and grim, gave her a precarious hope.

"I will see him now," she murmured, trying to regain her composure. Moving with exaggerated care on legs grown weak, she made her way slowly across the hall, her heart suffocating her with its beats. She paused briefly before the closed door, leaning upon it. The silence made a void of time. How long she stood there she could not tell, but feeling at last her limbs steadying to something much more under her control, she opened the door.

He stood, back to her, tall and black-haired, facing the bow window, where the heraldic cat device glowed in crimson blood above his head. "Miss Llewellyn," he said formally. His voice had something of the timber of the other, and she froze in hope and faint belief. The stilted correctness of his address swiftly disabused that fragile wish. It was Lord Falconbridge then, not his brother. "I am most entirely under obligation to your graciousness in seeing me."

Her graciousness, she thought. If he knew why she had fled him at the masquerade, would he still be using such fine language? If he knew what succeeded, would he even be here?

"I regret all the circumstances that have kept us apart. Some could not be helped. For most, I am fully responsible, and for those, I ask you to forgive me. I have not always, in my life, been a good man. In knowing you, I have found again the man I could have been, had not an overly indulged youth and the stubborn wrong-headedness I called pride led me down paths best not recalled. For my faults, I have tried to make amends. For my trespasses against yourself, I can only ask forgiveness.

She was grateful he still stood, back to her, motionlessly staring out the window. How could she answer him? "I. . . ." she began.

He turned and looked at her. It was he! He had come for her, against all opposition, he had come to claim her. "Will you marry me?" he said.

Her shock and her joy froze her in place. The silence spun out long moments.

"I see," he said gravely, breaking the silence at last. "It is too late. I regret the pain my presence must bring to you. Please believe me. You are the purest angel and the most beautiful being I have ever known. If I can do you any service, I am always yours to command." He picked up his hat and stick from the table beside him. "With your permission," he said, bowing stiffly.

"No!" she cried, crossing the room in quick strides, laughing and crying at the same time. "Yes! I will." She threw herself into his embrace, feeling the strength and warmth of him. "Oh, yes, I will. Please, please, never leave me again."

He drew her toward him tenderly, delighting in her slender trembling body pressed close to his, the soft feel of her hair as she laid her cheek against his heart. "No, never again," he whispered in it, "never again."

"We must tell Father," she said after a measureless time, suddenly looking up. "What will he say? Perhaps we should elope to Gretna Green. He will be angry. He will refuse his permission."

Vere smiled. "Little one," he said tenderly, "I believe it can all be managed without an elopement. Of course, if you would rather—" He looked down into her upraised eyes, remembering their dark, wild ride, and knew that she was remembering it too. He kissed her and felt her awakening passion as she returned it. A special license, he thought, as he held her against him and caressed the smooth curve of her waist, the sooner the better.

They stood together another ageless time, hardly daring to move or speak, each fearing to break the magic. At last, with regret, but with the knowledge that their embrace was only preamble, Vere released her from the circle of his arms. "Shall we speak to your father now?" he inquired with a smile.

"Yes," she replied tremulously, looking up into his eyes. "Mr.—"

"Vere," he responded, teasingly.

"Vere," she repeated, finding delight in pronouncing his name.

"Courtenay," he added, holding her uptilted face gently in his hands, smiling into her eyes.

"Vere Courtenay Fairfax," she completed, smiling back at him, pronouncing him in naming him: her own, her beloved, her one true knight. Clinging to his arm, they crossed the hall together, her resolution strengthened by the delicious warmth of his presence, the promise of unleashed passion to come.

"Father," she said, her voice strong and nervously high. "I wish your permission to marry Mr. Fairfax." They both sat facing him in the comfortable disorder of his study.

"Mr. Fairfax?"

"I shall not change my mind," she added boldly before he could reply. "I know I am pledged to listen to Lord Falconbridge's proposals, but my mind is made up."

"Is it indeed?" replied Sir Merlin, a small tic twitching noticeably at the side of his mouth. "You are going to marry—"

"Mr. Fairfax," she interjected.

"Mr. Fairfax," he mused. "You will not be dissuaded?"

"No," she returned bravely. "I am prepared to answer the same to Lord Falconbridge personally, as per our agreement."

"You intend to answer Lord Falconbridge's proposals," he said with something between a gasp and a sigh, "by stating that you are marrying Mr. Fairfax."

"Yes," she replied, her glance faltering as she caught Fairfax's quizzical expression.

"You are prepared to tell him—?"

"That I wish to marry his—relation, Mr. Fairfax." She did not intercept the startled look that passed between the two.

"Very well," her father said, and overtaken by a strange coughing fit, he walked quickly from the room, leaving them alone.

"I did not think he would be so amenable," Cat confided in Fairfax. "But why?" She sat in silence, wondering if her father had sent over to Foxearth for Lord Falconbridge.

"Well," said Fairfax, after a long pause, "I am waiting."

"Waiting," Cat replied in puzzlement looking up at him. "Then you are not—?" Her voice dropped in confusion.

"You are—" she began as dawning comprehension showed in her face. "Lord Falconbridge," she meant to say.

"Yes," he said and kissed her again.

DESIRE

WHERE true Love burns Desire is Love's pure flame;
It is the reflex of our earthly frame,
That takes its meaning from the nobler part,
And but translates the language of the heart.

Samuel Taylor Coleridge
1830